The

Remote

Country

of

Women

Fiction from Modern China

This series is intended to showcase new and exciting works by China's finest contemporary novelists in fresh, authoritative translations. It will represent innovative recent fiction by some of the boldest new voices in China today as well as classic works of this century by internationally acclaimed novelists. Bringing together writers from several geographical areas and from a range of cultural and political milieus, the series opens new doors to twentieth-century China.

HOWARD GOLDBLATT

General Editor

Bai Hua

Translated from the

Chinese by Qingyun Wu

and Thomas O. Beebee

General Editor, Howard Goldblatt

University of Hawaii Press   *Honolulu*

The

Remote

Country

of

Women

Originally published in Chinese in 1988.
Taiwan edition by Sanmin Publishers,
Taipei.

English translation © 1994 University of Hawaii Press
All rights reserved
Printed in the United States of America
99 98 97 96 95 94   5 4 3 2 1

Library of Congress Cataloging–in–Publication Data
Pai, Hua, 1930–

    [Yüan fang yu ko nü erh kuo. English]

    The remote country of women / Bai Hua : translated from
  Chinese by Qingyun Wu and Thomas O. Beebee.

      p. cm. — (Fiction from modern China)

    ISBN 0–8248–1591–2. — ISBN 0–8248–1611–0 (pbk.)

    I. Wu, Qingyun, 1950– . II. Beebee, Thomas O. III. Title.
IV. Series.

PL2895.A3465Y813 1994   94–9956
895.1'352—dc20   CIP

University of Hawaii Press books are printed on acid-free
paper and meet the guidelines for permanence and durability
of the Council on Library Resources

Designed by Richard Hendel

Bai Hua,
a photo taken by
Tak-wai Wong
in 1988

When a stream flows into a big river, it loses its purity

but gains breadth. When humanity walks toward

modernization, what is gained and what is lost? Here

I can only unfold to my readers the panorama of life

as it is and wait to hear their judgment.

—Bai Hua, June 18, 1993

Go, go, go, said the bird: human kind

Cannot bear very much reality.

—T. S. Eliot, "Burnt Norton"

The most irredeemable sin is caused by

the mischief of the fool.

—Baudelaire

I fear and hate any veil;

Yet all things are shrouded in mist.

I am no exception—

Only my soul, leaking through eyes of gauze

Soundless, colorless, shadowless, shapeless

Freely looking down at humanity

Including the self, made of flesh.

—Bai Hua

1

She was going on thirteen. Oh, beautiful Suna-mei! A crescent was waxing into a half-moon.

"One, two, three, four...." A group of boys and girls, all dressed in long shirts that looked like oversized blouses or undersized gowns, squatted beneath a row of ritual pennants on the hilltop and counted the vehicles crawling one by one around the bend of the hill like beetles. There were four cars: one black, two blue, even a red one. In their wake were two buses and three huge trucks. In the trucks sat People's Liberation Army soldiers, with guns in hand and bayonets flashing. It was scary. The children hushed up; even Geruoma, who was always laughing, frowned this time. Those naughty children often threw stones at trucks or intercity buses. Even the girls, aping the boys, tried to pee on the buses from above. But this time they did no mischief. They were too shocked. So many shining beetles and PLA soldiers carrying real guns. What a show. There was a saying, and it seemed to be true: in the outside world the more important the person, the smaller the car he drives, and the larger the house he lives in. Perhaps the tide of the great Cultural Revolution was pushing its way here.

The storm known as the Cultural Revolution had broken loose in the outside world when Sunamei was four years old. Since then, nine years had passed. She recalled how, when she was five, several Red Guards had run into her village.

Singing and shouting, they had gone from house to house and hung big posters on the walls. Stamping their feet and waving their hands, they had called on the villagers to rise up and make revolution. The grown-up villagers had responded with funny expressions as though suppressing a laugh. Who knew how to stand up and revolt? At least it had been a great party for the children. They had followed the Red Guards everywhere, singing, crying, shouting slogans. Some had even scooped red paint from the Red Guards' bucket and smeared it on their faces.

The villagers had prepared a dinner to thank the Red Guards. After the dinner, some Red Guards had asked a villager who knew a little Chinese, "What are you thanking us for?"

"For all the fun you've given our children. They don't often get to see youngsters from outside."

Not very pleased with this answer, the Red Guards took out their Little Red Books and read a sampling of Chairman Mao's quotations. The villagers nodded their heads, and the one or two Mosuo who could read even joined in the chanting.

Then the Red Guards asked, "Do you understand what we've been reading to you?"

"No." Those who had nodded now shook their heads.

The Red Guards seemed terribly disappointed. After assembling all the children, they gave each a red armband. Some children asked for extra ones. Then the Red Guards taught the children to mumble incantations like a Mosuo shaman as they thrust their Little Red Books over and over again into the air.

The next morning the Red Guards commanded the Mosuo, grown-ups as well as children, to persecute their commune cadres. The children balked, as did the grown-ups. They pretended not to understand the instructions. Even the few who knew a little Chinese became incapable of understanding a single word. Instead, the children simply stripped off their clothes and, plunging into Lake Xienami, paddled fiercely. Following the children, the Red Guards also jumped naked into the lake. In the water their skin appeared exceptionally white. Years later, many women still chatted about this in wonder and delight: "Oh, Ami! Those naked bodies were so white! As white as – oh my, whiter than milk. Even the blue lake could not stain them." After their blissful bath, the Red Guards marched off singing songs from *Quotations of Chairman Mao.* The waters of Lake Xienami once again calmly reflected the sky in mirror-like tranquility.

Women took the red armbands from their children and used them as diapers. Even now, right beside Sunamei, the little sister on Geruoma's back was wearing one of these diapers. The women were even complaining that the red satin did not absorb well.

After that bunch of Red Guards had decamped, the entire great Cultural Revolution became a story from far away. Horse drivers often brought laughable yet terrifying anecdotes about it into the village. Everyone loved to hear them. It was as if they were being charmed by ghost stories: they always listened with wide-eyed attention.

Now many more vehicles and soldiers were coming. Perhaps they wanted to force their Cultural Revolution onto the Mosuo village. Could the Mosuo possibly escape this disaster? Unlikely. The PLA soldiers were different from the Red Guards – they had real guns. Moreover, some big shots were also coming in their small cars. The children were excited and curious. They wanted those funny, terrifying stories acted out in their own village, right before their own eyes, and they wanted people they knew to be the actors.

The day before, a commune cadre had informed the villagers that the central committee was sending a team there. What was this central committee? They could make neither heads nor tails of such a thing. They were, however, quite familiar with teams. They had seen various teams. All those teams were like clouds blown in from outside: some rained a few drops; some thundered; others neither rained nor thundered. All the clouds eventually blew away; the blue sky and Mount Ganmu remained.

As soon as a team arrived, they began holding daily meetings: a cadres' meeting, a seniors' meeting, a women's meeting, a children's meeting. It was as though their words could never end and their characters could never be exhausted in writing. They performed a lot of tricks: a wave of shouting, a gust of criticizing, a surge of vilifying. Then they would dust themselves off, happily departing with folders full of criticism papers, bags of peanuts, dried fish, and whole salted pigs. No one ever remembered what they said at these silly meetings. Those who had been criticized didn't change a bit. No one felt a dismissed cadre had lost an arm and a leg or anything like that. Who wanted to be a cadre, anyway? Cadres were always having to stay up late.

The children still remembered those funny days. The strangest team was the one that had forbidden women to have babies. They put up posters that showed body parts and the formation of a baby in the womb. In neighboring Han villages they castrated women like pigs. They tried to persuade the Mosuo women to undergo castration, but no one would listen. The Han women had no choice except to scream like pigs being butchered. Dressed in white gowns, the men and women on the team stripped the women of their clothes, shaved their private parts, pressed them onto the broad slaughtering bench, held their hands and feet down, then used a shining little knife to castrate them. The innocent children got so excited that they jumped, stamped their feet, shouted at the top of their lungs. What a scene! The children were worried that the team wouldn't stay long enough; adults prayed for them to leave for fear they would get really warmed up and turn their scalpels on the Mosuo women.

The members of the team also wished to leave as soon as

possible because they had their own families. Some male team members, seeking pleasure, stole into Mosuo women's *huagu*. Afterward every one of them would give some gifts to his Mosuo lover and order her, "Don't tell anybody about us. If you do, you'll ruin me!"

Those Mosuo women did not understand why they could not reveal their joy to another person. "Afraid? If you were afraid you shouldn't have come to me. We haven't done anything shameful."

At that point, the team members wished they could sew the women's mouths shut. But instead they begged the women to tell no one – not a soul.

One night at midnight, little Sunamei bumped into a team member in her village. He was holding his shoes in his hand and tiptoeing as if stepping on thin ice. If anyone had said boo he would have tumbled down the stairs. When he met another team member on the path, the two of them told each other the same story: "I have been interrogating so-and-so...and we talked until late into the night." They mentioned only men's names. Why did they need to tell each other a man's name? Sunamei had seen both of them coming out of a *huagu*. At big meetings, such men always demanded confessions and repeatedly shouted an eight-character slogan: "Leniency to the confessors, severe punishment to resistors." Why wouldn't *they* confess, then?

Women who had affairs with those team members chatted among themselves afterward: "Although he can't speak our language, when he comes to play, he is certainly an old hand at it."

"During the day his face is cold as slate. Who could have guessed that last night in my *huagu* it would smile and drip honey?"

So the team of the central party committee came to camp around Lake Xienami. Its members deliberately chose to stay in Mosuo villages. No one could guess what they were up to. Did they want to remove another batch of commune cadres? Catch thieves? Castrate women? Who knows? The weather was fine; yet everyone's face was cloudy. All the cadres from the production team were assembled in the commune courtyard. Each of them brought his own sleeping bag and no one was allowed to go out. They were kept at the meeting for three days and nights behind the barred gate. The children learned from the car drivers that the team of the central committee really did not have a single soul from the central committee on it. The Cultural Revolution group of the central committee merely nominated a provincial party secretary as the team leader and the chairwoman of the provincial women's federation as the assistant team leader. It was said that they had come here to clear up the Mosuo mess. Two central committee members called Zhang Chunqiao and Yao Wenyuan had really lost their tempers this time and had written a lengthy article of tens of thousands of characters, which asked, "In China, the most advanced and most revolutionary socialist country in the world, why haven't we rooted out this most primitive, most backward, and most barbarous lifestyle?" Little Sunamei understood only the meaning of *root out* in this long sentence because she had begun to dig up grass with a shovel in the buckwheat field when she was very small. What did they want to root out?

The three-day (and night) meeting, in which the team leader asked Mosuo cadres to explain how the Mosuo matrilineal family was set up, amused and amazed the team members more than myths of goddesses. Young female team members blushed, male team members laughed with their heads shifting back and forth and their mouths hissing strangely. The Mosuo cadres at the meeting found this behavior most incomprehensible. "What's so funny about our way of life?" they asked. Every Mosuo cadre felt angered and insulted. When the meeting was over, all those Mosuo cadres had become drawn and sallow, like young buds struck by frost. Each of them took several team members to his village. Those glowing, ruddy faces turned to slate as soon as they entered the village. Among the five who came to little Sunamei's village was Gu Shuxian. Gu brought with her a squad of PLA soldiers to guard her abode day and night. She was a fat woman in her forties who wore over her mouth a sterile mask that made her look like a donkey. Little Sunamei thought, "She must be afraid of what might happen if she let herself loose to snap a mouthful of highland barley." Gu's quivering flesh made her gasp at every step she took. She wore a soldier's uniform, and a large Chairman Mao badge shone at her breast.

On first arriving in the village, Gu held a party meeting. It was already dark. Three party members and five team members, eight in all, attended the meeting in the pine forest along the mountain slope. A group of children in short linen gowns crept together toward the campfire. The children knew that the woman in charge was guarded by soldiers with pistols. Yet they neither thought they could be discovered nor believed the soldiers would really shoot them. They crawled to where they could hear the meeting and stayed put. They waited through two meals and did not hear anyone take the floor. The three Mosuo party members bowed their heads like sunflowers at night. The five team members were staring at them with round eyes, like toads squatting on lotus leaves. The children were getting tired but dared not leave. It was so quiet that the slightest movement would spook the meeting. Finally, Gu Shuxian could not bear the silence any longer. She ordered Suola, the Mosuo team leader, to interpret for her.

"Why is it so hard to take a stand? A Communist party member must take the lead in everything. We're not asking you to climb a mountain of swords or wade a flaming sea, but you must be trailblazers. Just think — everything is being done for *your* sake. We want you to live a decent, monogamous, legitimate life. What kind of life are you leading now? Only cavemen living ten thousand years ago had lives like yours, so chaotic that a child knows his mother but not his father. This is the residue of group marriage. You are party members. Aren't you ashamed of yourselves? This is far from the morality of a party member. We cannot put up with this anymore. Comrade Jiang Qing has given special attention to our team. Listen to the instructions of Comrades Zhang Chunqiao and Yao Wenyuan on how to accomplish your great historical mission. In the shortest possible time, by force or by persuasion, you must drag our Mosuo kinsmen out of the stone age and into modern life with the rest of us!"

Bima, a twenty-year-old female party member, said in a thin voice, "During the year of the Great Leap Forward...they said the same thing. But later – "

"What happened later?"

"The women and men who married ended up separating and returning to their mothers."

"I can assure you that this year is not the same as '58. If that year saw a storm, this time there will be a hurricane! We will not give up until we have carried the revolution through to the end!"

"I can take the lead in all things except – " Bima stammered, "except in this kind of thing. I...I...I can't take lead."

"Then you'll be expelled from the party!"

"So be it."

"So be *what?* You will still have to get your marriage certificate, even after you lose your party membership."

"I...I..." Raising her head, Bima suddenly found courage. "I don't see why the members of the central committee should give a damn about what's inside a man's pants or under a woman's skirt! We have been leading a decent, peaceful life, not a speck of chaos in it. No Mosuo has ever committed a crime, and none of us ever goes to court or picks a fight with her neighbor. Why are you forcing us to accept marriage? Why are you trying to separate us from our own kin and break up our matrilineal families? We are not accustomed to living in a family of strangers, separated from our own mothers and maternal uncles."

"Your head is on backward! Only monogamy fits current moral standards – can't you get that through your head?"

Nobody replied. Gu Shuxian roared out, "Understand?"

The three party members shook their heads in unison.

"Listen to me!" Gu Shuxian took off her sterile mask. Bits of white foam sprayed from the corners of her mouth as she screamed, "Without a marriage certificate, a man and a woman cannot become legal spouses. Men and women who 'sleep together' (what a vivid term) are committing a crime. When they are caught by the team, if they repent, they may get their food ration reduced; if they resist, they will be declared undesirables and sent to jail to reform themselves there! Now hear what I say: Everything I just said becomes effective immediately. Let's hold a mass meeting."

On hearing this, the eavesdropping children crawled back to the village. Like an impatient bird with seven beaks and eight tongues, in broken phrases and fragmented concepts they all tried at the same time to tell the adults what they had heard at the meeting. In spite of the verbal confusion, the message was clear that no one was allowed to make *axiao* anymore unless they got marriage papers and entered into a one-husband, one-wife relationship. On hearing that the team was determined to break up their extended matrilineal family, quite a few men and women started to weep aloud. They had a hunch that this time would be even more disastrous than '58.

At the mass meeting, Gu Shuxian read out loud the article by Zhang Chunqiao and Yao Wenyuan, which was immeasurably tedious, like the endless rumbling of a water mill. No one understood a word of it. Even Suola couldn't translate it. But no one was really sleepy. Thanks to the young eavesdroppers, the villagers already knew the gist of the article. Such a lengthy article was made simple and concise through the medium of children: a man and a woman cannot sleep together without official approval; also, when a man and a woman do not wish to sleep together anymore, they must go to the authorities to get a stamped, official paper. Otherwise, the officials will search your place and catch you.

After she had finished reading the document, Gu Shuxian asked the masses to discuss it. They sat through three candles, but no one said a word. Emphasizing each word, Gu repeated what she had said at the party meeting. Then she warned them, "Don't try to test the law with your own body. Adultery deserves the most severe punishment. If you do not want marriage, just stay in your own home and don't go out. Can you manage that?"

No answer. Perhaps silence was the best answer.

The older Mosuo rose first and exited the meeting place, followed by the women, the men, and the party members. The children brought up the rear. Gu Shuxian put on her sterile mask in a fit of anger and mumbled, "Let's see who is tougher! Let's see how long you can bear celibacy!"

She was going on thirteen. Oh, beautiful Sunamei! A grain of corn was about to bloom.

This occurred in the summer of 1975. A most peculiar, destructive revolution in China had already been dragging on for nine years, surpassing the length of the interminable anti-Japanese war of the thirties and the forties. If this could be called a flame, then the flame was dim but still smoldering. No one could really put it out. Moreover, these monsters who had illuminated themselves and burned others with this flame kept pouring oil onto the dying fire in desperation. So millions of Chinese were still being burned alive.

2

I gaze at her window. In the past it was pasted over with black paper; now a cloth curtain with tiny blue flowers hangs there.

So here I am again, in this place so familiar and full of affection. Oh, I can't help leaning against a plane tree on the sidewalk. I'm too weak to stand, and wounds cover my body like the scales on a fish. Torture, hunger, toil, lack of sleep, insomnia – all these have disappeared since yesterday. I can hardly believe the past is really gone; perhaps it has merely been suspended. During the past few years, I have adopted a sort of spiritual equilibrium that enables me to relegate any disaster – as soon as it has ended – to the status of nightmare. Reality only exists once I awaken from the nightmare. The din of the metropolis, the ceaseless flow of the crowds regardless of weather and time, the plane tree turning green, emitting its fragrance, the window on that third floor from which the light floods out – all this is real. Although reality is at hand, I can't go over and rush upstairs right now because I have no energy left. That lovable shadow in that window is her. No one but me would be able to tell that she is listening to music as usual. How often she used to turn on the record player stealthily and put that warped copy of Tchaikovsky's Sixth Symphony on the turntable. Every time it went around, the needle would move up and down once, distorting each quarter note by the interval of a sixth. She would turn the volume down so low that no one could hear it from outside. At those moments, when tears glistened in her eyes and a glass of hot water warmed her hands, she looked most beautiful, as though transfigured into the world of pure music. In the middle of all this vandalism, it was a miracle she could have a Tchaikovsky album. It was indeed a miracle, and I had brought it about.

The revolution of 1966, an entire nation gone insane, began with the savage destruction of cultural monuments. At that time I was an idealistic youth, a freshman at the College of Fine Arts, throwing myself into the revolutionary currents. Burn! We burned the Bamboo Slips of the early Qin; we burned the scriptures brought back by Buddhist Master Xuanzhuang from the Western Heaven (India); we burned the original works of Minangong, Tang Yin, Wen Zhengming, and Xu Wenchang. Needless to say, replicas of European Renaissance masters were all burned to ashes. Smash! We smashed the stone carvings and frescoes of the Sui and Tang; we smashed the fine porcelain art of the northern Song. Even human heads could hardly escape the fate of being smashed.

That winter I had been extremely lucky. The headquarters of the Red Guards had made me leader of the group raiding the Music Reference Library. At that time, the power of a group leader was indeed great; after all, Jiang Qing was merely an assistant group leader. I commanded my group of young warriors to remove everything from stacks and drawers, heap all the musical scores, albums, and tapes in the courtyard, spray gasoline on the heap, and then light a match. Just one match started a blazing fire. Around the fire we young warriors, holding Little Red Books to our hearts, chanted *Quotations of Chairman Mao*. I sincerely felt that we were creating an epoch, a great revolution that would shake heaven and earth. In a flash, what had been created through years of labor by the masters of world music was burned to ashes. Yet I firmly believed that we were merely eliminating the germs detrimental to humanity. From now on, the universe would be forever purged of such bourgeois music.

As the person in charge of the destruction, I was the last to leave that "slaughterhouse." Leaning against the wall in a dark corner, I watched with pride and satisfaction as the embers glowed – now bright, now dim – when a middle-aged woman wearing a worn-out padded hat and a faded, outmoded army overcoat, floated up from the basement. Unaware of me, she walked with dazed eyes to the embers, which were still emitting heat, and started poking around in them helplessly. I admired her boldness from the bottom of my heart, but at the same time I hated her for being so counterrevolutionary. How could I let her go on? I ran up to her, and she, like a chick in the shadow of a vulture, was immediately seized by sobs. Writhing on the ground, she turned a tear-streaked face toward me, stared at me, and sank into a state of abject terror. I acted the part of the victorious warrior pointing a bayoneted rifle at his captive.

"Who are you?"

"The library researcher."

"Why are you crying?"

"I...am...cry..." Her quivering lips were unable to get the words out.

"Why are you crying?" I took another step toward her.

Fearfully and cautiously she turned her back to me. Her eyes, like those of a frightened doe, looked over her shoulder at me, accompanied by fits of shivering. I didn't know why a sudden feeling of pity rose from my heart and my face became less stern. She whispered, "Have you ever listened to music?"

"What do you mean?" My revolutionary vigilance immediately made every cell of my body taut.

"If...you..." Her weak voice, like the chirping of a tiny bird, moved me to hear her out. "If you have a chance...listen to any of these albums in peace; you will understand how great those masters are. If you had heard any of them before, you wouldn't have treated them – "

"Ha – you have a lot of confidence in their bourgeois cultural superiority, don't you?" I sneered.

"Only if you listen to it will you understand. Please listen to it in peace – "

I kicked the heap of ashes, as if to tell her, "This heap of ashes will never make another sound." She understood my meaning very well. After wiping her shivering, dirty hands on her overcoat, she took from her bosom a single album, with Tchaikovsky's portrait on the cover.

"Still one... left, the only one. Since I can't protect it myself, you may take it and listen to it. Sooner or later ... you will find a record player. You must find a quiet place, although it's hard to find such a place now. You will find one, however; perhaps the upstairs room of a building whose capitalist owner has just been driven out."

I was quite at a loss as to what to do with this woman. Her audacity could only indicate either insanity or addiction to the drug of bourgeois culture; in either case, she was definitely beyond salvation, I thought. I grabbed the album from her and threw it to the concrete floor. The woman, who must have heard the sound of the album cracking, threw herself toward it and became hysterical. Holding the album in her arms, she roared in rage, "You, can't you leave even this last one unbroken?"

Out of curiosity, and with the generosity of a victor, I said with a smile, "Okay, give it to me. I'll listen to it. But remember, I can never be corrupted by it."

Her eyes full of confidence, she offered me the album with such solemnity that I wanted to smash it. Fortunately, her eyes were soon shut. With both hands touching her heart, she froze as if in silent prayer.

I wrapped the album in one of our revolutionary posters, took it secretly to my dorm, and hid it in the bottom of my suitcase, hoping to find a chance to listen to it. But then, fighting one battle after another, I completely forgot about it.

I gaze at her window. In the past it was pasted over with black paper; now a cloth curtain with tiny blue flowers hangs there.

Now she must be listening to that album. From her silhouette I can tell that the second movement is already underway.

It was she who made me take that forgotten album from the bottom of my suitcase. I should cross the street quickly, climb the stairs, knock at her door, fall straight into her arms, and lean against her shoulder, together at last, listening with her to that quivering of the human heart composed by Tchaikovsky. But I am too weak to move even a single step. A feeling of relaxation is incapacitating me, as if I were a swimmer approaching the shore. I want to call to her for help. Licking my parched lips, I find I have lost my voice. I don't even know how to shout or cry. In the surging waves of the metropolitan din, my tongue is as insignificant as the quivering of a bamboo leaf in the thunderstorm.

I began retracing my past. How did I get to know her? When did my love first begin? Three years ago? Yes, it was three years ago that I first saw this window. And before that? Where was I during the three years before those three years? Now I remember. That was 1969. That year we, the palace guards of Jiang Qing, were disbanded like captives who had surrendered their guns and, under the policy of so-called military training, were incorporated into the regular army, not as privates but as scapegoats, leading a half-imprisoned life on a farm. That bitch Jiang Qing finally abandoned us. Mixed feelings of anger, grief, insult, and a heavy sense of loss shattered all my beliefs. I was too tired to open my eyes and I hated to think about anything. I had no wish to repeat others' thoughts but had no thoughts of my own either. Thank heaven, my duty on the farm was looking after water buffaloes, a duty that enabled me to escape the drills in the scorching sun and other military training such as crawling, rolling, and fighting on the muddy ground. I did not even need to cultivate the earth with a hoe. Luckier still, my herd was a low-maintenance one. Gui Renzhong, a Ph.D. in chemistry and a former professor, was looking after a herd of cows. Although my buffaloes looked dirtier and clumsier than his cows, they made my job much easier. Gradually, I became one of them. In summer I would wallow in the muddy pond and then lie in the summer shade so that the mud on my body would dry and peel off by itself. In winter I would sleep on the sunny hillside, snoring to my heart's content.

Not long ago I had recited the *Quotations of Chairman Mao* and "The Three Old Articles" verbatim, but now every word of them sank into oblivion. What sort of things had I done during the Cultural Revolution? Had they been right? Which had been right and which wrong? Arguing, tearfully shouting revolutionary slogans, swearing to defend Marxism-Leninism and Mao Zedong thought to the death, fighting revisionism, breaking away from the Four Olds [old ideas, old culture, old customs, old traditions], wiping out all ox-demons and snake monsters, and smashing the heads of capitalist roaders. Furthermore, using one quotation to attack another, you seized my pigtails, and I spied on you. Then, like wolves who love to chase the scent of blood, we fell into wars with real bullets. We lived, ventured, thrilled for this sort of stuff. We even held Jiang Qing's stinking feet and carried her all the way to Tiananmen Square so that she could declare in her quivering falsetto, with an accent somewhere between those of Shandong and Shanghai, "My dear comrades of the proletarian revolutionary factions! My dear comrades in arms! On behalf of our great leader, I..."

Recalling her voice and its associations, I felt like vomiting. Ugh! What sort of creature was I? Where was I? What had I ever done? Aside from those endless troubles imposed on me, had I ever accomplished anything of my own accord? Was there a small space or a shred of time I could call my own? What should I even think about all this? Thinking always leads to a political judgment about right or wrong or to self-reproach, regret, shock, and depression. With a sudden turn of my body, I dropped my face on the soft, dry straw and fell asleep.

The public-address system of the farm was calling for "great unity, a great confederation of factions." Now my experience revealed its disguised message: now both the central leadership and the grassroots units were being torn by serious differences of opinion. Following Lin Biao's death in a plane crash, the entire nation had launched a campaign to criticize him. The propagandists, racking their brains, dug out all sorts of evidence to prove Lin Biao's long-hidden, wolfish ambitions, as though they had predicted both his plot to seize power and his death. Then criticizing Lin Biao alone became too monotonous, so they dragged Confucius in to play the role of Lin's henchman. It seemed odd that Confucius, who had lived over two thousand years ago, could be involved in Lin Biao's treason. But it was said that, after Lin Biao's plane crashed, many scrolls with the words *Restrain oneself in expectation of the restoration* were discovered hanging in his residence. It seemed that through his whole life Confucius had said only one unpardonable sentence: "Restrain oneself in expectation of the restoration," and that he had said it for the sole purpose of teaching Lin Biao how to seize power. Hence, Confucius became the chief schemer in the abortive coup d'état that had occurred in China between summer and autumn of 1971. Facing wave on wave of such filthy noise, I could only sleep to shut off my thinking. Fortunately, the coup d'état was a court intrigue that had no need of us monkeys to make havoc in the heavenly palaces. Right at this moment of my spiritual nadir, a beautiful girl was coming toward me with an empty knitted bag in her hand. For fear that she was a mere phantom, I rubbed my eyes: no, she was real.

Our first meeting was like a scene out of a pastoral romance. I, a cowherd of about thirty, had chanced on some good luck. Whether my courage came from long sexual starvation or was simply given to me by fate, I was bold enough to sit up on my grassy bed and call out to her, "Hi there. Come and sit by me for a while."

She narrowed her eyes and smiled sweetly, looking even lovelier with her nose wrinkled. Her pair of liberation shoes turned to point at me. Then she sat down beside me, as though she were my sister. It was the first time in my life that I had sat so close to a member of the opposite sex (except as a toddler, of course). I felt a bit uneasy. I pulled myself up in order to improve my appearance and posture; my bones, it seemed, had collapsed two years before.

Noticing my efforts, she tweaked my nose with her fingers. "Quit showing off!"

What? Such a fresh vocabulary. To a dropout from the political arena like me, her words sounded particularly human. It had been a long time since I had heard so human a phrase. I came alive again. The many meanings of her words left me with a feeling of infinite sweetness. And the smoothness with which she had tweaked my nose lingered for a long time.

From our chat I learned that she was no country girl but the "Thousand Pieces of Gold" daughter of the former deputy mayor Fang. Her father had been seized as a capitalist roader in 1966. After repeated criticisms, he had been sent to a cadre school for reform. His cadre school adjoined my farm. Each month the daughter, Fang Yunqian, came to see her father, a deputy mayor in the past but a good-for-nothing today. She brought him only some poor cigarettes and coarse cookies because anything good would be forfeited. A dog never changes its nature; how could a capitalist roader be allowed to enjoy comfort? Her mother had died when Fang Yunqian was five. Her stepmother was very young, and at the beginning of the Cultural Revolution she had declared herself a rebel and abandoned her family. At the criticism meeting she had mercilessly exposed the counter-revolutionary words and deeds of her husband and impressed the city as a woman warrior with a firm proletarian stand.

Strange – why hadn't I met her until today, when there had been scores of chances over the past twenty months? The field path, serpentine and long, had brought her to me at last.

She had been living on her own since she was thirteen. Although she had a brother, he had been sent to faraway Xinjiang. She was the only one left to guard their barracks – a three-room apartment, allotted housing for Deputy Mayor Fang after he had been driven out of the exclusive villa for senior officials. She went neither to school nor to work. No rebel organization would bother to take her on, and she didn't want to depend on any rebel organizations, nor on the official leadership. So she hid in the apartment like a mouse and went out shopping only before daybreak. She not only had learned how to cook for herself but had also assembled a private collection of classical novels, model operas, cooking recipes, Nietzsche's *Thus Spake Zarathustra,* and even a copy of *The Art of Healthy Sex,* which had been a rare book even before the Cultural Revolution. According to her, she had picked up all these books from outside the walls of the academic authorities like a scavenging mouse at night. Some of them had tumbled into the ditches and escaped their fate of being burned.

She told me of her treasure at our very first meeting. I don't know what gave me the charm to make her trust me at first sight. Her language and logic were entirely different from mine. Her mind was barren of any political conceptions. Her kind of thinking was utterly impossible to find in China at that time. She seemed to have been living in another world, where she had found the freedom of an insect in a cocoon – a freedom millions of other Chinese, along with myself, were unable to enjoy. I adored her. Once I had been a revolutionary hero who believed, "If we do not run the affairs of the world, who else can run them?" Today I not only admired her insect's freedom but was anxious to gain it myself. The radical change in me could be described by the poetic line, "The reversal of heaven and earth creates great elation." When I told her eagerly that I wanted to retreat into her cocoon, she laughed and gave no answer.

She looked at me as if I were a water buffalo covered with mud. Her eyes slowly grew larger; in them I saw something wrong with myself, and I started breathing faster. I wanted to escape from this strained situation, yet my limbs refused to obey me. Giggling aloud, she covered her mouth and jumped with mirth. I sank back onto the straw, feeling awkward and disappointed. What a shame. I felt like a thief caught in the act.

"Bye bye." Waving her bag at me, she left. When she got near the highway, she cupped her palms into a trumpet and shouted, "Will we meet again?"

Only now did God restore my strength. Cracking my whip, I shouted with the strength of a baby sucking its mother's milk, "Wait – for – me!"

Luckily I had memorized her address – street and number – while we chatted. Thank God! The moment the word *God* slipped from my mouth – from the mouth of a former Red Guard, mind you – my cerebral machinery started running. I had to think of a way to leave the farm and see her in the city. Zhuge Liang had passed away in A.D. 234. Had he been my grandfather, he would still be just as useless to me now. A man's imagination soars in such hopeless situations. Ancient Chinese in desperate straits always produced beautiful poetry and prose. Modern Chinese – take me, for example – have not a shred of literary talent. Pragmatically I thought of Zhuge Liang of more than seventeen hundred years ago, hoping he could give me wise counsel. But soon I reined in the blind galloping horses of my brain and the flames of romance died out.

What could I do? Ask for a furlough on account of a family emergency? Pity I hadn't enough material to weave even one lie. My family in the far north had perished in both name and reality. In the first year of the Cultural Revolution, while I was swelling infinitely between heaven and earth, my parents had shut the windows, turned on the gas and killed themselves. On hearing of their deaths, not only did I feel no sorrow, but I made an extremely fashionable wisecrack: their death weighed as light as a feather on me. A pair of bookworms, who knew nothing but how to bore into a heap of musty papers, had drowned in the rolling currents of revolution. My witty remarks won thunderous applause from the Red Guards.

Several years after their deaths, qualms of conscience arose with my disappointment. A belated but ever-deepening grief tortured me, like the hairshirt of an ascetic monk. Late at night I would crawl out onto the frozen lake to punish my heartlessness. Now, even if I viewed things from a purely pragmatic angle, I could use a family. Only then could I receive phony telegrams with messages such as "Father dying." If only they had survived and not died together, if they had still been alive, then they could die one at a time, so that I could use their deaths as an excuse to crawl out of this hell not just once, but twice.

In the little notebooks of the PLA representative on the farm, my name was surrounded by a cluster of question marks. Although I had made many sarcastic political remarks, they were clever net grazers and could not really be nailed down as counterrevolutionary. However, I had not performed any good deeds, such as informing on somebody, confessing the simmering slanders hidden in my heart against a certain political VIP or disclosing his secret crimes. Of course, there were other ways to build a good record. For example, you might have a heroic diary written beforehand. After setting a civilian house on fire, you could shout at the top of your lungs, "Long live Chairman Mao!" and jump into the flames to save the house. Or in the dead of night, jumping naked out of your warm quilt, you might cry hysterically, "Stop the class enemy!" and dash out of the room. Then you might use a spade to hurt yourself and produce a horrifying wound. You would then fall to the ground as if dying. When the rescuers came, you would groan in pain, "Don't worry about me. Go catch the enemy first!"

All these ploys were above my abilities. I was no actor. Even if threatened with death, I could not walk from the backstage area, where a normal person could still adapt himself, to the glaring lights of center stage. Moreover, I was terribly afraid of pain.

If I tried to ask for a leave, my request would be absolutely refused. "I want to buy some daily necessities in town." "Okay, write a shopping list, and we'll ask somebody to get them for you." "I need to have my watch repaired." "Whoever's going downtown on business can take it to the repair shop." "I want to have a look around town." "What? You are unwilling to devote all of yourself to labor reform?" Whatever reasons I fabricated would be refuted. They might even accuse me of "establishing counterrevolutionary connections."

Let's back up: Supposing they permitted me to go to the city, they would definitely send a good student to watch me, and this would not be much different from being followed by the KGB. The good student would record every word I said and every subtle expression of my face minutely in his secret book and then produce a profound analysis associating my behavior with the current situation of class struggle in society. His report to the leadership would doom me for certain. My remaining days on the farm would become even more productive. No. I must get rid of all these romantic illusions. What I needed was solid scientific experimentation. Right, I should ask for sick leave! I selected the farm clinic as my target, although I knew it was a tough stronghold.

There were two doctors in our clinic, one male and one female. The male doctor, a worldly-wise old hand in Chinese medicine, was surnamed Yu and called Shouchen. He was once a country charlatan, living on folk prescriptions and herbal pharmacy. More recently, because he had gained a secret prescription for gynecological diseases, he was retained as family doctor by an important bureaucrat. After liberation he had practiced traditional Chinese medicine in district hospitals. Since the beginning of the Cultural Revolution, he had been repeatedly criticized, the thin hair on his head had been completely plucked out by Red Guards, and he had cursed himself as worse than a pig or a dog. As a reward for such ruthless self-treatment, he was permitted to reform himself in the clinic. Every time he gained a generous amnesty like this, he kowtowed with extravagant words and tears. If in the past hunger and poverty had reduced him to the level of a dog, now fear was turning him into a wolf. He was on guard against every patient coming to see him. He put his hand around your wrist not to feel your pulse but to try to figure out what tricks you were playing in order to escape criticism and labor reform. When you stuck out your tongue, he did not even look at its coating but fastened his eyes on yours to gauge your mental disease, so that he could prescribe accordingly.

Nevertheless, I doubted Yu Shouchen had been born mean. A seed blossoms or grows thorny according to its specific environment. Perfect men, who are neither corrupted by luxury nor yield to power nor collapse under poverty, are a rarity. Take my case, for example: I was no perfect man. Pretending to be sick is cheating, isn't it? I admit I was cheating, but I couldn't feel ashamed of it. I was merely a pitiful, helpless being who was driven to cheat, and my cheating inflicted no harm on anybody; Lin Biao's cheating was spurred by his ambition – he was a snake trying to swallow an elephant – and his cheating had drawn thousands of people with him down into the abyss. Compared with Lin Biao's, my cheating was really nothing. This comparison cleared my conscience, and I started to play my tricks in a well-planned strategy.

Now let's turn to the female doctor: she was nearly forty. The fact that her husband had made her bear three daughters without loving her was enough to account for her neurosis. She considered every young and pretty female to be her enemy. In order to nip evil in the bud she would label any female a threat who gave her husband a lingering glance (that is, one that violated the three-second rule in basketball) and would punish her. She would even concoct evidence against her and report her to the PLA representative as a class enemy. She could not rest until her potential rival was punished with either political or physical death. Her husband was a manager in charge of the students' daily necessities on the farm. Each month, when he distributed sanitary napkins to the female students, she would volunteer to give him a hand. Her tigress stares sent chills down everyone's spine.

She understood perfectly well that her despotism over her husband was made possible by China's current political situation. She had collected both the examples of her husband's transgressions and the words to be used as evidence against him, and she herself would be a round-the-clock witness to his crimes. Even without such evidence, a wife who appeared in court (but at that time there was no official court, and the office of anyone in power could be used as a courtroom) against a political criminal played the multiple role of prosecutor, star witness, evidence, and lawyer.

This powerful lady was known as Liu Tiemei (Iron Plum). In her clinic, besides two doctors, there were two nurses, both selected from the countryside. The two nurses were descended from decent roots. Their ancestral line consisted of three generations of poor peasants, and none of their blood or non-blood relatives were in the ranks of the Five Bad Elements – landlords, rich peasants, counterrevolutionaries, criminals, or rightists. And, being illiterate, they were certainly purer and more dependable than those girl students. On the walls of their simple and crude clinic were nothing but color portraits of Chairman Mao with various facial expressions, in various uniforms, and in various revolutionary periods. On the wall immediately behind Doctor Yu Shouchen's chair there hung an eye-catching slogan: *Medical treatment should serve the needs of class struggle.*

The slogan seemed to say that, once you were denounced as a class enemy, medical art would not try to save you from death; it might even help you toward it. The slogan made any patient shudder.

This was the type of stronghold I was going to conquer. I had been a student of fine arts. Although I knew nothing about medicine, I seemed destined to study anatomy. Nevertheless, the day after I got my textbook on anatomy, the central party committee issued the document of May 16 to launch the great Cultural Revolution, and all my books were sacrificed to the fire god. Now I wished I had some knowledge of medicine. We had a genius on our farm – whenever he fainted, pretending to be sick, no one could detect the truth. But I dared not ask him for help. If I did, it would be not be much different from turning myself in. In fact, turning oneself in was less horrible than that. If you turned yourself in at the right moment, you could easily become a model confessor and receive clemency. Then you would be treated just like a model worker and be asked to give heroic talks everywhere. Besides, just as every American was looking for a chance to become rich and famous, every Chinese was looking for an opportunity to become a hero by informing on someone. You could definitely benefit from informing activities. If you didn't become a national hero, you could at least be liberated from arduous military training and toil. You could even become a grassroots leader or the like, gaining the privilege of issuing orders in a limited area, such as scheduling routine work and distributing daily meals. After all these calculations, I found there was no other way but to dig a tunnel to freedom by my own strength, in the heroic spirit of the Count of Monte Christo.

I gaze at her window. In the past it was pasted over with black paper; now a cloth curtain with tiny blue flowers hangs there.

3

She was going on thirteen. Oh, beautiful Suna-mei! Gathering beads of dew were about to flow in a stream.

The majority of the Mosuo put up with the clampdown pretty well. Men stopped their night visits to women. In the dead of night, Sunamei stole out from her *yimei* to watch the work team members parading in the village. They looked dreary, telling yarns one after another. She also groped her way to the *huagu* of the mature women to eavesdrop, but she couldn't hear any male breathing. Still, she was told that pairs of *axiao* had been caught in the *huagu* and in the woods. The work team forced the captives to accept marriage certificates and threatened to send the recalcitrant ones to jail for labor reform. Even so, one pair preferred going to jail rather than accepting a marriage certificate. The work team dragged this stubborn pair into the street for a criticism parade and hung worn-out shoes around their necks to insult them, even though the Mosuo could not grasp the symbolic meaning of those shoes at all. This was what the work team had accomplished in six months of bitter struggle along Lake Xienami. In addition, they had built a wall across the open-air hot spring to divide the bathing place into two compartments: the left one for men and the right one for women.

As things turned out, it was the work team who could not stick around anymore. They hurried through a summary report at the mass meeting, declaring that they had achieved a complete victory in the struggle to purify the family and marital life and that their victory was comparable to the liberation of Taiwan and the unification of the country. They declared that from now on, the Mosuo kinsmen could march shoulder to shoulder with the whole nation. The meeting was crowned with an entertaining program: a revolutionary wedding, sponsored by public funds, was held for those captured *axiao*. Each couple, now legally married, was given a single-door, Han-style hut containing cooking utensils, a quilt and two pillows, and Chairman Mao's portrait. The marriage certificate hung in its glass frame by the left side of Mao's portrait. Old Mosuo put on long faces while the brides and grooms, like marionettes, moved only when pushed by the team members. The children, however, always had fun, for they had never seen things like that before.

"One, two, three, four...," counted a group of boys and girls, all dressed in long shirts that looked like oversized blouses or undersized gowns, squatting beneath a row of *jingfan* trees on the hilltop and watching vehicles crawl, one by one, around the bend of the hill like beetles. There were four cars: one black, two blue, and even a red one. In their wake were two buses and three huge trucks. In the trucks sat PLA soldiers, guns in hand and bayonets flashing. It was scary. Luckily, this time all the cars, buses, and trucks were receding with their strange passengers into the distance. Resting her chin on her little hands, Sunamei tilted her head as she watched the troops disappear into the distance. She was thinking to herself, "Why did they have to be angry with us? Why do they take everything so seriously? Why do they insist that a man and a woman who come from different communities live together in a small hut? They must have eaten too much and have nothing to do. They came to interfere with *us;* we never interfered with *them.* Whatever they did, we let them alone. No one bothered to ask them anything." Sunamei sighed like a little adult. Her mood brightened, like the sky changing from overcast to blue skies. The clouds and mists were dispersing.

The six-month storm finally passed. Lake Xienami, like a smooth mirror, calmly reflected the sky once again.

The Mosuo were a simple people. They soon consigned the second political encroachment of the civilized world to oblivion, as if they were forgetting two invasions by mammoths or hordes of elephants. They healed instantly. No sooner had the engines of the departing work team started snorting than the *axiao* embraced each other. Apparently they had forgotten the taboos of heaven. Intoxicated, they embraced in broad daylight, during working hours in the fields. They believed that their ancestors and the goddess would forgive them because they had been forced to be apart from each other for so long.

Those who had been forced into marriage also started to walk out of their muddy huts, carrying their bedrolls to their own *yishe*.

She was going on thirteen. Oh, beautiful Sunamei! The husk of the spring shoot was falling away and the graceful green bamboo was emerging.

Little Sunamei had a point. Why had Gu Shuxian and her ilk so relentlessly wanted to tear up our *yishe?* Simply because these people were parts of a car. When cars come, they come; when cars go, they are gone. They all spoke the same words; the cars spoke the same words, too, and wore the same face. They couldn't understand the Mosuo tongue and the Mosuo didn't want to talk to them. Who could talk sense with a car, anyway? Cars only make a rumbling noise.

Sunamei understood all this intuitively. Was she right? Yes, but not quite. Gu Shuxian was indeed a cog in the political machine. She had to turn and move back and forth with the machine and make the same noise as the other parts of the machine. Nevertheless, she was made of flesh and blood, not of iron. When she was traveling in the red car, all the excitement and pride she drew from her power to decide others peoples' fate and to save the primitives ebbed away, and a strange feeling of sorrow gradually rose, overwhelmed her, and gave her a sense of defeat instead of victory. She had to admit that those silent Mosuo women and men were much more powerful than she because they did not fight their own bodies and souls. She wanted to cry but held back her tears, aware that her bodyguard, Xiao Wei, was sitting beside her and that her driver, Xiao He, could also watch her in the rearview mirror. She shut her eyes as if she were tired. Indeed, she was exhausted, although not at all sleepy. A desire burned inside her, a desire to be shocked. She felt dry and hot around her face, her neck, and her whole body. She forced herself to calm down so she could take the time to reflect on her life, as she frequently did.

With the help of a matchmaker she had been married to a local guerilla commander just before the victory over Japan. Her husband had married her not out of love but out of need. Before he found a wife, he had once complained to the county secretary, "I can't control myself anymore. If you don't allow me to marry, I'm afraid I'll commit some sort of sin."

Three years later, desire had turned to disgust. During the revolution, Gu Shuxian fully revealed her greed, calculation, vanity, and ambition. While her husband was following the field army marching to the central plains, she had been a student in the school for army dependents. In less than a year she had toppled the dashing political commissar and stepped into his shoes by spying on some women students and exposing their infidelity to their husbands at the front. When she assumed office, she adopted the severest methods to protect women: she dismissed all male staff members, except for a few aged cooks. She also invented a chain-protection system: anyone who discovered flirtation or adultery and did not report it would be treated the same as the sinners. Apart from being criticized in public meetings and having her hair torn from her scalp, she would have to carry sacks of grain during the military marches and mill flour all night when the army camped. Because of Gu's outstanding achievements, the husbands of the women students praised her highly as a woman of principle. But the students hated her. With tears in her eyes, the wife of a brigade commander complained to her husband about the tyrannical behavior of this woman political commissar. Her complaints raised Gu Shuxian's position higher than ever. Listening to his tender wife's weeping, the commander scoffed, "What she has done is for your own good! You can't go removing a political commissar of her caliber."

However, there was one man Gu Shuxian failed to win over: her own husband. He assumed a stony indifference and contempt toward her. When the troops stopped for rest and reorganization, Gu Shuxian would lead the wives of the higher-ranking officers on a round-the-clock march to the frontline troops. As soon as they stopped in a village close to the headquarters, many horses with leather saddles would arrive, with bodyguards to fetch the officers' wives. Only Gu Shuxian failed to send someone. That made her feel great. Why, she herself was a regimental officer and could ride her own horse to her husband's camp. By that time their marital relationship was already dwindling into just a name. She did not seem to care. "When I come, willing or not, you've got to sleep with me on the same plank, and I will press my naked body to yours, seducing you, terrifying you with the power of flesh. Then I will tell you about all the shameless scandals that happened in our school and about my investigative talent and my severe punishment of those sinners." Each time, long before she had finished the tedious account, her husband lay snoring in a deep sleep.

In 1949 her husband was demobilized. Luckily, as a civilian he was promoted to the position of provincial general secretary. He tried to talk her into a divorce, but she refused.

She stuck to him as revenge against his stony indifference and contempt over the past years. Once the provincial general secretary was interned in a hospital for a physical checkup and fell in love with a younger nurse. Gu Shuxian soon discovered their affair, and she immediately collected all the evidence against them. A woman's jealousy can make her much better than a professional detective. Nevertheless, she did not make a big fuss over it. Instead, she used a most ambiguous gesture to call her husband's attention to the fact: "I know everything about you. I have all the evidence against you in my hands. And so long as I breathe, you'd better not entertain any dreams of divorce." For her husband, this meant a complete blockade of his journey from hell to heaven.

Yet in public she always appeared as the most intimate companion to the general secretary. She loved to show off when her husband was with guests. "The general secretary loves my noodles. What's to be done? I'd better be his cook." "The general secretary does not allow anyone to touch his desk. What's to be done? I'd better be his secretary." "The general secretary does not allow anyone to make his bed. What's to be done? I'd better be his housekeeper. Although I'm a cadre with some responsibility myself, I just love to serve him. It's my whole happiness. I know – no matter how hard I try I won't really get anywhere in public affairs. However, I feel satisfied in having a loving husband. Don't you agree, darling?"

She knew that in front of the guests, he would have to say yes. She was also sure that in mouthing this yes he was wishing he could pounce on her in rage. He was forced not only to repress his anger but even to wear a pleasant smile. When the guests left he and she again became independent crags; they went to their separate bedrooms as if nothing had happened. If she had really cooked a bowl of noodles for him at that moment, he would have smashed the bowl in her face. Of course she would not even bother to try it. This so-called happy couple lived like this under the same roof for twenty years. During the Cultural Revolution, the husband was denounced as a capitalist roader and sent to a cadre school; she, having not worked at all in the past dozen years, became spotless and was chosen by the newly established revolutionary power structure – the provincial revolutionary committee – to be chair of the provincial women's federation. For the first time, husband and wife were drawn apart to a distance that matched their spiritual estrangement. Both sides felt not pain but relief. Gu Shuxian even felt better than her husband did because she now looked down on him from a commanding position. For many years she had been lower in rank than he. Now at last the tables were turned.

Her sojourn along the beach of Lake Xienami had destroyed Gu Shuxian's hard calmness condensed by years of hatred. She felt a tender sorrow rising from the bottom of her heart. She was disturbed by an emotion she had not experienced for many years. She was unable to figure out her past and present. She was particularly confused by the Mosuo life. Although the Mosuo did not live in a civilized way, it was impossible to change them, as if the long history of mankind and the influence of the majority races and their governments had no power over them at all. They, especially their women, were full of self-confidence. According to our social norms, they should have been cursed as shameless women, yet a queenly pride shone in their eyes. The ancestors of humanity had probably lived as they did. Suddenly, Gu Shuxian found herself admiring them. What she had heard about the rituals in which a Mosuo woman receives a man flashed through her consciousness like a movie, imprinting sharp, sensual images on her mind. She sighed. Then she warned herself and tried to control the wild horses inside her. She desperately wanted to recite a quotation but could not think of a suitable one. Her mind went blank and all the quotations blew away with the wind. She was suddenly overpowered by a desire she had suppressed for many years.

The driver, Xiao He, noticed in the rearview mirror that the face of the bodyguard, Xiao Wei, had turned ghastly pale. In spite of his shivering, Xiao Wei dared not move because his hand was held tight by the fleshy hands of the leading cadre, as she pulled it toward her breasts....

Such strange happenings were beyond the imagination of Sunamei and her fellow villagers.

She was going on thirteen. Oh, beautiful Sunamei! An obscure little flower, smiling gently with closed lips, was about to reveal her face. She was about to leap from the grassland, shining like a red star in the blue night sky.

4

I gaze at her window. In the past it was pasted over with black paper; now a cloth curtain with tiny blue flowers hangs there.

I had always been poor at physical education. I still remembered my participation in a race during my high school days. After a hundred-meter sprint to the finish, my heart was beating at twice the normal rate. A doctor's son once told me that after strenuous exercise your pulse and blood pressure rise steeply. Why not try this trick? So, I used my intuition to choose a lucky day and secretly reconnoiter the enemy position. Good, there were few patients in the clinic. I ran madly around the straw heap until I could hear my pumping heart. Then I hurried toward the clinic at a slow run. I could not let my heart rate slow down; on the other hand, the doctor was not supposed to hear my gasping, either.

Lowering my head and frowning, I walked slowly into the clinic and leaned listlessly against the door frame. Liu Tiemei saw me first and was not hostile, perhaps because I was not a woman. It was impossible for me to be a threat to her power over her husband. You see, gay people in China were practically invisible, even if many of them existed. Gay people did not arouse any suspicion because the common belief was that people of the same sex repelled one another; people of different sexes attracted each other. Nobody admitted the existence of such an abnormal phenomenon as homosexuality. It was all right for men to share beds and for women to be intimate. But communication between a man and a woman had to be conducted under the strictest supervision.

Liu Tiemei walked up to me and asked gently, "What's wrong with you, Liang Rui?"

"My...heart...is...beating wildly." It was true, my heartbeat started to accelerate because of my nervousness in front of her. I dared not look into her eyes. She held my wrist, feeling my pulse attentively. At that moment what worried me most was that my heart would resume its normal beat.

Doctor Liu turned to her nurse. "Give me a sphygmomanometer."

I felt a secret joy in my heart. My abnormal heartbeat had caught her attention. But as she wrapped the sphygmomanometer around my arm, a strange horror seized me: was it a noose in her hand? Could I still escape? As the inflated cuff tightened, the horror in my heart grew more and more acute. I almost fell into a swoon. When she took the sphygmomanometer off my arm, I experienced the relaxation of being set free from bondage.

She said coldly, "My dear young fellow! Why don't you take better care of yourself? You have no right to ruin your own body. Do you regard your body as belonging to yourself? No. It belongs to our great leader, Chairman Mao. Please sit here for a while for observation. Don't move."

I felt a chill penetrate me, from outside to inside, from head to foot, as if a bucket of icy water had just been poured on me. I did not know how long a while was going to take. Worse still, I was not allowed to move. Pretty soon my pulse and blood pressure would become regular. My scheming and desperate running had worked for a paltry five minutes. I had been on the verge of victory. If this Iron Plum wrote "transfer to the hospital" on my file and signed it

"Liu," I could dash to the intercity bus station. Who cared whether my pulse beat eight hundred times or eight times per minute? But – this unlucky *but* ruined everything.

Here I was, sitting on a bench, staring like an idiot at a corner of the room where a huge spider sat securely in her web while a tiny moth struggled in its corner. Should there be spiderwebs in a clinic? As I thought it over, there was really nothing strange about it. If creatures like Jiang Qing, Kang Sheng, and Yao Wenyuan could appear at Tiananmen Square, why couldn't a clinic keep a poisonous spider? I felt like that tiny moth, and the woman called Iron Plum was that huge spider. The spider sat still without a side-glance at the moth; her calmness angered and disgusted me. That tiny moth was me, utterly helpless, too weak to break free from those sticky filaments. It was better not to struggle. The more you struggled, the more the web tightened around you, and the sooner she could eat you. I had not suspected that I would be so powerless when my own fate was in my hands. I usually considered myself a strong man! Now she had drawn a circle on the ground and easily made me her prisoner. Could I still find a way out? Hmm, I was missing Mr. Zhuge Liang again, a man of superior wisdom who had died seventeen hundred years ago. What a good-for-nothing I was!

Then I noticed that Liu Tiemei and Yu Shouchen were nodding and whispering to each other. I could not read their lips and could hear them only very faintly. Although the faint sounds wove into a sheet of noise, I could not make out its warps and wefts. Their discussion, however, struck horror into my heart, numbed my hands, and even caused my ears to ring. They were talking about me for sure. I saw bullets shooting at me sporadically from the corners of their eyes. All of a sudden, I felt two snakes creeping from my armpits to my waist. I was at the point of screaming when I realized that these were two streams of cold sweat. After this shock I continued my tense waiting. I believed my situation was not so different from a criminal's awaiting sentencing in court.

Liu Tiemei came over and grasped my wrist fiercely – as if she were putting handcuffs on me. Again she tied the cuff around my arm. Like a captive deprived of his weapon, I surrendered my life to her disposition and thus overcame my fear. I even watched the rising mercury together with her, although I knew nothing about the line between normal and abnormal blood pressure. After the measurement, Liu communicated with Yu Shouchen in complicated hand gestures. Like a deaf-mute, she did it so fast and so skillfully that there was no way for an outsider to guess her meaning. She took off the sphygmomanometer, put it away in its metal case and closed the lid.

Then she said solemnly, "Chairman Mao teaches us: One must be loyal and honest to the party."

I repeated the quotation after her. Just as all priests represent Jesus, in China all politically privileged men and women, whether they were members or not, might well represent the party. I said *to the party* in a tone of sincerity. "I have learned this by heart."

"Before you came to the clinic, were you engaged in any strenuous exercise?"

"No."

"No?" Her eyes doubled in size.

"No." I also doubled the volume of my voice.

"Say that again."

"No! I swear to Chairman Mao!" Now I understood perfectly the possibilities of looking bold and self-assured.

"All right. You may leave now."

Released. Was I released for being guilty or innocent?

"Okay..." I looked at her expectantly, hoping she could write me a sick leave pass. If I couldn't leave the farm, I could at least take some rest on the farm. If I couldn't get full-time rest, then part-time rest would do.

"You may continue doing routine work. Just pay more attention to your nutrition."

I promptly seized the chance to show my cleverness. "May I have a day off to buy some nutritious food in town?"

"Leave your money with me. I'll ask our manager to buy some for you."

"Then..." I could not allow my sweat and pain to go for nothing, nor would I allow myself to be scared and shocked to no purpose. I said hastily, "Can you write me a few sick-meal tickets?"

"All right." She was pretty generous about this and gave me a whole week's worth of sick-meal permits and a few vitamin B_{12} tablets. Although a sick meal was nothing but a bowl of soft noodles, the tickets proved that I was not pretending to be sick and gave me hope for my next try. My first battle had not ended in complete defeat after all. But it had exhausted me, and I was listless for three days. I actually did become sick. But my efforts were not totally wasted. It was a necessary trial, and I had gained some knowledge about my opponents, Yu Shouchen and Liu Tiemei. I remembered one of the supreme commands from my days as a Red Guard: "We must look down upon the enemy in strategy but deal with the enemy seriously in tactics." Now I saw that the two doctors were not omniscient gods with three heads and six arms and that the clinic was not an impregnable bulwark.

While I was racking my brain to find a way to go to town, a major event related to asking for leave occurred on the farm. The protagonist was my roommate and colleague, a former professor of chemistry. I'd like to introduce this respectable elder man, Gui Renzhong, before telling his story. He was already sixty. I called him my roommate because he and I slept in adjacent cots in the huge dormitory. He was my colleague because he and I were both herdsmen. Every night I heard his wretched screams, which were not the voice of a human but a ghost's wailing in a midnight bamboo grove tossed by the wind. Gui himself could not make such shrill, quavering sounds except during one of his nightmares.

His wife Jane, a dozen years his junior, was a delicate, beautiful woman, a Hawaii-born lady of one-half Chinese blood, one-quarter black blood and one-quarter white blood. In 1965 she came to China from America with her husband Gui Renzhong. She was thrown into a panic by what happened in 1966. Her Anchor (Gui Renzhong's English name) was taken away from her. All their books, cosmetics, and expensive clothes were burned to ashes, and she was swept out of her house like dust. She found herself a survival nest in a janitor's closet beneath the stairs. In order to follow revolutionary trends, she exchanged her snow-white Russian blanket for a grass-green PLA uniform. You can well imagine how funny she looked — her natural brownish red curls simply refused to stay under her army cap. As soon as she tucked them in, they slipped out again. The watching Red Guards felt so provoked that they could not help clipping their scissors aloud. She went around pleading for Anchor, telling everyone that he was not guilty, not a spy. When they were in America, he had longed for his motherland, wept for his motherland, praised her Yellow and Yangtze Rivers. He had told her, "There's a paradise above, and there are Suzhou and Hangzhou on earth." Jane told people, "We came a long way from America to China. We even took a detour to Japan to avoid suspicion — isn't this the best evidence to show that Anchor loves China?" But nobody believed it, because she and her Anchor came from the dirtiest land, from the most reactionary, most treacherous of people: after all, at least eighty percent of Americans were CIA agents. Later, Jane was told about a newly emerged man of enormous power whose words could change any man's political identity, including that of a man like Anchor. After a long search, Jane finally located him.

He was short and fat, with protruding lips. After saying a

single word, "This – " he needed a pause to gasp for air. He loved to take off his shoes and sit cross-legged like a Buddha on the sofa, although his bodyguard had to assist him with every movement of his legs. The first time Jane went to see him, he did not allow her to be near him, perhaps for fear of catching U.S. imperialist germs. At a distance of twenty-six feet, she was stopped by a bodyguard with a pistol. After this important man had heard Jane's tearful appeal, rendered in broken Chinese mixed with English, he did not respond for a long time. Jane saw a pair of amazed, idiotic eyes flicker, and his eternally open mouth made a clucking sound as his Adam's apple slithered to swallow some saliva.

"I've heard your case. Let's talk…next…next time…."

His words gave Jane a glint of light at the end of the long tunnel. Three days later, she was summoned to see him again. This time there were no bodyguards, and the one who accompanied him was his wife – a thin, sallow hag with worry written all over her face. The important man stammered, "I'll find a way, find…a way…."

Overjoyed, Jane rushed forward to kiss his wife's reedlike, withered hand. Then she stooped to kiss his feet, which had long been freed from his square-toed leather shoes. He was suddenly shaking all over and seemed to be bending his hard-to-bend waist to help Jane up. Jane's face was washed by grateful tears. But at the same time, Jane was puzzled by him: he suddenly gasped fearfully and his swollen red face turned purple. She thought he was having a stroke or something; his two small round eyes were beaming bloodily bright. While Jane was at a loss, he fell like a huge sack of rice, crushing her to the carpet. A most unexpected and most horrible thing happened: That sallow, shriveled wife of his did not even try to stop the rape. Instead, she desperately held Jane's legs apart and with loud sobs begged Jane to obey her husband, to help him accomplish what he could not have done on his own.

Afterward, Jane was sent to a lunatic asylum, and there

she turned into the filthiest, ugliest, and most violent mad-woman. Dragging a long chain behind her, she cried in English over and over from the barbed-wire enclosure, "God! God! God!"

Jane's tragedy had become public news for every-one except her husband, Gui Renzhong. The very night I launched my assault on the clinic, Gui Renzhong saw a note on his makeshift brick pillow as he was changing for bed. He put on his glasses and hurriedly read it through. It said, "Your Jane is dying in Hospital 808."

Gui Renzhong hopped up like a locust, plunged toward the farm headquarters in his undershirt and shorts, and pounded at the door of the PLA representative, who threw the door open with an angry roar. "You! How dare you come to see me in your shorts?"

"PLA rep, look at yourself. You're also wearing shorts to see me, aren't you? And yours are flower printed."

The PLA rep touched his bare legs self-consciously.

"Well, what's up? In the middle of the night like this – "

"I want to ask for a furlough. I must ask for a furlough. I must – "

"Why?"

"Look, my Jane – "

He passed the note to the PLA rep, who smacked his lips as he glanced through it. Thinking it over, he raised his eye-brows and asked, "Who wrote this note?"

"I don't know. I found it on my brick."

"On your brick?"

"Yes. The brick I use for my pillow."

The PLA rep gave a cold chuckle. "Can the message be trusted?"

"What are you asking?"

"I'm saying, you'd better stay on the farm to reform your-self honestly."

"But my Jane, she – she is dying!" Gui Renzhong's tears gushed out. "She came back with me just to – "

"To what?" The PLA rep knew he was going to say "to suffer," and he waited to spring. When Gui Renzhong realized he was about to commit a terrible political error, he stiffened. Then – anxiety produces wisdom – he finished off his sentence in a most satisfactory way.

"She came back with me to...to be educated."

"That's right. She gets her education and you get yours. Both of you need to be educated. No furlough for you. Please go back to bed. Attention! About face! Double time!"

Gui Renzhong could do nothing but follow the PLA rep's commands. But he did not run back to his dorm. Instead, he dashed to the giant concrete statue of Chairman Mao that stood at the farm entrance, prostrating himself at the feet of the statue and praying silently. He knew that, if he pleaded with the PLA rep again, the consequences would be even more horrible. In his blurred consciousness, he gained a sudden realization that the Mao Zedong in a PLA overcoat was the great leader who commanded everyone, including the PLA representatives. He looked up at Mao Zedong, who stood gazing off into the distance, and said through his sobs, "Chairman Mao, you have always been generous and bighearted. Even if I am a poor sinner, my Jane at least is innocent. You should take pity on her for the Chinese blood in her. Now she is in danger of dying. I believe the message is true. Nobody would play a joke like that on me. She must be worried to death because of my absence. Although I am a poor wretch, enslaved by Western ideas, and have received many years of bourgeois education and sweated in America for U.S. imperialism, I have confessed my entire past and am willing to reform. The cows in my care are free of disease and disaster. They pass by every day; you must have seen them. Of course you've seen them because you are a great leader who knows everything. This spring I didn't get a wink of sleep for several nights running in order to take care of the newborn calves. At least these damned Ph.D. hands of mine were finally put to some good use. I received a dozen little calves and all are healthy and strong. I am atoning for my sins little by little. Now I've also learned how to milk a cow. But unfortunately my Jane is in danger in the hospital. I'm afraid she won't even have a chance to drink a cup of milk again. Oh, how she loves milk. She always told me how when she was small she went with her father on a journey to the American West. On a cattle farm, she could drink a large bucket of fresh milk at one meal. I knew the bucket she meant was merely a toy bucket, perhaps like a big cup. Chairman Mao, I beg you, please put in a word with the PLA rep for me. I beg you. What a benevolent man you are! It's a pity you haven't met my Jane. If you had met her, you would be very fond of her. She is such an innocent, lovely lady, and she loves our country so profoundly. In America if she had heard someone speak ill of China or the Communist party, she would bash his head in with her high heels.

"She was born in poverty. As you know, not all American girls are capitalist young ladies. Her father was a sandwich man. I'm sorry, Chairman Mao, I don't mean that her father was a bread with sliced meat. No. What I mean is that her father was a humble man who made his living by hanging advertising posters on his body, front and back. Jane grew up in the midst of discrimination and insults. Chairman Mao, you should take pity on her for the fact that she left all her relatives and friends to follow me to China. She strove to march toward the bright future. Now she has no relatives around and no friends to comfort her in sickness. Chairman Mao, don't you know that? During the Korean War she, like her father, hung a placard before her with the Chinese character *Renmin Zhongguo hao!* and another behind her with its English translation 'Bravo, People's China!' For such a trifling thing, she was held in custody for three days, as she was too young to go to jail. Chairman Mao, I wouldn't dare to bring up what I've just told you at meetings because people would think I was trying to evade my own crimes or trying to gild my face in order to win their sympathy. Chairman Mao, I see you are smiling. You're not blaming me. I beg you, please issue a supreme command to the PLA rep on my farm: 'I agree to Gui Renzhong's request,' or 'lift your noble hand and let Gui Renzhong pass!'"

"How dare you give directions to our great teacher, Chairman Mao?"

Where had that voice come from? In great panic, Gui Renzhong kowtowed: "I deserve to die ten thousand deaths. I deserve to die ten thousand deaths!"

"Old Gui, why don't you ask Chairman Mao for leave directly?"

Now Gui Renzhong saw it was I who stood in front of him. "It's you! Please tell me, can I, such a sinful man, ask for leave directly from Chairman Mao?"

"Why not? Isn't Chairman Mao the wisest?"

"Of course. So you mean I can ask him directly?"

"Yes, absolutely."

"They won't add another crime to my record, will they?"

"No, no one will."

"Is that true?"

"Yes." I said all this completely out of sympathy and indignation, with no intention of ridiculing or teasing him. I wanted him to be able to break out of the prison farm to see his Jane before she breathed her last. As for the consequences of such an act, I had not even considered them.

Gui Renzhong again knelt on the ground, looking up at the lofty statue of Chairman Mao under the starry sky. He said with reverence and awe, "Chairman Mao, can you grant me a couple of days leave? A couple of days will be quite enough. My Jane will recover as soon as she sees me. I know she will be all right after seeing me. I'll tell her, 'See, Jane, your Anchor is perfectly all right, isn't he? He's growing stout, free from any diseases and misfortunes. On the farm, the leaders take good care of me. I eat well, live well, labor and study every day. Labor and study are essential parts of me.' I assure you, Chairman Mao, these are the words I'm going to say to her, nothing else. I do not wish to hurt her feelings. No. I won't divulge the dark side. I swear to you, I'll come back on time. Chairman Mao, may I leave now? Have you granted my request?"

Chairman Mao smiled beneath the lofty starry sky but said nothing. Gui Renzhong looked at me with a puzzled expression.

I said, "Chairman Mao has already approved your leave!"

"He did? Did you hear it?"

"I saw it."

"You saw it?"

"Right. And you saw it, too."

"I also saw it?"

"Yes. Look, Chairman Mao has stretched out his right hand, hasn't he?"

"Yes, yes. He has stretched out his gigantic right hand."

"That means: 'Comrade Gui Renzhong, you may leave now.'"

"'Comrade Gui Renzhong'? Did he call me comrade?"

"His face speaks for itself, doesn't it?"

"Yes, his expression does say so. Comrade!" Gui Renzhong laughed merrily like a child, two streams of tears gliding down his cheeks. "Then, Chairman Mao, for how many days may I leave?"

"He has indicated a definite number, hasn't he?"

"Really? Tell me, how many days?"

"Look, his right hand has stretched out five fingers, hasn't it? Five days, you may leave for five days."

His tears gushing like a fountain, Gui Renzhong kowtowed loudly on the lawn and bowed several times – almost touching the ground each time. Then he dashed toward the entrance. I called him back.

"Get dressed."

"Oh, right. I'm not dressed yet." He turned to run toward our dorm.

Sitting on the granite steps beneath the great statue, I looked into the night sky in bewilderment and frustration. I longed for those ceaselessly twinkling stars to turn into a hurricane, showering either stones or fire. I was willing to suffer. If we Chinese do not fear living in a world such as ours, why should we fear death?

I watched a well-dressed Gui Renzhong run out of the entrance and dart toward the highway. I knew there wouldn't be any buses or trucks on which he might beg a ride at that hour of the night. But I did not stop him. Any attempt to stop him was meaningless. He would not listen to me anyway. Better let his short legs carry him to Jane, his beautiful Jane, his intelligent Jane, his good-hearted Jane, the Jane who loved him at the cost of her life.

That night I did not go to bed; instead I sat at the foot of the great statue, looking up into the starry sky. How beautiful. Those countless stars – they were forever shining bright. Even when the sun came out during the day, they were still shining on us, although we could no longer see them with our naked eyes.

I gaze at her window. In the past it was pasted over with black paper; now a cloth curtain with tiny blue flowers hangs there.

The following evening, Gui Renzhong was brought back by the PLA rep. He received a good beating. Supposedly the torture had been done in private by the enraged revolutionary masses and the PLA rep had not been present. In fact, it had been a well-designed persecution. At a large-scale criticism meeting, facing waves of storming slogans, Gui Renzhong stood in the center of the stage, spotlights mercilessly focused on his blood-scabbed brow. The PLA rep ordered him to confess his crime.

Lost in deep thought for a long time, he gradually revived with a quite unexpected, childishly sweet smile. He announced happily to the audience, "It's not her, nothing like her at all. That woman is not my Jane. How could she be compared with my Jane! It's all a big mistake. My Jane is not in Hospital 808. She is not sick. She is in perfect shape. Now I do not need to worry anymore. Comrades, I am grateful to Chairman Mao."

I stuffed my cap into my mouth just in time; otherwise, I would have burst out crying, howling like a flood that had burst the dam. The meeting could not continue. It was dismissed, and Gui Renzhong was asked to write a self-criticism. Five days later, Gui Renzhong received a speck of ashes in a shoe box. On the shoe box was pasted a picture of Jane, taken when she had first stepped onto Chinese soil. The PLA rep told him, "This was your wife." Gui Renzhong held the box in his hand, mute and tearless, and bowed numbly to the PLA rep.

God had finally heard Jane's cry. Perhaps she had seen her Anchor and recognized him, even if Anchor had failed to recognize her. But when she recognized him, her soul had left her. God invited her to enter paradise. When she met God, what kind of questions would she ask, and how would God respond to them? I believed God's answer would be like this: "My dear daughter, if I could explain what is happening in China, then God would no longer be God, and China would no longer be China."

To the day I die, I will never admit that I had created a tragic practical joke. No, it was not a practical joke. I swear it to Chairman Mao.

I gaze at her window. In the past it was pasted over with black paper; now a cloth curtain with tiny blue flowers hangs there.

5

Now she was thirteen years old. Oh, beautiful Sunamei! A sickle-shaped moon had waxed into a full boat.

Five girls from the community were going to remove their linen gowns. On New Year's Eve they gathered under a row of pine trees along the lake in a place appointed for the annual meeting for thirteen-year-old girls. Every year there were up to a dozen thirteen-year-olds. In the previous years, Sunamei had been allowed only to stand watching at a distance. The bonfire on the grassy land and its reflection on the lake were like two large blooming flowers. Young maidens were dancing beneath the pines in a circle like a group of fairies. They opened their throats, singing unabashedly to the sky, as if they were already grown women. Their swaying arms and leaping legs churned the blazing fire into a dazzling sight. Then the girls sat and boiled tea by the fire in earthen kettles no bigger than their fists. Like the sixty-year-old *dabu,* they narrowed their smiling eyes and sipped hot tea with inexpressible satisfaction. They were drinking wine, too. Their cheeks, burned by flames and wine, were red as azaleas.

Now she was thirteen years old. Oh, beautiful Sunamei! A bud the size of a grain of corn was starting to bloom.

Now Sunamei came to know the magic power of wine, fire, and strong tea. Gulping down a bowl of wine, she felt herself instantly turned into an adult. She embraced her good friend Geruoma and bit her cheek fiercely. Geruoma shrieked like a devil, and all the other girls covered their ears in fright. When they realized what had happened, they laughed and jumped on Sunamei and pressed her to the ground. Although she could hardly breathe, she felt great joy. She loved being pressed like that, as if all her bones were being loosened. When she struggled out from beneath their weight, she gave a long cry to the stars in the sky and on the river. The crispness of her own cry startled her. Cupping her burning cheeks in her hands and watching the crackling flames, she had a sudden desire to tear off the shapeless linen gown that she had worn for the past thirteen years and to plunge naked into the lake. Although the winter was severe, she believed even the water could not make her feel cold. While she was dreaming wildly, her friends held her hands and danced around the bonfire again. Sunamei began to sing in a voice that even she found pleasant and beautiful. However, the song she took the lead in singing was still beyond her full comprehension.

> A pair of silver pheasants
> > perch on the golden barley stalks.
> On the golden barley stalks
> > one upon the other the two fold into one.
> Taking wings to the blue sky,
> > the one becomes again a separate pair.

Sunamei's heart beat with excitement as she thought about the five girls, who had just reached thirteen, becoming five women in pleated skirts. How would it feel to wear jade bracelets and silver earrings, to have her waist wrapped with a broad, rainbow sash, to let long strings of beads hang from her neck, and to crown her head with a heavy set of ornaments and a wig? She became intoxicated. All the girls became intoxicated. They held each other up, singing and dancing.

Three boys were going to enter manhood the same year with the five girls. Oh, no – they could not become big men but would remain boys. Although they were gathering just on the other side of the hill, no one could hear their noise. Were the boys reluctant to become men? Were they not happy to take off the linen gowns? Were they not willing to wear pants? Ah, cowards. Because no one could hear their singing and foot stamping, it would be better if they could mimic a donkey's neigh.

The roosters started crowing at last. What lazy roosters. They must have nestled themselves beneath the hens' warm backsides and overslept. When the bluish morning glow appeared on the river, the five maidens, as if at a sign, suddenly held each other, weeping. No one knew whether their tears were shed in joy or in sorrow.

The bonfire had burned out. A sheen of light smoke merged into the mist drifting in from the river. The woods before the dawn were inexpressibly beautiful and mysterious, as if some elf or spirit were about to appear.

As they were parting from each other, Geruoma whispered to Sunamei, "Sunamei, you are so beautiful. I bet you'll have a hundred *axiao*."

"Really?"

Sunamei felt a bit chilly on the way to her own *yishe*. The wind crept along her bare legs and into her whole body. Like a pair of icy-cold rough hands, it groped all over her warm body. She was thinking, "Why do I need that many *axiao*? True, my *amiji* Zhima has had a lot of *axiao*. Every month at least three men go to her at night. Those *axiao* never help us grow crops or herd cattle. Do they come just to tell her stories? Are they good storytellers, like Awu Luruo? But how can she lie in bed with her eyes wide open from dusk to dawn, listening to stories? My eyelids would fight each other."

Sunamei was told that *axiao* always bring presents such as bracelets, necklaces, and sashes. But those presents are for exchange. A woman gives butter, wine, lumps of tea, melon seeds, candy, and popped rice in return. She also learned that a woman can boil tea with her *axiao* alone in the *huagu*. Nevertheless, they need time to sleep. Without sleep they will have no energy for next day. But there is only one bed in the *huagu*. Can a woman sleep with an outsider in the same bed? Men snore in their sleep. All her uncles snore thunderously. Can a woman fall asleep with a snoring man? There must be something terribly interesting a woman can do when her *axiao* comes. Otherwise, Zhima would not be so happy. Each night, as soon as Zhima hears a little stone rolling along her roof, she opens her door quietly with sweet smiles, lets her *axiao* in, and then bolts the door behind him. Once Sunamei tried to push it open but failed. Why bar the door? She wanted to hear stories and share their strong tea. Listening to the women's bantering, Sunamei had figured out that receiving *axiao* was a most joyful thing. The eyes of mature men told her they were all willing to be a woman's *axiao.* If a man did not want to be an *axiao,* he would have no other place but the cowshed to sleep at night, for no *yishe* set up beds for mature men. But sleeping in the cowshed is a bit humiliating.

When she arrived home, Sunamei saw the *yimei* crowded with all her relatives and neighbors. All were beaming with happiness. Only Sunamei, feeling somewhat at a loss, wanted to cry. Flames danced in the fireplace. Little animal-fat lamps were lit before the hearth god and the kitchen range for ancestral worship. The *daba,* a tall, lean priest under a felt cloak, squatted by the fireplace, hanging a bunch of colorful statues. Among them were the gods of clouds, wind, rain, thunder, mountain, and water and the snake god, the horse god, the dog god, the tiger god, and so on. They looked both fearful and attractive.

Sunamei saw that the horse god had five legs. Why five legs? It was true that she had seen a five-legged horse before. But Awu Luruo had explained to her that the one that can stretch out and draw back is not a leg. What is it, then? Awu Luruo would not tell her. In fact, a he-horse has only four obvious legs, and its fifth, often withdrawn inside his belly, is hard to see. But the fifth leg of the *daba*'s horse god was diagonally posed, noncontractible, and nonmovable. And his snake god was funny, too. Why does his snake have fat buttocks? Nobody has ever seen a fat-bottomed snake. Did his snake get fat buttocks in becoming a god?

Under those gods was placed a row of porcelain bowls, each containing a different beverage: wine, milk, pure water, tea, and sugar water. One of them even held a green twig. The *daba* was muttering incantations that neither Sunamei nor the Mosuo adults could understand. Perhaps even the *daba* himself did not quite understand them. Sunamei had been to several *zhaijie,* but they were all skirt-dressing ceremonies for others. Today's ceremony was for her, and she was the center of attention. Ami took her by the hand and led her to a place between *youshemei* and the fireplace where a large salted pig and a sack of grain lay. Sunamei stood with one foot on the pig and the other on the grain. Ami asked her to hold a silver bracelet, strings of beads, earrings, and other jade pendants with her right hand and to grasp yarn and linen with her left. No one told her what all this was supposed to mean. Was it a good wish for her to have all this wealth throughout her life? She thought it must be. Ami, who was Sunamei's birth mother and known as Ami Cai'er, did not look old yet. She stripped her *mo* of her linen gown and left her nude in front of the crowd. For the first time in her life Sunamei saw that her skin was extremely pure and white. And for the first time she discovered that her breasts already protruded, although only like egg halves. She did not feel cold at all. Yet she bit her lip in embarrassment and did not dare face the surrounding eyes. From the top of the door, Ami took down the new set of clothes she had prepared for Sunamei: a high-collared short blouse with gold embroidered hems and a pleated white linen skirt. She beat the clothes against the door several times, as if she were afraid some bugs might have crawled in. Ami Cai'er first put the skirt over Sunamei. When the skirt fringe covered her feet, Sunamei suddenly felt much taller. Then Ami put the blouse on her and tied her waist with a colorful sash with beautiful designs. In the end, Ami smoothed Sunamei's nestlike, entangled hair with a wooden comb and crowned her with a heavy headdress.

The *daba* was praying fervently to his many gods and to the Hearth God of the house. Then he blew on the wool string in his hand. This exhalation was said to be the breath of God. With this breath, the string became a talisman. The *daba* tied this string around Sunamei's neck because she had reached thirteen, the age that gives a woman's body a soul. This talisman would prevent her soul from flying away prematurely. Awu Luruo had once told her that the wool string around the neck of a thirteen-year-old girl is also a reminder that her ancestors had come thousands of miles to Lake Xienami with herds of sheep. It tells her not to forget the hardships they had experienced.

Ami asked Sunamei to call in the big black dog. At Ami's bidding, she fed the dog some rice and a piece of pork. Then she repeated after Ami, "My dear dog, a human being is too delicate and cannot brave endless winds and storms. A human being can live only thirteen years and does not know how to receive *axiao*. But you dogs are tough, and able to bear all kinds of hardship. You know living means suffering, and you live for sixty years at least. The goddess takes pity on us and lets us exchange our lives with yours. Hence, human beings enjoy longevity. We are grateful to you, so we feed you and treat you like a member of the family. We share whatever we have with you."

These words touched Sunamei's heart. With her arms around the black dog's neck, she kissed its wet nose. After giving the dog her thanks, Sunamei kowtowed to her ancestors, to the hearth god, and to all her relatives. She thanked her ancestors for giving her a soul, and the hearth god for keeping her from cold and hunger, and all her relatives for their kindness in the past and their continuing protection, like woods protecting a frail wildflower.

Now all her family began helping Sunamei serve rice cakes, melon seeds, popped-rice candies, and buttered tea to entertain the guests who came for her ceremony. Sunamei walked in front of Ami. She was not used to the change yet. The headdress was heavy and the new clothes stiff. Every movement produced a gentle rustling. Asi (great-grandmother) was sitting at her usual place on a piece of warm yak hide at the head of the fireplace. Asi had seldom spoken during the past few years, and her throat always made a sort of gurgling sound while her hands counted a string of black beads. Today Asi looked exceptionally happy. She seemed to be smiling. When Sunamei knelt before her, she raised her hands and touched her all over from head to feet. Sunamei knew Asi did so not because of her blindness but because touching was her special way to convey love. Sunamei was the youngest of Asi's lineage. Today Asi touched with her own hands the fourth generation.

Before the visitors left they all took out their presents. Some had brought Sunamei shuttles for weaving bands. Some gave her glossy silk thread. Some gave her new clothes, necklaces, bracelets, and linen. Every present was delivered with beautiful wishes.

One said, "Our present is as thin as a little stream; yet when you become *dabu,* this stream will grow into a big river."

Another said, "These bracelets that never wear out embody the friendship between our *yishe* and yours."

Another said, "Linens never wear out; the land will produce forever. With your strength and capability, you will never exhaust what you have. If you save what you produce, it will pile up like a mountain."

"Silk embroidered on linen is like flowers and sunshine

on the grass. The shadows of worry, no matter how dark, disappear."

"With our own eyes, we see your beautiful body, the body of a lucky mother. We hope you bear nine daughters and nine sons."

On hearing these wishes, Ami grinned from ear to ear. She took Sunamei by the hand and saw the guests off at the gate. She thanked them for coming, for their precious presents, and particularly for their wishes, which were far more precious than any presents. After the guests left, all the members of the *yishe* sat around the fireplace, with the women on the honorable right-hand side, and the men on the left. Sunamei felt like a newly blooming flower and all happy eyes were fixed on her. Ami led the *yishe,* though he was not the first in seniority – Asi was still alive and healthy, and there was her *ayi* as well. Although Sunamei had no *amizhi,* she had three *amiji.* The youngest among them was Zhima, only sixteen years old. Being the most beautiful, charming lady in the whole *yishe,* Zhima filled the courtyard with her laughter. Even at night, her *huagu* could not seal in her merry laughter. Sunamei often thought to herself, "Do the men vie with one another to be with Zhima just to hear her laugh?"

Ami was a capable woman. However, she had just passed fifty. She had given up her *huagu* and moved to the communal *yimei.* She forbade her steady *axiao,* Zhabosi, to visit her. She told him frankly, "I am no longer in the age of blooming; my years of childbearing have passed. The house responsibility alone is heavy enough for me to shoulder. You men, unlike women, do not look old even at sixty, and you can still visit young girls' *huagu* if they open their doors to receive you." Zhabosi felt sad, and he cried, too, although he was a big, powerful man. Sunamei was with Ami the night she said good-bye to Zhabosi. She grasped Ami's skirt and felt pity for Zhabosi. Zhabosi could not come anymore. On each of the previous thousands of nights, he had stayed in

Ami's *huagu,* and Ami had never received another *axiao.* Now he couldn't come anymore. Where could he possibly sleep? Could he go to the *yimei* and lie amid the snoring sounds of her old uncles? In any case, he could not come to Ami, for "Do not come to me anymore" had been said by a Mosuo woman. A woman has her *huagu;* a man does not. A man may come in only if a woman opens her door to him. If a woman refuses to open her *huagu,* a man either stands out in the cold or leaves. Here, the *yishe* belongs to the women. Women are hosts, and men are guests.

When Zhabosi tried to hold Sunamei in his arms, she screamed, even though she overheard from Zhima that Zhabosi was her *ada.* Sunamei thought, "What is *ada?* and what does *ada* mean? What is his relation to me? He neither provides me with food and drink, nor works in our fields. He is merely a guest, isn't he? He is merely my Ami's guest, and a night guest at that." When Zhabosi left, Ami moved out of her *huagu* and left it vacant. Ami actually told Sunamei that her *huagu* was waiting for a *mo* – a girl of thirteen.

Now she was thirteen years old. Oh, beautiful Sunamei! Round dewy beads were beginning to flow in a stream.

The breakfast after her thirteenth birthday was exceptionally sumptuous. Ami first served a chunk of salted pork to the ancestors on the altar and spilled a cup of wine and a handful of rice on it. Then she said in a strange, quivering voice, "Dear ancestors, my ancestors who came from the prairies beyond the horizon and whose souls returned beyond the horizon, you drove away tigers and subdued leopards heroically. You opened a path in the cliffs to the Jinsha River. You removed the hilltop in order to grow barley. Now you have another woman who is ready to pass on the line from generation to generation. After she accepts the soul the goddess blessed her with, she will begin to have passion and love, and the charms to attract men. Like a sapling, she has already spread her treetop in the golden sunlight. She knows where to extend her branches and when to bloom and bear fruit. Let her live naturally in this world. Beauty is being natural. My dear ancestors, please bless her, teach her, and enlighten her. Please let her learn the secret of life and open its only door as soon as possible." After the prayer, Ami began serving food to everyone. Although on that day Sunamei was the moon surrounded by stars, Ami did not give her a morsel more than the other members. However, everyone's portion today was larger than usual.

After breakfast, Ami took Sunamei to all the other *yishe* to wish them a happy New Year. Sunamei could hardly remember how many *yishe* she had visited. Everywhere she received the same hospitality, the same rich food, and the same good wishes. Many women of her generation looked her up and down as if they had never seen her before. Were they attracted by her new apparel or by the person in that apparel? She took a bite of whatever Ami asked her to eat and a sip of whatever Ami wanted her to drink and gave replies in the way Ami had taught her. In the past, men had never wasted their glances on Sunamei, but today she looked different in their eyes. Men looked at her in the manner they looked up to *amiji* — with tenderness, affection, and respect. Sunamei's heart was trembling with joy, like a flower in the breeze.

Back home, Ami led Sunamei by the hand, walking toward the East Wing Bowers. Ami walked slowly in front and Sunamei followed a step behind. Although without a smile, Ami's face, bright and calm, assumed the same countenance as last year when she had taken Sunamei to worship the goddess. Sunamei had started climbing the stairs of the East Wing while still learning how to crawl. Yet today she felt odd, as if she had never been up there before. Why was the pinewood handrail along the stairs full of scars? Ami's steps slowed on the stairs; she seemed to be recalling the moment she herself had turned thirteen. Had Ami felt happy or sad when she turned thirteen? Not until today did Sunamei notice that the tenth step of the stair was a board much thinner than the rest, and it squeaked each time it was tread on. Sunamei thought, "Why didn't I notice that before?" She had hopped up and down countless times, merely to exercise her legs. And she had also climbed step by step stealthily in order to overhear her *amiji*'s secrets.

Finally, Ami opened the lock of the *huagu* next to the staircase. She then gave the little key to Sunamei. Sunamei's heart jumped. Her own key. Although the key was tiny, it could lock a room, and from now on no one but she alone could open that room. This tiny key could simultaneously lock up her privacy, like that of *amiji*. All the keys of their *yishe* hung at Ami's waist. She is the *dabu* who took charge of and distributed the wealth of the community.

The *huagu* had been swept spotlessly clean. The logs in the fireplace at the center of the room were ready to be lit. A gray earthen pot sat on the iron tripod. A bamboo bucket for buttered tea, a pot of tea leaves, and a pot of salt were placed on the hearth. To the left of the fireplace was a wooden bed. And on the wall hung a round mirror the size of a big bowl. Ami, holding Sunamei's hand, stood for a while at the open door of the *huagu,* as if she wanted Sunamei to carefully examine the room that now belonged to her. Ami's gentle white cat pushed its way in and squatted at the edge of the fireplace, calling them. Ami stepped in, and Sunamei followed.

As soon as Ami opened the bamboo trunk beside the fireplace, the clothes and fabric that had been given to her caught Sunamei's eye. Everything inside was brand-new. Ami handed the trunk key to her, too. Now Sunamei had her second key. The straw on the bed was newly spread. Atop the straw was a large piece of thick sheepskin and a folded blanket with red-square patterns. Sitting on the bed, Ami asked her, "Sunamei, isn't this room beautiful? From now on you will live in it. Are you afraid?"

"Yes, my dear Ami." Sunamei had been sleeping in the *yimei* all her life. Like a little kitten, she had nestled among her aged *awu* and *ayi* and a crowd of children. Every night Asi's whistling snore had sent her to dreamland right on time. She had dreamed all sorts of things. Some had been pretty awful. But whenever she woke up she could hear Asi's snoring and her *amu gemi's* and *amu geri's* mumbling, which eased her mind and sent her back to sleep.

Ami looked at her favorite *mo*. "Don't be afraid, Sunamei. Someone will come to keep you company."

"Really?" Her wide eyes full of fright, Sunamei asked Ami, "Is he going to be a stranger?"

"A stranger in time will become an acquaintance."

"No, Ami. You come sleep with me."

"I'll do no such thing. Sunamei, you are thirteen years old."

"But Ami, I am still young. Does any man really want to be my *axiao?*"

"Sunamei, you are no longer a child. The moment you begin living in the *huagu,* you become a woman. Please remember, this room is assigned to you by Dabu Ami. Now you are the mistress of this room, and you are your own mistress. You have complete freedom to receive anyone or decline anyone, all according to your heart and will. The men who come to visit you in our *yishe* belong to you. You control this *huagu,* as well as the key hidden next to your heart. Please take care never to lose the key. In the courtyard of the Mosuo, no matter how heroic men may become, none of them will dream to take the key from a woman. A woman is a human being who produces human beings. *Mo!* Sunamei, please remember! Remember – " Ami's tone and voice reminded her of the *daba's* sacred prayer. She was trembling. "Ami, I have learned it by heart."

"Please repeat it to me, Daughter."

Sunamei stammered back everything she had been told.

Ami nodded in satisfaction. She embraced Sunamei and

said to her, "The Mosuo work in the field during the day to produce clothes and food and make love at night both to continue their line and for enjoyment. They are their own masters during the day and remain their own masters at night. Only love and true appreciation of love produce joy. Lack of love and failure to appreciate love bring misery. You cannot be taught to love; you can only experience love, body and soul."

Sunamei nodded in bewilderment.

Ami laughed. "You nod, don't you? But, no, you still don't understand. You will not understand my words until later. The most important thing is that no matter how much joy a man may bring you, you cannot surrender to him the self that belongs to you. Sunamei, always be your own mistress!"

Still Sunamei did not quite understand why Ami had to warn her repeatedly. Remember: a Mosuo woman is her own mistress. She thought, "Besides the room Ami just allotted to me, what else belongs to me? I possess nothing. The property of the whole *yishe* is guarded by the cluster of keys hanging on Dabu's waist, isn't it? I myself have only a thirteen-year-old body and an active, inquisitive mind. But Ami's words seem to say that my body is covered with silver and gold."

Sunamei did not notice when Ami walked out of the *huagu* and left the body that now belonged to her alone in the little room that also now belonged to her. But she now saw how she had come to exist in this human world. She knew she had reached the door of mystery; although it was still shut, she guessed that the location of this mysterious door was nowhere but in herself. What was shut inside the door? She gave her imagination free rein. Imagining gave her a lot of pleasure. She could barely control her tears of joy. The key to the door is in your hand, isn't it, Sunamei? The lock is already open. That door to mystery and to the self is waiting for you to push it open. A slight push will give you a crack of light. Then you may peep through that crack. But, for now, Sunamei neither wanted nor dared to push that door. Even if she desired desperately and had not the slightest fear, she could not. Her conflicted state of mind confused her. Perhaps she did not feel the urge. She was waiting for that gust of warm wind that made a flower suddenly open.

She kept waiting, quite bewildered, knowing that her only hope was pinned to a long wait. Her body was satiated with waiting. Night came quietly. She thought, "Was I waiting for the night? Now night has come. No. Night deprived the little *huagu* of its brightness, and even the little round mirror shut its eyes. Then it was dead still. Was I waiting for the stillness? No." Gradually she detected a stream of noise. Her ears became eyes. She simultaneously heard and "saw" the elders and the children in the *yimei*. Yesterday she was one of them. Now she was an observer: Asi starts her whistling snore that hangs like a haze hanging over children's dreams. The burned wood sinks in the fireplace, turning into dark-red embers. The big black dog is going on patrol in the courtyard, its gentle steps almost inaudible. The five mules are still in their mangers, munching heartily and snorting.

The *huagu* next to hers belonged to Zhima. Sunamei heard and "saw" her come home, unlock the door, come in and make a fire. Soon her little teakettle started singing. Was it for these noises Sunamei was waiting? No. Then she heard and "saw" Cili, Zhima's *axiao*, pass her door to stand in front of Zhima's *huagu*. A gentle push made the half-shut door give a loud cry, "Gee – wa," like that of an innocent baby.

Cili, a tall, ruddy-faced man, fished on the eastern bank of the lake. Every night he canoed across. He had started coming to Zhima's *huagu* a month ago. His body always carried the pleasant smell of fish. He entered speechless, nor did Zhima say a word. She poured tea for him. Then they sipped tea together. Sunamei was puzzled. Cili did not tell Zhima stories, although a fisherman should be able to recount tales of the lake or under the sea. To him, handed-down tales plus newly made-up ones must be like fish caught in a net. Yet he neither told stories nor spoke to her. He drank and drank and then sucked on his water pipe. The bubbling sound from the pipe seemed endless. How stifling. Sunamei leaned against her bed, bored. All they did was drink and smoke, smoke and drink.

Sunamei recalled that, when Asi was strong enough to stroll along the lake, she had often taken her along. Asi had said, "For every person on earth, there is a star in the sky." She asked Asi, "Which star is mine?" Asi said, "Since you haven't put on a skirt, how can you have a star?" Now I have put on a skirt. Asi, tell me, which star is mine? Sunamei looked into the night sky. She found it. Her star was sending a message with its twinkling. It was a bright green star. Its light shone straight into her heart. She wanted to catch it and hold it with both hands above her head. Oh, she understood at last: It's you I'm waiting for. Rising up onto her tiptoes, she found herself extremely light. The lightness amazed and pleased her. She felt like she was floating, flying toward the green star on the peak of a mountain, and the star was speeding toward her. But the moment she stepped on the mountain peak, her star stopped. There was still a great distance between them. She started flying again, and her star sped toward her again. She was flying among rivers of stars, like countless snowflakes. She could not tell which star was hers any longer. Every star looked half like hers and half not. Worried, she started to fall. Perhaps when she landed on the ground she would be able to tell which was hers. But, being too light, she had lost the power to fall. Her body floated like a sheet of paper. Finally, she forced her body downward. Placing her two feet together, she landed on a plain. Then she saw the green star that belonged to her again, still so far away. Suddenly she heard a strange noise, a noise she had never heard before, which deprived her of the power of seeing. In fact, the noise simply woke her from her fantasy of flying in the starry sky. She listened again intensely and found the noise coming from Amiji Zhima's *huagu*. It was Zhima's voice. It wasn't like crying or weeping or groaning or sighing. Sunamei had never heard such a noise from Zhima before. She seemed to see Zhima being borne up toward the starry sky. But Zhima was not chasing after the star that belonged to her, for she herself was a big, bright star. Zhima ended with a long, contented sigh, which dispersed suddenly like morning mist. Then the man breathed heavily several times. Finally, their rhythmical breathing faded away. Supporting herself with one hand against her head, she heard all this. She was shocked, as though it had thundered near her; although the flash of lightning had disappeared, her heart was still beating fiercely.

Taking off her new top, new skirt, and heavy headdress, she burrowed naked under her blanket. Cili's snores made the partition between their two *huagu* hum like an airplane. Lying on her back, she touched her thin, small body. Looking up at the beam in the roof, she seemed to know that she was waiting for a male, for a man who would be the first to offer his love as her *axiao*. The embers in the fireplace were covered by ashes. Only the big white cat's green eyes still shone. What was she waiting for?

Now she was thirteen. Oh, beautiful Sunamei! The husks were falling off the spring sprout and the green bamboo was emerging.

What year was it when Sunamei reached thirteen and became a Mosuo woman in a long, pleated skirt? She did not know, and there was no need for her to know. Antiquity, long forgotten by many nationalities, is still the present reality of the Mosuo people. Sunamei is only thirteen years old, but her people are more ancient than the legendary Yao and Shun. During the time of Yao and Shun women had already become dependent on men. E Huang and Nü Ying wailed for their lost husband: Oh, my heaven! Their sky had fallen. Today the teardrops on bamboo in southern China remain the best evidence of their obedience.

While Sunamei was entering the age of thirteen in this primitive manner, the modern world was entering the year 1976.

She was already thirteen. Oh, beautiful Sunamei! An obscure little flower with pouting lips was about to reveal a smile. Popping above the grass, it shone like a red star against the blue night.

6

I gaze at her window. In the past it was pasted over with black paper; now a cloth curtain with tiny blue flowers hangs there.

Jane's death caused me to abandon my long-planned strategy for attacking the stronghold of the clinic. During the night, Gui Renzhong often shone his flashlight on Jane's portrait on the cover of the box containing her ashes and stroked it affectionately. Jane's beauty was, indeed, beyond description. It reminded me of the full-blooming golden chrysanthemum in tropical sunlight, particularly when her face beamed with happy smiles. As Gui Renzhong kept Jane's ash box beside his pillow, I was lucky enough to share his happiness. Each time after admiring Jane's beauty, I could not fall asleep for a long, long time. In turns the fierce, insane Jane in rags and the pure winged angel on the palm of God appeared before my eyes until I was utterly exhausted.

As the saying goes: a leaky house confronts one rainy day after another; a disabled ship is struck head-on by a storm. Poor old Gui had suffered another misfortune!

The PLA rep was extremely conscientious, never relaxing his vigilance over us odd-job workers who did not participate in collective labor. He hammered over and over again: "Never leave any dead corners."

The cowherds, duck tenders, fishpond watchers, and

cooks were regarded by the PLA rep as ideologically loose men, and he believed our minds would grow sprouts with the slightest relaxation in political study. Therefore, he never gave us a moment of peace, saying, "Even those from a working-class background will turn revisionists if they make themselves comfortable – let alone these stinking number 9's, who were reluctant to reform themselves."

Every night, after feeding the cows and water buffaloes, all the odd-job workers had to get together for political study – a fixed system that could not be changed even by a thunderbolt. No absences were allowed. And everyone had to give speeches. Actually, this type of study was not so hard to cope with. The moment the leader finished reciting a supreme command, you took the floor. First you wished Chairman Mao a long life three times. After Lin Biao's death, you no longer needed to wish for "Great Assistant Helmsman Lin's good health," of course. But you could not forget to chant, "Learn from Comrade Jiang Qing." You could perform this stereotyped ceremony in slow motion, stringing it out for at least three minutes. Then you recited at least three supreme commands between murmurs of admiration and tears of excitement. Of course, you might pause from one emotion to another. Pauses meant you were thinking, and no one dared to hurry you up or cut in during your slow buildup of genuine proletarian feelings. After all this, you spoke about the results of your study, such as how you felt the greatness and foresight of the supreme commands in influencing Chinese and world revolution, blazing our path, and inspiring all genuine Marxists and Leninists to fight bravely for the realization of their ultimate goal of communism. To give your speech some depth, you might first denounce Soviet revisionism and U.S. imperialism and then engage in some self-criticism. If you were afraid of saying something wrong, you could cite Chairman Mao's quotations from the beginning to the end of your speech. In so doing, not only would you avoid possible mistakes, but all your listeners would have to regard you with love and awe because "One of Chairman Mao's words has the force of ten thousand." Quite a number of people could easily compose songs of quotations or string quotations into essays or plays. In those days everyone, no matter how stupid, acquired this particular knack. The old scholar Gui Renzhong remained an exception. He read Chairman Mao's works with honesty and effort and after each reading contemplated what he had read. If there had been a library nearby, he would have checked out a thousand books in order to test the truth of Mao's latest supreme command. Studying, meditating, and researching silently by himself, he would have been all right. But he was far too inquisitive. Each time he asked a question, my palms turned sweaty. Who could make him understand that to ask questions was just asking for trouble? One could safely say, "I have no questions," for it had been officially announced that we must carry out Chairman Mao's instructions whether we understood them or not. Not only did your inability to understand them simply betray your inferior ideological level: no one even dared to doubt their truth. But Gui Renzhong was different. He asked questions with such straightforwardness that I wanted to warn him late at night. However, I dared not. If I warned him, he would surely report my words honestly at the meeting. I could not afford to take the risk.

It was by asking such a question that Gui suffered his greatest misfortune. That day we were discussing a supreme command:

Except for the desert, wherever there is a crowd of people, they can be divided into the left, the middle, and the right. And it will remain so for ten thousand years.

Every one of us put on a show of excitement, gratitude, praise, and self-criticism. When the PLA rep asked, "Any questions?" we chorused, "No, Chairman Mao's instruction is a universal truth that can be applied to the four seas. It is easy to understand but infinitely profound. It requires more than a lifetime to grasp the whole truth of it."

But Gui Renzhong refused to follow the flock. He raised his hand.

"Report!"

My heart jumped into my throat and I held my breath. What sort of question would he raise? Although a Ph.D. in chemistry, he was no wiser than a four-year-old in politics.

"Our great leader Chairman Mao teaches us, 'Honesty is a scientific attitude; self-deception and ignorant arrogance cannot solve problems.'" Pretty normal. I relaxed a little. "I want to ask a question."

"Please! All questions are welcome in our discussion." The PLA rep crossed his legs. I grew nervous again.

"Chairman Mao says, 'Except for the desert, wherever there is a crowd of people, they can be divided into the left, the middle, and the right. And it will remain so for ten thousand years.' Marx, Lenin, and our great Chairman Mao Zedong, these three, coming together, can be considered a crowd. In this crowd, who is the left, who is the middle, and who is the right?"

No one present at the meeting, including the PLA rep, had expected such a question. It was as if old Gui had thrown a bomb into our midst. For a while we were so flabbergasted that no one knew what to do. But Dr. Gui Renzhong was examining each of us with his sober, naive eyes, believing his question was really a hard nut that even the PLA rep would not be able to crack. He rubbed his hands together. Even the PLA rep failed to give an answer. After a long, uncomfortable silence, he pounded the table, rose to his feet, and left.

A quarter of an hour later, the loudspeaker came on. Several of Mao's quotations regarding severe punishment of counterrevolutionaries were followed by a call for an emergency assembly. The recording of a bugle call spread ominously in the air above the farm.

Undoubtedly, the question raised by Gui Renzhong was the most vicious crime of sacrilege. Workers of the entire farm stood indignantly in the canteen, a straw-thatched shed, waiting for the PLA rep to denounce Gui Renzhong's crime. The denunciation was kindled by a sudden roar: "Drag the counterrevolutionary Gui Renzhong to the stage!"

This unprecedentedly large criticism meeting lasted more than three hours. Everyone knew old Gui's suffering, but none dared to show him a shred of sympathy. Group after group pledged their loyalty to Chairman Mao before the square table where old Gui was bowing low as a dwarf. In order to demonstrate their revolutionary action in front of the PLA rep, they put on all sorts of masks. A poet, famous at home and abroad, denounced Gui Renzhong between short sobs and long wails, as if he were at a funeral. A well-known playwright simply charged headlong toward Gui like a goat. Fortunately he was unable to climb the table. Nevertheless, he had fully demonstrated his hatred for the criminal who dared to attack the great leader. A few howling females jumped on the table to pull old Gui's hair and pinch him. An old spinster, taking advantage of the chaos, sprang up on the table and pulled the old man's private parts fiercely, parts that should not be touched by females other than his own mother or wife. The searing pain made the old man scream for help. A historical opportunist, who had pretended to be a Communist when the Communists won the upper hand and had yielded to the Kuomintang when the Kuomintang gained power, dashed forward and pushed down the bench on which Gui Renzhong was standing. As Gui fell, the mob jumped onto him with strange shrieks, and everyone tried to stomp on him. Finally, I shouted at the top of my lungs, "Chairman Mao teaches us, 'We must fight with words, not with physical force.'"

This shout stopped the feet that were determined to trample Gui's body into marmalade. The mob could not make out whose voice it was but believed it must be the PLA rep's. Who else but the rep would dare to shout such a quotation at such a moment?

Old Gui's head was bleeding. His right leg, limp as a noodle, could no longer support his weight. Obviously, it was broken. The PLA rep could only adjourn the meeting and order Gui Renzhong to write a self-criticism. Later, Doctor Yu Shouchen asked the PLA rep what was to be done with the broken leg of Gui Renzhong, that dirty dog? The PLA rep issued three directives: one, his leg should be treated in accordance with the principle of revolutionary humanism; two, the cows herded by Gui Renzhong should be assigned to someone else; and three, Gui's written self-criticism must be completed and handed to the PLA rep's office as soon as possible.

Using traditional Chinese medical arts, Doctor Yu set Gui's broken bone and splinted his leg with boards. Instead of feeling bad, old Gui relished the little happiness brought by this misfortune. Now he needn't go out to work anymore. Every day he could stay in the empty, spacious dorm with his Jane. Squatting on his quilt and facing the wall, he wrote his self-criticism on a washboard placed on his knees. He always took a serious attitude toward self-criticism. Each time he would go through his four volumes of Mao Zedong's works. When he wrote something satisfactory, he would pause and read it emotionally, nodding and swaying, as if he were not writing a self-condemnation but a beautiful prose poem like the "Ode to Yueyang Palace" by Fan Zhongyan.

One night, when Gui Renzhong lay his tired body down on the bed and stretched out his broken leg with excruciating pain, he asked me in a tiny voice, "Do you remember whether the one who wailed like a funeral guest was a man or a woman?"

I knew he meant that great poet. Out of his extreme love for the great leader, the poet had so distorted his pitch and tone that it was hard to tell his gender. But I could not tell him the truth. I only said, "Sorry, I didn't notice."

I gaze at her window. In the past it was pasted over with black paper; now a cloth curtain with tiny blue flowers hangs there.

With a broken leg, it was unlikely that Gui Renzhong would make any big trouble. So it was up to me to scheme at night how to conduct my campaign against the clinic.

Gui screamed again in his nightmare. It was already one o'clock in the morning. Someone yanked open our dorm door. A chilly wind filled the room quickly, as though a swarm of practical jokers had dashed in and pulled away all of our quilts. Most of us were jarred awake, slinging a flood of curses.

"It must be Piglet!" They thought the man who had opened the door was Zhu Zaizhi, a college student majoring in world geography.

"Damn it! How many times does he have to pee in one night?"

"We should tie his bladder with a string."

"Let's write a petition to the PLA rep and ask him to transfer Zhu to another dorm."

I knew Zhu, a weak body plus a pair of thick glasses for myopia on his nose, a little guy who drank a lot of water. Then I heard someone speaking the words in my mind.

"How can we blame him? He has a kidney problem and the food here is so bad. Can anyone really tie his bladder up? Why don't you try it on yourselves first...."

We laughed. A few sound sleepers were awakened by the laughter. An old teacher, struggling to clear his sticky eyes, sat up and asked in amazement, "Is the Cultural Revolution over now?" His question aroused another bout of uproarious laughter. One could taste many flavors in this laughter. Of course, they were dominantly bitter and sour.

Someone teased the dreamer: "Supreme command: 'We must carry the proletarian revolution through to the end!' We order you to carry your beautiful dream through to the end!"

Several bouts of laughter that night made it hard for me to fall asleep. Our ancient masters observed that happiness may be brought by an intelligent mind. Perhaps my happiness was coming, for I had gained some insight from Zhu Zaizhi's bladder trouble. Right, I must try my trick. It was half past four – the perfect time. I started coughing fiercely. I discovered that feigning a cough was the easiest thing in the world. The more one coughs, the itchier one's throat becomes, and the more one wants to cough. In less than fifteen minutes, someone started protesting. "Who is coughing? Do you have to be so loud?"

"I ... I ... I can't help it. My chest aches," I said with more coughing, pretending to be helpless.

"Your chest aches?" Another guy jumped up from his bed and cried, "Damn it, you must have TB. You might infect us all!"

"Get up and go to the clinic!"

"Our clinic doesn't have an X ray."

"Have them write you a permit to see doctors in town."

I answered their concerns with more coughs, nearly bringing up my heart and liver in the process. With great effort, Gui Renzhong moved his splinted leg over and turned to face my back, which he pounded gently.

I said to myself, "I do not feel the slightest shame for deceiving those inhuman beings at the clinic. And I am merely playing a joke on all of you other guys. But to deceive old Gui troubles my conscience." Gui said no words to me but hammered my back gently. I could feel him suffering for me. But there was no way I could tell him the truth. It would be useless even if I begged him a thousand times not to report me. He would act like a toddling child who tries to stop an unwelcome guest from seeing his father by saying, "My father said to tell you he's not home."

The following day I did not go to the clinic. I coughed through another night. Old Gui thumped my back all night, without stopping for a minute. As my cough worsened, half my dormmates got really angry with me, although the other half were still sympathetic. Half blamed me for not going to the clinic; the other half defended me by saying, "We should understand his dilemma: if he goes to the clinic, old Iron Plum will chase him out like a class enemy who feigns illness."

Hearing such weighty support, I coughed more fiercely and, to express my grievance, even gave my cough a sobbing edge.

Three days passed. Still I stayed away from the clinic. I went on coughing for five days straight, and old Gui hammered my back for five nights. The whole dorm rose up in indignation and called me a coward.

"What are you afraid of? If you are really sick you should go see the doctor. If you are not playing tricks, why do you need to be afraid of her? Your case will be tuberculosis, pneumonia, or lung cancer. Please go. Old Iron Plum won't bite. Maybe she'd wait on you like her wounded uncle."

Still I answered with more coughing. For me the situation was not so intolerable. During the day I could take a nap in a haystack. Within five days, I guessed, at least fifty people had reported my illness to the PLA rep: "Although as an unremolded intellectual his death would be a trifling matter, still the health of his dormmates involves our reform, and reform through labor is a part of the fate of the great proletarian Cultural Revolution. And it can also affect the health of our PLA rep, who, as the representative of the proletarian headquarters, visits our high-ranking leaders.

The consequences are unthinkable. We have sworn to protect the health of our PLA rep and wish the leaders of the proletarian headquarters a long, healthy life."

This type of toady harangue sounds extremely repulsive today; but back then the PLA rep found it perfectly normal and pleasant. The reports eventually aroused his attention. He first asked the informers in an accusatory tone: "What did Doctor Yu and Doctor Liu say about his case?"

"He hasn't dared to go to the clinic."

"What?" The PLA rep was genuinely surprised.

"He's afraid the doctors won't believe he's really sick."

"That can be determined by a physical exam."

"But the clinic on our farm doesn't have an X-ray machine."

"Why can't they determine his illness without an X ray? The human factor is the most important one. Our Eighth Army went through eight years of the War of Resistance, defeating the Japanese devils with rifles and millet only. You intellectuals, how can I ever make you understand?"

"But a doctor cannot see...the lung."

"Mao Zedong thought is a microscope, isn't it?"

Silence.

"Is it really necessary for him to have an X ray?"

"Yes. I was told that when Chairman Mao has his annual checkup, he has several X rays taken," a freshman in the performing arts from the Drama Institute related reverently.

"Where did you hear that?" Overcoming his shock, the PLA rep found it hard to believe.

"The fiancé of...the daughter of...my brother-in-law ...serves in the central guards division of Zhongnanhai."

"Oh." The PLA rep sized up this actor who had not yet had the chance to show himself on the stage. The information about his relatives' connection with Zhongnanhai [the residential place for the highest state and party officials] definitely put him in a favorable light. The PLA rep's state of mind gradually improved.

"What's your name?"

"Song Lin."

"Ah, I think I know you. You're in the manure company, aren't you?"

"No, I am in the vegetable company."

"Well, please report yourself to the farm propaganda office tomorrow. You probably know how to write criticism speeches."

"Yes. I can also sing model operas."

"Good. My eyes aren't that bad, are they?"

"Of course not. You can see everything."

"Certainly. Otherwise why would the leadership entrust me with such an important task? Our farm has twenty-one returned Ph.D.'s and sixty-seven professors in the category of reactionary academic authorities. College graduates and high school students like you number more than a thousand. Do you think these stinking intellectuals are easy to handle? Sometimes they may look like pitiful lambs, but actually they are more cunning than monkeys. If I didn't have a diamond drill, how would I dare take over these broken pots? Now – what did you come here to report?" Distinguished personages certainly have a poor memory. The PLA rep had sunk into self-admiration and had totally forgotten the petitioners' request.

"We beg the PLA rep to show some concern for a sick student who has been coughing for days."

"Give him permission to have a checkup in town."

One word from the PLA was enough to relieve the clinic of all possible political responsibilities. Old Iron Plum wrote a transfer without checking my throat. When I first held it in my hand, I nearly revealed my true self. Spiritual elevation made me forget to cough for a whole minute. In order to remind Iron Plum to observe me, Doctor Yu gave a little cough. His cough alerted me first. I immediately started coughing loudly.

I coughed all the way out of the clinic. Even then, I

walked with measured steps, coughing all the time, for I knew their eyes were fixed on me.

Back at the dorm, I took my only suitcase out from under the bed. Fetching a few clothes, I found the record album and took it out, too. Of course, I punctuated my packing with constant coughing. After packing my daily necessities (a worn-out toothbrush, a half-empty tube of toothpaste, a wash towel, and a quarter of a soap bar), I climbed on to the bed and leaned over old Gui to say good-bye.

"I'm leaving now, old Gui. Take care of yourself."

"It's you who should take care. Have a good rest in town. Only the rich can afford to have TB: You must have nutritious food." Groping around in his quilt, he took out a small, dirty parcel and handed it to me. "Jane forced it into my hands at the moment we were parted from each other. I never ate it. Now I'd like to give it to you because you need it more than I do." With these words, his tears started to flow. How could I accept this precious gift from him, even though I didn't know what was wrapped inside?

"No – how can I accept this? It is the only thing Jane left you."

"Yes." He grasped my wrists. "You must take it with you. If you don't, I'll never again regard you as a friend." He thrust the hard parcel into my hands.

"I can't – how could I?"

Old Gui rose in a rage. "All right. Give it back to me. If you look down on me and my Jane, give it back." I was stupefied by his angry roar. I neither remembered to cough nor dared to return the parcel. I held that little thing with both hands, my tears welling up. I hadn't expected that my long-dry eyes could still produce tears. In order to repay his kindness I thought I should give him something in return. But what did I have? Being not only a pauper but also a political swindler, what could I offer him? No, that wasn't true. I had my sincerity, just as old Gui had his. "Old Gui, I have nothing to give you. But I can leave you a bit of advice. Don't trust people too easily. Believe me, this advice is vital for you."

"I really trust too easily?"

"Yes!"

"Oh?"

"Don't you remember how we trusted Lin Biao all those years? In his preface to Vice Chairman Lin's instructions, the editor used thirty-six superlatives, saying that he held highest the red flag of Mao Zedong thought, that he was the most loyal to Chairman Mao, the most arduous in studying Chairman Mao's works, and the best in applying Mao's words to practice, and the most advanced model for us to look up to. Now Lin Biao still occupies one superlative in our memory: the greatest swindler in history."

"But – Lin Biao is dead, isn't he?"

"That's true. But – " I wanted very much to say "are those who remain alive all trustworthy?" but I swallowed my words.

"The swindler is dead. Thanks to Chairman Mao, that swindler is dead. What a pity that an airplane was smashed."

"That's right. . . . I've got to leave now."

I left him with coughs. Coughing all the way to the long-distance bus stop, I measured one thousand, five hundred, and sixty-two paces – a distance that had been silently measured by many an inmate yearning for freedom. Luckily, a dusty bus was passing. I jumped on it. Seeing no acquaintances, I resumed my normal, healthy appearance. There were no vacant seats, and even the narrow aisle was heaped with all kinds of sacks and with piglets tied with ropes; I could hardly find a space to put my feet. But pretty soon, I felt like a winged angel.

Fields, clouds, and trees flanking the highway flashed by and inspired me to sing. However, I hated to sing quotations or model operas. I was racking my brain for something to sing. Humming, I distilled a tune in my throat. It was hard to find a melody suited to my vocal cords. Not that I didn't love singing. I had always loved singing. But because I was immediately ridiculed for being out of tune every time I opened my mouth, my enthusiasm was naturally dampened. After a while I no longer dared to sing in public. I recalled that, when I was enrolled in the Institute of Fine Arts, I had always loved to scream a few lines in the public bathhouse. I believe that public bathhouses have the best acoustics. Even a dry throat can produce the self-intoxication of a great soloist. It was said that the Russian operatic bass Chaliapin first discovered his singing talent because he happened to scream in a public bathhouse. My train of thought gradually led me to a familiar tune, one that I used to scream in the public bathhouse but that had long since faded from my mental horizon. It was a beautiful, sentimental tune that I had learned when I went to sketch in Shanbei with my professor. It should be performed on a vast plateau with a fully open throat. But I was always out of tune when singing in the open air. Only in the echoing public bathhouse could I achieve the musical effects of the wide-open spaces. My musical feeling now came alive. I was intoxicated in a vacuum without self, without time, and without space. My vocal cords started quivering and a deep breath rose from the bottom of my abdomen. A song finally broke out of my mouth:

Sweet brother is going to the West.
Your loving sister has no way to hold you here.
But to spend a hot night together
I'm taking off my flowery panties.

I never knew I could sing so beautifully, with portamenti and trills.

The bus jerked to a stop. Unaware of the astonished glances from all the passengers, I thought someone might have been run over by the bus.

"What's the matter? Hit someone?" I asked the driver.

The driver asked angrily, "What unit do you belong to?"

"The East Wind Farm."

"Where are you going?"

"To the hospital in town."

"Oh, I see." Something suddenly dawned on the driver. "Why didn't they send somebody with you?"

"Why should they?"

"Does your farm really trust you like that?"

"Why not? I'm no scoundrel who doesn't pay for his bus ticket."

"Revolutionary comrades!" The driver turned to the passengers and said sternly, "For our mutual safety, I suggest we tie this patient up so he won't hurt anyone when he has a fit."

Before I knew what was happening, passengers from both sides had reached out and bound me with the ropes that had been used to tie the piglets. It all happened as fast as in the saying, No time to cover your ears when it thunders. Kicking and struggling desperately, I yelled, "Help!... You dirty dogs! I'm not a patient! I'm not sick!"

"See, just as I expected," said the driver complacently. "Whoever has this kind of disease behaves like a drunkard who will never admit he's drunk. Stop up his mouth."

The young woman conductor took the kerchief from around her neck and covered my mouth with it. A whiff of smelly sweat made me nauseous; yet I had nowhere to vomit. Romantic novels always say that the cloths a woman uses to wipe her perspiration are fragrant silk. Never believe those silly descriptions. A woman's perspiration smells no better than a man's.

Those butchers had really done a good job. They gagged me and tied my feet, too, so I could neither struggle nor shout but only curse them in my heart. At the same time, the piglets were now running rampant because the ropes holding them had been transferred to my body. They burrowed around under the passenger seats, squealing. What a lucky day for them. Damn it! But why did they tie me up? What gives them the right? Why? Why? While these questions gnawed at me, those who had tied me up leaned back comfortably and snored. The bus, like a drunken peddler, ran with a constant rattling and ringing. Perhaps its hood or engine parts were loose.

Gradually I came to understand why they were treating me like that. They thought I was insane. Who else but a madman would dare to sing a provocative, sexy song in the land of China in the year 1972?

That thought calmed me down.

I gaze at her window. In the past it was pasted over with black paper; now a cloth curtain with tiny blue flowers hangs there.

7

Sunamei's first *axiao* was slow in coming. Although she had been a skirt woman for half a year now, men seemed to ignore her existence. She was an obscure, tiny blossom; only the huge, colorful flowers dazzled men's eyes. Her *amiji* Zhima was a full-blooming, pollen-laden flower. Men could smell her fragrance from a distance. Her shining eyes could hook a man's heart (those were Ami's words). As soon as Zhima appeared in a crowd, she became the full moon in a starry sky. In contrast, Sunamei was a pale glowworm. She was too close to Zhima; the moon shone too brightly. Zhima was like a broad, singing river; Sunamei was merely a babbling brook winding in the woods. Ami Cai'er knew her *mo*'s mind and tried to console her every day. "You are still young, Sunamei. You are still too young." Each time Sunamei heard this she wanted to cry her heart out.

The twenty-fifth day of the seventh lunar month is the most solemn festival for the Mosuo to pray to their goddess. On that day men and women climb Mount Ganmu in pairs. Amiji Zhima invited Sunamei to go along. "Sunamei, you can go with us. Geda will get two horses ready on the eve of the festival." A stout and honest man of forty, Geda was a horse driver and Zhima's latest *axiao*.

"Fine, Amiji."

The night before the festival, Geda brought over two horses. Tying the horses in the shed, he went straight into Zhima's *huagu*. Behind the partition, Sunamei heard Amiji

Zhima and Geda frolic throughout the night. If they did not tell any jokes, why were they having such a good time? They bit each other like a pair of two-month-old piglets. Screaming and howling, they tumbled out of bed onto the floor.

Sunamei did not hear the first crow of the roosters, for she had just sunk into a sound sleep. Amiji Zhima gently tapped at her door.

"Get up, Sunamei. You may go ahead with Geda. I want to prepare some food before I leave."

"Amiji, please go with us. I want to ride with you," said Sunamei as she was getting dressed.

"No, Sunamei. You two go ahead." She turned to Geda. "Be careful. Don't scare my little Sunamei."

"That white horse of mine is steady enough." Geda's voice was quite gritty.

"I don't mean the white horse, I mean you, you black donkey." Sunamei knew her *amiji* was teasing Geda for his swarthy complexion.

Geda chuckled. Amiji Zhima slapped his back. Geda chuckled again. As Sunamei stepped out of her room, Geda grabbed her around the waist quite unexpectedly and flung her easily over his shoulder. Greatly surprised, she grasped his head. But when her hands touched his beard, a strange feeling made her let go instantly. She almost fell from his shoulder. Geda stretched out his other hand and supported her waist as he carried her down the stairs. Geda took the white horse from the shed, without stirrups or saddle. First he placed Sunamei on the horse and then led it toward the gate, which Zhima had already opened. Coming out of the gate, Sunamei laid her face against the horse's sleek neck. Once outside, Geda jumped on the horse so swiftly and lightly that Sunamei was not aware that he was already behind her. Geda held Sunamei with his left hand as he let the horse trot very slowly, perhaps in order to give Amiji Zhima time to catch up.

As soon as Geda was mounted, Sunamei was enveloped by man's strong, hot breath, a mixture of the bitter smell of tobacco, the sweet flavor of licorice roots, the hot taste of wine, and the thin, sour smell of sweat. Although it was the first time she had breathed such a mixture of air, she got used to it very soon, and it felt homely and pleasant. Perhaps it was just an accident that Geda covered her small right breast with his hand. Sunamei, however, became excited as well as embarrassed. Leaning her head against his open, hairy chest, she felt obliged to say something. "How nice it would be if Amiji could go together with us."

"She is waiting for an *axiao* she loves even better than me."

"What?"

"You don't believe me, but I know. Before daybreak, she can receive another *axiao* without delaying anything. My red horse is so fast that before we're halfway there, she'll catch up with us."

Actually, Sunamei did not doubt Geda's words. Amiji Zhima's beauty won her numerous *axiao*. But it was hard to imagine how Zhima's heart could take in so many men.

It was the hottest season of the year. Dawn was the coolest time of day. Promising crops whispered in the morning breeze. Geda started singing softly. His low but heavy voice echoed like a bronze bell. With his mouth against her left ear, Sunamei felt as if she were sitting in a huge cavern. Morning stars looked like dew hanging from the cliffs.

> I am visiting Mount Ganmu
> > with my dear *axiao*
> as if we were drifting upon the clouds. . . .

Sunamei had not learned how to sing in antiphonal style with men yet. After a pause, Geda sang the female part in a falsetto:

> Green vines and oak trees twine together;
> Butterflies and flowers share their joy.

Sunamei felt ashamed of herself. How could a skirt woman not know how to sing?

> What are you thinking, my sweetheart?
> Your beloved man is right by your side.

> Happiness leaves lingering ripples, my dear
> sweetheart.
> How dare the tranquil lake forget the orgy of
> the waterfall?

> Hand in hand we walk, sweetheart.
> The path is always too short for us.

> Sweetheart, I may wither someday like a flower.
> I hope you'll collect my petals out of love.

Geda's falsetto turned sorrowful, like that of a wistful woman. But a moment later he became himself again and called to Sunamei.

"Sunamei! Can you see Mount Ganmu now?"

"Yes. On the horizon." It was already sunrise. A giant lion was squatting beneath the heavenly curtain.

"Does it look like a black lion?"

"Yes, it does."

"Have you heard the tale of Ganmu?"

"No."

"Do you want to hear it?"

"Yes."

When Geda loosened the reins in his hand, the horse got the message to slow down. Geda narrated with feeling into Sunamei's ear:

"Once upon a time, Black Bottom Dam was a flat prairie, and Lake Xienami was located in its center. All kinds of animals and birds inhabited the lake area. They lived in joy and harmony. White swans, unfolding their wings, circled around and glided across the lake in pairs. The female and male monkeys, embracing each other, tumbled along the hill sides. Even tiny red dragonflies knew how to arch their bodies to join with one another, head to head and tail to tail. These beautiful sights caught the eye of a goddess who often bathed in the lake and of a god named Hawa who frequented the lakeside for fun. The two of them wanted to live like all other creatures in nature. The goddess took Hawa as her *axiao,* and Hawa took the goddess as his. They met during the day, swimming naked in the lake. When night came, they embraced on the grass. Their love for each other was beyond description."

Sunamei's heart started shivering. Faintly she visualized that intimate, unspeakable scene. Geda continued:

"One day, Hawa invited the goddess to meet him on the southern bank of the lake. He waited and waited until the stars came out, and dew fell on the grass like rain, until all that was left was a pale moon in the night sky. But the goddess failed to come, and Hawa was so sleepy that he could hardly keep his eyes open. As soon as he fell asleep, the goddess arrived. She was late because two other gods, Warubula and Zhezhi, had intercepted her on the way. With great effort she got rid of them and hurried to meet Hawa. But before she could explain why she was late and how Warubula and Zhezhi were waiting for her on the northern bank, the roosters crowed, cuckoos started singing, white swans spread their wings, the east grew light, and the dawn bloomed like a flower. Seeing one goddess and several gods still lingering in the human world, the angered sun issued a command forbidding them from returning to heaven. They were nailed to the ground by the sunlight and petrified into mountains. Look, Mount Ganmu was the goddess, and surrounding her are Mount Hawa, Mount Warubula, and Mount Zhezhi. They are all waiting for the night, when they can meet behind the back of the sun. When the jealous Warubula saw the goddess sleeping with Zhezhi, he flew into a great rage. With a fearful roar, he cut the thing off Zhezhi's body, the thing a woman does not grow. From then on, the goddess ignored the jealous Warubula, forbidding him from approaching her. She fell in love with Mount Hedigu and wanted to sleep with him, and, when the tyrannical, jealous Warubula attempted to stop her, she said, 'If a woman is not willing, stop your daydreams. No matter how much gold and silver you may possess or no matter how strong you are, I am my own mistress!'

"Sunamei, this is the myth of our goddess. Do you like it?"

"Yes, very much – but some places I don't quite understand."

"Which places?"

"Why does Warubula want to cut...the thing a woman does not grow...off Zhezhi's body?"

Geda burst out laughing, as if Sunamei had asked a most stupid question, confusing her even more.

"Why can't I ask this question? Why not? I should ask about whatever I don't understand, shouldn't I? Zhezhi was wearing pants, so it would be much easier to cut off his hand. Why did Warubula need to cut off that particular thing?"

"You'll know some day, when you have an *axiao*."

Why would she need an *axiao* to gain such knowledge? Sunamei did not pursue the question further for fear of seeming even more stupid.

In the east, a flood of rouge appeared. The parallel ditches at the foot of Mount Ganmu gradually came into sight. They resembled a Mosuo woman's ruffled skirt.

Pointing to the canyon between two mountain ridges on the way to Zhebo Village, Geda asked Sunamei, "See that? What does it look like?"

"Sorry, I can't tell."

Geda stretched his right hand under Sunamei's skirt and touched her legs. "Now do you see?"

Geda's suggestive act did trigger her imagination. The two ridges did resemble the supple, slender legs of a woman. A round mound protruded in the place where the two legs converge. Sunamei dragged Geda's hand from beneath her skirt.

"How does it feel?" Geda laughed crudely.

"What's all this laughing about?" Amiji drew up speedily on horseback. "What fun you are having."

"I'm trying to help Sunamei find the goddess's legs, but she can't figure it out."

Zhima looked at him askance. "When a woman looks at a woman, her eyes are, of course, less observant than those of a man who looks at a woman."

"Heh, heh!" Geda chuckled.

"Heh?" Zhima mimicked him.

When they reached the hilltop, the pilgrims had already made bonfires; wafts of white smoke rose to the sky. Lama and Daba were reading sacred texts and incantations. Their murmuring sounded like mosquitoes buzzing around flower bushes. Tying the horses to the trees, Geda followed Zhima and Sunamei to kowtow before the shrine of the goddess, who sat atop a stag equipped with a splendid leather saddle. She had a crown on her head, and she carried an arrow in one hand and a lotus flower in the other. The stag's tail seemed to dance in the wind. Her face resembled the full moon and a vertical eye of wisdom grew between her eyebrows. Sunamei wanted to laugh but held back, for she suddenly remembered the goddess who caused violence among men. She guessed that the lotus flower in the goddess' hand was meant to attract *axiao* with its fragrance. But why the arrow in her hand and the bow at her waist? Were they to punish Warubula for his sin of wounding Zhezhi? Sunamei felt the goddess' appearance was tender and dignified, like that of

Amiji Zhima. After the ceremony, they rode behind groups of worshipers along the lake path and circled the lake once. Lovers started their singing dialogues. The songs they improvised became less and less familiar. Sunamei couldn't fully appreciate them. Like creatures in twilight, women and men were all orgiastically intoxicated. Pairs of *axiao* were like two waterfalls rushing down the mountain, anxious to find a merging place so they could collide into a single surging wave and then lie together and float in the direction of the sunrise.

In a woods carpeted with green grass, paired *axiao* embraced tightly, lying beneath the trees. The warm stars started glowing like embers. Twigs and vines drooped like curtains. Amiji Zhima and Geda were sleeping between the two horses. A tired Sunamei fell asleep as soon as she leaned against a twisted tree trunk. On awakening, she found her blouse wet through with sweat. Standing up, she shook the wild seeds from her skirt. A gust of cool wind swept past her. The stars calmly looked down over the hilly woods. Spurred by curiosity, Sunamei, now perhaps the only person awake, stepped gently as a shadow over the soft grass to observe the *axiao* sleeping. The first couple she met were Amiji Zhima and Geda, who were sleeping naked together, as if they did not know that stars gave light and that eyes, accustomed to darkness, could still see. Amiji Zhima was lying on her back, one leg bent slightly. Pillowing his head on Zhima's shoulder, Geda seemed to be bending face down, snoring thunderously, with one hand on Zhima's breast. Sunamei found Amiji's sleeping pose very charming. The slender limbs below her waist indeed resembled the two mountain ridges near Zhebo Village, including the small, dark, swelling mound between. Amiji Zhima was as beautiful as the goddess. The horses, like two stone statues, were motionless, resting with their eyes shut. Sunamei wanted to leave them, yet her feet refused.

Did having an *axiao* simply mean two people of different

sexes sticking together naked, with no fear of being seen or touched? As if struggling from a boy's embrace, she pushed aside a sapling and walked away. She tried to avoid looking at those naked beings, those fishlike couples; yet it was impossible, for they were scattered everywhere. She even saw a pair rolling like one down the slope. They seemed to have forgotten how deep the canyon was. Had it been ten thousand feet deep, they still would not stop. Sunamei felt the urge to warn them. But her throat was too dry to make a sound. She could only watch helplessly as they rolled in slow motion down the slope. She saw their feet sway like fish tails.

Sunamei wandered in the woods like a sleepwalker. Suddenly, clusters of women and men's begging cries and hysterical screams astonished her and chased her back to her original spot on staggering feet. Covering her burning cheeks and lying on the grass, she tried to collect herself. She could neither see nor hear anything. Tears trickled along her fingers to the grass. "I am not crying. Why should I cry?" Still the tears trickled. She did not know when they stopped. She saw herself riding a stag with an arrow in her left hand and a lotus flower in her right. She wore a tall, shining crown; the stag wore a necklace with bronze bells and red tufts. Flowery white clouds lifted the stag's hooves. She heard the wind whistle past her. She laughed happily. Then she recalled that the goddess in the shrine did not laugh flippantly with her mouth wide open, so she closed it. Mount Warubula gradually turned into a naked man with horns, laughing savagely, reaching out to stop her. She drew back her bow and shot an arrow at him. With an eerie howl, Warubula retreated and became a mountain again. Then, Mount Hawa appeared on her left, with a black, hairy chest. He was lying on the ground but sat up on seeing Sunamei. Clapping his hand on the grass by the lake, he invited her to sit down so he could tell her something. While Sunamei hesitated, Zhezhi appeared on her right with a troubled face. Covering his genitals with his hand, he turned away from her. In the distance, Mount Hedigu glistened in the rosy sunlight. In the flood of golden rays, a handsome young man appeared, wearing a silver helmet and ancient armor. He reached out to her, smiling tenderly. A sudden excitement overwhelmed her and made her unable to hold the stag. She knew she was waiting for a man but had not expected it would be a charming prince. He was handsome and had good manners. Those naked men were too crude, although all men were naked before their *axiao*. She felt she loved Hedigu better; he was different from the others. The stag, who knew the human heart, dashed toward Hedigu. Sunamei threw down her bow and arrow, jumped off the stag in front of Hedigu, and plunged into his arms. Hedigu embraced her. Suddenly she grew very tall and could rest her head on his shoulder. She returned Hedigu's embrace. Seeing the handsome Hedigu slowly close his eyes, she closed hers. Now Ami's words rang in her ears: "Only love and the appreciation of love can produce happiness. Absence of love brings only sorrow." "This must be love. I know what love is now." Ami also had said, "Love is something that cannot be taught. One must experience love, body and soul." "Now I am experiencing it, am I not?" Forget the past and shut out the world of colors. But what was she really going through? Did flames burst from her inner body? No, her emotions weren't like flames but like the water of a thermal spring flowing through her body. No, not her body, but her soul. Body and soul were quivering, made smooth and pliant by the hot spring. Although reluctant to open her eyes, she knew Hedigu was quivering like her. Then she moaned, "Ami, I love! I know what love is." Suddenly, she felt her skin had a tinge of smoothness. Opening her eyes, she saw Hedigu was naked, a naked man in her arms. She shoved him aside, only to find that she was naked, too. She did not know how she had gotten naked like that. When had she taken off her clothes? No, she hadn't taken them off. Then why weren't her clothes on her body any more? Just as Hedigu was embracing her, she woke up.

Amiji Zhima and Geda stood before her. The sun popped its laughing face through the treetops. Thousands of slanting rays shot between leaves and branches. She was too shy to look at herself, a naked woman in the sunlight. When she realized that she did have her clothes on, she rose to her feet, rubbing her still drowsy eyes. Meanwhile, she found herself before the mountain peaks, still tiny and obscure, like a rat under the cloak of a lotus leaf. In contrast, Amiji Zhima had a tall body, a pair of eyes emitting infinite self-confidence and charm, and two long, springy legs. Even Sunamei was attracted to her, not to speak of the men. Geda caressed Zhima's body with eyes of love and warmth. Tidying up her hair from the back, Zhima cast him a languid but bewitching eye. Geda gently held Sunamei with one hand and lifted her onto the white horse.

"You may ride by yourself now. I'll ride with Zhima on the other horse." Thus saying, he jumped on the red horse, bent low, and stretched out his arms to Zhima. Giggling, Zhima sprang into Geda's arms. Holding her tight, he tapped the ribs of the horse with his boot heels. The red horse, raising its head, galloped away with a loud neigh.

Holding the reins tightly, Sunamei did not allow the white horse to run after them. The horse, carrying her like a burden, trotted downhill. She seemed to drop straight from the blue heaven to the grassy earth. The sky above was suddenly overcast. Clenching her teeth, she checked her tears. She was determined to send her tears back or make them dry in the rims of her eyes. She declared to herself, "Now I am a skirt woman!"

8

I gaze at her window. In the past it was pasted over with black paper; now a cloth curtain with tiny blue flowers hangs there.

Damn my luck! Not until the bus had arrived at the terminal in town did they take the towel from my mouth, untie the ropes, and push me off the bus. To test my throat, I shouted with all my strength,

"Who are you! How dare you treat me like that? You – "

I could hear my voice was still loud and clear. Nothing wrong with my vocal cords. Yet everyone ignored me. Each passenger went his own way; the driver and conductor left after locking the bus, as if I were a mute and my shouts did not exist. How could they treat me this way? But they had. Could I bite their ears off? I must let them know I was not a madman but a TB sufferer – to be honest, someone impersonating a TB sufferer. Of course, I could not reveal the truth. I merely shouted, "Chairman Mao teaches us: 'Seek truth from the facts.'" Prefacing my remarks with a recitation from the *Quotations of Chairman Mao* would make me invincible. Otherwise, the masses could ask me, What is your attitude toward our great leader Chairman Mao? Such a question would strike me dumb. "I have come to town to treat my tuberculosis. How could you have tied me up like a madman? You criminals!" But they ignored me. Only a few passersby, totally ignorant of my case, stopped to watch me, snickering. They must have thought I was a clown, or else why would I be imploring law and justice in a lawless, godless state? This train of thought brought a sour smile to my face. Who cared, if my goal of reaching town had been realized? I spit fiercely and then rubbed the saliva into the ground with my feet. My action declared the end of a most humiliating journey. In the end, I had squeezed myself out through the narrow gate.

I gaze at her window. In the past it was pasted over with black paper; now a cloth curtain with tiny blue flowers hangs there.

I remember the first time I went to look for her. I was standing beneath this same tree and spying at her window from the same angle. Unable to see any light, I could not be sure whether she was in and whether she lived alone or with someone else. Although I was just a country bumpkin, I was smart enough to find her place by the address she had given me and to figure out that the window pasted over with dark paper must be her cocoon. As if floating on the clouds, I climbed upstairs and stood by her door to eavesdrop. Nothing could be heard. My attempt to peep was also doomed: the keyhole was stuffed. I knocked at the door. After a long moment, the door opened a chink, letting out a slim shaft of light. Although the door was unlocked, it was held by a chain. Perhaps recognizing me, she unhooked the chain and opened the door wide. I had expected our meeting to be a beautiful scene, as in movies and plays: she would utter cries of surprise, and I would be too thrilled to say a word but would shuffle my feet with lowered head. The reality was entirely different: she showed no surprise, and I didn't, either. It seemed my arrival fit her expectations perfectly.

Wrinkling her nose, she extended one hand. "Hi, come on in. Don't be shy."

Yielding to her gentle tug, I stepped into her cocoon.

"Take a seat."

Where could I possibly sit? There was only a dilapidated iron bed in the middle of the room. A shapeless quilt, which never needed folding, was heaped on the bed. And, she was sitting on that bed, holding a pillow that looked like a gray cat. Looking around, I found the room needed no modifiers. The classic description, "a home with four bare walls," was perfect. Seeing my disappointment, she sneered and stood up to drag me over.

"Take a seat. Don't pretend to be more foolish than you are."

I could well imagine how foolish I looked. My last haircut had been done in what was called the toilet-seat style with a pair of rusty scissors by a classmate who knew nothing about haute coiffure. My clothing consisted of a most fashionable threadbare army coat and blue pants too short to cover my bare muddy feet in worn-out liberation shoes. From my shoulder hung a large, stupid-looking, mud-colored satchel that contained the album wrapped in several layers of old newspapers.

I too sat down on the small iron bed. The bed gave a shriek – of welcome or of protest? Most likely the latter. She stood up and then sat down next to me. The iron bed gave out a helpless groan. She took out a delicate Yixing teapot from under the bed. She took a sip, wiped it with her hand, and passed it to me. I thirstily sucked down a huge mouthful. From the slurping noise, she knew I had drunk up the whole pot. She grabbed it from me and said, "A bumpkin indeed! How can you guzzle tea like that?"

In great embarrassment I saw the leftover tea leaves in the pot. The tea was warm and strong. I asked, "May I have a bowl of cold water?"

"Don't humiliate me. I have plenty of tea. But the way you drink shows your lack of culture. You need to become more civilized." In the little kitchen she put a large handful of tea leaves in a large mug; passing it to me, she said, "Take it and drink to your heart's content."

Holding the hot tea mug, I laughed. But soon I realized that act 1, which I had performed impromptu, had come to an end. What should I do for the next act? "Tomorrow I've got to go to the hospital for an X ray," I said anxiously. "You know, I'm...not sick at all. The X ray will expose me instantly. But it's nice to play hooky for a change. Even if I have to return tomorrow, this will still have been a rewarding trip." As I pronounced the phrase *rewarding trip,* I purposely slowed down its rhythm and polished its tone with tenderness and sad emotion. Like a poor actor, I cast a slightly flirtatious glance at her. She gently patted me on the back. Shaking me, she said mischievously: "Supreme command: 'Since you are here, be at ease.' No need to worry. Don't go to the hospital. I'll take care of your X ray, your medical report, and all the rest."

Wow! My eyes grew wide with surprise until they were larger than those of a cow. Hard to imagine that a little girl, dwelling in her deep bower, could have such power. Sequestered inside a cocoon, what influence could she possibly exert on the outside world? It was no less severe than our reformatory farm. Between human beings there was only surveillance, exposure, informing, and slander. Where could one find sympathy or personal friendship? Was one really able to find a friend willing to write a false medical report (the term *friend* was generally regarded as outdated and reactionary)? You could never seduce old Iron Plum into doing such a thing.

"Don't you believe me? If not, there's the door. Bye, bye."

"It's not that I don't believe you, but I *dare* not believe you."

"You dumb country bumpkin. You still believe that everybody behaves the same as when you were a Red Guard – when people blindly believed everything they were told and conscientiously did their evil. It's strange that even today you are still under a deception, failing to see that every member of the central committee has been wearing two faces since the very first day of the great Cultural Revolution: one for the Red Guards and the masses, the other for their cronies. Please remember, bumpkin, not all shining planets try to reveal themselves. On the contrary, those who shine brightest on others squat in the darkest shadows. The hoi polloi like us, with no luster to decorate us, have to protect ourselves from the strong rays and create a shadow so that we can put our hands behind our backs and get a little warmth. Except for this tiny warmth, what else is left to us? Never mind. Why should I get sentimental over something like this? Don't laugh at me."

"I feel the same way sometimes. I can suddenly become sentimental over things that have long bored me to death. So I'd never laugh at you. What strange creatures human beings are. Really strange. But...where can I stay for the night?"

"Here, of course."

As simple as that? Dear heaven! So simple. "Come with me." A male and a female living in one cocoon. How could such a complicated matter become so simple? Many sages and virtuous men in Chinese history had expounded on this topic. One emperor after another had established religion, law, and the courts through senate, ministry, and constitutional congress. Civil courts had sentenced thousands on thousands of sinners, and talented scholars had written mountains of classics, popular novels, and dramas. Yet stealing into her cocoon was unbelievably easy. I'll bet she didn't know China could even claim the great sage Confucius, even though the entire nation was consuming tons of paper and ink to criticize him, or perhaps she was not conscious of the fact that she and I belonged to different sexes. I remember once she told me she had read a great many novels and found that most of them based their romances on a certain ethic. Perhaps she was merely bragging. In fact, she had never read any love stories. I stared at her flabbergasted, and she suddenly spewed the tea out of her mouth with an irrepressible laugh.

"Look at yourself in the mirror. You're like the farmer brought before a judge for pulling up railroad spikes to use as weights for his fishing nets." She read me well enough. I hadn't read Chekhov's work to know what kind of appearance the farmer had made before the judge. But I was sure she was not flattering me. "Why don't you put down your wretched satchel?"

She snatched it from my shoulder. As she was about to throw it into the corner, I held her hand. "Don't break it!"

"What, except for quotations, what else do you have in it?"

"My medical transfer permit – "

"And half a cold bun."

"No. A record album."

"An album? *Shajiabang Riverside? The Red Lantern? On the Dock? Taking Tiger Mountain by Strategy?*"

"None of those." I cut her off for fear of hearing the titles of all eight model operas. "Tchaikovsky."

"Tchaikovsky?" Her eyes lit up. I have never seen the eyes of those who came to an oasis after a long journey in the desert, yet I believed the eyes of the dusty wayfarer would be just like hers at that moment. She patted my cheeks with her soft little hands. "Gorgeous. How wonderful you are! You can get a Tchaikovsky." I took the album out of my satchel and tore away its wrapper. The portrait of Tchaikovsky appeared on its cover, a man with thoughtful, wise eyes and a typically Russian beard.

"Oh!" She felt Tchaikovsky's face and said affectionately, "Old Tchai, it's really you, my old man Tchai." How could she address Tchaikovsky as "old Tchai," as if he were an old Chinese man with whom she was acquainted? I was a bit jealous. How did she get to know him so well? I, a university student, seemed to be less knowledgeable than a junior-high schoolgirl. I had never even heard a note of old Tchai's compositions. Nevertheless, it was I who had preserved this album from the vandalism that was still going on.

"Superb! How did you keep it till today?"

"I..." I dared not tell her the truth. The truth could be too true for her. Any image, too true to reality, becomes monstrous. It could reduce my status of being superb to that of being barbarous. Countless precious albums, tapes, and composition books had been burned to ashes by one stroke of a match. Yet then I thought I was behaving like Lin Zequ, our national hero who had burned all the opium from foreign ships with such dignity. Now I could give her only an ambiguous answer: "Purely by accident. Pity, it has a crack."

"Oh." She seemed to understand my situation and stopped pursuing the truth. Perhaps she was guessing that the album was associated with personal tragedy and did not wish to awaken my sad memories. This was indeed a grave mistake. However, the misunderstanding had already arisen. Let her misjudge me.

Closing her eyes and holding her hands to her chest, she said solemnly, "Let me sit in silence for a while before I listen to it."

Looking at her uplifted, angelic face, I had no idea what she was thinking. But I could be certain she was trying desperately to lead her soul to tranquility. Gaping like a fool, I gazed at her lips, which turned red from excitement. Had I ever had such pure passions? No. What passion I had once experienced was of another kind, a fervent, hysterical impulse. But, although at that moment she looked like a calm lake on the surface, the depth of her soul held subterranean flames. I was amazed that a cracked album could stir such terrific waves in her heart. How could it? But how were we going to listen to this album? Could it play itself? Of course not.

As I was puzzling the matter over, she opened her eyes and said softly, "Come with me."

I followed her. She opened a door to another room, a room filled with worn-out sofas, broken chairs, old quilts, and other items. It smelled moldy, and each footstep stirred up a cloud of dust. From the dust and broken furniture she pulled out a makeshift ladder, obviously homemade with poles and sticks, and passed it to me. I shouldered the ladder and hurried away from the dust. She asked me to carry it to the narrow bathroom and place it in the square roof opening made for the convenience of plumbers and electricians. She climbed up the ladder into that hole and dragged out a transistor radio. Passing it to me, she then took out a four-speed phonograph made in Czechoslovakia. So, she had hidden her treasures in the attic. We wiped the dust from the machines and plugged them in. As soon as the radio was turned on, a line from a model Beijing opera spilled out:

"This woman is indeed unusual...."

She quickly turned a dial, cutting off Ma Changli's trailing voice rather brutally. Finally, she used a snow-white, fine cotton kerchief to clean the album gently. Her movements, full of love and care, made my cheeks burn. What a sharp contrast between us. Now I understood the power of contrast in the artistic world. In the past, I had known only that the contrast of shadow and color could produce a special visual effect of merely technical significance. Who would expect it could sometimes shake a person's soul?

When the crystal needle started hissing along the turning album, she supported her chin with both hands, gazing at the light reflecting from the dark, rotating record.

Before I knew it the music rose, like a troubled man's sighing or moaning. Because I was a nonmusical person, it took a while before I could hear its warm, beautiful theme, a theme that in the most sensitive listeners produced a heartrending pain or streams of hot tears. It sounded like a forbearance, a stubborn will to suffer through thorns, gravel, blunt-edged, serrated knives, grains of salt, and sharp bits of ice. I couldn't help but be conquered by the sorrowful passions of Tchaikovsky conveyed in that cracked album. A vast tide pushed me irresistibly. With its push I slid into the depths of the sea. I shut my eyes submissively and yielded myself to it. Besides its effect, what emotions had I experienced before? There were some, but so shallow, so tasteless. The flow of the sorrowful music embraced me, drowned me, lapped at me. I was willing to perish in its rise and fall. Tiananmen Square, surging with a sea of people, arose in my sight. Although thousands on thousands of people had once trooped across Tiananmen, waving flags and quotations in unison, their vigorous actions had now become chaotic and sluggish. The splendid past scenes of Red Guards crossing the Yangtze River had now became a pitiful scene of struggling for life. Those heroic fights had turned into monkeys rioting in a swamp. The distorted scenes flashed back, the faded colors reappeared. All fragments, nothing but fragments. The sonorous music bore me up again and again from my distress. I had never been moved like this before, had never gained so many insights, had never rid my brain so thoroughly of waste. I felt heavy as well as light, sorrowful as well as happy at the same time – a mixed feeling of rising and sinking. Once past its painfully cramped stage, the music marched over vast spaces with resolute, frank melodies. Then it returned to stillness with a lingering depression.

A long moment passed before I knew my eyes were still closed. Opening them, I turned to Yunqian and found her lapels were soaked with tears. She did not weep or sob. Her tears just seeped out. The record player ticked to a stop. The world inside the cocoon was frozen in a void. We sat in the grim hollow for a long time. Then I uttered a helpless sigh, a sigh that sent a chill up and down my spine.

After another long pause, Yunqian stood up, turned off the light, and quietly opened the window facing the street. Pale moonlight poured in, and the world outside the cocoon quieted down at last and became an inhabitable place. Fresh air filled the room at once. I walked to the window and looked at the shaded path in the dim streetlight. There was not even a dog's barking — only some loose, big-character posters rustling in the wind. She looked at me with tears in her large eyes. As if by magic, I could see my own image clearly in her pupils. She said softly (only to me), "Only at this time of day do I open the window. Like a jailer, I open the door of my own cell and let my eyes out for relaxation. During the daytime, inside the window is a small jail, and outside the window is a large prison. I'd rather imprison myself in the small one, all alone. Only my imagination is free. Here, I can exist for myself. Stepping out of it, I have to exist for others. All my behavior and words have been denied by others. Although the prisoners in the large prison, with their own complaints, hardships, and unspeakable sufferings, are pitiful men, their pitifulness turns them only into starving wolves, waiting for their chance to tear up any among them who appears weaker and more pitiful. In order to avoid becoming so cruel, I try hard not to visit the large prison. In order to protect yourself there you have to be vigilant and pretentious all the time, never blink. It's too exhausting. Why should life be so exhausting? Every minute they are ready to take you out. Why do they demand that hundreds of millions of people must be spotless? Is it that a human being lives just to avoid making mistakes? Without any defects, can one still be flesh and blood? What is sin, after all? If life is full of sin, then no one should be called a sinner. If they demand that others be spotless, how about themselves? Have they never committed any sin? Are they really as pure as plaster statues? Certainly not. They are vicious hunters who set snares for animals. They hear the painful cries of the captured animals in the snares as music. Isn't this the greatest sin in the world? When snares are set everywhere, can they themselves still walk without obstacles? Ah!" She heaved a deep sigh, deep as the sound of wind coming from the autumn woods. One could imagine thousands of yellow leaves falling with the wind. "Again I've squandered my emotions over things that have long bored me to death. You are incorrigible, Fang Yunqian. Don't laugh at me!" She sneered at herself, helplessly shaking her bobbed hair.

I gaze at her window. In the past it was pasted over with black paper; now a cloth curtain with tiny blue flowers hangs there.

She and I stood on the borderline between the small jail and the large prison. Under the lingering effects of Tchaikovsky's booming symphony and a young girl's heartfelt monologue, I seemed to dwindle to a tiny speck, a spiritual pauper. I had never experienced such a pleasant mental pain before. Against Tchaikovsky's Sixth Symphony and Yunqian's philosophical deliberations, anything from my mouth would seem either redundant or foolish. Even if I spoke for a whole night, my words would not carry one-tenth of the weight of hers because her words were not spoken, yet flowed like spring water from a deep valley, nurturing the natural flowers of wisdom grown in the dark woods. I alone had the luck to watch the glistening of those flowers. I went up close to her, and she gradually moved her tearful face to my shoulder and held me in her arms, quite naturally. Soon my face was covered with her tears and with mine. Then our burning cheeks dried her tears and mine. I felt her soft lips nibble at my face and neck; she was looking for my mouth. She kissed it greedily. For the first time in my life I learned that kissing did not mean a simple touch of the lips. I imitated her clumsily. Then, I became even more ravenous in kissing back.

Suddenly, a shriek like a bayonet thrust itself into our world, and we shoved each other away in horror. Not until three seconds had passed did we realize that someone was shouting in the street loudspeaker.

"The latest supreme command! Attention, revolutionary

comrades! Please get up immediately! We are going to broadcast the latest supreme command!"

Yunqian shut the window at once and walked silently to the iron bed, sitting on it. I followed her to distance ourselves from the shouting. When I sat by her side, she grabbed me. I could feel her blazing body turning icy cold, shivering.

I gaze at her window. In the past it was pasted over with black paper; now a cloth curtain with tiny blue flowers hangs there.

Holding each other tightly, we fell onto the narrow bed. What happened next I can't recall clearly. However, I remember she was not the experienced fox I had expected but a virgin. I was disappointed, depressed, upset, troubled with all sorts of self-questioning. Can I do this to her? Is it legal? Is it right? What if someone catches us? If I do it, what will she think of me, and what will I think of myself? How can we face each other in the morning light? All the pleasure I could have possibly enjoyed was swallowed by the flood of these endless questions.

As expected, she looked wronged, as if she had lost something or exposed her soft spot to me. We dared not even look at each other. From the corner of my eye, I watched her in a sorrowful state of mind. While I was doing my morning toilet, she cooked our breakfast silently – two bowls of oatmeal and some toast. She covered the floor with old newspapers and sat on them. I hesitated because every page of the newspaper carried Chairman Mao's portraits and his supreme commands in bold print. Sitting or wiping your feet on them would be sacrilege. However, when I saw the window pasted over with black paper, I saw how I really was in a cocoon and could be seen by nobody else but her and how she could be seen only by me. With a faint grin, I sat down beside her. We nibbled our bread and sipped our gruel. After eating, I offered to do the dishes in the little kitchen. When I returned, Tchaikovsky's symphony was again radiating in the cocoon. Sitting on the iron bed, looking up at the bulb that shone day and night, she was warming her hands with a glass of hot water. She seemed to have transcended herself and was lost in music, her eyes reflecting the rays of the light.

With every turn of the record, the needle jumped once, creating an extra quarter note and an interval of a sixth not written by Tchaikovsky.

So that is how Yunqian and I started living together. She forbade me from getting in touch with the outside world except when, wearing a big mouth cover, I went to the farm periodically to deliver my medical reports, with the seals of the hospital and the chief doctor, to the PLA rep. She alone shouldered the minimal diplomatic work required for our survival. Each time I handed in a medical report with the words, "contagious tuberculosis, positive," the PLA rep treated me like a ghost. Holding my report at arm's length from his eyes with tweezers from the clinic, he gave it a hasty glance and sent me away. He would say, "Chairman Mao teaches us: Do not hide your disease for fear of the doctor. Because disease befalls you, take it easy. All right, take advantage of the treatment. You may leave now." I stretched out my hand for him to shake, but he merely waved goodbye. I suppressed a laugh. He was always lecturing us on the supreme command, "Fear neither hardship nor death." Yet he wildly feared death. In the thirties, romantic novelists resorted to this incurable disease to create tragedies for their lovers. But tuberculosis was no longer a dangerous disease in the seventies.

"Leave now or you'll miss the bus to the city." Only then did I realize that I was a patient with a contagious disease. The PLA rep never asked where I was living or what I was doing for money or whether I was still making revolution in the depths of my soul. His indifference gave me the cover I needed.

Where did I get all these medical reports? During the years of white terror, how could there be a hospital or doctor who would dare to commit the crime of forging reports to help a petit bourgeois intellectual escape labor reform? Yunqian told me the following story:

She got my medical reports from a chief doctor who was currently the child of fortune. This doctor had once lived in the apartment opposite Yunqian's. Now he had moved to Red Hill Village, famous for its celebrity dwellers: newly promoted ministers, bureau chiefs, major actresses and actors of model operas, and doctors who had gained their merits by curing the diseases of the nouveau riche. Doctor Jia Songli belonged to the last group. Early in the Cultural Revolution, he had been tortured nearly to death because he had treated capitalist roaders and reactionary academic authorities with his excellent knowledge of medicine. Worse still, he had studied in Germany as a young man. At the mere mention of Germany, those class-conscious, vigilant party members would naturally associate him with Hitler. Their imagination well surpassed that of poets, and Jia Songli was tortured as a scapegoat of the long-dead Hitler. Every day he had to dress up like Hitler, with a little moustache on his lip and a tuft of hair drooping from his forehead. He wore a tall hat and carried a gong. Giving the Nazi salute with his right hand between the beats of the gong, he paraded along the route designated by the revolutionary rebels. If he slacked off at all during his parade, they would make his route even longer and his hat even taller and heavier (by putting some pig iron inside). However absurd Jia Songli's performance looked, it inspired no laughter at the time. Even the street urchins were shocked rather than amused by his show. After each parade he had to drag himself to his upstairs room. No one, not even his wife, would lend him a hand. Yet little Yunqian often came to his rescue, calling him uncle, asking after him with charming smiles, sharing her food with him, giving him cups of hot water, and even sending him local papers published by all sorts of factions. To her, his Hitler moustache and tall hat were invisible.

In 1969, when one of his old capitalist-roader patients became a VIP member of the proletarian headquarters, Jia Songli was promoted because he was indispensable to the VIP's health. Ridding himself of Hitler's little moustache and tall hat, he became a man of merit to the proletarian headquarters. The chairman of the revolutionary committee at his hospital happened to be a former student who had once attempted to kill Jia; he never dreamed that Jia would return to the hospital alive. When Jia resumed his work in the hospital, the chairman, to show his goodwill, appointed Jia as the chief doctor. Whatever Jia demanded, he would agree to. In fact, Jia did whatever he wanted first and informed the chairman later. Jia's rehabilitation not only was a severe blow to the chairman's morale but also was a political threat because of a strange thing he had done in the past.

That strange thing had occurred during the first winter of the Cultural Revolution. At that time, the chairman of the revolutionary committee was the general of the Rebels of the Municipal Medicine Circle. The headquarters, set in the former dean's office, became his private court as well as his pleasure palace. One night, the general and his underlings gave Jia Songli the third degree, trying to force him to confess his participation in Hitler's Beer-Hall Putsch. Jia Songli appealed repeatedly to them that he had no knowledge of history, had never heard of the putsch, let alone been part of it. Of course, his appeal was interpreted as resistance, which must be met with corporal punishment. So they forced Jia to kneel on the floor with eight heavy bricks on his back. Dismissing his case, the general summoned a young female doctor named Lu Xiu. He then ordered his underlings to leave and to bar the headquarters entrance from outside. What about Jia Songli kneeling on the floor?

Well, the general considered his teacher little more than a broken chair. He believed his teacher would never pick up his stethoscope again in this life. Even if he survived, he would be politically dead. A politically dead person was little different from a pig or a dog, whose existence held no threat to human beings. Therefore he did not give a second thought to performing the following interrogation right before his teacher.

"Lu Xiu. How do you feel now, my old classmate? What you refused me for five years I gained easily last night, didn't I?" Although pale, Lu Xiu was still beautiful. She sobbed but refused to answer. "You can't blame me. I had hoped that we could love each other equally, like old classmates, and I pursued you patiently. But you wouldn't accept me. Not even I could foresee that today I would become the master of your fate. Your crime is very grave."

"I was innocent. It was by accident, a slip of my pen, that I wrote a slogan incorrectly."

"The evidence of your crime is in my hands, but I haven't shown it to anyone else. You can still be saved, if you – "

"No! No!"

"No? You already did it with me last night." The general grinned.

"That was forced. You drugged me. What you did was immoral and illegal."

"Illegal? Immoral?" He laughed savagely and swiveled in his chair.

"You had your way; won't you please let me go? I won't – won't report you – "

"What?" he shouted. "Will the sun rise in the west tomorrow? *You* report *me?* Go ahead and try. If they don't accuse you of class revenge, you will still be labeled a class enemy who attempted to corrupt a leader of the revolutionary rebels. In the end I will remain what I am!"

"But you already did it to me."

Jia Songli's back and knees ached terribly. He endured

the pain as sweat dripped to the floor. Yet as he listened to this strange interrogation, the pain in his heart overwhelmed his physical suffering.

"Yes, I did. And I want to do it again. I want to do it when you are awake, not in a coma. I want you to react like a woman. I want you to twist, to groan, to hold me tight."

She wept in indescribable sorrow. A pitiful young woman, trembling with fear like a hare cowering before a wolf, she appeared absolutely hopeless and helpless. Her weak nerves had gone numb.

Jia wanted to leap up with a roar and smash the general's head with the bricks on his back. Yet he knew he was unable to stand up. And he knew few people could stand up at this moment. He wanted to die. Although people turned into various strange creatures in stories he had read, none could match this general. His boldness shocked him but also won his admiration. Now he saw that boldness belonged to a man in power who had nothing to fear, and displayed itself in front of the weak. Once he realized this, Jia Songli felt he was being humiliated more than the young woman was. He sighed. "I am weak, weaker and more pitiful than a woman. No. I am a dead man, dead in body and soul." He found it impossible to believe he was still a feeling man with a memory, and this former student of his definitely treated him as subhuman. This, then, was not really a case of the general behaving like a brute before an actual witness.

Jia Songli found no way to tell Yunqian what the general then did right in front of him. The general never imagined that Jia Songli, a man once sentenced to death and a nonbeing with eight bricks on his back, would stand up again. Wearing his white gown, he came back to work at the same hospital, a real human being. To the student-general-chair, Jia's return meant not just the restoration of a job but the appearance of a living witness to his crime. It was too late for regrets – the sun indeed had risen in the west.

Don't think I'm digressing – this tale is closely linked

with my survival in the cocoon. Without the rebirth of Jia Songli, where would I have gotten my medical reports? And without medical reports, how could I have bathed in the wonder of Tchaikovsky's music with Yunqian? Without him, I would be basking in the sun by the filthy pond with my water buffaloes.

What did our shared life mean? What moral standards should it be judged by? What consequences did it have? I was beset with these questions, or rather, these questions could have arisen at any moment of our carefree pleasure to kill my joy. But Yunqian seemed never to mind any of this. She followed her instincts. Because she needed me, she dragged me out of the terror and chaos of the large prison into her little cell. Her cell became a small jail with imagined walls and regulations, like our ancient ancestors who drew a circle on the ground to declare it an enclosure. Inside our small jail, we were free, much freer than hundreds of millions of other Chinese. Because inside the large prison, every Chinese mind becomes a more impregnable prison cell; we opened the doors of our minds inside our cell, at least partially.

Water conduits, gas pipes, and electric wires were our only links to the outside world. Of course, the hysterical shouts from the loudspeakers on the buildings, the jarring sirens of the police cars, the sounds of wind and rain, crying, and model opera arias could still be heard faintly. Those noises warned us constantly that our flimsy cocoon was surrounded by the larger prison, as if located at the bottom of an iron barrel. Yunqian seemed to see and hear nothing. She concentrated all her knowledge and strength in hiding herself, in making herself inconspicuous, in order not to be noticed by anyone. Public attention was detrimental during those years. Even radicals of the hour, hardly self-conscious, realized that then was not the right time to show off. We never attempted to make any friends. Actually *friend,* a politically ambiguous term, had long been purged from the modern Chinese vocabulary. A person who was not a comrade must be an enemy. Did we feel lonely? Yes, a bit. We passed the time reading worn-out books, sometimes exchanging them to share our sympathy for the underdog and our jealousy for the victor, our curses on the evil forces that block the unity of the lovers and our worries for weak, helpless heroines.

Once when Yunqian was out shopping, I opened the window slightly. A fresh, biting wind immediately blew in a slogan: "Supreme command: With a population of eight hundred million, how can we stop fighting?"

I shut the window at once, but my mind remained agitated for a long time and arguments crept into my empty head. Why does a population of eight hundred million need fighting? Can we live without it? According to this logic, today's world, with a population of over four billion, can never enjoy a moment's truce. If that is so, then is there any hope for a peaceful future for humanity? Then I began to understand the logic behind the Cultural Revolution: stirring up fights, masses fighting masses, fighting with the pen, fighting with fists, fighting until each side died and rotted. Endless fighting produced a philosophy of boundless pleasure in fighting heaven, in fighting the earth, in fighting men. Perhaps only the spectators experienced the boundless pleasure in such fighting. That pleasure surpassed that of Tang Minghuang and Yang Guifei as they watched the cockfights and cricket fights. They were more amused than the Roman emperors who watched the gladiator contests, because modern methods of fighting were too wondrous for even generals hardened by major wars to imagine.

Now the theory of class struggle was inadequate, and new theories of fighting were churned out daily. Although the old class enemies in China had been all but annihilated by execution and imprisonment, rather than diminishing, the fighting grew more savage than ever. In order to prove the eternal nature of class struggle, some hack theorists invented batch after batch of new class enemies. The bourgeois rightists of 1957 were their first invention. Then followed the newly emerged counterrevolutionaries, the class enemies, the crawling insects who dare to bomb the proletarian headquarters, the dutiful sons and grandsons of the landlord and bourgeois classes, the loyalists, the army troublemakers, the May sixteenth elements, the Mongolian people's party, the escaped landlords, rich peasants, reactionaries, criminals, and rightists. Yet even these were not enough. Lin Biao added all other counterrevolutionaries and called for a sweep of all the ox-demons and snake-spirits. The moment Jiang Qing called someone a bastard, that bastard would be thrown into jail. Now it became clear that class division had become obsolete in this great era of fighting within such a large population. Any person with some historical knowledge would know that in the 1940s Hitler put into practice a similar theory on an international scale. Being more candid than the Chinese leftists, he declared a war in which an inferior race would be wiped out by a superior one. In recent years, while the foreign telescopes were all aimed at the Milky Way, our telescopes were aimed at the Chinese people. While foreign microscopes were examining germs, those inside China examined human thought. But what was I doing thinking like that? Hadn't I already withdrawn myself from the world outside the window?

All this thinking must have made my mouth gape like a fool's. Yunqian opened the door quietly, and before I knew it she was by my side, laughing. She pushed me to the floor, embracing me tightly and pressing her lips to mine. I was brought back to the reality of our cocoon. Every time she came back from a necessary outside trip she would embrace me passionately and give me all her love. Perhaps each time she escaped from the large prison back into our small cell she felt she was returning to a utopia known only to us. She particularly cherished this cocoon because it was a small but noble land inside which another citizen – me – loved rather than fought.

I gaze at her window. In the past it was pasted over with black paper; now a cloth curtain with tiny blue flowers hangs there.

What a cocoon, solitary but cozy, dim yet bright, cramped but free. Inside it, we tried to shut out spring, summer, autumn, and winter, shut out the clouds, sun, rain, and snow, shut out worries, troubles, and noises. On each revolution, the needle jumped on the cracked record, producing extra quarter notes and sixths. They were the consequence of a minor mistake among numerous grave errors committed in my life. I could tolerate it in Tchaikovsky's music by pretending it was a deliberate masterstroke done by a mad conductor. Why shouldn't I tolerate it because some people were still distorting the musical composition called history? The 33⅓ needle jumps per minute gave me an insight: discordant noises outside the window were filling up all space and time and penetrating people's conscious, and even subconscious, minds.

Sometimes I entered a meditative state of mind, like an ancient sage. This was different from the self-criticism prevalent in China, of course, which was nothing but self-flagellation, self-justification, and self-deception. Self-criticism was a gesture of surrender to those in power, and it was largely brought about by torture, shackles, and isolation. There were some who offered self-criticism out of loyalty or flattery. A sage's meditation occurs under no pressure. He examines himself according to the morals he is willing or obliged to accept. The most serious question I put to myself was, Am I now a deserter?

"Yes, I admit I am. I am a deserter who has escaped from the largest civil war in Chinese history."

"Why do you want to be a deserter? What a shame."

"I've become deaf to those jarring terms. I do not wish to wear those conceptual shackles. Because I am already in jail, why do I need to wear so many shackles? I no longer know whose soldier I am, nor whom I should attack. Because I have been deprived of my freedom, it is impossible for me to make even a blind attack. Moreover, I am utterly exhausted.

"There's an important point – why? Do you really want to watch idly while the fields of socialist China grow wild with weeds? What's to be done about China's future? Is it possible that the Chinese people will grow cows' stomachs so they can ruminate, with half-shut eyes, after each fill of fodder? What are our glorious victories?"

"What does *our* mean, anyway? What are the enemy's defeats? Who are the enemies? What is honor? What is shame? I no longer recognize their meanings, and my spiritual burden has been released. All the colorful political concepts could no longer shine like gold necklaces and jade bracelets. They were nothing but chains and shackles."

"But look what dirty tricks you have used."

"So what?"

"You deceive people."

"Deception is pretty normal, isn't it?"

"Pretty normal?"

"Not only normal, but fashionable."

"Fashionable?"

"Yes, it suits the current fashion. The magnificent background is nothing more than a paper curtain. I merely play my inescapable part of a clown in the melodrama, adding a few improvised funny lines. What I've done is in perfect harmony with the gist of the drama. Furthermore, I've never blocked any genius actor or actress' free performance or the development of the plot. The actions of my minor role, natural and concordant, fit perfectly into the libretto. Why should I feel out of place?"

"Then why do you think the background is merely a

paper curtain? It is the great mountains and rivers of our ancient country."

"No, I think it is even more illusory than the paper curtain. In the sunlight I often see the most fashionable, brightest color as black and the shadow as a dazzling light."

"That's your own illusion."

"No. I believe many people feel the same as me."

"Really?"

"Really. But they are flexible enough to adjust their intuitive vision to accord with established concepts."

"Then why don't you adjust yours according to the established rules?"

"I jumped off the treadmill designed for the white rat."

"What?"

"A treadmill designed especially for a little white rat. As soon as the rat gets into the wheel, he has to pedal like mad. The rat believes it's making great progress, but in fact it remains right where it started, only its eyes are so dazzled by the spinning wheel that it can't get off. Some white rats keep pedaling until they are too tired and fall off from exhaustion. Some pedal until they vomit blood and die, but their wheels keep spinning."

"What a cruel game."

"Yes, very cruel. Nobody can escape this wheel, including its designers, who crawl into it in order to show others how to do it. The moment the wheel starts spinning, they know they have made a deceptive device that, in spite of its speed, stays forever in the same place. However, in order to prove they are making progress, they must keep going. It is impossible for them to stop anyway. They are eventually deceived by the speed they make and become more fanatical in their pedaling. The image of the wheel becomes blurred. The power of inertia pushes and stimulates the flying feet and overexcited nerves, pedaling, pedaling until the wheels burst or their hearts break.... Fortunately I was still alive when I fell off that wheel."

I often stole to the window and poked a small hole in the black window paper, as if piercing the walls of a stronghold. Then I behaved like a clown who had not washed the colorful paint from his face, hiding behind the scenery to watch the silly games he had just played, parodying a made-up monkey. The clown takes obscenity for pleasure, cruelty for bravery, hypocrisy for respect, urine for tears, excrement for the elixir of life. Such a performance provided not only superb entertainment but also precious experience of life from a philosophical angle. The play was heightened by enthusiastic support, inexhaustible flattery, and endless confessions.

Every morning at six o'clock, when Yunqian, lying on her stomach, was still sound asleep, I tiptoed barefoot over to the window to see the most fantastic episode of that life-long drama.

Precisely at six o'clock, an old hag appeared, carrying a vegetable basket and dragging a pair of liberation shoes while she went barefoot (*liberation* – what a glorious term). She had her army cap on crooked (the VIPs who reviewed the parades of the Red Guards at Tiananmen Square all wore this type of army cap, although some of them were civilians; this type of cap, like the halo surrounding a god's head, emitted rays of sacredness and purity). With numerous Chairman Mao badges pinned to her chest, she looked like a Soviet general. I was worried that the weight of those medals would break the old woman's crooked back. Her oversized blue blouse was so worn out that the crowded badges could bump each other freely, producing a bell-like music. She laughed to herself constantly. God knows why she was so happy. She was picking up green leaves dropped by vegetable carts (thank heaven, nearly all the carts spilled a few leaves or a handful of turnips along the way). Whenever she picked up a leaf, she burst into excited laughter. Laying her basket on the ground, she would flip up the back of her long skirt and slap her backside, shouting, "The situation is not merely good. It is excellent! It's getting better and better."

If she found a whole cabbage or something, she would jump even higher and shout even louder: "The enemies grow more rotten day by day, whereas we become stronger and stronger."

The people on the street paid no attention to her, except for those in long queues, who stared at her silently. In fact, they were staring at the greens in her basket, admiring her for having gleaned so much. Although the lines she shouted were obviously improvised, they created a unique and powerful artistic effect at the right moment, like a film editor joining two shots into a montage. The watchdogs, no matter how sensitive they were to class struggle, did not interfere with her, because her lines demonstrated no political problems, had no ulterior motives, and were all quoted from the political classics. Who dared to say our situation was not excellent? Who dared to say the enemies were not growing more rotten daily? And who dared to say we were not getting stronger and stronger with each passing day? If you blamed her for her inapt quotes, then how would you explain the statement that "Chairman Mao's works are a universal truth that can be applied to the four seas"? So the old hag won her freedom to perform. Every day she went onstage like a sophisticated actress at exactly the same time and place. Her precision was like clockwork. By and by her image was printed on my memory. I drew a sketch of her without even having to cast a glance at her. I was quite proud of myself. The sketch captured not only her image but also her inner spirit. But when I showed my sketch to Yunqian, she unexpectedly rose in a rage, for it showed her I was peeping at the outside world. The large world seemed still attractive to me, or I was still too easily captured by it. It was definitely a dangerous tendency.

She said to me sadly, "Why are your hands so restless? The window cannot shut you in, and even I fail to attract you."

"I want to draw."

"Why don't you draw me, then? I'll be your model."

With tears streaming down her face, she slowly undressed. An entirely different Yunqian appeared before me. Instantly I asked myself why I had never seen she was such a beauty. I had seen authentic works as well as replicas of nude sculpture and painting, and I must admit they all showed well-proportioned, beautiful bodies as well as the value, strength, and confidence of a human being – yet the one in front of me was not an artistic representation but a living body with a soul. Moreover, she loved me with all her body and soul (although she had never expressed her love in words). To me, this was most important, surpassing the beauty of Venus created by any master hand. How I had neglected her in the past. After one hysterical impulse, I had simply slept by this snowy, perfect masterpiece created by nature, never caressing her with a loving glance. During a sketching class at school, I had the chance to draw two female models, both married women with children. Honestly speaking, they had aroused a powerful sexual desire in my youthful, restless body. When I stepped into the sketch room, my face grew ghastly pale. Shaking all over, I was unable to pick up a pen or hear the professor's words. Of course, my reaction to the naked females revealed the awakening of puberty. When I started looking for their shapes and lines, I gradually calmed down. Recalling the loose muscles of the two models as I stood before the body of Yunqian, I felt extremely ashamed of my adolescent impulses.

I embraced her gently and whispered,

"Yes, I will draw you, but not now."

I lifted her easily, and I was so alive....

I gaze at her window. In the past it was pasted over with black paper; now a cloth curtain with tiny blue flowers hangs there.

9

"Sunamei! After worshiping Goddess Gan-mu, your eyes become even brighter, like midnight stars."

"Sunamei! After worshiping Goddess Ganmu, you shoot up in a twinkling, like a sapling in May."

"Sunamei! After worshiping Goddess Ganmu, your waist sways like willow twigs in March."

"Sunamei! After worshiping Goddess Ganmu, you spread your fragrance far and wide, like a bud ready to bloom."

"Sunamei! After worshiping Goddess Ganmu, you bring back her smiles."

Sunamei was pleased. So many people admired her – women and men, peers and elders. Although Ami did not say anything, she looked her up and down with closed smiling lips and kissed her cheeks affectionately. Sunamei looked at herself in the mirror a couple of times a day. Amazed by her own change day by day, she couldn't help shouting into the mirror, "Sunamei, you really are pretty!"

When autumn came, the heaviest job was cutting millet under a summer sun that never wanted to set. Three communities brought in this harvest. Sunamei joined the ranks of the adults, squatting in the fields, cutting and cutting. The withered stalks of ripe millet sang a rustling tune to the movements of the sickles. When adults of the three communities joined together, the work site heated up. Apart from singing, they made love jokes – sexual puns that made Sunamei's cheeks burn. These grown-up women's explosive laughter not only provided the best explanations but also added to their charm. The smells of sweat and tobacco from male bodies simmered in the air like hot wine. Sunamei worried that the harvest would soon be over, and then she could not hear those jokes any more. Those men and women, older than she, demonstrated such surprising talent in making jokes. Witty remarks simply rolled off their lips like pearls. Every metaphor taught Sunamei new shades of meaning. She was so intoxicated by those sweet, obscure comparisons that she wanted to swoon. She never dared to laugh out loud at the jokes. She was there simply to cut the millet mechanically with two hands; she let the sweat from her face trickle down through her breasts and soak her waistband.

On the threshing floor, men and women, surrounding a large heap of barnyard millet, let their flails rise and fall in unison. In the center, Amiji Zhima swayed to the rhythm of the flails. She looked so energetic, swaying as she flailed; sweat soaking the upper part of her skirt, her reddened face shined in the late sunlight. The men glanced at her arms with sleeves folded high up, at her swaying buttocks, at her brown feet beneath the ruffles of the skirt. Sunamei was thinking to herself, "How wonderful if I were the one standing in the middle! I know how to do it." She beat her flail fiercely. The giggler Geruoma laughed loudly, without restraint. Sunamei found this cheap because Geruoma had passed the skirt ceremony together with her. How could she still laugh like that? A foolish laugh, like a girl under thirteen. What's so funny, anyway? Do you have beauty to display? Zhima had the beauty of a pollen-emitting flower; Sunamei did not, and that was what annoyed her most.

Night fell. Men stayed on the threshing floor to guard the millet. They lay their sweat-soaked bodies on the dry straw and covered themselves with fur cloaks in the fashion of the Li nationality (the Li call them *cha'erwa*). Women brought them food. Watching the men eat heartily, the women forgot their own exhaustion. Some men showed off the waistbands and pants their *axiao* had made for them as they praised their fine needlework and good hearts. Some men begged or grabbed little gifts from women to test their love for them. Sunamei wore a new waistband and a new kerchief she had embroidered in expectation of someone's begging for or grabbing it. Grabbing was better, for it revealed the lover's irrepressible passions. When the men had eaten their fill, the women picked up all the bowls and pots. They left individually rather than in a group, as they had come. The men also left one by one in different directions. Everything seemed natural, as if there had been no deliberation. In fact, some of the bowls and pots were shattered when the lovers met and hugged each other too eagerly.

Sunamei had not yet learned the language of the eyes. She did not yet know the secret of a planned accidental meeting. With self-confidence, she chose to walk alone on a quiet path. The path led her to a small river, flanked by a row of saplings. She did not feel hot, yet wanted very much to bathe her sweaty body in the icy water. It seemed an endless job to pinch away the bits of straw from around her neck. Although she could not hear any man following her, she was positive that he must be stalking her at a distance. There must be a man attracted to her, perhaps two or three taking her path. The river sang aloud to accompany her. Oh, she could hear noise behind her. She became too excited to walk steadily, and her feet banged against each other. When she was certain the noise was footfalls – the footfalls of a man – she nearly shed tears of joy. This proved her attractiveness as a mature woman. She pulled her shoulders back. Imitating Amiji Zhima's carriage, she let her skirt sway like waves but held her body steady as if she were borne up by the clouds in the sky. She could feel the man behind gazing steadily at her back. She knew her back was full and broad. The footsteps came nearer, hesitated, and then stumbled. Sunamei pretended not to hear, as if she were listening only to the singing of the river. She was guessing who it could be. One by one, she reviewed the most robust and interesting men in the fields, as well those on the threshing floor that day. Was it Nazhu, who could put coarse jokes into delicate words? Perhaps it was Nacuo, who could make his muscles roll like a woman's body. If not them, it must be the best singer, Azha, whose voice made Sunamei's body thrill. The footsteps caught up with hers. Her anxiety matched her joy, and her heart nearly stopped beating. She was waiting, waiting for the appearance of a pair of coarse or gentle hands and a burning hot body, waiting to be thrown onto the short grass. Then – as she expected – she felt her head kerchief being snatched away. Turning to look, she saw a boy no taller than she. It was Bubu of the Adi community, a boy who had just put on pants. As if falling into a deep pond, Sunamei pushed him away, grabbed back her kerchief, and screamed, "You! Are you a man? A bare-bottomed cock!" The bare-bottomed cock was audacious enough to hold her waist.

Sunamei shoved Bubu to the stones. Then, straddling him, she beat him with her quivering fists. Kicking his feet, Bubu cried aloud like a baby. Sunamei stood up and ran away like an arrow, along the path of the river to the dark woods. She dashed heedlessly into the woods like a deer startled by gunfire. Covering her head with her hands, she tunneled through the dense branches. She did not stop until she came to a spot where the branches were so thick that no noise from the outside could sink in. Then she grabbed a young sycamore tree and cried to her heart's content. She had never been so sad and had not cried like this since her tenth birthday. She was disappointed in herself and hated all men. Do you have eyes? Why are you so blind to my beauty?

Above her, a bird cried. Becoming as ashamed as she had been enraged, she immediately stopped crying and dried her tears with the back of her hand. Quietly she squatted and groped for a round, heavy stone the size of a dove's egg. Lifting her face, she was searching for the bird who dared to mock her. High concentration lit up her eyes. She discovered a long-beaked stork, resting in the woods after a day's catching of loaches. She saw it scratch the mud from its claws. Sunamei cast a look of hatred at it, tiptoed, and then jerked her body, flinging the stone at the stork. She had good aim, having hit a sparrow with a stone at age five and small fish in the shallows many times. The long-beaked stork was frightened off, a tuft of its breast feathers falling off. The victory relieved Sunamei's bad mood. She walked out of the woods slowly. When she saw the big black dog of her family sitting by the roadside, it was like seeing a kinsman. Throwing her arms around its neck, Sunamei said, "How did you know I was here? You were afraid I would lose my way, weren't you? Good dog! Good, good dog!"

Tears welled up again; she choked back her sobs. Although the dog had been her friend since her childhood, a dog after all was just a dog. Wagging its tail, the black dog ran ahead and Sunamei followed. By the time they reached home, it was already midnight. She saw her *ami* waiting for her at the entrance. "Sunamei," Ami held Sunamei in her arms and asked softly, "where is your *axiao?* Why don't you bring him home? This is something to be proud of, you know. Mo, you should bring him home with good manners."

On the verge of collapsing into Ami's arms with a cry, she held back her tears, recalling she was a skirt woman, not a little girl wrapped in a linen gown any more. She merely said angrily, "For me, all men are dead!" Then she dashed through the yard and up the stairs, plunging into her *huagu*. She sat paralyzed on the bed, covering her face with the sheep's wool and lying motionless until daybreak.

From fragrant autumn to chilly winter, Sunamei's pinched face showed no smile. Quite unexpectedly, the silent anger made her look more mature and more beautiful. Like a patch of azaleas blooming on the mountain peaks, beautiful Sunamei rose before the men from dozens of miles around, making them look up to her and seek a path to reach her. When the swinging festival came in the first lunar month, Sunamei deliberately asked that her swing be five feet longer than the others. As soon as she got on, the swing flew high above the heads of the audience. The ruffles of her skirt danced like lotus leaves in a storm. Her self-confidence rose with her body. She giggled heartily, her calves flashing from under her flying skirt. She could hear, from beneath her feet, that the clapping and cheering for her were much louder than for any other woman. It was true this time. She tasted the sweetness of the truth. She was really flying, clouds and sun whirling overhead. Among the laughter and cheers she discerned men's sincere praises. Her intoxicating laughter, like a stream breaking its dam, ceaselessly poured down.

"Is she the Sunamei from Youjiwa Village?"

Sunamei swung away, giggling.

"Is she the *mo* of Cai'er? Oh!"

Sunamei swung back, giggling.

"Like a lotus flower shooting above the water at night."

Sunamei bent over. One forceful pedal, and she flew to the sky again.

"How wonderful if I could have her as my *axiao*."

Sunamei looked down at the uplifted faces and giggled.

"She must have chosen her own *axiao* long ago."

Sunamei swung over people's heads and soared to the sky, giggling.

"I would be content if I could drink a little tea in her *huagu*."

Sunamei swung down, giggling.

"I am going to look for her tonight."

Sunamei flew away, giggling.

"Do you really think she wants *you?*"

Sunamei, lowering her body, swooped down, strewing her laughter among the admirers.

"Do you really think she wants *you?*"

Sunamei was flying away.

"Do you really think she wants *you?*"

Sunamei deeply inhaled the wind from the steppe.

"Do you really think she wants *you?*"

Looking down at the men who were quarreling over her, Sunamei laughed. "I shall decide who I want."

Sunamei let her swing slow down by itself. Slower and slower, until finally the swing stopped and Sunamei jumped down, giggling. She ran away, still giggling, chased by hundreds of men's loving eyes. She ran toward Youjiwa Village, like a black phoenix butterfly flying into the deep green woods, having dazzled people's eyes with its crazy waltz.

Hooves clattered like firecrackers. Sunamei felt there was a man on horseback behind her. The clattering suddenly slowed down. "Pa-ta, pa-ta." A horse's hot breath nearly licked her back. She did not turn her head, but moved aside to make way. Yet the rider did not pass her. Tightening the reins, he let his horse circle around Sunamei. Sunamei lifted her head in anger, only to see a smiling face, the face of a forty-year-old man, a ruddiness penetrating through his darkly tanned skin. The face was covered by black stubble, the eyes were bright, a few red veins in them betraying the strength of wine. Around his waist was a wide belt with six wallets. On the brow of his chestnut horse hung a small round mirror, and the horse's mane was decorated with scarlet tassels.

"Sunamei! I want to stay in your *huagu* tonight."

"If you dare to come – " Sunamei did not expect she could give such a mature reply. It was calm, neither condescending nor humble, neither too proud nor too shy. Lifting her face and with eyes wide open, she replied in a voice neither too loud nor too soft.

"I am Longbu of the Kezhi family. That's just what I wanted to hear." With these words, he turned his horse to leave. Sunamei saw Longbu leaning into the saddle as he galloped away. A waft of wild odor from his body dispersed in the air. The horse galloped swiftly, yet Longbu bent down to light a cigarette and turned to blow Sunamei a smoke ring. Then, in the manner of a Mosuo male courting the female, he shouted, "Ah – hi – hi!" The sonorous sound echoed in the air for a long time.

Sunamei laughed. She was laughing at her own pretense. She had acted like a woman who had already received at least five *axiao*.

10

I gaze at her window. In the past it was pasted over with black paper; now a cloth curtain with tiny blue flowers hangs there.

One afternoon in May, I went to the farm to send my monthly report to the PLA rep. On my way back, I chanced on Gui Renzhong. Why hadn't I noticed him the moment I got on the bus? Because he had changed beyond recognition. The former cowherd now had his formerly messy hair neatly parted in the middle and pasted thinly over his scalp, with an excess of pomade (too old-fashioned). He wore a brand-new khaki Mao-suit and a pair of fashionable leather shoes, but he still held the shoe box that contained Jane's ashes. His new appearance so confused me that I felt like a twelve-foot Warrior Buddha too tall to touch his own head. Gui, one of the old intellectuals undergoing labor reform on the farm, had slicked back his hair in a style that even newly promoted cadres dared not follow. He dragged me to the vacant seat by his side and whispered mysteriously, "Little Liang, I have moved to the city."

"Moved to the city?" How could he possibly move to the city? How could he obtain permission? Was he capable of solving the problems of housing, registration, food rationing, and the other dozens of official coupons for daily necessities? In particular the coupons were the privilege of city residents, closely linked with their life and death. Without those coupons you couldn't even buy a roll of coarse toilet paper. A city was different from the countryside, where one could rub his bottom clean simply with a lump of dry clay.

Seeming to guess my doubts, Gui put his arm around my shoulder and said, "Housing, residential registration, grain ration – everything has been solved. I even got a ticket for three ounces of cooking oil for this month. Three whole ounces – that's quite a lot. They also gave me all kinds of coupons for daily necessities. One of them is for buying women's sanitary pads. Although I can't use it myself, I was told it could be secretly exchanged for eggs. One sanitary-pad coupon is worth two brown eggs."

"Really?" I was dumbfounded. How could he have suddenly risen to blue heaven?

"I owe everything to Chairman Mao's wise diplomatic policy. To tell you the truth, I must start with 'ping-pong diplomacy.' Now China is ready to have a dialogue with imperialism. Kissinger and Nixon have both visited China. At the banquet in honor of Nixon, the song 'America, the Beautiful' was played. It was fantastic, a glorious victory for Chairman Mao's great diplomatic line! In the past, it was absolutely correct to ignore the Americans and fight them mercilessly; now it is equally correct to hold banquets for them, so as to demonstrate fully the style of our great nation. As to Chairman Mao's great strategies, I've never had the slightest suspicion. Now it all becomes clear, doesn't it? We have swapped Soviet revisionism for U.S. imperialism. Now Soviet revisionism has become our number 1 enemy, and U.S. imperialism number 2. Of course, number 1 and number 2 need to be treated differently. We must attack number 1 first. While attacking number 1, we may as well put number 2 aside or even get them drunk with some mao-tai wine. After wiping out Soviet revisionism, we can turn back to annihilate number 2. We can do it; we can definitely do it. This is indeed wisdom! The strategy is known as the one-front war. In war we must fight one battle at a time; at dinner we must eat one mouthful at a time. These are not my own words, but Chairman Mao's original – "

"Old Gui, I know all this. But how could you move from the farm to the city? Tell me how. Why did a meat pie drop from heaven right into your mouth, and how is it that you were looking up at the moon with an open mouth at that very moment?"

Gui Renzhong rubbed his hands in excitement and joy. "I owe my luck to Chairman Mao. Long live Chairman Mao! Long live Chairman Mao! However, we cannot use idealism to perceive things in the world; otherwise the party's patient teaching and our hard reform achieved under the guidance of Mao Zedong thought would all be in vain. We must look at the world as whole and shape our viewpoints from the angle of the general strategy of world revolution. This matter concerns not the fortune or misfortune of any one individual but the needs of revolution and the needs of the party."

"But what does all this have to do with *you?*"

"Did you know I once studied in America and even received a doctoral degree there?"

"Yes, I know. I heard that at least fifty times during your confessions."

"That's right. I received a Western-enslaving education and was poisoned through and through. My experience led me to admire the American lifestyle, and, as a bourgeois intellectual, I stank and putrefied wherever I went. I really was rotten to the core and hard to change. If not for the party's patient education, reform, rehabilitation – "

"Old Gui, I know, I know all this. But I want to know how you can – ?"

"In America I had a lot of classmates. They are all better off – damn it, see how deep my bad roots go! As the saying goes, 'Different vines bear different melons; different classes speak different languages.' What does *better off* mean? It implies the possession of cars, houses, high position –

money, in a word, the comforts of fame and fortune. But fame and fortune are the root of all evils. How dare I say they are better off? The sinister implication is that I am not doing well. How can I complain? Isn't it a good thing to remold oneself into a new person under Chairman Mao's leadership in the most revolutionary country in the world? Of course, it is a good, a very good, an extremely good thing. It is one's greatest happiness. What does material wealth count for? Spirit and revolutionary will are the most precious wealth. I feel infinitely honored to stand in the ranks of the Chinese people, even in the status of being reformed. I should look down on American cars, houses, fame and fortune, etc."

I dared not cut his self-criticism short and had to let him go on. I had lost my curiosity. Who cared why he was moving to the city? I shut my eyes. He continued to lash himself.

"Chairman Mao teaches us: The further the socialist revolution develops, the more desperately people resist, the more they show their antiparty and antisocialist faces. My case proves the truth of Chairman Mao's wise teaching. What I said a moment ago revealed the antiparty, antisocialist nature hidden in my bones. Come to think of it, I am truly shocked. Despite my having suffered so much and undergone so many criticism meetings and written thousands of self-criticisms, I remain the same – am I going to meet my judge in the other world with such a stubborn, granite head? It's difficult. It is harder to remold an intellectual's thought than it is to climb the blue sky!"

Uttering a long sigh, Gui murmured for a long time with tears all over his face. I knew he was very sincere in all this. He would be very much annoyed if I interrupted him. The bus was crawling in the warm sunlight, and I felt a bit too hot in my worn-out sweater. However, I dared not move for fear of affecting his faithful confession. The jerking of the bus soon put me to sleep. I don't know how much time had passed before I heard a voice in my ear.

"Little Liang, aren't you listening to me?"

He shook me awake. I nearly burst out laughing, seeing his tearful face leaning against my shoulder. "Old Gui, please don't get too close to me. I have TB."

"I'm not afraid. I'm immune to all germs except decadent ideas." I dared not challenge him. One word from me would kindle another tedious self-criticism.

"I have an American classmate named Thomas Eliot — not the modernist poet who won the Nobel Prize in 1948 and died in 1965. My classmate Thomas Eliot is an important nuclear physicist in America, very famous — infamous, I mean." (He added *infamous* hurriedly in order to show his critical attitude. Naming was a simplified version of criticism.) "Through Kissinger, he passed a list of the Chinese scholars who had studied in the United States to our government. A small number of them are designated as eminent scholars. Unfortunately, I was one of the most famous, the most infamous — this is the root of my evil; otherwise, I could be reformed more easily. Thomas Eliot is coming to visit China soon. He plans to spend two hours in Gui Renzhong's residence. This creates a tense situation, for where is Gui Renzhong's residence? My residence of course is your residence, as well as everyone else's residence. We feel comfortable and warm living together in communist style. But the Yankees think differently. If they saw me living in a barn, sleeping with dozens of others on one long platform, running after our cows with a whip, they would slander China, saying that we persecute intellectuals. We and they have different, or opposite, concepts of suffering and happiness. We need to treat our own people and foreigners differently in order to avoid leaving loopholes for our enemies. For this purpose, the leadership assigned me a house, which was said to be first owned by a garment merchant and then used as the consulate of an eastern European country. At the beginning of the Cultural Revolution, the diplomats of the revisionist countries were all chased out. So the garden lay in waste, the roof grew weedy, the rooms became dark with smoke as Red Guards roasted their chickens inside, and the floor had several burn holes. But everything has been repaired now. Because it was an emergency, no one dared delay. Within a week, everything in the house was properly installed except for the hopeless garden. It was pretty hard to rebuild the garden because all the flowers, birds, fish, and insects – the pets of the leisured class – had practically been annihilated. However, the comrades working in Foreign Affairs were truly capable. They transplanted a plot of Lucerne lettuce and dozens of green cabbage. The green vegetables and the Lucerne with purple buds were quite a sight. I can tell Thomas that we Chinese utilize every inch of our land to produce for the revolution and to create beauty at the same time. Liang, you must pay a visit to my place. You know, they even assigned me a 'servant.' Don't be surprised. The duty of this servant is limited to opening the door for Thomas when he arrives and making us coffee and serving dessert. Then when Thomas is leaving, he needs to open the door again and hold his car door, bowing a good-bye. Please, come with me to see my house. Oh, no – excuse my slip. I meant the socialist state house assigned to me at the moment by the leadership."

"Okay. A chance to do a little sight-seeing."

When old Gui and I got off the bus at the terminal in the town center, I found his broken leg had completely recovered. You wouldn't have known his leg had once been fractured unless you knew the story. In high spirits, old Gui took me to the street in an area known as the French Concession before 1949. He pressed the doorbell of a large villa. On the square marble column by the iron door hung an enamel plate that read, *Gui's residence.* This small plate no doubt ran counter to the order of the day in revolutionary

China. It should appear only when it was needed for filming life in prerevolutionary society. But now they were not making a movie. I was so astonished by what I saw that my eyes nearly popped out of their sockets. Odder still, a robust man wearing a sort of Western black uniform of the old days opened the iron gate. I guessed he must be old Gui's servant. This servant shot a fierce stare at old Gui. "Why did you come back so late? Do you know what time it is?"

Gui's high spirits vanished with a shiver. "The bus – the bus – it's very hard to catch. If you don't believe me, you can – ask – him."

"Who's he?"

"Little – Little Liang, a comrade from our farm."

"I expected you home early so we could rehearse. You went to the farm just for that shoe box?! Damn it, you stinking intellectual, making such a fuss about nothing."

Rehearsal? I was puzzled. Was it true that old Gui was going to perform on stage?

"I'm to blame. I'm to blame – " Old Gui bowed low several times. "Rehearsal is easy for me. I can manage it in a minute."

"How long is your minute? I need to fetch my son from kindergarten."

"Take it easy. We can start the rehearsal right away."

"Take it easy? If we don't hurry up, we won't finish before dark!"

"Let's begin, then. Little Liang, you came at the right time. Would you please play the part of Thomas Eliot?" He hid Jane's ash box in the vegetable garden.

"Me? Play the part of Thomas Eliot? I'm no actor."

"You have only a few lines. Now please go wait outside the gate." He pushed me out and locked the door. "Little Liang, press the bell now."

Following his instructions, I pressed the bell. I had never touched a bell before and felt quite excited. How wonderful was this tiny gadget that rang at merely the gentlest touch.

Wanting to test the magic power of my finger, I pressed it for about ten seconds. Old Gui's servant yanked the door open and roared, "What's wrong with you, you bastard? Who's going to pay for it if you break it? Even if you can afford to pay for it, who could come and fix it in time? The American devil is coming here in three days. We can't afford any damage."

Like a child who had broken his toy, I looked at the finger that had brought this horrible reproach. To challenge this servant, I pressed the bell and released it in a flash. The bell gave a crisp ring to prove it was still in perfect working order.

Old Gui said apologetically, "This young man's a bit careless. Let's start again." The servant slammed the door shut. "Look at your watch and don't press for more than three seconds," Gui shouted. "Now start." I watched the time and pressed for three seconds. The servant opened the door with a long face.

Old Gui reminded him, "Bow deeply. Then extend your right hand to invite the guest in with the words, 'Are you Mister — ?' Little Liang, please tell him, 'I'm Thomas Eliot. I came from America to see my old friend Gui Renzhong.'"

The servant stood erect and glared at me: "Are you Mister — ?"

"I'm Thomas Eliot. I came from America to see my old friend Gui Renzhong."

Old Gui reminded him of the next line: "Say, 'Please come in, sir. Mr. Gui is waiting for you.'"

Imitating Gui Renzhong's manner, but with an angry tone, he said, "Please come in, sir. Mr. Gui is waiting for you — "

"Say, 'Here is Mr. Thomas Eliot!'"

"Here is Mr. Thomas Eliot!"

"Very good, very good," old Gui said cautiously to the servant. "But you'll play your part even better if you assume a little more politeness and show a bit more respect."

"What? More politeness and respect? I'm already polite and respectful enough."

"All right. Do it the way you want." Gui Renzhong came in from the sitting room to shake hands with me. "Tom, long time no see. Tom, how are Mary and the kids?"

I didn't know how to reply. Old Gui improvised lines for me. "'How are you, Gui? Where is Jane?' Oh, no! Little Liang, you can't ask that. If you do I'll be at a loss for an answer."

I didn't know whether to laugh or cry. "Of course, *I* don't need to ask about Jane; I'm not the real Thomas. But I'll bet you anything Thomas is going to ask about her. He won't just stick to the words you've made up for him."

"That's true." Slapping his brow, he found himself in a dilemma. "If he really asks that, I – I can only try my best to avoid it. Little Liang, come try it out on me."

I said in an affected foreign accent, "Dear Gui, how are you?"

"Fine, Tom. I'm fine. See, I look well, don't I?" He stretched out his arms expansively to show his vitality. There was a tearing sound, as the thread at the joint between shoulders and sleeves came undone. Old Gui said in haste, "It doesn't matter. I know how to sew it. Thanks to our labor reform, I've learned all sorts of things. Tom, I'll bet you don't know how to sew. I believe you don't do any manual labor. The aristocrat class is ignorant because they are clothed and fed by others – "

"What are you saying?" The servant cut off Gui abruptly. "How dare you lecture our foreign guest? How can you use our terms to deal with foreigners? They would seize this case as an example to say that we are criticizing them. Why are you such a bumbler?"

"I'm sorry. Let's try it from the beginning again. I guarantee there'll be no bare thread around the sleeves on the real occasion. Don't worry. I'll sew them with thread from the quilt and I won't make such large motions. Little Liang, come on, let's try again."

"Gui, where's Jane? Where's our beautiful lady Jane? Why didn't she come to meet me?"

Tears streamed from poor old Gui's eyes. However, he managed to avoid the question pretty well. "Tom, my old friend, you — you look the same as always. Please come in." He led me to the sitting room. The servant withdrew to the kitchen to make coffee for us.

The sitting room was newly painted; a crystal chandelier hung from the ceiling, a grand piano stood in a corner, and a landscape watercolor print was on the wall above the piano. Who knows where they had gotten it all? In the niche of one wall was a pedestal. In the past, it must have supported a sculpture, perhaps a nude, but now it displayed a brightly colored clay sculpture of Wu Qinghua, the heroine of the revolutionary ballet *The Red Detachment of Women*. The ballerina held a rifle and tiptoed on one foot. The plusher sofas were covered with fine drawnwork; however, from the words *The Red Flag Hotel,* one could easily tell that the furniture in the house was really borrowed.

"How come you're living alone, Gui? Where's Jane?" As I sat back into the sofa, I repeated my earlier question.

Holding back the tears, old Gui complained, "Little Liang, please don't make trouble for me. Why do you have to cling to that question?"

"It's not me who's clinging to this question. When Mr. Eliot sits down in this spacious house, he'll naturally think about your family life and find it odd that you're living alone here."

"All right. Go ahead and ask."

"Gui, where's Jane? Why doesn't she come to greet me?"

"Thomas," with great effort old Gui mumbled, "sorry, Jane, Jane — she hasn't come back from work yet."

"Oh, can I go see her in her office before I leave?"

"Uh, of course — of course not."

"Why not?"

"She is – is – not in this city."

"How can that be? Don't tell me you two have to work in two different cities? Why don't you talk with the authorities? Shall I talk to them for you?"

"No. This is a trifling matter. We are willing to – "

"Willing? I don't get it. How can you two be willing to be separated by your jobs? Please tell me what city Jane is working in now. I can easily postpone my itinerary one day and go with you to visit her."

"No – thank you, Thomas, but that won't be necessary."

"Gui, I can see you are hiding some pain."

"No, not at all, Thomas." Old Gui was caught unaware.

"You must be hiding something from me. Jane has passed away from this city, this state, this world after being tortured, hasn't she?"

Sobbing and sobbing, suddenly old Gui howled like a reservoir breaking its dam. Frightened, I stood up and shook him. "Old Gui, stop behaving like this. Look who's coming!"

The servant carried a lacquer tray into the sitting room. "What's the matter?"

Old Gui stopped his crying immediately. His mouth twitched.

"Nothing. I stepped on his foot accidentally during our rehearsal."

Seizing one foot immediately, old Gui cried heartily.

As the servant moved coffee cups, saucers, sugar bowl, and milk jar onto the coffee table, old Gui gradually stopped sobbing. "Spoons, coffee spoons."

"What? Since the cups are so small, why use spoons? Bad habit."

"It's their custom."

"Custom!" The servant went angrily back to the kitchen for spoons.

"You should hand coffee to the guest from his left," old Gui cautiously told the servant.

"Why not from the right? Your American guest is a rightist."

"This — is their custom."

"This is custom and that is custom. Okay, we're just putting on a show. When it comes to anything real, how can we do things according to bourgeois custom? Damn them!"

"Of course, we're just playing."

"Now I'm off work and I have something else to do." Removing his narrow-collared old uniform, the servant warned old Gui, "You have to sleep on the floor, because the bedding is borrowed from the Red Flag Hotel, and we must keep it clean."

"Okay. The floor here is much cleaner than the platform we share on the farm."

Pointing to me, the servant said, "You can't spend the night."

"I have my own place."

"No smoking!" The servant warned the master of the house.

"Yes, sir." The host answered the servant in awe and reverence.

"Do you know how to use a flush toilet?"

"Yes, I do."

Walking toward the door, the servant commented, "I knew you could. All class enemies are just dreaming to restore their lost paradise. This house is your little paradise now, but don't mistake a dream for reality!" The servant walked out. Old Gui and I heard the clanking of the iron gate. Old Gui was racking his brains about the knotty questions he must face in the upcoming visit. I sank back in the sofa, feeling extremely miserable and sorry for old Gui for being forced to play such a part. Yet he seemed quite happy, unconscious of the cruelty of his tragicomedy. He was good at reducing the mental burden forced on him to achieve some sort of spiritual lightness. He was always trying to sort out daily events like tangled thread. Although he never found the beginning or end of a single thread, he always believed he had found it. His explanation was that this was revolution and every happening during the revolution was rational. Revolution was a sharp knife that could cut through a tangled thread in no time.

The doorbell rang and old Gui sprang up in fright. I signaled him to sit down and offered to open the door. At the door stood a healthy-looking woman of around thirty. She looked strange: her pants were not loose enough; her blouse was a bit too tight around the waist; and her black heels were somewhat too high. I suspected she even used a little makeup. She belonged to the type of women whose youth had gone but who would never be visited by old age, a type of beauty that reminds you of fading smoke over the wide expanse of the wasteland.

"I'm looking for Professor Gui."

The title *professor* surprised me because I hadn't heard it for years. "Do you know him?"

"I will when I see him."

"Well – please," I said.

"What's your relation to Professor Gui?" Xie Li asked.

"Comrade. We're comrades at the same farm."

"Oh, I see." She smiled and said, "Please."

"After you." I became more polite.

The woman went straight into the sitting room and offered her hand to Old Gui. "You must be Professor Gui Renzhong."

"Not worthy of the title. I am old Gui."

"Let me introduce myself. I am called Xie Li, 'xie' as in *xiexie* [thanks] and "li" as in *molihua* [jasmine flower]."

"Do you want to talk to me about something?"

"Show me around the house first, will you?" Before old Gui could say yes, she walked upstairs and downstairs, inspecting every room and wall cabinet, including the bathroom and kitchen. When she finally stood downstairs in front of old Gui, she measured him up and down several times in the manner of someone buying a mule at the cattle market. Then she took out a form and passed it to him.

"I was born into a poor family. Age, thirty-two; education, middle-school graduate; marital status, single. Here's a description of my political behavior. Everything is recorded there clearly."

Taking up the form too nervously, old Gui groped through his pockets but failed to produce his eyeglasses. Finally, he found them in his pants pocket. That pair of glasses of his also had a terrible background; they had originated in New York. At Gui's very first criticism meeting, as the Cultural Revolution was starting, they had broken a "leg" – a bad omen that foretold Gui's destiny of breaking his leg. The first broken leg was supported by a little bamboo stick and wrapped with fine enamel-insulated wire. Old Gui carefully cleaned the cracked glasses with a dirty handkerchief. Blowing on them, he wiped them again before putting them on. Then he started reading the form in a murmuring voice, but quite solemnly. "*Name: Xie Li.* Right, 'xie' as in *xiexie* and 'li' as in *molihua. Sex: female.* No doubt about that! *Birthdate: June 1944.* Oh, thirty-two years old. When you were born we hadn't yet won the anti-Japanese war. Yes, Japan surrendered in August 1945. But it was impossible for you to receive a Japanese-enslaving education. As a child of one or two, you had only a blurred picture of the world occupied by the Japanese aggressors. In the year of liberation, you were only five years old. While you were acquiring the power of memory, red flags were fluttering over your head. *Education: enrolled in the Peace Street Elementary School at age seven* – of course, this was a school set up after Liberation. *Enrolled in the Number 6 Junior High School at age fourteen* – no problem. *Failed to pass the university entrance examination* – lucky you didn't. Chairman Mao teaches us, 'Higher education must be reformed.' After secondary education, one needs to do some practical work. You became an assistant in a shop. Although Confucius was born into a declining noble family of slave owners, he didn't attend middle school or college, either. He started his career doing service at funerals, perhaps as a trumpet player. Li Shizhen of the Ming dynasty picked mountain herbs for quite a number of years before he was able to write his famous *Guide to Herbs.* Much earlier, the great inventor, Zu Chongzhi, never received secondary or higher education. In America, Ben Franklin was once a printing-shop apprentice and a paper boy. In Scotland, James Watt was just an ordinary worker. Maxim Gorky was completely self-taught. It is said he attended school for only two years. According to this, you seem not to have read many books – good for you! You don't suffer much from intellectual poisoning. *Behavior during the political movements: a clear attitude and firm stand in every political movement.* During the campaigns of the Three Antis and Five Antis, you performed 'Catch the Big Tiger Alive' in a joint show for the kindergartens. During the purge of counterrevolutionaries, you reported a suspect to the police because you saw him wearing a pair of dark glasses like a spy. During the antirightist campaign, you exposed your music teacher because she had taught her students a performance called 'Butterfly Lovers.' At the criticism meeting, you bravely denounced that evil teacher, even pulling her hair in your excitement. During the Great Leap Forward, your group yielded the highest output of steel. During the economic hard times of the 1960s, you defended the honor of the country to a foreign reporter: 'We eat meat every day. There's no such thing as starvation in China, not even for a rat. Look, that's one over there, isn't it? Right under the desk.' It was impossible for the foreigner to quarrel. However, when the reporter started taking snapshots of big-bellied children drinking large bowls of thin soup, you rushed forward, grabbed his camera, and exposed his film. Afterward, you were praised by the departments of Foreign Affairs, Security, and Education. You should have been awarded the title 'Chairman Mao's good pupil,' but, considering that your model deed could not be promulgated abroad, they gave you only a certificate of merit, framed in glass. The moment Chairman Mao kindled the great proletarian Cultural Revolution, you threw yourself into the revolutionary currents, lashing out at imperialism, revisionism, and all reactionaries, as well as at the capitalist roaders. You followed Chairman Mao's strategies closely. You joined rebel organizations such as 'Headquarters of the Workers Rebelling to the End,' the 'Regiment of the Lord's Whip,' the 'Detachment for a New World,' teams for 'Exposing the Bottom Line,' the 'Hurricanes,' and 'Fighting with Words and Defending with Weapons,' the 'Writers' Association Defending Jiang Qing,' militant groups such as the 'Magic Club,' the 'Ambitious Men,' 'The Impassioned,' the propaganda team of the 'Great Union,' and so on. You have held the posts of number 5 servant and number 2 servant, head of the Defense Department, the Intelligence Department, the Propaganda Department, the Munitions Department, and the singing and dancing troupe. You have been on the revolutionary committee of the Four New Things Shop as its senator, chair, and representative of the Workers' Propaganda Team. All these glorious deeds have won my high esteem. Comrade Xie Li, you are a person red to the core; whereas I (sigh) have been black from birth. If only I could be reborn. Little Liang, are you taking all this in?"

"Yes, I am." I was shivering the whole time, in a state one might describe as shivering without being cold. Best to compliment her with a line from the model opera: "This woman is indeed unusual!" Old Gui not only expressed his respect for her but shook her hand cordially on returning the form. "Nin – " Old Gui had changed *ni* [you] to the honorable term *nin* [you] to address her. "You [*nin*] have come here for – ?"

"Especially for you."

"For me?"

"Yes. Marx says, 'Only by emancipating all of humanity

can the proletariat ultimately emancipate itself.' You need help."

"That's right. I remain an unreformed intellectual."

"I am well informed about your past and present. Losing your wife at your age left you lonely and helpless. You need help, particularly political help. Judging from your history, you belong to the most vulnerable category in today's society."

"True, true."

"You don't even dare speak to those who come to check your water meter or collect your electricity bill."

"True, true."

"Because they are the proletariat; whereas you are the bourgeoisie."

"True, true."

"If a gang of children came to throw stones at your door, singing, 'Imperialist reactionaries are running away with their tails between their legs,' you would not chase them away."

"Right. I'd be afraid of getting hit by the stones."

"But I would."

"Yes. You are proletarian, brave – "

"That's why I came to talk with you. Let's open the window of our hearts and speak candidly. You and I have both passed the age of courting. Furthermore, the practice of murmuring love before the flowers and under the moon, which is nothing but bourgeois sentimentalism, has been swept into the ash can of history. What I really mean to say is that you and I should get married. Don't be nervous; just listen. Our marriage must obey the situation of revolution. Now you are single, living in a spacious, gardenlike villa. When your foreign friend comes to see you, he will definitely have questions about your personal life and ask after your family. Then it is hard for you to give an answer."

"Yes, that's right."

"If I am your spouse (not your lover), you should call me

'Mrs.' in front of foreigners, and I should sit right by your side." As she spoke, she sat close beside old Gui, and he was so scared that he put his hands on his knees, not daring to look at her even out of the corner of his eye. "He would find no excuse to ask about your former wife," she continued. "Our marriage will benefit you, the state, and the revolution. If I am your wife, I can defend your public as well as your domestic affairs. Any bastard who dares to bully my old man will learn that my old man may be timid, but I am not. With me standing right before them, who dares to fart? I'll stick a carrot up his ass right on the spot. I'm famous all over town."

Old Gui shuddered in spite of himself.

"Think it over for ten minutes or so. Don't think I want to gild myself in your glory. What glory do you have to gild me with? Nothing but black dust. I'm willing to do this purely out of self-sacrifice. Gui Renzhong, a chance like this will never come again. One minute's wrong choice yields lifelong regret." Thus saying, she put her hand on old Gui's shoulder, who turned his frightened eyes to me. Being exceptionally smart, Xie Li said, "Chairman Mao teaches us that one must think independently."

Old Gui's eyes withdrew from me timidly. "Let me think – think – it over."

"Only four minutes left."

"I am much – much older – than you."

"I know. Let me ask you this: What is the principal requirement for revolutionary marriage? Answer me."

"Of course, it's – revolutionary – ideals."

"Don't you have revolutionary ideals? Don't you want to wipe out all imperialists, revisionists, and reactionaries? Don't you – ?"

"Yes, of course I want – "

"That's all you need, my dear revolutionary companion."

Giving old Gui's head a pat, Xie Li stood up and went

outside. Opening the gate, she shouted, "Comrades in arms, unload."

Neither old Gui nor I had noticed the two and one-half-ton truck parked outside. At Xie Li's command, three husky men jumped down from the truck. One carried quilts and pillows, the other two followed empty-handed, although one of them seemed to have a large roll of paper in one of his pockets. In high spirits, Xie Li led them into the sitting room, handily flipping on the crystal chandelier and all the side lights. I suddenly realized it was already dark and that Yunqian must be waiting for me anxiously.

"Look how wonderful your new wife is. She's brought her own bedding with her. This king-size sheet is brand-new. So are the silk comforter and nylon mosquito net. These pillow cases are embroidered, not with flowers but with quotations. Look at this one: 'Never forget class struggle.' And this one: 'Be vigilant against revisionism.' If you think you don't have to keep politics in command while you're sleeping, you're wrong. The noose of class struggle must be tightened at all times. Take them to the upstairs bedroom." Xie Li waved her hand decisively.

"They — ," old Gui said anxiously, "they won't let me sleep on the bed. They told me to sleep on the floor so I wouldn't dirty the hotel comforter."

"But things are always changing. Now I'm here. How dare they forbid us to use the bed? The bed is for sleeping, isn't it? Today it's on the bed of the bourgeoisie that the proletarian will sleep. This is called 'The joy of reversing heaven and earth.' I can sleep in the bed, and so can my husband." The man carrying the bedroll made a racket with his hobnailed shoes as he went up the stairs.

"Now for the formalities."

"Formalities?" Gui looked like a monkey trussed up by a hunter. "Now? Here?"

One man took out a stack of marriage certificates

stamped with the seal of the district revolutionary committee, and the other took out an ink pad. "Write this." Xie Li started dictating: "His name is Gui Renzhong."

"*Gui* as in *rich?*"

"No. *Gui* as in *chrysanthemum.*"

The man tore up the first certificate and wrote Gui Renzhong's name on a new one. "Bride's name?"

"You son of a bitch, how dare you forget my name?" Xie Li slapped the back of his head.

With a wry expression, the man wrote down Xie Li's name. "Now place your seals here and here."

Xie Li took a huge seal from her pocket and the man helped her stamp it on the certificate. Confused, old Gui said, "All my possessions were taken away at the beginning of the Cultural Revolution."

Xie Li said quite generously, "No matter, a fingerprint will do." The man seized old Gui's forefinger and pressed it on the inkpad. Just like Yang Bailao being forced to sell his daughter while he was drunk, old Gui appeared miserable and lost, his eyeballs quivering in their sockets. He was forced to press a small, blurred fingerprint on the certificate. Xie Li gave him a noisy kiss on the tip of his nose.

"For a revolutionary wedding, everything must be simplified. Let's break out the beer, mao-tai, and brandy from the cabinet, and the stewed pork, roast chicken, and ham from the icebox and celebrate!" She had a marvelous memory, hardly forgetting anything she had inspected.

Old Gui stood up and waved her off. "That won't do. My foreign guest is coming in three days."

"I know," Xie Li said, "for a two-hour visit. One bottle of wine will be enough."

The three men acted at once, taking out a case of beer, three bottles of mao-tai, two bottles of brandy, two roast chickens, two plates of ham, and three plates of stewed pork. When they started unscrewing the bottles, I patted old Gui's shoulder and said in a low voice, "I have to go now."

"You — you're leaving?" Old Gui stared at me in horror. He was afraid of being left alone. What would he do if I left? I stood up to leave.

"Young fellow," Xie Li said, "Why not drink a glass of wedding wine?"

"No, thanks." I walked outside. Old Gui followed me and picked up the shoe box he had put in the vegetable garden. With a look of fright, confusion, and loss, the kind of look one might wear after a catastrophic earthquake, he asked in a low voice, "They must be actors and actresses from a show company. They're merely playing games with me, aren't they?"

I laughed quietly and patted his shoulder. A show company? Actors and actresses? Playing games? But the fact was they did not come from a show company. They were not actors and actresses. They accurately represented certain groups of people on the rampage in China. They were not playing games. If they had merely been actors and actresses from a show company, things would not have been so terrible. But I avoided Gui's question. Putting on my large face mask, I went into the vastness of dusk. I heard one of the men old Gui took to be actors singing (doubtless with his wine glass raised on high): "I drink a bowl of wine and bid Mother good-bye...."

Holding the shoe box containing Jane's ashes, old Gui stood at the gate. His shadow blurred gradually, merging into the darkness of the night.

I gaze at her window. In the past it was pasted over with black paper; now a cloth curtain with tiny blue flowers hangs there.

11

Longbu of the Kazhima family was a rich caravan man. He had been to Dali in the south, Lhasa in the west, the ferry in the east, and Tibet in the north. He fell in love with Sunamei, for little Sunamei was far more bewitching than all the women he had been with before. Not only her tender cheeks and her eyes cool like stars in the sky but her entire disposition – whether revealed through a frown or a smile, a lifting hand, or a kicking toe – every part of her body, and every one of her movements stirred his heart. The pouty little mouth must be the fountainhead of honey. Longbu alone discovered Sunamei as a red jewel encased in a layer of green moss. Turned out of the moss, she would be red like a drop of fresh blood. Only Longbu had detected Sunamei, a wondrous flower hidden in budding clothes, which a ray of sunshine would make bloom like a flaming sun.

That night Longbu, carrying a heavy leather sack, walked up to the gate of Sunamei's family. It was tightly bolted. He attempted to find footholds for climbing on the earthen wall, but it was solid and smooth. He picked up a sharp flint and started chiseling. Hearing the noise, the big black dog, dragging a long chain inside the yard, ran about barking. Longbu took a handful of pork from the sack and threw it over the wall. The dog shut up. Longbu went on digging. Soon there was a shallow indentation the size of his big toe. He tied one end of a rope to the sack and the other to his waist. He leaped up and hung from the top of the wall by his hands. He saw the black dog gnawing on the piece of skinned pork. Longbu hauled the sack to the wall by the rope and then let it down into the yard. He followed, but now that he was inside the yard he didn't know the way to Sunamei's *huagu*. He couldn't go ask the *yimei,* nor did he dare knock on the door of just any *huagu.* Then he saw a figure emerge from the shadow of a column: it was an older woman. Obviously, she had watched Longbu jump in. He walked over to her, carrying two bottles of fruit wine and six lumps of tea. He was overjoyed to see that she was none other than Sunamei's mother, Cai'er. He gave her the presents and said in a low, reverent voice, "I am Longbu of the Kazhima family. These little things are inadequate to express my respect, but please accept them for the sake of Sunamei."

"It's you, Longbu. Sunamei has never been touched by a man. Please be careful."

"I will, Cai'er. Thank you for telling me."

"A man like you won't really love Sunamei as she is now."

"Cai'er, I love the present Sunamei as well as the future Sunamei."

"Go to her, then. The first door by the staircase leads to her *huagu.* Has she left the door unlocked for you?"

"I believe she has." As Cai'er retreated to the *yimei* with the presents, Longbu went upstairs with his sack. Sunamei had been waiting for him anxiously for a long time. More than once she thought maybe Longbu had merely toyed with her and forgotten his promise by that evening. If he remembered a former path, a former family, a former door, and a former girlfriend, he might not come to her anymore. Just then, she heard footsteps on the stairs. She hastily put on the skirt she had just taken off and sat with her legs dangling over the side of the bed. Her *huagu* was so quiet she could hear her heart beating. Was it Longbu, or Amiji Zhima's *axiao?* Or Amiji Ama's *axiao?* But Ama's *axiao* had already arrived, and Zhima's had gone out on business. It must be Longbu. It must be he. Covering her jumping heart with her hands, she walked to the tenth step, a thinner board. Its squeak under her tread stopped her. Then it dawned on her: how could he know where my *huagu* is? What if he steals into a wrong door? Shall I go out to meet him? No, that would cheapen me. Sunamei did not dare move. Then she heard someone's voice right outside her door. It was Zhima. "Is that you, Longbu? Are you looking for me?" Sunamei's heart almost stopped. Longbu did not answer. "Come in. This is my door."

Longbu said, "This little object cannot express all my respect for you, but please keep it for Sunamei's sake." Sunamei's heart fell back in place from her throat. She crawled to the door and softly unbolted it.

Amiji Zhima was giggling. "I know. I saw everything at the swings. Your eyes, kindled by Sunamei, did not burn blindly, did they? Later, you chased after her on your horse. See, I saw everything. Longbu, you really have a good eye. But tonight you must be careful. Sunamei might think it great fun, knowing nothing about the fierce love of a man. She could jump up and bite off your nose."

"She – really has no – am I her first *axiao?*"

"Yes. All right, I'll accept this bottle of wine." Zhima went into her own *huagu*. Longbu stood outside Sunamei's door, for a long while, without trying to push it open. He was amusing himself by imagining how he could possibly avoid Sunamei's teeth. He touched his nose absentmindedly. The door opened with a slight touch. He saw Sunamei shrink back into a corner of her bed, like a little girl before the age of wearing a skirt. Taking a box of matches from his breast pocket, he struck one and lit the oil lamp on her dresser. Like a naughty child on awakening, the lamp light slowly stretched and lit up the whole room. Longbu poked the dying fire in the fireplace and rearranged its logs. Soon the little fire grew big. Big flames led small flames, flames linked with flames. He filled the small teapot with water and took out a lump of tea from his sack. He then broke off a piece and tossed it into the pot. Then he fetched dried beef, melon seeds, popcorn, and candies wrapped in colorful paper. He did all this while his eyes were glued to Sunamei. When the water was boiling, he curled his legs before the flames and smoked a cigarette. He passed one to Sunamei, but she shook her head with a smile. Only then did Longbu break the silence: "Sunamei, I'm not being a bad host, am I?"

Sunamei flushed with embarrassment. She had reversed their positions. She should be the host, not Longbu. Swiftly, she jumped off the bed and sat by the fireplace, serving wine and tea to Longbu. The white cat hopped into Longbu's lap, receiving him as a member of the family. The bowls, having stood idle in a corner for more than a year, finally found their usage. Longbu served wine and tea to Sunamei. She bravely drank one mouthful after another with him. Her cheeks burned. Setting the cat by the fire, Longbu gently stroked Sunamei's soft hands with his large ones, rough as horse-tooth stone. Worried, Sunamei lowered her head. She did not know what would happen next. Longbu looked as if he was not going to do anything. Then, he pulled her lightly over to his side, letting the drunken girl lean against his chest. He sniffed again, and again a maiden's fragrance came from Sunamei's neck. Without knowing it, Sunamei laid her face on Longbu's hairy chest. She did not know when and how he had unbuttoned his shirt, but she was not frightened by the strong heartbeat of a man. Actually, it felt natural to be so close to one, and she experienced none of the shock she had suffered when she saw Amiji Zhima and Geda sleeping nude on the night they went to worship the goddess. She thought to herself, "How did I pass the long narrow bridge I thought I could never cross? How did I get to sleep on the bed? How were my clothes stripped off? How did Longbu's sleek, bare arms seize me like a lamb?" She was not aware of all this, as if neither she nor Longbu had moved an inch. He did nothing that would make Sunamei feel embarrassed or wild. He called her name softly all the time, and every action of his was extremely gentle. There was nothing that would alienate her or shock her with the pleasure of another person. He kissed her gently, and she kissed him gently. She felt the strong smells of tobacco, wine, and hot sweat, pleasant and intoxicating. He kissed her more and more passionately, and she returned his kisses more and more passionately. Then it was no longer he kissing her or she kissing him. They were locked in one mutual kiss, hardly breathing. Every cell in Sunamei's body was relaxed, and every nerve that could hamper a maiden's joy was anesthetized. Her eyes lost their luster, and she felt a need for Longbu to hold her tighter and tighter. Longbu was already holding her tightly, but not tightly enough. Sunamei was pleading with her groans.

Longbu supported her legs with his arms, whispered into her ear, "Sunamei, my dear Sunamei, please bite the lump of muscle on my shoulder. Bite it!"

Obeying his words, Sunamei bit the protruding hard muscle on his left shoulder. At first she merely put it into her mouth, not understanding why she needed to bite it at all. Suddenly, Longbu grasped her waist with one hand and drew her to him. Sunamei's teeth bit so fiercely that Longbu gave a low groan. He knew his shoulder must be bleeding. Sunamei opened her sleepy eyes, let the lump of muscle slip from her mouth, and rubbed her lips over his neck. She held his broad back even tighter. Her tense legs became relaxed, so as not to be in Longbu's way. She submissively received him — no, not received him, but invited him.

Zhima seldom had a night all to herself. In fact, she didn't sleep the whole night. But contrary to her expectations, she did not hear Longbu shout for his nose, nor Sunamei scream and weep. She murmured to herself, "Longbu, Longbu, what a man you are!"

Before daybreak, Zhima heard Longbu say to Sunamei behind the partition wall, "Tonight I'll bring my bedroll here. Is that all right with you?"

Sunamei replied tenderly, "Fine."

12

I gaze at her window. In the past, it was pasted over with black paper; now a cloth curtain with tiny blue flowers hangs there.

May and June should have been the peak of the blooming period. I still remember: azaleas bloomed and withered; roses bloomed and withered; tulips bloomed and withered; cherry blossoms bloomed and withered. But now China has no flowers to bloom anymore — and thus nothing more to wither, either, of course. Everything looks fantastically bare. All month I have been worried about old Gui. This month was his honeymoon with that dragon woman. How had the two of them received Thomas Eliot? It must have been an improvised farce, impossible to perform. After all, the visit took only two hours, and two sixty-minute sessions are easy enough to get through. Old Gui must have suffered through that one-act drama like a senile actor who keeps forgetting his lines. Fortunately, that woman could create her role and her lines and avoid expanding her supporting role so as to become the main character. Old Gui had to serve as her interpreter. It was difficult, impossible, even, to understand things in China, particularly in the China of today. For example, in his own home old Gui was allowed only the floor to sleep on. No matter how much Xie Li invited him with curses, he dared not touch the bed — I understood him perfectly. But could foreigners possibly understand his behavior? Another example: Xie Li and her comrades in arms could pocket marriage certificates, printed and stamped by the local power bureaus, and legalize a marriage more easily than pairing a she-rabbit with a he-rabbit. The bride, Xie Li, taking advantage of her political superiority, had beaten the drum and gong with her tongue and had issued a mere two- or three-word command to nail old Gui and herself together in a marriage certificate, effective immediately. She had simply enthroned herself in his room with all her belongings. Why had her class origin become so important? How had her lack of education turned into political capital? Could a foreigner understand any of this? No, impossible. Therefore, we must compile a dictionary of Chinese fiction especially for foreigners; otherwise, the Chinese novel can never travel outside our national boundaries.

Yunqian absolutely forbade my seeing old Gui and advised me to kill my dangerous, childish curiosity. In fact, I cared only about old Gui's life. When human feelings in a society drop to the freezing point of indifference, that society is bound to collapse. What importance life holds for every individual. Isn't the fate of a state and nation embodied in the fate of its countless ordinary individuals?

Before I went to the farm to turn in my medical diagnosis for June, my legs carried me to old Gui's gate in spite of myself. No need to press the button, because the huge iron gate was wide open. From outside I had already heard signs of a brawl in the living room. Disturbed, I entered and climbed the stone steps leading to the scene. At first sight, I saw the servant sitting on a couch. His earlier humble appearance had given way to an air of complacency and solemnity, as, wearing an old Mao suit, he watched with a scoffing smile while Xie Li jumped and screamed. She then stood defiantly with her hands on her hips. Her three comrades in arms stood behind her, hands likewise on hips.

She railed, "It isn't that easy! Move? I am the wife of Professor Gui Renzhong! The foreign guest has taken our pictures, which must have appeared in the American newspapers. The background of those pictures is this very house. Think of the international scandal if we were forced to move out!"

"Not a bit of it," drawled the servant. "The foreigners will never know about it."

"I'll ask my husband to write to Mr. Thomas Eliot."

"Go right ahead. But let me warn you that your letter will be delivered directly into my hands. Then you will be found guilty of the crime of treason and imprisoned, and I'll let you stay there to wear out the bottom of the jail." His voice showed no malice.

"No, wait a minute. I can't write to Thomas Eliot; I don't even have his address. As soon as he stepped out the gate, I handed in his identity card. It was you who took it." Now I saw old Gui slink out from behind the grand piano with his shoe box containing Jane's ashes. "You good-for-nothing, shut up and stand aside!" Xie Li shouted at old Gui.

The servant spoke at a slow, measured pace: "You must move out today. The hotel is sending men over for the furniture, utensils, and bedding. Men from the model opera troupe are coming to get their grand piano. The Friendship Store will reclaim their carpet, scrolls, and paintings."

"Ugh." Xie Li wrinkled her nose. "Very well, move us. Have everything moved out. This old dame can sleep on the floor!"

"I'm afraid even you can't even do that. This house belongs to a VIP. Do you know the one I mean? She came to inspect the work and living conditions in our city. Everything in the house has to be rearranged by tomorrow — it all has to be done up in green tones. Between you and her, which old dame is tougher?"

Xie Li lost her voice. Rolling her eyes, she suddenly got an idea: "All right, we'll move. But you must give us an apartment suitable for a married couple."

The servant took a letter out of his pocket and passed it

to old Gui. "Gui Renzhong, here's a notice for you from the farm. Read it out loud."

Before he fished the letter out of its envelope, old Gui's hands were shaking so hopelessly that the letter and envelope rustled like falling leaves. "Gui Renzhong: On reading this notice, report with your dependents immediately to your team for reeducation." Silence hung over the room, with no sound but that of the servant's scratching of a match, lighting a cigarette, and puffing smoke rings. The paper in old Gui's hands was still shaking.

"Dependents!" Suddenly Xie Li uttered a cry, as if she had just come to life. "You can't throw a family dependent into the street. Gui Renzhong is a Stinking Ninth, a bourgeois reactionary; but I am third-generation, urban working-class, one-hundred-percent proletarian revolutionary. You had better make sure the way you're treating me is politically correct!"

"You may be counted as Gui Renzhong's dependent."

"What do you mean, *counted as?* I have a marriage certificate, legal and binding. Why do you say *counted as?*"

"The housing problem of Gui's dependents should be solved by the leadership of Gui's unit. Gui Renzhong belongs to the East Wind Farm. They will take charge of you. The farm has plenty of land to put up a thatched shed, and no shortage of work or tools."

"But I am a registered city resident and have the right to urban supplies," shouted Xie Li at the top of her voice.

"That depends on whether you want Gui Renzhong or want city residence and urban supplies."

Xie Li threw herself onto the sofa in a fit of anger. Turning her head to old Gui, she said, "Speak up, you! What do we do?"

"You should – don't follow me to suffer on the farm. In fact, we're not really married."

"What? You dirty dog! You want to abandon me?"

"Facts speak louder than words. In the past month you've

– snored every night while I lay wide awake on the floor waiting for dawn. I couldn't sleep – "

"Ha! You really are a virgin of fifteen. Give it to me!"

"What?"

"The marriage certificate." Old Gui took out the wrinkled certificate and handed it to her. She said, "I'll take care of it. Since you're not qualified to be a proper husband, I'll deprive you of your conjugal rights. I'm not divorcing you because I know you have lots of school chums in America who might want to visit you again, and you are incompetent to deal with them." She turned to the servant. "Say, my old man has a lot of classmates in America. Many of them, more important than Eliot, are big shots in politics, the military, Congress, and news agencies. One after another, they're going to ask to see my old man. Have you thought of that?"

"Of course we have," the servant said smugly. "Any foreigner coming to our country must apply for a visa first. If we delay his visa one day, we'll gain enough time to evacuate a house, borrow decent furniture and silverware, get proper food from special shops, transfer Gui Renzhong back from the farm, and even let you two remarry. One day is plenty of time. You only used a quarter of an hour to marry him, didn't you?"

"You're not afraid of the inconveniences?"

"No, of course not. We have lots of trucks and plenty of time. No need to worry about us."

At the mention of trucks, three of them pulled up to the entrance. After putting down the loading ramps, strong porters rushed into the sitting room like a flock of crows. Feeling threatened, Xie Li quickly ordered her three comrades in arms, "Hurry! Pack my stuff and move it out. Don't let them haul my things away as public property." Her three men dashed upstairs like gangsters, and soon the house was filled with dust and the rumbling of furniture. People inside fought brutally, knocking into each other, punching and kicking each other, cursing each other's mother and father. Xie Li led her three comrades in arms, arguing over her so-called private property. Words were not strong enough, and the three men fought savagely until their blood ran. A rare opportunity. If you can grab something by force or deceit, go ahead. The controversy over the genuine owner of an embroidered curtain got the two warring parties into a bloody fight. In the end, a beautiful art treasure was torn to shreds. When the chaos died down, the house had been stripped to its bare walls. In the sudden stillness, only three people were left in the vacant sitting room: old Gui, carrying Jane's ashes in a shoe box; the servant, holding a ring of keys, ready to lock the house after our departure; and me, trembling in fear. "May I leave now?" old Gui asked his former servant with respect.

"Yes, you may."

"I'm not taking even a needle of public property with me."

"All right. Please go." The former servant shook his keys impatiently.

"Thank you very much for all this. Good-bye."

"Don't mention it. We're all doing things according to revolutionary principles."

Old Gui walked over to me. "Little Liang, you were sent by the leaders of the farm to get me, weren't you?"

"No. I was on my way to the Farm to give my monthly medical report, and merely dropped in to see you."

"Oh. Good – we're going the same way then."

"Yes."

Old Gui and I walked silently out of the sitting room. His eyes surveyed the house where he had lived for a whole month – if it could be called living. The vegetables transplanted to the courtyard, unable to adapt to the desolate wasteland, were already withering. I heard the noise of shutting windows and locking doors behind us. On the bus, old Gui's face gradually lit up. He said, "Little Liang, I still think the farm is a much better place for me. I feel at home there; those brown cows seem to be fond of me and I feel comfortable with them, without any ideological burdens. A bourgeois intellectual like me should suffer hardships; otherwise I feel uneasy, remorseful, and ashamed. Don't you agree?"

I didn't answer. At that moment, a powerful impulse was impelling me to speak from the bottom of my heart, out of concern for him, with words more penetrating than those I had spoken last time. But he beat me to it. "Thomas didn't ask me any tough questions, as if he knew everything already. He only looked me in the eyes from beginning to end. That day I behaved so well that the leadership of the Foreign Ministry praised me, saying I looked very cheerful and displayed the normal state of mind of a prominent intellectual. They particularly mentioned the part of my talk concerning my contempt for Western material comforts, as being concrete and sounding real and sincere. And when Thomas asked about the attacks on intellectuals during the Cultural Revolution, I replied, 'It's true, but it's a necessity, just as a mother spanks her own children. It doesn't matter if the spanking is a little harsh, for the mother's intentions are good.' He said, 'Perhaps the mother you're talking about is a stepmother.' I refuted him with a stern face: 'No, no! She's our real mother.' The leadership particularly approved of these words. They said that, because I love the party and the motherland, I shall be allowed to meet my other schoolmates from abroad." A feeling of satisfaction carried him away as he said this, licking his upper lip.

Fortunately, I had suppressed my impulse to reveal the truth.

I gaze at her window. In the past, it was pasted over with black paper; now a cloth curtain with tiny blue flowers hangs there.

When we got off the bus and turned down the road leading to the farm, we met an execution vehicle – actually a
military truck – flanked by armed soldiers. Behind the
driver's cab stood a criminal tied crisscross with ropes. A
placard stuck erect in the ropes behind his back rose above
his head.

"Someone is going to be executed?!" Old Gui pulled me
over to the side of the road.

"It looks like a woman."

"Yes, it is. It's Liu Tiemei from the clinic, isn't it?"

"Liu Tiemei? How can that be?" No matter how hard I
tried, I could not link the image of Liu Tiemei to the con-
cept of a criminal about to be executed. But soon I recognized her, too.

The execution truck was moving slowly. In the distance,
the public meeting of the farm collective had not yet been
dismissed. The sound of shouted slogans rose and fell. The
truck was drawing nearer and nearer. Liu Tiemei was wearing a new set of clothes, something I had never seen her
do before. Although it was a hot day, she had slipped on a
flimsy red wool sweater over her cotton-print blouse and
had draped a white gauze scarf over her shoulders. Her hair
was combed and shone brightly; a small bunch of nameless
wildflowers was pinned to her hair above the temple. She
appeared carefree; a naive smile hung from the corners of her
mouth. As she looked down at me and Gui, her expression
betrayed a condescending pity for us. On the death sign
were the words *Counterrevolutionary Murderer Liu Mei*. Perhaps the judicial authorities had thought Tiemei [iron plum
blossom], her first name adopted from one of the model
operas, was definitely a model name for revolutionaries and
should not be profaned by a criminal. So they had restored
her original one-character given name and circled both it
and her surname with vermilion. The Four Olds [old ideas,
old culture, old customs, old habits] had been abolished at

the beginning of the Cultural Revolution. Who would expect an old custom like a death placard with the name of the victim circled in vermilion to be continued without question? Liu Mei had even been permitted, according to her wish, to put on a set of new clothes, wear a bunch of wildflowers, and have a feast – all this according to ancient custom that may well be prehistoric.

Old Gui was terribly frightened, as if he, not Liu Tiemei, were to be executed. Shivering, he kept murmuring to himself, "How could she have murdered someone? How could she have murdered someone?"

"Right. Why did she murder someone?" I asked myself. It was impossible to associate her present image with her former life.

"Who did she murder?" old Gui asked me.

"Good question. Who did she murder? Most likely, she murdered Qin Guangming."

"Her husband? How could she murder her own husband? Impossible."

"Quite simply out of jealousy. She said long ago that sooner or later she would turn Qin Guangming [bright light] into Qin darkness. Now he has certainly turned to darkness."

"Can that be true? "

Old Gui gaped for a long time. Not until we came to the farm did we learn that Liu Tiemei's victim had not been Qin Guangming – the eternal case of murdering one's spouse – but Yu Shouchen's wife, Jin Xiangdong. Why had she killed Jin Xiangdong? (Yu Shouchen's wife was not a young woman but had a fashionable name. Originally, she did not even have a first name and had been legally registered as Jin's. At the beginning of the Cultural Revolution, Yu Shouchen had written a formal petition to change her name to Xiangdong [facing the east], to imply that her heart turned toward Mao Zedong.) Jin Xiangdong was born ugly, and the older she grew the uglier she became. Why had Liu

Tiemei, a young woman, killed such an ugly old hag? Was it possible that she and Qin Guangming were caught having an affair? A childlike curiosity drove me to search for the truth.

But a complicated love-murder case demanded more than a few words of clarification, and I dared not stay long on the farm, for it was a hotbed of trouble. Fortunately, I met Song Lin, a freshman at the College of Theater and Drama, who perceived my curiosity at a glance and took me to the Propaganda Office. Closing the door behind us, he whispered, "You are dying to learn the details of the case, aren't you?" I nodded. "They have been working on this case for a whole month now. Today, after the final judgment, she was sent to the farm for a public trial. Finally, they identified her officially, and she was ready for execution. I work in the Propaganda Office. The pavilion by the water is the first to receive the reflected moonbeams. Taking advantage of my job, I not only read through her file but also secretly wrote a play based on my readings. I'm sure my play is a timeless masterpiece, but, if anyone reads it, it will be criticized like poison weeds. Worse still, my head may have to be patched up."

"Why? Your play is based on real persons and real events, isn't it?"

"You stupid fool! After years of the great Cultural Revolution, how can you still behave like a guest from America? As if anyone were allowed to write about real people and real events! The more realistic it is, the more your writing will be vilified. Haven't you read Yao Wenyuan's important article 'On Realism'?"

"Too many articles for us to read, published simultaneously by our two newspapers and one journal [*People's Daily, Liberation Army Daily,* and *Red Flag*]. And even if I were to read them, I can't keep anything in my head."

"We're not allowed to write about real people and real events, not even about the real deeds of the members on the party central committee of the Cultural Revolution, who are correct at all times. Anything we write that breaks the rule cannot be let loose on the public. Those are the principles you must learn by heart. It's a matter of life or death."

"Then why did you write the play?"

"My hands were itching."

"So, it's a biological problem."

"That's right. Isn't your curiosity also a biological problem?"

"Yes. All right, your hands were itching, so you wrote it; my mind is itching, so I want to read it."

"You may take the script with you as long as you read it while squatting in the hospital latrine."

"Thank you so much."

"Wait. First you must write me out a receipt."

"What kind of receipt?"

"Write the following: 'I am keeping the script of the play *Flames of Passion* of my own accord. Every word Song Lin wrote fully expresses my own imagination and thoughts.' Liang Rui, month, day, year."

"Why should I write such a thing? I don't even know the plot yet."

"Well, to be mean is to be generous. The human heart is hidden beneath the skin. Who knows whether or not you will report me for public criticism after you've read it? If I have your receipt in my hand, I won't worry. Good for both of us. As the saying goes, two locusts are tied to one string — you cannot fly away, and I cannot hop away. If you want to read it, write the receipt. If not, you may regret it your whole life."

"I'll write it. You're awfully clever."

"If I wasn't, how could I be invincible?"

Song Lin put a slip of paper in front of me and passed me an uncapped fountain pen. I wrote down everything he said. Then with one hand I turned it over to him, while with the other I took the script, which I stuffed into my bag as Song

Lin opened the door for me. "My duties keep me from seeing you off."

"See you later." I left.

I gaze at her window. In the past, it was pasted over with black paper; now a cloth curtain with tiny blue flowers hangs there.

Yunqian was angry with me for bringing home the script because she hated it when I was curious about anything. It wasn't worth signing a contract with the Devil in order to satisfy one's curiosity. But once I started reading her the script, her anger vanished.

Here is the original script, just as Song Lin wrote it:

FLAMES OF PASSION

ACT I

Time: Month X, day X, year X. Night.
Place: A strange clinic on a strange farm in a strange country.
Characters (in order of appearance): DOCTOR L, DOCTOR Y, and the SERPENT from the Garden of Eden.

As the curtain rises, DOCTOR L *and* DOCTOR Y *are sitting upright on the stage, reading attentively in murmuring voices. The* SERPENT *slithers in through the window.*

SERPENT *(female voice):* This isn't the Garden of Eden. And where are the naked Adam and Eve? Why have I come here? Perhaps there's some snake medicine in the cabinet. Yes, there it is: a martyr from my serpentine family, preserved in a glass bottle. Even without life and power she looks real, raising her head, lashing her forked tongue, and dexterously twisting her body. She is trying to warn people:

"I am a venomous snake. Be careful, everyone." Thank heavens, I am no ordinary snake. In fact, my venom is made from all kinds of seductive potions to catalyze people's sexual desire, jealousy, hatred, courage, and pride. They are classified as number 1, number 2, number 3, number 4, and number 5, respectively. If I prescribe the right seductive thing for the right person at the right moment, I will conduct all those tender, glorious, and heroic dramas in the arena of human life. Look at this respectable pair: the two of them seem pure and honest. Actually, they both lost all human feeling long ago. Every cell in their bodies has abandoned its original function and turned into a stronghold in which to seal the self and protect it from outsiders. However, I can turn them into Romeo and Juliet, Othello and Desdemona, Hamlet and Ophelia, Pan Jinlian and Ximen Qing, even Shi Xiu and Pan Qiaoyun, although letting them retain their own appearances. Now please watch closely how these two beings talk.

The DOCTOR *acts as if she were reading scripture. She reads and converses with her neighbor at the same time. Of course, the actress is highly skilled and can use a husky voice and perked-up ears to deliver and catch the necessary information without interrupting her reading of Chairman Mao's works. No doubt she should have a female voice because she is a woman. But because of years of shouting at her patients — including at her husband, who to some extent is also her patient — her voice has become hoarse but dignified, barely feminine. This lack of femininity is also caused by the fact that as a female she has had little chance to flatter her boss and has never had a lover. She is too chaste for anyone to find an unclean spot. She vigilantly stands guard over other female bodies as well. Any potential flirting eye will be destroyed by her hateful stare.*

L: Doctor Y...blah, blah, blah (*"blah, blah, blah" indicates their recitations of Mao's works*) Comrade Qin Guangming...blah, blah, blah...

SERPENT: She is talking about her own husband.

L: Comrade Qin Guangming has never set high standards for himself...blah, blah, blah...At every opportunity, he allows himself to be eroded by bourgeois thought...blah, blah, blah.... When I caught him...blah, blah, blah... he not only refused to make revolution in the depth of his soul but also refused others' help. He defies the slogan *leniency to those who confess* and resists to the end. Treating patients at the clinic from dawn to dusk in the service of the revolution, we can only study Chairman Mao's works profoundly at night...blah, blah, blah. This is a great disservice to him. My heart keeps jumping to my mouth as I sit here reading. I know I must undergo self-criticism. As one must read Mao's works with all one's heart and soul, my wandering thoughts reveal my disloyalty to our Red Sun...blah, blah, blah. But I fear Qin Guangming will be seduced by a bad woman...blah, blah, blah....

Y: Don't worry...blah, blah, blah.... We are living in hard times...blah, blah, blah...and in a dismal place...blah, blah, blah.... I bet he dares not even imagine that sort of thing...blah, blah, blah....

L: I don't know...blah, blah, blah. Bourgeois thoughts are pervasive. I am a decent, politically staunch comrade in arms and a life companion for him. Yet he shows no interest in me at all...blah, blah, blah....

Y: How can that be? A person always climbs high; water always runs downhill...blah, blah, blah.... He should have enjoyed the sweetness of putting politics in command of the relationship between husband and wife...blah, blah, blah....

L: He is no longer a child. Strong liquor tastes better than mother's milk...blah, blah, blah....

Y: Why should *you* have to suffer?...blah, blah, blah ...These strong emotions will affect your study and your work. Why don't you change places with him...blah,

blah, blah.... Let him be you and you be him...blah, blah, blah....

L: Blah, blah, blah...What do you mean by that?...blah, blah, blah....

Y: Blah, blah, blah...I mean...blah, blah, blah...let him worry about you and snoop on you and lose sleep over you...blah, blah, blah.... That way, you can transform passive defense into offensive action, can't you?...blah, blah, blah....

L: Which wouldn't be such a good thing for me. He doesn't give a damn about me...blah, blah, blah.... Even if I jumped into a well and rotted there for three days and nights, he wouldn't come looking for me...blah, blah, blah....

SERPENT: See, now she needs a bit of seductive potion number 1.

Y: I don't mean you should jump into a well...blah, blah, blah....

L: Not jump into a well...blah, blah, blah...hang myself from a beam, then?...blah, blah, blah....

Y: Why do you always have to think of death?...blah, blah, blah....

L: Should I think of living, then? As long as I am alive, I am a mote in his eye...blah, blah, blah.... The conflict between the bourgeoisie and the proletariat is irreconcilable. It is a struggle to the death.

SERPENT *(aside):* There sure is no chance of changing *her* without drugs!

SERPENT *creeps along the wall toward* L. *She pops her head out from under the desk and stretches her fangs into the cup close to L's hand (in that strange country no state employee can tear his or her hand away from a teacup). After injecting one drop of seductive potion number 1, the serpent retreats under the desk.*

Y: Blah, blah, blah.... You must live, live better than he does!

L: Blah, blah, blah.... Don't I live better than he does now? Every year I am chosen a paragon for the study of the theory and practice of Mao Zedong thought...blah, blah, blah...I have reported more than a dozen cases involving self-inflicted wounds and fake diseases by people attempting to escape reform through labor...blah, blah, blah...and have I ever missed my chance to speak at meetings where the paragons talk of their heroic experiences?...blah, blah, blah.... He's living better than I?...blah, blah, blah.... Is that what you think?...blah, blah, blah.... Then your mind has gone moldy!

Y *(hurriedly)*: No. I meant you should live even better. Ten or a hundred times better than he does...blah, blah, blah.

SERPENT *(aside)*: Why isn't she drinking yet? Further delay will really foul things up.

L *takes her cup and, sipping a little, scrutinizes it immediately.*

L *(to herself, in amazement)*: Why so sweet? I put in only a pinch of cheap tea dust. How can anything be so tasty at twenty fen an ounce? Anything sweet and tasty is suspicious. Only a bourgeois loves sweet and tasty things.

L *gulps down several mouthfuls at one go.*

L *(completely forgets her reading of Mao's works; her voice grows tender)*: Tell me again, Doctor Y: how can I live better than he does?

Y *(puzzled by the pitch of her voice and its musical tones, which seem strange because he hasn't heard them for years, he retreats tactfully)*: What I meant is, you should live like a stainless-steel screw, screwed into the machine of the proletarian dictatorship so that the great machine can run properly...blah, blah, blah....

L (*disappointed*): Really? No, you must have meant something else. Did you say I should live more *happily* than he does?

DOCTOR L *makes eyes at* DOCTOR Y. DOCTOR Y *is flabbergasted, as if he had caught a snake while groping for an eel.*

L: That I should be more *relaxed* than he is?

DOCTOR L *casts one glance after another. Leaving his seat,* DOCTOR Y *steps up to* DOCTOR L, *trying to feel her pulse. Seizing her chance,* DOCTOR L *grabs his hand and pulls it to her breast. Astonished,* DOCTOR Y *struggles free and returns to his seat, gasping.*

SERPENT: Doctor Y's sexual desire is not strong enough to overcome his suspicion and anxiety. I'd better give *him* some drugs, too.

SERPENT *pops her head out from under* DOCTOR Y'*s desk and injects a drop of seductive potion number 1 into his cup through her fangs. Just then, in order to calm himself,* DOCTOR Y *gulps down several mouthfuls. He immediately puts on his spectacles to scrutinize the cup.*

L (*sweet as honey*): Y – please tell me, tell me, tell me. What a naughty fellow you are. If you had the nerve to say it once, don't take it back now. You mean I should live more freely than he, more romantically, more sensuously, more passionately, and more self-fulfillingly than he, don't you? Hmmmmm?

Y (*the drug is beginning to take effect*): Yes. Can you? Do you dare?

L (*slants her eyes flirtatiously*): Who's going to stop me?

DOCTOR L *extends her arms, much like Desdemona when Othello finishes his account of his heroic deeds at the sea.*

Y (*the drug has not had its full effect on him*): Please don't let the others see us like this. If they do, at best we would be denounced at large criticism meetings and then sent to the prison rock pile.

L: Nobody will see us, for nobody can imagine you and I would…blah, blah, blah…(*from now on, "blah, blah, blah" means something other than that they are reciting Mao's works*) any more than he can imagine the two pillars outside our clinic door coming together of their own accord.

Y (*his dry, sallow face gradually suffused with the color of pork liver*): What you say is quite true.

Once more DOCTOR Y *goes to* DOCTOR L. *But this time he behaves like that dandy Ximen, who approaches Golden Lotus when Old Woman Wang excuses herself and locks them in.*

DOCTOR L *unbuttons her blouse. Her modern outfit saves her a lot of time over Golden Lotus. Besides, she does not wear a beautiful and seductive red undergarment like that of Golden Lotus. As soon as her blouse is opened, a pair of shriveled, baggy breasts flop out.*

SERPENT (*aside*): They do not need to steal the forbidden fruit. That has gone rotten a long time ago. Neither do they need to cover themselves with red flowers and green leaves. The narrow hospital bed for examining patients will do. Adopting a most economical method, they fold themselves up, one on top of the other, like a double-decker. Of course, there's nothing new between her and herself or between him and himself. But between she and he or he and she, everything is brand-new. Therefore, their love is most passionate.

Blackout.

SERPENT: Blackout! Apparently even the electrical generator lacks courage and needs a drop of seductive potion number 4. But if I go to the power plant, the best episode will be over before I get back. It's better to stay and listen to the sensuous music in the darkness.

Curtain falls.

ACT 2

Time: Twenty days later. Night.
Place: DOCTOR L's home.
Characters *(in order of appearance):* SERPENT from the Garden of Eden, DOCTOR L, J, Q, DOCTOR Y, etc.

As the curtain rises, SERPENT *is alone onstage, coiled in the middle of a square table in the center of the stage, thrusting its head high, swaying complacently.*

SERPENT *(aside):* The break in the play is to show the passage of time, as well as to omit repetitions that are not really worth seeing. It's better to hide such vulgarity between the acts. The love between L and Y can be called missed love, stolen love, and forgotten love; it also can be denounced as adultery, illicit intercourse, secret communication, ignoble combination, rape seduction, etc. From the very first day, it became an endless circle. Although their sexual contacts repeat themselves only mechanically, the lovers do not tire of them. To L and Y, their every lovemaking, like the mesh between two newly lubricated old gears, always seems fresh and new. But for our audience it is a different matter: a word repeated three times will bore even a dog to death. No matter how brilliant the director, he dare not allow a three-minute kiss in the movie. The explicit love scenes can recall only the monotonous motions of the crankshaft in a dull cylinder. Therefore, techniques such as fade-in, fade-out, or symbolism are often used. They are supposed to leave the audience's imagination some room to maneuver: the more obscure, the more suggestive. Is it not true that our audience can well imagine what L and Y are doing now in private, and what they will do next? The divine dragon reveals only its head, not its tail.

Because of the imaginative power of the director, the second act of the play is set in L's home, when L's husband has gone to the city to buy the month's supply of sanitary pads for women laborers. Again L suffers a sleepless night. She suspects that Q must have a mistress; the recent change in herself convinced her that no matter how austere the circumstances, human lust floods irresistibly. The cinders of L's jealousy immediately burst into flame. On top of that, Y, although close to hand, cannot experience joy with her in a comfortable double bed. Y's wife, J, seems suspicious. Even the most stupid wife on earth is sensitive to her husband's infidelity. Y cannot find an excuse to be absent from home for even one night. Now L is coming. Look: her brows are heavily knitted, and her steps are hesitating. She looks more a woman now than ever before.

SERPENT *turns and goes under the table.*

L *enters.*

L: I'm thirsty, thirsty, thirsty!

Shakes thermos, then teapot. All empty.

L: Q! Oh, he's gone to the city. Buying a ton of sanitary pads takes all day and — *night!* (*The actress should particularly stress the word* night.) He didn't even put the pot on to boil, forcing me to drink cold water.

SERPENT *(aside):* I know which cup she is going to use. I must give her a combination of seductive potion number 1 and seductive potion number 2 to add fuel to her fire.

SERPENT *spits two drops of seductive potion into a cup. As expected,* L *takes that cup. Filling it with cold water under a tap, she drinks it down at a single gulp.*

L: Delicious. Tastes like iced sweet-sour plum juice. How shall I pass the night? How shall I pass it? I'm asking *you,* L! How can I tolerate all this? What is Q doing? I can neither know nor see nor feel, nor guess which bitch he is stuck on. *(Maliciously)* I hope he gets stuck inside her and they can't be separated, until some children drive them into the street, throw stones at them, and parade them on carrying poles, making an exhibition of them in broad daylight. What is Y doing now? There, too, I can neither know nor see nor feel. But I can well guess that he is sleeping with that filthy old swine J. *(Hysterically)* Oh, my God! Why do I see them as clearly as if I were standing at the foot of their bed? You are torturing me. All of you are torturing me, you damned men and women! How I wish I could snatch away your quilts and scorch you with a red-hot iron! I'll tell J, tell her to her face: "Y is mine. Y loves *me* from the bottom of his heart. He loves *me.* He belongs to *me.* I need him most, just as he needs me most."

SERPENT's voice: How about Q? Who does Q belong to?

L: He's mine! Can there be any doubt? I am his lawful wedded wife.

SERPENT's voice: J is Y's lawful wedded wife.

L: That's beside the point. *(Looking around)* Who is speaking, anyway? Who are you? Your words are flatulent and irrelevant.

SERPENT's voice: First of all, I admire your honesty – honest people are so hard to come by nowadays. However, except for you, all the people recognize the marriage license as valid. What can you do about it?

L *(in extreme sorrow and exasperation):* Yes, what can I do? What can I do?

SERPENT's voice: Here she comes, Y's legitimate wife. J has come.

L *(shocked):* What? J has come? Can she possibly be coming here? What has she come here for? What can I do for her? Ask her to forgive my sins?

SERPENT's voice: You've committed no sin, have you?

L: No. I've committed no sin. What sin have I ever committed?

SERPENT's voice: She is knocking at the door.

Sound of knocking.

L: She really has come. Should I open the door or not?

SERPENT's voice: Why don't you open the door? Are you afraid of her because you feel guilty? Are you her moral inferior?

L: By no means! I want to look her in the face, and she has arrived just at the right moment.

L *opens the door. A haggard, deranged J enters.*

J *(listlessly):* Sister L, I'm sorry to bother you so late at night. Don't blame me, for I have no choice but to come talk with you.

L: You – at this hour of the night you come looking for me?

J: I've come to beg you to return my husband to me.

L *(in a sudden rage):* What did you say?

J: Please return my husband to me. I beg you.

L: Who has robbed you of your man? Who? How dare you come to my house to look for your man? I'll squash that swinish face of yours. Go ahead, search the place! Where is your man? Do you need to go to court?

J: For your sake and the sake of my husband, let's not go to court. Better to resolve the matter privately. Sister L, his heart is in your place.

L: In my place? I've never seen it. All his organs, including his bowels, grow inside his own body. Go find him, ask him. Why ask me? Go away! Get out of my house.

J *kneels on the floor and kowtows to* L.

J: One's head should touch the ground only when one dies. Now I kneel and kowtow to you. Please give him back to me and to our children.

L *(turns her back):* You recognize only your own suffering, your own misery. Don't I suffer, too? Aren't I miserable? You say his whole heart is in my place. I must say that not even a tenth of his heart has been given to me. We're merely behaving like thieves, hiding like a pair of wild rabbits. *(As she speaks she is overwhelmed by sorrow. She weeps, snivels, and blows her nose with her fingers, then flicks mucus onto her feet).* I cannot live without him. Sister J, please give him to me. I beg you. You and he have never lived happily together anyway. He doesn't even want to speak to you. Why keep a mute?

L *also kneels.*

J: No, no! *(Screaming)* No! He and I are legally married, companions for life. We have had sons and daughters, and a large part of us is already buried in the earth. Let you have him? No, that will never do. He is mine! No matter how many criticism meetings I have to endure or how much you promote proletarian ideology and eliminate bourgeois thought, he is mine. A husband cannot be regarded as common property. I am not bourgeois, and he is not my capital. He is the blood father of our children, and I am their blood mother. You cannot break up our family, Sister L!

Kneeling on the floor, both women wail loudly. They move closer to each other on their knees and finally embrace each other, wailing together in heartrending grief.

SERPENT *(aside):* What? Can they possibly be reconciled? No, of course not. But they have achieved a momentary sympathy for each other. So the rhythm of the drama begins to slow down, as in a suffocating storm when the sky neither clears nor opens up, and it is hard to reach the climax of lightning and thunder. From this point on, the reconciled parties will continue quarreling, pleading, fighting. The three of them – no, the four of them – will hassle each other to death. This kind of protracted war can produce fifty TV series and take an audience to the end of its tether. No, no such dull TV series. What I need are Shakespearean characters, with distinctive personalities and stunning climaxes. L and Y both need seductive potions number 3 and number 4. Otherwise you, the merciless audience, will clatter your theater chairs the way Chopin plays his funeral march. One after the other you will leave, and only a sleeping boy, with a lollipop in his hand, will remain. Because the situation will brook no delay, I must act promptly.

SERPENT *creeps out from beneath the table and squeezes drops of seductive potions number 3 and 4 into the cup.*

L: Don't cry, sister. Let's stop crying. We are both victims of Y, Sister J. *(As she speaks, she breaks into tears with a new wave of sorrow.)*
J: You're right, Sister L. Let's stop crying and stand up.

They help each other up. L takes the cup.

L: That cursed man of mine has gone to the city and is not back yet. He didn't even boil any water for me. Sorry, I have to offer you this cold water. Your body fluids have all drained through your eyes. We doctors of Western medicine are extremely partial to drinking water. Apparently you don't like water. That's why you look so old for your age, and why your skin has lost its luster.

J *(full of gratitude):* Quite true, Sister L. I don't like water very much.

L: Drink some, then. Wet your throat first.

J *takes the cup and has a sip. Then she passes it back to L. L swallows a big mouthful.*

J *(now coming back to her senses, she feels something wrong with the new relationship between them.)* Sister L, I must make my stand clear: my man belongs to me. He cannot be shared, and his heart cannot be shared, not even a shred of it. Not even the most wretched woman in the world could accept something like that. Now I must be leaving.

J *stamps her feet fiercely and turns to leave.*

L: Wait!

DOCTOR L *dashes forward to block the door with her body.*

J: Let me go, you shameless woman. Whore.

L: You're the whore. A whore even pigs or dogs won't touch, a whore too cheap to be sold...

Playwright's note. – Because such abusive language will be censored by any government, no matter its ideology, one hundred eight characters are here omitted.

J: You're the whore, selling pussy openly. You've slept with a thousand men, thousands of men....

Playwright's note. — Urgently omit 213 characters.

L: You, you're one! I – I'm going to split you in two!

L's lips turn from livid to white. Slowly she bends over and her hand, like a snake, wraps itself around the handle of the ax by the door. In a flash, the ax is raised high.

J: Ah, you want to murder me? Okay, I don't want to live any longer. Go ahead, kill me!

J rushes head-long at L, who quickly steps aside. J's head smashes against the door. Quick as lightning, L brings down her ax and gashes the back of J's skull horribly. Blood splashes all over L's face.
The theater lights dim. (Playwright's note. — Although murder occurs often in our lives, actual murder scenes are not allowed in works of literature and art. Fortunately, the lights on the stage can be dimmed instantly.) The lights come up again gradually. The audience first sees a cup on a square table, and then SERPENT's *head emerges above the cup.*

SERPENT *(soliloquy):* L has finally removed the greatest obstacle in her emotional life. Obviously, she knows that what she has done is a crime that makes it less possible for her and Y to be united. But she chose to be a criminal. Without killing J, she could hardly keep on living. So she killed her. Calmly she cut her archenemy's body into ten large chunks and put each one into a plastic bag. Then she cleaned the floor, changed her clothes, and washed her face. She then dumped J's head into a huge earthen pot to boil for soup. Look, my dear audience!

The spotlight moves to a lighted stove. On the stove is a huge earthen pot. Squatting before the stove, L fans the fire. The spotlight moves back to the desk, illuminating the cup and SERPENT's *head.*

SERPENT: She needs some seductive potion number 5.

L *(soliloquy):* I can't have him anymore. I can't have him anymore. No love. No love forever…forever…forever. *(Bursts into hysterical laughter)* But I've vented my hatred. People in this world won't understand: how dare a woman split another woman with an ax? How dare she calmly dissect her body into ten pieces? How dare she carefully clean all the blood off the floor? And how dare she boil the woman's head in a huge pot for soup? Why aren't I paralyzed with fear? Why aren't my hands shaking and why isn't my heart beating fast? Why don't I even care about the consequences? All these questions are for you fellows. Go think hard about them. Do your research! Study your sociology! Open your criminology books! Investigate! Measure out the murder scene! Put every shred of evidence through chemical tests! Read the fingerprints! Search for the murder weapon! Round up the witnesses! Cross-examine the criminal – cross-examine *me.* Hold a public trial to denounce *me.*

L *empties the cup at one gulp.*

L *(in a carefree manner):* I will not confess. You cannot force me to open my mouth, not even with an iron bar. Without my confession, however, you still can sentence me to death. In order to demonstrate your talent, loyalty, and firm proletarian stand, one by one you climb onto the platform to expose my crimes born of your imagination. You will write a tedious court verdict, attributing murder to the vicious tide of bourgeois corruption. *(Waltzes around, singing)* Tra-la-la…

Q *pushes the door open. Sunlight follows him into the room.*

L: So you've finally come home. Which bitch did you spent the night with?

Q: Hey, stop talking nonsense. I'm dead tired. Next time, you'd better go with me into town.

L: There won't be a next time for us anymore.

Q: What?

L *(smiles mysteriously):* No next time for us anymore!

Q: Why not?

L *(laughs loudly):* Because I am going be shot. *(Imitates the executioner)* Ready – aim – fire! Pow!

Q: What nonsense are you spouting, so early in the morning?

L: Though I do not have the beauty of Chen Bailu, I will recite her lines: "The sun has come out! But the sun is no longer mine. I am going to sleep now."

Q: Are you mad?

L: I'm perfectly fine, never saner than today! Come see what this is.

She drags Q over to the pot. Q is horrified.

Q: Agh! A human head!

L: You're the abnormal person here. A human head is a human head. Why make such a big fuss over it?

Q *(his teeth chattering):* Who – who – whose – head?

L: Why? Can't you recognize it? It's not boiled out of shape yet. It's J's head, you know, Y's wife.

Q: Why – why – did you – k-kill her?

L: No comment. Wait until the written verdict appears. Now, your duty is: first, call Y over here; second, report me to the police.

Q dashes out.

L *(soliloquy):* Who says I am mad? Can a madwoman be so calm as to accomplish whatever she wishes to do? What I've achieved another person would have to overcome ten thousand obstacles before even trying. Overnight, I demonstrated a will, a strength, and a talent more powerful than Hitler's on the eve of his attack on Soviet Russia. Now I see what it means to defy world condemnation, I recognize what decisiveness is and what composure and bravery are. The potential daring spirit and strength of a person is usually wrapped up in a cocoon – especially of a woman. If she does not have the courage to defy world condemnation and act decisively and opportunely, she can never achieve anything outstanding. Take the example of the First Lady of our strange country. A few years ago, she was known by hardly a handful of people throughout the nation. Occasionally one might hear, through the grapevine, that she was helping a few actors and actresses to reform the old Beijing Opera. Who could expect that one morning she would expand her rehearsal stage to the whole land and assign dramatic roles to all its people, big shots and small potatoes alike? No one could escape his role. In this nationwide tragicomic farce, full of grief and ecstasy, she handily wiped out several old love rivals, together with those who knew her early private life. But she dared not murder them herself. She finished off her enemies without getting a spot of blood on her dress, and she never tasted the pleasure of chopping her enemy's flesh with an ax. She is no match for me. No match at all.

Y *enters as if in a trance.*

L: Here you are. Now the obstacle between us is removed. Look, this is your wife's head.

Y *(covers his eyes):* Agh! You – you cruel-hearted beast!

L: Coward! Put down your hands. Open your eyes wide like me and look reality in the face. When you shut your eyes, do you think all the things in the world disappear? Do you think others no longer see *you?* Instead of letting ten thousand people stare at you like a blind dog, you might as well fix your eyes on them to beat back their stares.

Smiling proudly at everything, you will shock them even more. Let them wake up out of their fog and salute you. Come on, Y. Now you can hug me without any fear or worry, right in front of your wife. She cannot peck at you any more. Come on! *(Extremely sweet)* Come – darling!

L steps to pull Y over to her. Y shrinks back in horror.

Y: Agh, don't! Don't come near me!
L: Coward! Why were you always so audacious before? Why did you seduce me in the first place, if you were going to be so timid today?

Noise is heard outside.

L: They're coming. I must put on some makeup and wear my new clothes. I am going to get married again.

Exit L into the bedroom.

Y: Monster! Monster!

Y is experiencing extreme pain and grief. Q rushes in with several policemen. L enters from the bedroom. According to the principle of Three Prominences [positive characters, heroes among the positive characters, and major heroes among them], *a ten-thousand-watt stage light should be added.*

L is wearing a cotton-print blouse, covered by a thin red-wool sweater. A white gauze scarf is draped over her shoulders. Her well-combed hair is raven black, and she wears a small bunch of nameless wildflowers above one temple. Her carefree manner makes her look innocent; a naive smile is at the corners of her mouth. She strikes a heroic pose.

Tableau, held for a long time. Orchestral music. Blackout.

A spotlight is cast on the square table. Coiled on the table, SERPENT *holds its head high in triumph.*

SERPENT *(soliloquy):* My dear audience: Before the curtain falls, please allow me to say a few words. I know you all hate me and regard me as the true culprit in this murder case. I understand your feelings. But because I have not yet been prosecuted in court, and also because one cannot find a lawyer in this strange country, I need to present my own defense. My defense is actually a famous quotation that is absolutely convincing: "The materialist dialectic shows that the external factors are conditions for change; the internal factors are the essence for change. The external factors take effect only through the internal factors. An egg, at a suitable temperature, turns into a chicken, but temperature cannot turn a stone into a chicken because their essences are different." That's my entire defense. In a country where there is no judge, no jury, and no public prosecutor, I can only invite you, my respected audience, to make a fair, appropriate judgment. Thank you.

The curtain falls. End.

I gaze at her window. In the past, it was pasted over with black paper; now a cloth curtain with tiny blue flowers hangs there.

As soon as we had finished the play, Yunqian complained, "It's thrilling, but too exaggerated. And not realistic, not realistic at all."

"I think it's *extremely* realistic. It truly reflects reality."

"Not at all. If you don't believe me, read it to other people. If a single person thinks this play is realistic, you win the bet."

"Unfortunately, I wouldn't dare read it to anybody else. But even if I did, I'd still lose the bet."

"Because the play is unrealistic."

"No. It is only because the play is truly realistic that I am bound to lose."

"Why?"

"Over the past twenty years, millions of people here have acquired a false sense of reality."

"You are a superman, an exception."

"I am no exception. The tableau of L before her arrest in the play coincides perfectly with my last image of Liu Tiemei. The verisimilitude of this art stuns me. Song Lin has accurately captured the spiritual transformation of Liu Tiemei between the clinic and the execution truck. His artistic representation is concise and convincing."

"Is that serpent also real? Isn't it simply a figment of the author's imagination?"

"Although it is purely imaginary, I believe in its truth." I gazed at Yunqian in excitement.

"You really are an ideal audience." Yunqian kissed my eyes.

I gaze at her window. In the past, it was pasted over with black paper; now a cloth curtain with tiny blue flowers hangs there.

13

Longbu was back on the road with the caravan. His posts got farther and farther away from home. Correspondingly, Sunamei's waiting for his return became longer and longer, and her longing for him more and more desperate. An inexpressible feeling of emptiness seized her. During Longbu's absences, Sunamei weeded the fields wearing the beads, bracelets, and earrings he had given her. The sun dancing on the shining ornaments gave her a sense of pride before people. However, she preferred relishing, in her moments of solitude, the sweet feelings Longbu had left her in those intimate nights. During the day, she refused to join the youngsters' dances by the lake or the antiphonal singing in the woods; instead she retreated early to her own *huagu* to sink into the smells of tobacco and wine and the senses of Longbu's body. At night, she would awake at the slightest clattering of hooves. Although she fully understood that Longbu could not be back yet, her heart still trembled in excitement, hoping for a miracle – Longbu's early return. But the miracle never occurred. In the fields, on the way home, along the stream, Sunamei's sneer turned away the men's passes and metaphorical insinuations. She could not forget Longbu for even one second. This capable but staid, middle-aged man unknowingly had aroused her strongest passions. Like an inundated piece of land, each time she enjoyed the pleasure of being penetrated to the point of satiety, yet she longed for the rush of another surging flood. She believed there was no man who could erase the impression Longbu had left on her senses.

This time Longbu's post was too far away. He did not return for two months. On the east side of the lake there lived a lad of eighteen named Yingzhi, who walked thirty *li* to the Youjiwa Village every evening, hoping to see Sunamei. He believed that, if Sunamei saw him, she would have to listen to him. And if she listened to just one word from him, she would continue listening, as she did to the song of the river from which she could hardly tear herself. Yingzhi ran to her village ten nights in a row, but failed to see Sunamei. Many people dissuaded him from such a foolish pursuit: Sunamei was unwilling to see him. Even if he met her, she would not listen to his babbling. He ignored them.

Yingzhi had begged Sunamei's childhood friend Geruoma to put in a word to Sunamei for him. For this purpose, he brought Geruoma a silver ring set with a pine-green stone. Geruoma did not accept the present, and just giggled. Yingzhi was confused and his wrist ached because of holding the ring in his palm too long. Instead of taking the ring, Geruoma covered her laughing mouth and wiped the tears from her eyes. She laughed and laughed through three pipes of tobacco. Perhaps her stomach ached from laughing too much. Finally, she said, "I don't have the luck to wear this precious ring. How could Sunamei ever listen to me? You'd better ask somebody else to help you. Yingzhi, why don't you drink to your heart's content at the stream by your feet, instead of seeking the dew on high cliffs? You may stay at my home tonight. My *huagu* is pretty warm."

"Thank you, Geruoma. If there were no Sunamei born in the Youjiwa Village, I would rest at your home." Turning her back, Geruoma ran away giggling.

Yingzhi had also asked Sunamei's *ami* Cai'er for help, bringing her ten lumps of tea. Cai'er received him warmly and invited him to drink wine. But when he expressed his desire to see Sunamei, Cai'er said to him earnestly, "Yingzhi, you are a handsome man. In all of Xienami, one cannot find another man so handsome as you. But you know, a man's beauty is not on his face. I don't know where it is – only his *axiao* knows. And even his *axiao,* although she knows it, cannot say it. My daughter Sunamei already has an *axiao.* Her heart is placed in Longbu's tobacco pipe, and no one can touch it, unless Longbu throws it out. Moreover, Longbu is a good-hearted man. Each time he comes back from his journey, he brings a large sack of food, clothes, and other things to show his respect for me. Besides, Sunamei's *ami* is not Sunamei and cannot be her master. Although her eyes, nose, mouth, full breasts, and soft waist, plus the particular thing a man loves, were given by me, they were separated from my body at birth. I have no right to make any decision for her."

"Does Sunamei know I want to see her?"

"The whole village knows."

"As long as she knows, the trips I made are not in vain. Ami Cai'er, please tell her Yingzhi has been here again."

"Alright, I'll tell her."

One day, Yingzhi met Sunamei's Amiji Zhima on the way. Carrying a large bundle of dried grass, her body was steaming with sweat. Grabbing her bundle, he said to her, "Zhima, let me carry it for you. You look tired."

"You are Yingzhi, aren't you?"

"Yes, Zhima. How beautiful you are."

"Many men praise my beauty with the intention of getting into my *huagu.* You alone do it for some other purpose."

"But it is true, Zhima, your beauty is born, not brought about by my praise."

Biting her lower lip with her pearly teeth, she looked at Yingzhi with a naughty smile. "Is Sunamei more beautiful than I?"

"One cannot compare one person's beauty with that of another. A lantana has a lantana's beauty; a camellia has a camellia's beauty."

"What you say is true. Yingzhi, do you want to see Sunamei?"

"Zhima, are you teasing me?"

"No. I am the person who can let you see her."

"How can I thank you, then?"

Zhima shook her head, and said with a smile, "Come at midnight. I will keep the gate and my *huagu* open for you. Do you know which room is her *huagu?*"

"Yes, the one by the staircase."

"Have you ever knocked at it?"

"No. I know it's no use, for many men have tried."

"Please come tonight. Between my *huagu* and hers is one board. You come to my *huagu* first. I won't keep you."

"I will come. Let me carry the bundle home for you."

"No, thanks. I am not tired." She beheld Yingzhi in admiration. "You really are a man of perseverance."

To Yingzhi, the time from evening to midnight was no shorter than three years. By the time midnight finally arrived, he had kicked almost all the pebbles on the roads and paths around the Youjiwa Village, counted all the households and trees dwelling in the village as well as the stars in the sky, called the names of Sunamei and Zhima ten thousand times. He pushed open the gate that led to Sunamei's *huagu*. As expected, it was unbolted. He threw in several pieces of pork through a narrow opening to bribe the black dog. The dog did not even snort, wagging its tail as a gesture of welcome. The young man climbed the stairs to the *huagu*. He paused at Sunamei's door, resting his hands on the door and leaning his face against it in order to listen intensely – Sunamei was sleeping soundly. Then he pushed open the door to Zhima's *huagu* in the darkness. Zhima jumped off her bed. She held Yingzhi's shoulder and took him to Sunamei's door, whispering: "I can only give you a chance to see her. I heard you say, if only you can see her. ..."

"Sunamei!" Zhima knocked gently at Sunamei's door.

"Eh?" Sunamei was alert. "Amiji Zhima?"

"It's me. Open the door, Sunamei."

"Is there something you want to tell me?"

"Yes."

Sunamei opened the door, and Yingzhi strode in. Striking a match, he lit the little lamp. "Yingzhi wants to have a look at you...." With these words, Zhima went back to her own *huagu*.

Sunamei, her clothes draped over her shoulder, was annoyed. "Get out!"

"Sunamei, people say you are a woman of feelings and sober thought. I doubt it. In the past I saw you only at a distance, but today I find only your beauty and not your tenderness. That kind of beauty does not appeal to me.... All right, I'm leaving. Sorry for disturbing you. Please accept my apologies." Although Yingzhi stepped out, he kept his hand on the doorknob.

For a while Sunamei could not speak; her self-esteem had been injured. She knew Zhima had heard everything. Tomorrow the conversation would be known to the whole village; the day after tomorrow to the whole world. People would gossip: the single-minded Yingzhi was dying to see Sunamei; one word from her drove him away in disappointment. Sunamei said in a challenging tone, "So you're leaving. Then why don't you move?"

"You told me only to get out, not to go away. I do what you say. If you say *go away,* I will go away." Sunamei did not say *go away,* or anything else. The one inside and the one outside the door, locked in a stalemate, listened together to their quickened breathing. "If you do not say *go away,* you should say *come in.*" Sunamei did not say *come in.* "If you do not say *come in,* I will invite myself in. If you don't say *don't come in,* I will come in." Sunamei did not say *don't come in.*

Yingzhi entered the *huagu* and shut the door. Before Sunamei knew it, Yingzhi was embracing her tightly. He tore away the clothes draped over her shoulder. Yingzhi surprised her like a summer storm, and Sunamei resisted and then accepted him. The rain that had held its power for so long poured down without forming visible threads. Apart from the lightning, there were low, heavy, dark clouds smelling of fish. The hot rain poured ceaselessly, the universe was submerged in water, forests swayed in the water and streams overflowed. Sunamei suffered the violent rain joyfully, her tears and the rain flowing together. Twice she wanted to jump up with a scream; yet she was motionless under the weight of hot rain and clouds. The rain gradually let up and the thunder vanished. Yet the clouds remained. When the dark clouds drifted and thinned out, Sunamei, like a willow sapling that had exhausted its madness, dripped beads of glistening water in the sun. She opened her eyes, seeing the lamplight small like a bean. The naked, white Yingzhi was lying by her side, tender words flowing from his wet lips into her ear.

"Sunamei, have you ever seen a shooting star at daybreak? When all other stars turn gray, the shooting star slants down with its flashing tail. I have been watching it every evening outside your window. But you cannot see it, for you are dreaming. Sunamei, do you know how little weeds grow during the night? They shoot up with dew on their heads, singing a gentle bubbling song and flipping their tiny leaves. I can see them while I squat at the foot of your wall. You cannot see them because you are lying right above my head."

Sunamei laughed happily. She was amused by Yingzhi's words. Naturally she was comparing him with Longbu. After making love, Longbu always sank into a sound sleep, but Yingzhi was different. He made Sunamei feel like the water on the ground after the storm; having found its riverbed, it flows softly on. She knew Yingzhi must also be tired. She blew out the lamp and embraced him. To save his breath, she covered his mouth with her hand. Body and soul, Sunamei accepted Yingzhi. Soon they fell sound asleep, the stars outside the window were shooting down, and the weeds at the end of the wall shooting up.... They could no longer hear or see.

When you are expecting a miracle, the miracle never comes. It comes only when you forget or even fear its appearance and the miracle turns to its opposite. Longbu returned ahead of schedule. When Yingzhi and Sunamei were sound asleep, he knocked at the door.

"Who is it?" Sunamei woke in surprise. From the knocking sound, she could tell: Longbu had come back.

"Who else could it be?"

Sunamei nudged Yingzhi awake.

"Is someone in there with you?" Longbu had guessed it. Sunamei did not reply; she did not know how. "I hurried back at night without going home first. I am terribly thirsty. Can you give me some tea?" He waited patiently. Sunamei opened the door. Yingzhi sat by the fireplace, rearranging the firewood, and the white cat was washing its face with its paws. Longbu laid a heavy sack on the floor. "Oh, it's you, Yingzhi."

"Do you know me?" Yingzhi looked at him, a little tense.

"How could I fail to recognize you? I attended your pants-wearing ceremony." The white cat jumped into Longbu's lap.

"Oh..." Yingzhi shaped his hands like a chimney and blew on the fire through them.

"Give me a hand, Sunamei." Longbu untied his sack and Sunamei took from it wine bottles, granulated milk, dried beef, cookies, and lumps of tea. Longbu poured out three bowls of wine, divided the milk grains that had been fried in butter into three shares, and cut three beef chunks of equal size. "Drink, Yingzhi." Longbu took up a bowl. Yingzhi drank his, but Sunamei only sipped at hers. After a long silence, Longbu again poured wine into the three bowls. Sunamei's eyes darted back and forth, from Longbu to Yingzhi. Longbu seemed scarcely to notice. "Yingzhi, have you ever been out with the caravan?"

"No."

"You won't see much of the world without that sort of experience. You know, every road is a book. Young man, you should go with me on one of the journeys, visiting the dam at Lijiang, the city of Dali, the boulevard in Xiaguan. It's really an exciting world, where you meet all sorts of men, hear all sorts of languages, and see all sorts of bizarre clothes. Oh, and those spectacular plays! They show movies every day, even during the daytime, in a closed dark room. The women of the Bai nationality are really beautiful, as clean as clouds after a rain. They wear white dresses decorated with red flowers from collar to cuffs. But you cannot touch them. One touch would invite a stare or a curse. This journey of mine has been a bit tiring. I'm exhausted — " Speaking as he drank, he gradually shut his eyes. Leaning against the wall opposite the warm fire, he seemed to fall asleep.

Yingzhi whispered to Sunamei, "I have to go."

Sunamei shook her head, waving her hand slightly to indicate her unwillingness for him to leave. She thought Longbu would not see this. But somehow Longbu was able to catch her message with his eyes shut. Pushing the white cat aside, he jumped up. "I have to go now." Before Sunamei was on her feet, he was already down the stairs. Sunamei stayed motionless, staring at the fire for a long time; Yingzhi gazed at her face. The big white cat stroked their faces with its fluffy tail.

The following night, when Longbu again came for a visit, he found his bedroll and sack lying in front of Sunamei's *huagu*. After carefully hanging a gilded necklace on its doorknob, Longbu shouldered his belongings and walked slowly downstairs and out the gate.

14

I gaze at her window. In the past, it was pasted over with black paper; now a cloth curtain with tiny blue flowers hangs there.

Again the time had come for me to take my medical report to the farm. As I shut my eyes and reminisced on the bus, the scenes and images flashing through my memory were all associated with Gui Renzhong. Nothing else could intrude, no matter how interesting or sensational: Old Gui following a herd of cows, each with eyes of grief and loyalty just like his. Old Gui looking up at the lofty statue of Mao with boundless faith. Old Gui prostrating himself on the ground out of sheer joy and excitement at his five-day leave. Old Gui raising a shriveled hand to get a chance to ask questions at the meeting. Old Gui massaging my back with his gentle hand while holding his broken leg. Old Gui wearing a brand-new suit and moving slowly toward me like a paper doll. Old Gui being forced to put his fingerprint on the marriage certificate like Yang Bailao. Carrying Jane's ashes, he follows me out of the villa, a playhouse designed for foreigners, his face showing no trace of misery or humiliation, only the relaxation of a shy actor who finally gets off the stage. The moment I thought of him, my heart was wrenched with pain as if a vulture were tearing out my entrails with its talons. His life would be an endless tragedy caused by his personality, or rather by his ignorance.

But could one possibly call an internationally renowned scholar ignorant? Still, I found it hard to explain the series of tragedies caused by his ignorance. He was a man of freedom in the realm of chemistry, an expert on chemical combinations, not a high school student who merely knew that H_2O = water. Why, then, did he remain such a childish simpleton? I believe a child being stolen at infancy and raised by a pack of wolves could grow into a wolf child and feed on carrion. But could an adult — and a sophisticated, top intellectual to boot — also become a wolf man? I was puzzled by this strange phenomenon. Although the Chinese, almost without exception, were being wolfified and pigisized to various degrees, until today there were few men like old Gui who had deteriorated so much and still continued to bump their heads against walls without realizing they needed to turn around. I felt he needed someone to enlighten him, like a bodhisattva, someone to drop purified water on his brow from a willow twig to wake him up at the edge of the cliff, someone to make him understand that "if a man cannot speak like a man in front of men, a man will never speak like a man in front of Satan." He needed someone to let him know that the statue was high because its steel frame was large and so it consumed more cement. But who was here to enlighten him? A bodhisattva was merely a Buddhist god that did not really exist as a physical being in this universe; therefore, he could not be produced by way of chemistry. I alone could save old Gui, and I felt obliged to bring him out of the wilderness. To refuse to save him would be inhumanly cynical and cruel. He had suffered enough. Now it was time for me to help him swim the bitter sea.

With these thoughts, I felt a shining halo over my head, and my noble sentiments so thrilled me that my eyes filled with warm tears. It would be difficult to catechize him face to face. Better to write it out so he could read it over and over. I took out a notebook from the satchel and wrote the following:

Old Gui:

I have been worried about you for some time. How are you? You aren't doing fine, I know that, because you are too naive, far too naive. Although no irregularity in a chemical reaction can escape your eye, when confronted with the false phenomena of the sacred in life, particularly with certain wooden idols, you quickly lose your power of perception. Worse still, you exalt those false images with a dreamlike enthusiasm. Each of us has a prison in his mind, but yours is much more fortified. Why don't you try sticking your head through the iron bars to see the vast sky beyond the prison? Sometimes just one more step will lead to a new world. I sincerely hope you accept my advice. Turn it over and over in your mind, pondering it like the tables, formulas, and equations you have mastered before. You will understand my message. May one opening (insight) lead to one hundred openings.

Your loving student,
Liang Rui
Month x, Date x, Year x

I folded the message into a butterfly bow and thrust it into old Gui's hand as I was leaving the farm. I whispered, "A letter for you."

"A letter?" He reacted strangely.

"For you alone to read."

"Me alone?" His expression grew even more strange; he stared at me pitifully.

"Yes. Read it several times. Think things over. Then burn it...."

"Burn it?" His voice became as dry as withered leaves.

I asked him another three times to burn the letter before I walked away with a relieved heart. I was lucky in having to wait only a minute before a bus came. As I dozed during the ride, I wore a broad smile because I had made progress.

A beautiful new world was unfolding under my feet. I was imagining how old Gui looked on his awakening: his forehead must be radiating wisdom and his eyes becoming clear like a fountain, his face washed by tears of gratitude for me.

The screech of the bus sent me flying to the roof and then dumped me back into the seat. My head and buttocks hurt badly. An accident? A two-car crash, or someone run over? The moment I straightened myself out, the door opened and in stepped two men. To my surprise, one was the defense leader of our farm; the other was his guard. The farm's defense office was like the state's Department of Police, plus the Department of Security, plus court and prosecutor. Its leader had the power of minister plus judge plus prosecutor. All four eyes sized me up. "Liang Rui, get off the bus!"

"What's happened?" I stood up.

"*You* can ask that?" The leader was in a rage. "No nonsense now, roll yourself out of here!" Roll? Of course I actually walked out. As soon as I was off the bus, they snapped handcuffs on me. They used a fashionable new method: pulling my right hand over my shoulder and twisting my left behind my back, they locked my two hands together. I don't know why I asked them, "Why shackle me like that?"

The guard said, "This is called 'Su Qin Carrying His Sword'. What a bumpkin you are." Of course I was a bumpkin; after all, not everybody has the right to exercise dictatorship over others. The Chinese, with their high culture, love to do everything in style. The Western Lake in Hangzhou has ten scenes of beauty. So everywhere in China people try to imitate it, as if without ten scenes a place would not be worth seeing. Refined literary names for the beautiful scenes stimulate a man's appetite for sight-seeing. The bodies of a cat and a snake roasted together carries the name Dragon Fighting the Tiger. The body of a butchered chicken decorated with a tomato is called Phoenix Facing the Sun. Inventing beautiful names to match cuisine is understandable, because the names may serve as appetizers.

But why did they need a heroic name for the manner in which they shackled me? Could that also stimulate people's appetites? It sure seemed to. Although it didn't take long to shackle me and push me into the jeep, in that short time I attracted a large crowd. There were no villages on either side of the highway, so where did they come from? Did they spring out of the ground? China has certainly earned its fame as a country with a large population. The onlookers were excited to see that I, who was being devoured by the beast of power, was not one of them. Their happiness seemed to show their favor for the power and their complicity in the act of devouring.

The jeep returned along the route it had come. It took at least a mile to throw off the onlookers. The springy seats of the jeep could by no means be compared with those in a luxury car. In less than five minutes I tasted the heroism of Su Qin Carrying His Sword. My wrists, elbows, and back ached intolerably. I started groaning, as I tried to guess what crime I had committed. Had they discovered my illness to be false? No, impossible. As long as that head doctor was still in power, he would take responsibility. Even if they had found out the true nature of my illness, did they need to stop a passenger bus to arrest me? Had my affair with Yunqian been discovered? No, even more unlikely. We were always hidden in our cocoon. Who would bother worming into it to catch us? Even if we were discovered, at most we should only be criticized for behaving immorally before marriage, a defect that can be corrected through education. I sorted through my entire short history but failed to find any crime, mistake, or even an error of omission for which I deserved to be arrested. I was certain they had made a mistake in arresting me, producing another miscarriage of justice. Yet they had to have some reason to arrest me! Yes — suddenly it came to me in a flash. Perhaps the message I had passed to old Gui had fallen into the wrong hands.

No, impossible. Absolutely impossible. After all, I told him the letter was for him alone to read. Even if the message upset his three loyalties and four infinite loves, he would not report me so fast. I had repeatedly told him: "Read it several times. Think things over. Then burn it." If he had read it twice and thought things over for three minutes before reporting, they still could not have arrested me so fast. Unless he reported me the moment he read the first line, as if he had discovered a dagger on unfolding the sheet. I thought it utterly impossible – a hundred times impossible, a thousand times impossible, ten thousand times impossible.

But the facts taught me that it was possible – a hundred times possible, a thousand times possible, ten thousand times possible.

Before the jeep arrived at the farm, the huge shed had already been prepared for a large criticism meeting. Their experience in handling such meetings was truly admirable. When I was escorted to the shed, I looked up and saw an extra-large banner hanging across the stage: *Criticize the Active Counterrevolutionary Liang Rui,* which already determined the nature of my crime and put a tall criminal's hat on me. Therefore, as soon as I entered, like a famous Beijing Opera actor striking a pose as the embroidered curtain rises, I received an uproarious welcome. Slogans showered down on me like a storm and hundreds of fists were raised in my direction, stretching and withdrawing like cannon barrels. Being denounced by the pointing fingers of thousands gave me the sense of being a star. Suddenly I felt like a great president with a sky-scraping hat. Swarms of people on tiptoes, squeezing and nudging each other, pushed forward to catch a glimpse of me. I was escorted to the stage. Holding my head high, I stood there in the heroic pose of Su Qin Carrying His Sword. Hysterical shouting distorted everyone's voice; I could not make out what they were shouting. When my head was thumped by a fist, I guessed they were shouting for me to lower my head. So I lowered my head, unable to see anything but my toes.

The solemn voice of the PLA rep rose above the din: "Chairman Mao teaches us: 'When the old reactionaries are wiped out, new ones will grow. If we lose our vigilance, we will suffer a great loss.' 'The trees want to be still but the wind will not stop.' 'Never be so bookish and naive as to treat complex class struggle as a simple matter.'" From the quotations he recited I could tell the ordeal I was about to go through, and my body froze from the inside out. The PLA rep continued in a voice quivering with indignation: "Comrades, revolutionary comrades! Don't some of you think the Cultural Revolution has carried on too long? Don't some believe that all cow ghosts and snake-spirits have been wiped out? And don't some blame us for shooting mosquitoes with cannons or creating a storm in a teacup? I hope those comrades will draw a lesson from this active counterrevolutionary. Comrade Gui Renzhong, would you please come to the stage?"

The words *comrade* and *please* used by the PLA rep created a disturbance in the meeting. I was unable to see but could well imagine: being surprised by the favor, Gui Renzhong's legs turned soft. It took a long time for him to reach the stage. The PLA rep said to him, "Please read to our comrades the reactionary manifesto of the active counterrevolutionary Liang Rui!" Manifesto? If I weren't shackled, I'd have dashed over to tear him into pieces. When did I ever write a reactionary manifesto?

Gui Renzhong started in a funereal tone. "Comrades! Active counterrevolutionary Comrade Liang Rui – No! He is not a comrade but an enemy. Taking advantage of us being bedmates, he wrote me a letter in an attempt to shake my revolutionary belief. Before I had read it through, I smelled something fishy and immediately handed it over to the PLA rep. Now I'll read this reactionary manifesto – "

Old Gui's reading shocked me. Did I really write that? How could I have written something like that? Could I have been so careless as that? Now even *I* was finding the message to be extremely reactionary. Before old Gui had finished it, I was already soaked in sweat. Then the model fighters of the farm vied to take the stage. Nearly all of them became professional speakers, delivering elegant criticisms with associations, allusions, political theories, and class guidelines. Each heightened his speech with a grave face, harsh tone, and grandiose terminology, as well as with physical gestures such as beating the chest, stamping the feet, and spraying saliva in all directions. Although I had expected such expertise, I could not help shouting bravo in my mind for their penetrating analyses and apt associations. Let me give you some samples:

"Comrades, my revolutionary comrades! Listen, what kind of words are these: 'How are you? You aren't doing fine, I know that. Because you are too naive, far too naive.' Do these words sound strange or new? No. They smell reactionary. Chairman Mao teaches us, 'Reactionaries are waving their hands at you.' What does *waving their hands* mean? The message 'How are you? You aren't doing fine, I know that. Because you are too naive, far too naive' is a typical example. The author cunningly hid the supplement to the sentence. Too naive with whom? It is obvious that his spear is aimed at our great leader Chairman Mao, at the great, glorious, and flawless Chinese Communist party, and at the revolutionary masses. The beginning of his message exposes his inveterate hatred toward them." At this moment, the speaker could not help shouting from the bottom of his heart: "Long live our great leader Chairman Mao. Long, long, long may he live!" The audience echoed his words with the force of thunder and lightning.

Another example: "The phrase *irregularity in a chemical reaction* sounds exactly like the counterrevolutionary Hu Feng. Is the author *really* talking about chemistry? No.

Counterrevolutionaries know the importance of putting politics in command. Some of our comrades are naive enough to complain that we have overemphasized politics. The counterrevolutionaries have done it much more than we have! The author then talks about the false phenomena in life, particularly those of the sacred! Attention, comrades! What are these false phenomena of the sacred in life? What can be called sacred in life? What else if it is not our loyalty to the great leader and our belief in revolution? But he does not stop there. Listen to the next line: 'You exalt those false images with a dreamlike enthusiasm.' Notice the arrogance of this counterrevolutionary, who assumes the reactionary intellectual's pose of 'I alone wake while the whole world sleeps.' He is slandering the great, stormy, revolutionary movement we are currently carrying out as the false dream of a single individual. How vicious he is! If we tolerate *him,* who can we not tolerate? Down with the counterrevolutionary Liang Rui!" Another wave of slogans resounded in the shed.

Another example: "This counterrevolutionary is extremely vicious. He attacks every happy man living in our socialist China for having a prison in his mind. What does the mind prison refer to? It refers to the fundamental principles of Marxism-Leninism-Mao Zedong thought. He has issued a reactionary call for us to step out of the prison, saying 'just one more step will lead to a new world.' What new world is he really talking about? No doubt, the so-called Free World. This counterrevolutionary Liang Rui must be a running dog of U.S. imperialism. We can be certain, without any investigation, that he is a spy of the American FBI. Down with U.S. imperialism! Down with Soviet revisionism!" U.S. imperialism and Soviet revisionism were a matching pair. Each phrase sounded incomplete without its partner, even in slogans.

Another one: "'May one opening lead to one hundred openings.' What does that mean? No doubt it is a reactionary password. Be open to whom? His first opening seems to be toward Taiwan and Taiwan's spy organizations. This first opening will then lead to U.S. imperialism, French imperialism, British imperialism, Soviet revisionism, and so on: more than a hundred openings. How dangerous one opening is, my comrades!"

Yet another. "The reasons Liang Rui joined the American FBI and Chiang Kai-shek's spy networks to sabotage our socialism can be traced to his class background." When did I join these spy organizations? How did I join them? Did I have contacts to introduce me? Who? Where? I searched my mind in earnest. "Both his parents were reactionary intellectuals. The moment the great Cultural Revolution started, they committed suicide to resist the revolutionary campaign and to show their deep-seated hatred for the Communist party. Liang Rui has buried hatred in his heart because of his late parents and has attempted to revenge them at every possible turn. Now he is honing his sword. Shouldn't we hone ours?!"

There were too many wonderful speeches to display them all here. But they unexpectedly calmed me down, and I pondered them with pleasure. But old Gui was scared almost to death; I could hear him shivering. His report on me, his vigilance and his loyalty had won him little forgiveness: nearly a third of the criticism speeches were directed at him. For instance: "Why did the counterrevolutionary choose you? You must have something in common, stinking together." "How did you collaborate with him? Why did he call himself a student of yours? Why? You must have taught him his counterrevolutionary schemes." "It is to your credit that you exposed him in time and regained your political head. However, the fact that he chose you and you alone proves what a dark, reactionary soul you have." "Your relationship with him has exposed your ugly soul to the broad daylight. Don't entertain the idea that you are different from him. You and he are wolves of the same pack!" Although my hands were shackled, I took pity on old

Gui, fearing he would be too scared to live this thing through. It was true that the PLA rep had a higher understanding of policy, for he said in a conciliatory tone: "Comrade Gui Renzhong – " The term *comrade* dragged old Gui from the enemy side over to the ranks of the people. It was a reprieve from death. "Of course, he has made his own mistakes. But mistakes are different from crimes. Everyone makes mistakes. But he has performed a meritorious deed by trusting in the strength of the party and helping to root out a counterrevolutionary." I heard old Gui give a sigh of relief. "However, he must undertake serious self-criticism in order to cast off his birthmark and his old bones." Could old Gui cast off his birthmark? Could his old bones be remolded? I doubted it.

That night I was sent to the second prison, along with the evidence of my crimes – the message I had written and all the criticism speeches delivered at the meeting. My way to prison seemed simple – no delay caused by red tape, no torture to obtain a confession. Everything – all the procedures from arrest to incarceration – was boiled in one pot. If only other matters in our country could be performed in such an efficient manner. After they checked my ID card and the evidence against me, the prison gate clanked open. I was driven in a prison car for quite a few minutes before reaching the cell allotted to me. The prison was obviously a big one. Two guards walked me to a changing room, where they ordered me to strip. As I took off my shorts, the two suddenly jumped me, kicking and pummeling me. I only had time to give a desperate cry: "Hey, I have TB!"

"We wouldn't spare you if you had cancer!"

I gaze at her window. In the past, it was pasted over with black paper; now a cloth curtain with tiny blue flowers hangs there.

When I came to, I was prisoner number 809999 in cell number 10045. My first discovery was that my hair had vanished. Cell number 10045 had an area of approximately ten square meters. Why *approximately?* Because I did not have any measuring tape with me. I was the fifth prisoner in that cell. Those who had arrived earlier treated me quite politely in that cell, not like in the prisons described in nineteenth-century European fiction, where old prisoners bully the new ones, nor like the KMT prisons shown in Chinese movies, where the prisoners love and live harmoniously like one big family. I stretched my limbs. Luckily, they still moved. My number was printed on the chest of my prison suit. It was so long I read it several times for fear of being beaten for not knowing my so-called identity.

"Number 99!" Who was number 99? I was obviously number 809999. A young man pointed at me. In the confines of the room, his finger nearly scratched my nose. "Hey, number 99, they're calling you!"

"Ah!" So the numbers could be shortened by leaving out the first four digits. Had they arrived at the figure for my savings account in the same way, I would have suffered a tremendous loss.

"You must reply 'Here!' *Here* means you are in this cell, not escaped or dead. Listen, number 99!"

"Here!"

"That's it. What are you in for?"

To avoid their contempt and insults, I said audaciously, "Double agent. A spy of the American FBI as well as for Taiwan."

"Too common." He laughed. I saw the number on his chest was 809998. His laughter sounded like the cry of a baby duckling, quite pleasant. "Do you know what kind of man I am?"

"No, I don't."

"Do you know what kind of man he is?"

Number 98 pointed at number 97 – a shy young man with feminine brows and a pale face.

"No."

"Or what kind of figure is he?" Number 98 pointed at number 96 – a sleepy-looking man in his forties.

"No."

"Or what kind of fellow is he?" Number 98 pointed at number 95 – a boy of about fifteen, whose prison sleeves were too long and dangled like those of a classical Beijing Opera actor.

"No."

"See, there's peak beyond peak, heaven beyond heaven. Don't be so cocky. Number 97, although he looks like a delicate bookworm and blushes at coarse words, is a very famous man. He is the big counterrevolutionary who once held a nuclear device in his hands and attempted to blow up City H."

I burst out laughing. "Don't make me sick with your lies. How can one hold a nuclear device in his hand? How could he lift it up?"

"You don't believe me, do you?" Number 98 detected my surprise. "That's why he was brought in. Ask him yourself."

Number 97's face flushed. As he smacked his lips, two lovely dimples appeared on his cheeks. He said, "It's true."

"It's been more than five years now, hasn't it?" Number 98 asked.

"Five years, three months, and four days." Number 97 recalled the date exactly. He took a newspaper clipping from his underwear and pressed it into my hand. Unfolding it carefully, I saw the striking red headline:

A Great Victory for Mao Zedong Thought. City Cracks Giant Criminal Case. Counterrevolutionary Thug Feng Minzeng Attempts to Blow up City H with a Hand-Held Nuclear Device!

Two full pages vividly described how the young university student had contacted a Russian exchange student named Natasha, who had given him a nuclear device from the USSR by the fifth piling of the Ming River Bridge and had expected to blow up the city on National Day. On behalf of the Soviet government, Natasha gave him ten thousand rubles. For future communication, she left him a button-sized transmitter. Thanks to the luck that always follows our great leader Chairman Mao, the remote control of the device malfunctioned because of dampness, and the attempt failed. With the rise of the proletarian Cultural Revolution, the rebels exposed and arrested this dangerous enemy with the telescope and microscope of Mao Zedong thought. The nuclear device, which sank to the bottom of the river, is being retrieved, while the button transmitter was swallowed by the thug's mother. Although revolutionary medical workers dissected the mother's body, they failed to find it. In all likelihood it passed through her system, and revolutionary rebels in charge of the sewer system have expressed their determination to pursue the matter to the end.

"What do you think of that?" Number 98 asked me.

"Well, mine looks ordinary by comparison." My case had been decided simply by public criticism, and the two huge pages of a printed newspaper definitely carried more weight.

"Number 96 can't be slighted, either. Although his stay here is short, he is profoundly learned. He has published an important work during the Cultural Revolution. Maybe you've heard of it."

"What work?"

"*The Ouyang Dictionary of Self-Criticism.*"

"A true hero does not like to show off his past glorious deeds," said number 96. "Were it not for the shortage of paper, the circulation of my dictionary would have been comparable to that of *The Quotations of Chairman Mao.*"

"Yes, I read the publisher's advertisement somewhere in a rebel newspaper. If your dictionary helps propagate Mao Zedong thought, and you look like a man of foresight, how did you wind up in prison?"

"Don't flatter me. If I really had foresight, I wouldn't be here. My knowledge was insufficient and the power of foresight is precisely what I lack. I committed a mistake by including many of Lin Biao's words. I never dreamed that Mao Zedong's constitutional successor would fall so hard. Strangely enough, his fall implicated me as a trumpeter for the ambitious Lin Biao and a schemer for his restoration. Could I deny the crime? Could I refuse to confess? Because everything is printed in black and white, I willingly admitted all my crimes. My heart, my mouth, even my toes agree that I deserve punishment. China has a proverb: If a man does not have a long-term plan, he must be beset with immediate troubles. It's true."

And number 95 – what sort of figure was he? He turned his body to face the wall.

"He is a renegade."

"What? A renegade?" Although I was not normally rowdy, I found myself shouting.

"Yes. In 1938, he escaped from Yan'an to Xi'an. When he stopped at Wuhan he joined the KMT central spy network, thus betraying the revolution and selling party secrets."

"Is this some kind of joke?"

"It's no joke. I'm merely giving you his background."

"But he wasn't even born in 1938."

"You know that and I know that, but the men who sent him here don't know that – "

"Who are you talking about?"

"Zhang Guotao."

"Zhang Guotao. You mean *he* is Zhang Guotao?"

"Yes, no doubt about it. *Zhang* as in the combined characters *bow* and *long*, *guo* as in *fruit*, and *tao* as in the word for *waves*. Granted, the last two characters of his name are only homonyms with those of the historical Zhang Guotao."

"He should appeal. It can't be hard to explain such a simple thing, is it?"

"Who can he appeal to?"

"To the prison director."

"The director cares only about locking up prisoners, not about reviewing cases. None of us has had a trial – " I started laughing convulsively. I laughed and laughed until the guard roared and struck me with a leather whip. But as soon as he left I recommenced laughing, and this time sobbing as well, although I covered my mouth with my hands so that my laughter would not be heard. When I stopped laughing out of exhaustion, I heard number 95 sobbing. "How about you, number 98?"

"I'm a riddle."

"A riddle?"

"Yes, a riddle."

"How can a man be a riddle? What kind of riddle?"

"I don't know myself – I was an elementary school teacher who traveled to Beijing to make revolution. One day, following a crowd of my countrymen, I squeezed into the Jiangsu Room of the Great Hall of the People. It so happened that Kang Sheng, adviser to the central cultural revolutionary committee, was receiving rebel representatives from Shandong Province. I never dreamed I might see such a big shot in my life. You know, during the anti-Japanese war, Kang supervised work in Shandong – land reform I was told. He was a daring man of power and carried out a policy of annihilating the enemy. People said his maxim was *Where does the soul go if the body no longer exists?* I looked at him, smiling like an idiot and with tears of joy started clapping madly. I was obsessed with catching his attention, with letting him know how I had worshipped him all this time. Thank heavens, he noticed me, even though he was pretty far away. He pointed and asked in our Shandong dialect: 'Who is that man?' It was just like the poetic line: 'The native dialect remains, though the hair turns gray.' I was too thrilled to stammer out a sentence. 'I – I – ' The crowd opened up, and I squeezed my way through to him. As I stood watching him, his face dropped quite unexpectedly and he told his bodyguard, 'Have you ever seen him before?' The guard said no. Narrowing his eyes as if focusing a camera, Kang reminded me of his lovely nickname, the 'Chinese Dzherzinsky.' I once saw Dzherzinsky in a Soviet movie called *Cyclone of Hatred*. When his eyes fixed upon a reactionary, the reactionary could never run away. Why did Kang look at me like that? Just like Dzerzinsky – well, it might not be bad to have an X ray because I have no disease to fear. For reasons known only to God, Kang suddenly said, 'This man is a riddle. Arrest him.' Before I understood his words, I was gagged by the guard and bundled off to prison. This is the third prison I have stayed at. After all these years, maybe Kang has forgotten to guess the riddle. But I have been guessing.... The more I try, the more confused I become.... Why am I a riddle? How can I, a human being, be a riddle?"

As his words trailed off, he closed his eyes and sank into deep thought. I believed he was continuing his guesswork. I wished I could help him find the answer. Soon I came to see that, if an old Bolshevik like Kang could not solve the riddle, then I, an ordinary person, could not possibly do so. It was clear that the man was indeed a riddle, in the sense that every Chinese man is a riddle. The most solemn task facing the nation and the party is to guess this riddle. Of course, not everyone has the right to solve it; however, everyone has the right to join the guessing game to avoid having himself be written off as a riddle. Only a few conjurers have the power to create and declare answers to riddles. The connection between a riddle and its answer is top secret. Millions of people deprived of the right to solve riddles, together with those who keep the logical connection between riddles and their answers secret, are forever sitting on pins and needles. As the saying goes, "Misfortune befalls a man while he is sitting at home." Who knows when you may be written up as a riddle for wild conjecture? Even those few who have the right to create riddles and declare answers, and those who hold the secret link between a riddle and its answer, enjoy no peace of mind. Besides the very few at the top of the pagoda, all other players shiver in a state of wakeful puzzlement, for they know best the conspiracies hidden in the handkerchief of the master magician. I heard many legendary tales in prison. (Even thick prison walls cannot block the spread of tales. Perhaps that is the way ancient tales such as Yi Shot Down Nine Suns and Kuafu Chased the Sun have survived along with eternally suffering humanity. They possess not only infinite charm but also the power to transcend space and time.) Of course, although believable, they cannot be put on trial for truth. For instance, I once heard a tale about a member of the central cultural revolutionary committee and a member of a provincial revolutionary committee. I will record the dialogue as follows:

"Old W, don't worry. Even if the flood swallows 9,599,999 square kilometers, on the heights of the last kilometer you may sit fishing away."

"Old L, please don't talk like that. I feel just the opposite way, like someone who has been forced to sit on the edge of a well, waiting for a fateful push."

"You worry too much. How could that ever happen?"

"One morning you or I may go to jail in chains."

"Stop pulling my leg."

"Want to bet?"

"Yes, how much?"

"Well, a carton of Colorful Butterfly, the best cigarettes your province produces."

"And what's your stake if I win?"

"A carton of Great China."

Soon after, they were both sent to prison. L lost a carton of Colorful Butterfly to W, and L's follower sent it to W's prison in Qin City.

Take the case of Lin Biao and his die-hard followers like Huang, Wu, Ye, Li, and Qiu: In one moment they were climbing up to the ruling peak, a single step from absolute power, beneath one man but above many millions of people. Then they fell into the abyss, and to the Chinese people, it was like a dramatic nightmare.

The neighboring cell on our right also held five criminals. These five inmates all belonged to the same unit. Let's call them A, B, C, D, and E. A came to prison because B exposed him; B came because C informed on him; C came because of D; D came because of E; and while in prison A wrote heaps of information to implicate E. Because of their mutual hatred, A, B, C, and D quarreled fiercely and fought bloodily. But when E was thrown in they became reconciled. Instead of quarreling and fighting, the five of them sat in a circle, playing Passing the Flower to the Drumbeats. By turns one of them would beat his thigh like a drum. Then A, B, C, D, and E would pass the flower – a dirty handkerchief – as quickly as they could. At the stop of the drumbeat, the one holding the kerchief had to describe the most delicious food he had ever eaten, with gestures and noises to convey the color, flavor, and smell of the food. A was from Sichuan. He said the dish he loved most was twice-cooked pork. The thin, transparent slices of pork colored with red pepper, tender ginger, and green garlic are cooked together with thin slices of hard bean curd. The dish tastes peppery, spicy, boiling hot, and salty all at once. He mimed eating it with hissing noises, oil dripping from his mouth, tears welling up in his eyes, and snot running from his nose. His performance was so brilliant that his audience felt they truly had shared a complete Sichuan dish with him.

When it was D's turn, as a native of Guangdong, he performed the eating of baby mice. In the fields one catches a nest of pink baby mice that have not yet opened their eyes. They can do nothing but twist their tiny heads and huddle together, making cute little squeaks. To stress the eating ceremony, one must put the tender mice on a snow-white six-inch plate. If you snap a color picture of them, the white and pink will form the essence of an artistic work. Then one puts a small cinnabar cup on the table, pours it two-thirds full of excellent soy sauce (Guangdong natives call it Sheng-chou), and then adds a few drops of hand-ground sesame oil. To complete the ritual, one prepares a pair of ivory chopsticks. When the gourmet sits down at the table, his eyes fill with the pink flower pattern created by the darling babies before he even picks up his chopsticks. One must eat the dish with a style known as "three cries." If one fails to achieve the three cries, the mice are blamed as weaklings without enough vitality and liveliness. What are the three cries? The first occurs when the ivory chopsticks pinch a baby mouse, which lets out a crispy cry, *zhi!* The second occurs when one dips the mouse into the cup, and its tender skin is stung by the sharp soy sauce with a sizzle. The third occurs when one puts the seasoned mouse into his mouth and it gives his last cry of *zhi!* When the body of the mouse is rolled on the tongue, it becomes soft as a dumpling, and as it touches every corner of one's palate, all one's senses make the saliva ooze. Everything sinks to oblivion, and all one's nerves concentrate on the passage from mouth to esophagus to stomach. Particularly the stomach because the bowels, having moved ahead of time, can hardly wait for the well-chewed, bloody baby mouse. If I had heard such a thing before coming to prison, I would have puked. But my living in an era that tests a man's courage to eat human hearts, plus the hard conditions of prison, where I lived on seven ounces of coarse daily rations, made me willing to seduce the singing sparrow to come down, and I would have swallowed it, feathers and all, if I could have. Under such circumstances it is a pleasure to hear someone describe in a most civilized manner how to eat baby mice who have not seen the light of day. I greedily relished every detail told by anyone on the subject of cooking and eating. The man charged with the crime of attempting to bomb City H with a handheld nuclear device collected a great many recipes.

Through sleepless nights, he talked about how to cook and eat special dishes. In my childhood, although ghost stories kept me awake because I was afraid that a headless female ghost would sit on my face with her bare bottom, I loved to hear them. Similarly, in prison I loved to hear about food, even though I knew that each spiritual feast would excite my digestive system without a crumb of real food to satisfy it. I would suffer shivering limbs, cold sweats, and insomnia. It is well said that a man is a mill and that his hunger stops only when he sleeps. During the sleepless hours, hunger attacks you ten times more frantically, seizing every nerve and pinching every blood vessel. You thirst for something more than water, for some solid substance. You would swallow a stone if you could in order to fill your emptiness.

I was jealous of number 96, who had compiled *The Ouyang Dictionary of Self-Criticism,* for he told me in privacy that his wife smuggled in a large tube of White Jade toothpaste every other week. The tube actually contained condensed milk — as I found out through careful observation. Every day before bedtime, he would squeeze some condensed milk into his mouth under the pretext of brushing his teeth. Although it did not help his empty stomach, it was a comfort for his digestive and nervous systems. My sense of smell was particularly keen. Moreover, he and I shared a wooden block as a pillow. So when he fell asleep, his mouth would open to release all his hidden smells. Condensed milk in a toothpaste tube made me think of his capable wife; then thoughts of his wife led to thoughts of my Yunqian. What was Yunqian's relationship to me? It did not matter whether or not she belonged to me. The question was, Could she smuggle a tube of condensed milk to me through the mercy of the prison director? But before she tried this backdoor, she must first learn that I was in prison and where my prison was located. Pity, she had no knowledge of my present situation. Every night the smell of condensed milk from number 96 threatened my whole existence. It kindled flames of starvation, which burned night after night, until I wanted to commit suicide. One midnight, unable to put up with it anymore, I shook number 96 out of his sound sleep. "I am going to report you."

"Nonsense!" He woke up from a muddled dream. "What can you report me for?"

I whispered into his ear, "Condensed milk in the toothpaste tube."

"What?" He sat up speechless. I had hit a nerve. If I made a fuss over it, at least his secret lifeline would be cut off, for the warden would no longer allow any toothpaste to be brought to his cell. "What do you want, then? Half of it?"

"No. I don't want to take advantage of you."

"A citation of merit? If you want that, you're making a terrible mistake. Because the warden would hate you to the marrow. You know I got these tubes with his special permission. Even if I could no longer get them, you wouldn't benefit from my misfortune. Instead, he'd find a pretext to put another set of chains on you."

"I want only to know how your toothpaste is brought to the prison and why the warden gives you special permission."

He straightened his body into a more comfortable position and said proudly, "My wife is pretty, and the warden is willing to help – "

"So the cost of your toothpaste is very high."

"I don't know, I don't know – no matter how high the cost is, it's no concern of mine. She does it for me anyway."

I didn't pursue the question any further. With a sigh I let my head sink back onto our shared wooden pillow. Instantly a concrete image of Yunqian rose before me. I wanted her passionately. She overwhelmed my physical hunger. In my mind our cocoon became dearer than a house of gold. I regretted that I had not enjoyed it fully and had never tidied it up: my lethargic attitude toward life. I had always thought our stay together to be mere coincidence, not something for life. I had listened to Tchaikovsky's Sixth Symphony numerous times. Although each listening had thrilled and intoxicated me, many of the notes had escaped me, making it impossible for me to string those themes together in my memory. And although Yunqian and I had spoken often, we had never touched on anything profound. I hadn't even asked her whether our intercourse was love. If it weren't love, what was it? To tell the truth, when I lost her I missed her body most. I had indulged myself with her body, even making experiments according to *The Art of Healthy Sex*. Most of our experiments were not very successful because the written techniques were not universally applicable. Making love is like painting. Technique alone cannot produce a masterpiece. The masterpiece needs to be completed by the soul, even if it is only a splash of ink and some simple color. Apart from longing for her body, I also longed for the spirit of her body that stimulated my desire. That is a female's most essential spirit. Those smooth, warm arms of hers, like two melodies merging together, gently circled my head. My face lay at the bottom of the valley between two soft mounds. I breathed to the rhythm of her heart. Because of her soul's longing, her body yielded to me, a gift of gratitude. No wonder the Chinese classical novels regard man's joy and woman's love as forms of gratitude. Beneath her right breast there was a black mole — the only idea of her body I retained. Otherwise, she gave me only abstract memories. Even those abstract memories were mere illusions exaggerated by my sexual impulses, without clear outline, shade, or color. Many times I made up my mind to see, draw, and memorize her body so that I could behold her as a whole in her absence. But each time my effort was sabotaged by my uncontrollable sexual drive. When my desire ebbed, my vision vanished. How stupid I was. Just like the monkey king eating the peaches of immortality and Pigsy chewing ginseng, I remained a primitive man. Would I have another opportunity to be close enough to her to admire her generous love in the way I admire Rodin's sculpture? Could I still, half drunk and half sober, explore every inch of her body with kisses: every line, the smooth curves of her waist, and the dark valley hidden from sight?

I couldn't understand how number 96 could tolerate such an exchange – using his beautiful wife's body to bribe the warden simply for a supply of condensed milk in toothpaste tubes. I would let myself be gnawed to death by hunger night after night before accepting such a deal.

Believing I was intimidated and no longer dared to report him, he went back to sleep. Suddenly I found his appearance despicable as he exhaled the smell of condensed milk from his gaping mouth. In my mind's eye, his swollen face transformed itself now and then into a hog's face with its black bristles burned off. Although I had never seen his wife, I drew a sketch of her in my imagination. She was very beautiful and pleasantly plump. Wearing an awkward smile and biting her quivering lips, she shut her eyes, tilted her head, and used her hands to push away the warden's hairy chest in helpless resistance. Disguising her pain and disgust, she put up with him, like leaping over a chasm, hoping this would be the last time. It would be over, it would be over soon.

I would refuse to pay the price number 96 had sacrificed and not only for condensed milk. If it were for doughnuts, roast chicken, seasoned cakes, rice, braised pork, cooked pig feet, boiled dumplings, or pies filled with crabmeat, even if it were for freedom or for Yunqian herself, I would still refuse.

I gaze at her window. In the past, it was pasted over with black paper; now a cloth curtain with tiny blue flowers hangs there.

15

After becoming *axiao,* Sunamei and Ying-
zhi, like a pair of bamboo shoots after a warm spring rain,
pierced through their husks one morning, high above all the
other bamboo around them. They swayed in the rosy morning sun; every leaf glistened with pearly dew. They suited
each other so well that no other men dared to court Sunamei, and Ami Cai'er woke up more than once from her
dreams with happy laughter.

Yingzhi had grown up in the same *siri* as Sunamei. He
was not rich. Unlike Longbu, who came each time on a
giant horse carrying a large sack of food, Yingzhi, having no
horse, could come only on foot with a few gifts. But Yingzhi
could bring Sunamei a happiness that differed from the
mature passion of Longbu. They were two flames of youth
come together, circling and teasing and burning stronger
and stronger. They were full-fledged white cranes on the
lake in May, feeling fresh and excited over every flight and
landing. They were a melody gliding past groves of reeds as
the water surface, shattered by playful indulgence, gradually
grew calm, and the silvery moon, replacing the golden sun,
shed its light on their bodies. The stillness of nature at this
moment was their sweet, long solitude. Ami Cai'er trea-
sured those moments of solitude most. As she grew older,
she felt more keenly that the space of a woman's heart is not
so big after all. It accepts only a few men, or rather, one
man. All other men are merely shadows, and some are

merely mildew left on the memory, recalling an unpleasant experience.

Sunamei's eyes brightened, her waist and thighs grew supple, her breasts arched, her laughter grew clear, and her songs sonorous. Many women gossiped about her out of jealousy. But their reverence for Goddess Ganmu made them accept their own fate. They knew it was Ganmu's favor that had created another Zhima. No, she was even more attractive than Zhima. Neither men nor women could resist her smile. While dancing, whenever she stood in the middle, the team surrounding her would change its rhythm and pattern according to her example or at her subtle suggestion. She had such self-confidence. Every movement of her hand and her foot was precise, graceful, and charming. What surprised people most was her singing. Previously, hardly anyone knew she could sing; like her personality, her song had been obscure. Now, not only did her voice make the girls of Youjiwa Village silent like cicadas in the cold, but her capacity for improvising amazed all the villagers. When they heard her singing, they intoned the name of the goddess. Oh, Goddess, because you bless her with beauty, why did you also give her all the wisdom? Goddess, being an omniscient overmother, declined to answer such silly questions raised by people on earth. And especially when Sunamei stripped off her clothes and plunged into the open spring to bathe, whoever saw her would utter a cry of amazement: Ami! you must have come from heaven, Sunamei.

Luo Ren, deputy head of the county cultural bureau, was visiting Youjiwa Village. He stayed with Team Leader Sula for several days. It was rare for a cadre to stay in a small Mosuo village, and, because he came not from the local county but from County H, the news quickly spread from door to door. The whole community was trying to guess the purpose of his visit. Luo Ren was a short, bespectacled, thirty-year-old man of the Han nationality. He could speak the language of the Li nationality, which the Mosuo also spoke. He was bold enough to eat Mosuo preserved pork as well as Li boiled tripe. He was not only skilled in the dances of the Li, Mosuo, and Tibetan nationalities, but could also play the flute, stringed instruments, the accordion, and a type of mouth organ called *kouxuan*. Because he knew how to weave the half-singing and half-wailing language of love through the quivering of a bamboo reed, by playing the *kouxuan* he could make the Li girls blush and hide themselves in the woods. He could also join in the singing dialogues with Mosuo women in the Li language, boldly using even their most erotic terms. However, no one had ever heard of his having an *axiao,* not even for one night of romance. Luo Ren never dared to try, because his *axiao* would tell every woman she saw all about it the following morning. As a Han, a cadre, and a party member, he would be disciplined for the slightest misbehavior. At the very least he could be expelled from the party or even sent to a farm for labor reform, thus losing the freedom of a cultured man in a small town. It was said that once a twenty-year-old Mosuo girl had earnestly invited him to spend a night in her *huagu.* She assured him over and over, "I know you are a cadre and a Han man, and that the party forbids your visiting *huagu.* But if you come, I will tell no one, not even my *ami.* If you are afraid, you may come in the small hours and I'll come out to meet you. I can bring you a set of my *awu*'s clothes so no one will recognize you. No one will see you.... If you don't want to do it in my *huagu,* we can get a horse and ride to Mount Hawa. Near the summer pasture on the mountain is a row of empty wooden cabins. If we bring a box of matches, we can make a warm fire. There, no one will see or hear us. I will make you happy, let you touch my body at your will. I know how to make a man happy. If you don't believe me, try now. Touch me while I shut my eyes. Please come to my *huagu* or climb Mount Hawa with me. I have a horse and will bring wine, cookies, dried beef...."

But when she opened her eyes, Luo Ren had long disappeared. From then on, Mosuo women gossiped about Luo Ren's lacking a penis. One woman was said to have groped in his crotch when he was off guard. However, such tales were denied by team Leader Sula, who said that the commune secretary had once passed through City H on his way to the provincial capital for a conference. Because he was Luo's old friend, he had shared a meal in his house and had seen his wife and children. The children were not convincing because the Mosuo never cared about which man's seeds led to their birth. But seeing his wife was powerful evidence. If he really lacked that thing, how could she stay with him? But Luo Ren remained an ambiguous man in their minds. They even discussed ways of seducing him into taking a bath in the spring so everyone could have a clear answer.

What had Luo Ren come here for this time? People were curious, although they knew he was not involved in imposing marriages or castrating women, but that he engaged in delightful things like singing and dancing. He had visited the village a few years before, collecting ancient tales from Daba and other elders. He had filled a dozen notebooks. Later he stopped his research in this area, for anything ancient belonged to the category of the Four Olds. Those notebooks had caused him to endure more than thirty criticism meetings, and all his hair had been yanked out. This time when he came to Youjiwa Village, he wore an old army cap, never daring to take it off. Several girls schemed to snatch it away to expose his bald head, which must have resembled a piece of grassland grazed by sheep after a frost. But those girls knew that Luo Ren was a smart man who only appeared dull. It was nearly impossible to seduce him to take off his pants, and it would be no easy matter to remove his cap. In fact, one audacious girl, instead of taking off his cap, wound up with her own skirt pulled down in public. Their tactics did not seem to be working.

Luo Ren seemed to have no special mission this time. During the day he helped the women with the weeding, and in the evening he joined the dances in the clearing. He loved to play his flute vigorously with the team dancing behind him or pluck strings and sing with the girls. But when the crowds cheered for Sunamei to sing, he lifted his eyes and fixed his gaze on her passionate lips. Sunamei's lips were a bit thick, like two full-grown orange segments. Yet they contained not juice but coursing blood that gave them the transparent red of pomegranate seeds. Today she looked exceptionally happy. During the dance she followed Luo Ren and changed her dancing styles and patterns like a kaleidoscope. Some were purely her own invention. The dozens of young men and women in the dance were extremely excited. As their sweat cooled them down, their singing rose. Sunamei sang an improvised song to a traditional tune, expressing the hot spring of happiness in her soul. Yet her happiness was tinged with a trailing sorrow. She sang,

> White clouds bend down to the river
> Embracing the flowers along the bank
> Before white clouds turn to rain
> Flower petals wither away
> Carrying tears of white clouds
> > They sink gradually in the stream.

Before she could finish the lingering trill, Luo Ren's string broke. He gazed at Sunamei as if in a trance. He found it incomprehensible that Sunamei's soul could produce such a tragic effect at the extreme of her happiness. She was a flower in full bloom. In spite of the beauty of her voice, what made her a talented singer were her exceptional sensitivity to art and her soul. It was rare to see such a genius born in such a remote place, among such a primitive people.

"Sunamei," Luo Ren said. "I'm going to call on Dabu

Cai'er of your family. Shall we go together?" "Yes." Throwing on her *cha'erwa,* she kindled a torch from her friend's hand and led Luo Ren away by the hand. All the young men and women dispersed with their torches, like lava flowing through a hilly woods viewed at a distance.

Luo Ren stumbled behind Sunamei, so she stopped now and then to wait for him. She led him over ditches and ridges. She was so familiar with these paths that she could find her way home with her eyes shut. Entering the gate, they found Dabu Cai'er searching for missing hens. Those lazy bones, blind at night, must have been sleeping at the foot of the wall. She picked them up by their wings, and they screamed their surprise. Dropping them into the chicken coop, Dabu Cai'er asked out of habit, "Mo, is that Yingzhi?"

Sunamei giggled. "Someone passed away in Yingzhi's village. He has to help wash the horse for the funeral."

"Who is it, then?"

"He is an *axiao* I found for you." Excitement made Sunamei forget hierarchy.

"Dabu Cai'er!" Luo Ren hurried to the side of Cai'er. "It's me, Luo Ren. I've come to see you."

Cai'er slapped Sunamei's back. "Comrade Luo Ren, please come to our *yimei* and have some wine."

"Have the children and elders gone to bed?"

"Yes. It's late."

"Ami, why not go to my *huagu,*" suggested Sunamei. "I have some wine."

"Good idea." Cai'er let Sunamei go ahead to make a fire. Then she took Luo Ren in and sat in front of the fireplace. Sunamei poured two bowls of wine for them. Cai'er said, "You've been away from Youjiwa Village a long, long time. We miss you badly. How are your wife and children?"

"Fine, thank you."

"Is the Cultural Revolution still going on outside?"

"No end in sight."

"Still terrifying?"

"Not any more. Like a sky covered with brooding clouds, it can neither thunder nor clear up; it is just stifling."

"How could Chairman Mao think up such a fantastic idea? What is he thinking now? Does his wife still rule at court?"

Luo Ren suppressed his laughter. Unable to answer, he remained silent. Cai'er, however, had no interest in getting an answer. "We Mosuo don't like fighting. The stone cannot be kindled. Though it can be split in a fire, it seems they do not intend to burn it any more...."

Sipping a little wine, Luo Ren changed the subject. "Sunamei, the singing and dancing troupe of our county has been reestablished."

"The singing and dancing troupe? What is that?"

Sunamei was still too young to have been to Yongning Dam and Yongning Street. How could she know anything about a singing and dancing troupe? Ami Cai'er explained, "It is a group of people who make their living by singing and dancing."

Sunamei giggled, betraying disbelief and amazement. But she had to believe it because it was from Ami's mouth. "Are there really people who make a living from singing and dancing?"

"Yes, quite a few. The provinces and Beijing have even more of them." Luo Ren looked at her face burned red by curiosity and the fire.

"Those people must lead a merry life."

"With a lot of hardships."

"Do they work in the fields?"

"No."

"Then, where do the hardships come in?"

"They have to undergo hard training."

"Training? Training for what?"

"The skills of legs, waist, and voice – "

Sunamei giggled again. She could hardly imagine how

such training could tire a person. "Because they practice every day, I guess they are all good singers or dancers."

"Not really. Singing and dancing require talent. A wooden club cannot learn to dance and sing even in a thousand years."

Sunamei laughed. Pulling a stick from the fireplace and holding it high, she amused herself by imagining the way a club would dance. When the teapot screamed, she poured tea for Ami and Luo Ren. "Brother Luo, do you think I have talent?"

Luo Ren took a look at Sunamei, her eyes radiating with self-confidence and pride. He said slowly. "I can't tell – " He shut his eyes as he drank his tea.

With a cunning wink, Sunamei fixed her eyes on Luo Ren's face and challenged him. "Brother Luo, I don't think you are telling the truth."

Meanwhile she held his hand and scratched his palm with her fingertip. Luo Ren was so startled that he spluttered out a mouthful of hot tea into the ashes. Dabu pinched Sunamei's thigh. With an exaggerated cry, Sunamei fell into Ami's arms. "Ami, you are so mean. Look, my thigh is turning purple." Holding up her skirt, Sunamei bared her slender, white leg up to the thigh.

Luo Ren thought admiringly, "The body and limbs of a Mosuo woman are indeed given and nurtured by the goddess. It is said that children born to two mutually loving souls must be beautiful. It's the truth, isn't it? Their sexual congress, devoid of social and psychological burdens, is like two springs from the woods merging together."

Sunamei feigned a cry: "Ami does not want me any more. All right, I'm going to the city. Brother Luo Ren, please let me join the singing and dancing troupe so I can earn my living by song and dance. How cruel my *ami*'s heart is! Am I not the flesh of your flesh? Am I not a root of our *yishe?* Brother Luo, please take me away. Please take me away!"

Ignoring her complaint, Ami smiled, stretching her hand

to feel her bare thigh. Sunamei jumped up, held Ami by the neck and gave her cheek a playful bite.

"Mo, Sunamei!" Ami embraced her and asked affectionately, "Do you still want to go?"

"No. I'll never leave you."

"But Ami will die one day."

"No. Ami will never die. Ami can't die."

"Death, life, birth, these are not things one can allow or forbid. Sunamei – " Ami was shedding tears over a nameless sorrow. "Dabu's key must be left to you – "

"Ami!" Sunamei held Ami desperately, as if she were dying.

Leaning against the wall, Luo Ren looked tired. His eyes, hidden behind half-closed lids, were fixed on mother and daughter as they gradually calmed down.

"Luo Ren." Ami addressed him. "You came to Youjiwa Village to take my Sunamei away, didn't you?" Her voice, although quavering, carried a dignity that forbade him to lie or avoid answering.

He replied honestly, "Yes."

Sunamei raised her head from Ami's lap and looked at Luo Ren with wide-open eyes and closed lips. He straightened up and said somberly to Ami, with his eyes on Sunamei, "Sunamei has a rare talent. Like a flower growing along a stream deep in a dense mountain forest, even she, like the trees, stones, and flowing stream, is unaware of her beauty and importance. It would be a great pity for her to bloom and wither there. Ami Cai'er, Sunamei will become a star. The whole county will know her name and thousands of people will spend money to watch her sing and dance. She will bring honor to you, to Youjiwa Village, even to Xienami and to the entire Mosuo people."

Sunamei's eyes lit up. Looking at Ami, she saw her eyes grow dim and sad. She could not understand why Ami was not as excited as she. For the first time, she had learned that people will spend money to watch others sing and dance.

And for the first time, she had realized that her dancing and singing could be exchanged for money. She would not only hear praises from her kinsmen and neighbors but also win thousands of admiring glances from an unknown audience. She thought, "How wonderful that would be! From the ancient times to today, has there been a Mosuo woman luckier than me? How many talented Mosuo women have bloomed and withered like a flower by the stream in a deep mountain woods. I will break into the outside world with my singing. I will stride into the outside world with my dancing. I was told by Longbu, a caravan man, that the outside world is endless. It has thousands, millions of interesting people – but why does Ami look worried?"

Ami watched Sunamei's face glow with confidence, hope and eagerness. She became even sadder. Luo Ren said, "Ami Cai'er, today things are different from in the past. The highway is complete, and a day will be enough for you to visit our county. If Sunamei follows me to join the singing and dancing troupe, when you miss her, you can go to her. When she wants to see you, buses are always available. What are you worrying about?"

Shaking her head, Ami Cai'er said softly, "The outside world is entirely different from ours. I am afraid my *mo* will not be able to adapt to it."

Sunamei let out another giggle. "I am accustomed to all sorts of living conditions. Ami, you forget that, when you wanted me to look after pigs, I looked after pigs, and, when you wanted me to herd cattle, I herded cattle. When I was ten, you sent me with a Tibetan family to drive the cattle to pasture high in the mountains: I went, didn't I? I slept in their tent and drank their strong buttered tea. I got used to their ways of living in no time, didn't I? I also learned to sing their songs – "

"You were still a child then. Now you are grown."

"What's the difference? If someone tries to bully me, I will simply run home. Whether by bus, or on horseback, or neither, no matter how long the road is, it cannot scare Sunamei."

"Quite true," agreed Luo Ren. "Sunamei learns fast and will adapt to any surroundings in time. And I will take care of her."

Ami, her eyes shut, seemed not to hear any more. Sunamei told Luo Ren, "Leave Ami to me. I can persuade her. I have made up my mind to go. You know I am good at singing and dancing. You must take me with you. Thank you for your kindness, Brother Luo." The world before her eyes had suddenly broadened.

Finishing his wine, Luo Ren said, "Ami Cai'er, thank you for the wine and tea. I must be leaving now."

With some surprise, Ami Cai'er said tentatively, "I thought you were going to stay in Sunamei's *huagu?*"

Luo Ren laughed. "Sunamei does not like me."

Jumping up, Sunamei challenged him. "If Sunamei likes you, what will you do?"

"I will stay."

"Okay, please stay." Beating the dust off his clothes, Luo Ren turned to leave. Sunamei grabbed him from behind and gave his back a big squeeze before letting him go. Looking up at the *huagu* from downstairs, Luo Ren saw Ami Cai'er staring at the flames in the fireplace in bewilderment; Sunamei, twisting her hips and swaying her skirt, was already starting her performance.

16

I gaze at her window. In the past, it was pasted over with black paper; now a cloth curtain with tiny blue flowers hangs there.

We political criminals were now allowed to step out of our cells and participate in collective labor in a large courtyard encircled by high walls. Blockhouses with embrasures stood on the southeastern and northeastern corners. The guards thrust the barrels of their machine guns through those embrasures so that even prisoners with the poorest eyesight could see them. From beyond the wall we could hear sounds of the human world: cars honking, children crying, women quarreling, police sirens screaming. We could also hear flocks of pigeons whistling across the sky. When I first stepped into the blue sky, I nearly fainted. The waves of city din that had bored me in the past were now beautiful melodies.

Our job was breaking stones, delivered during the night, into thumbnail-sized gravel. We were told that the job was to implement Chairman Mao's supreme directive, "Dig the tunnels deep." It was magnanimous of them to assign such a glorious task to us wretched criminals so as to give us a chance to do penance. The prisoners of each cell sat in a circle on the ground, each with a fist-sized hammer on a bamboo handle. The hammer was pretty springy and one careless knock could smash one's fingers. So we pleaded with the warden to return our leather belts during the day so we could use them to hold the stone and avoid smashing our fingers. We promised to return the belts when the day's work was done so they did not have to worry about suicides or stranglings. Our request was accepted. From then on, our hammering din became part of the prison scene. Our inmates, taking advantage of the loud noise, boldly enjoyed their fireside talks. I had not expected this sweaty job to give us so much freedom.

Our circle's conversation was excited by a six-year-old girl. As soon as we entered the vastness of the yard, we surveyed our new world. The northwestern corner was inhabited by female prisoners. Although both male and female prisoners were placed within range of the machine guns, male prisoners darted their glances at the females, and the females cast theirs at the males, as though playing a courting game.

Number 96, although he wore a sleepy face all day long, became invigorated the moment he entered the yard, revealing the true man who had compiled *The Ouyang Dictionary of Self-Criticism*. Locating his seat in the southeast but facing northeast, he selected the best vantage point, and thus established his superior position. It was he who first discovered that there was a six-year-old girl among the female prisoners, smashing stones with a small hammer. We hotly debated the girl's status – was she the convict, or was it the young mother by her side? At first we all agreed: we took it for granted that the mother had been arrested. Because no one would take care of the child, she had brought her along to the prison. This reasoning seemed natural, for there were historical precedents. But our conclusions were soon negated by number 96. As he was able to see from his vantage point, the little girl had a prison number on her chest; her mother did not. Nor did her mother wear prison clothes. Out of her love of cleanliness, she had merely hung a prison gown over her blue-dotted white blouse. And she was wearing leather shoes. All these were clues that she was not a prisoner.

When number 95 – the fifteen-year-old Zhang Guotao – heard that a six-year-old convict was incarcerated in his prison, he scoffed and laughed. But no sooner had he started arguing than he realized how dangerous it was for a prisoner to laugh in broad daylight. If caught, he would get a good beating. He suppressed his laughter and even shed a few tears. We now had a satisfactory answer about the little girl's status. But the question of what crime she had committed was equally puzzling. What was the answer? We were anxious to find out. Like students sitting for a university entrance examination, although our hands were hammering stones, our minds were being gnawed by mice.

Our number 98 – the riddle Kang Sheng had failed to solve – suddenly said, "Listen, they are talking about this behind us."

Number 98's ears were truly sharp. We immediately pricked up our ears like rabbits. Behind number 98's back sat A, B, C, D, and E – the five inmates of cell number 10046 – and E was saying something expansively. It was hard to measure the power of our senses. However, almost magically, our erect ears, like radar, caught the acoustic signals amid loud hammering, soft gossiping, and the musical din of the human world. And, as if our ears were equipped with Dolby, all unwanted noises were filtered out.

E was saying, "I discovered the truth at last. I pieced together the tips I gathered from my right and left sides, ridding them of falsity to seek the truth...."

D cut in with a strained voice: "If you had learned how to get rid of falsity to seek the truth earlier, I wouldn't be in prison."

E struck back: "Do you want to hear it or not? D, what a damned fool you are! Okay, I'll shut up and let you tell the tale."

A, B, and C said in chorus, "Go on, go on. Don't take it personally."

E insisted, "Okay, I'll go on, provided nobody interrupts me again."

"Don't be so fussy."

"This little girl called Lingzi is six years and forty-five days old...."

"Show off!" D cut in again.

"No, I just want to be accurate. On the night of her sixth birthday, her grandma was boiling an egg for her in the kitchen. The little darling had to play all by herself in the room, practicing the paper folding Grandma had taught her. As Grandma dropped the boiled egg into cold water for easy shelling, she heard a terrible smashing sound and thought that little Lingzi had broken their only thermos: 'Good lord, there's a thermos shortage in the market nowadays. What will I do?' When she came in to have a look, she reeled in horror: Little Lingzi had created a terrible disaster. She wished Lingzi *had* smashed their thermos. But the sound was of Chairman Mao's sacred plaster statue shattering into bits. Holding a folded paper boat, Lingzi stood blaming Mao, as if he had made the trouble: 'Look at you! Just look at what a mess you've made!' It took a while before Grandma, who had collapsed, came to and realized how critical the situation was. She picked herself up and bolted the door and then staggered around to find a sheet of red paper with which to gather the debris carefully, all the while begging forgiveness. After putting the wrapped debris under the bed, she held little Lingzi in her arms and whispered, 'Lingzi, why didn't you break anything else but *him?*' Lingzi said with dignity, 'I wasn't trying to break anything. I was trying to put this cap on Grandpa Mao. I was afraid he might catch cold.' Panic-stricken Grandma tried to cover Lingzi's mouth, but in her haste she covered her eyes instead, and the little girl's voice grew even louder. Aware of her mistake, she moved her hand down. 'Lingzi, Don't talk like that! If people hear you, they'll never let you get away with it. You know your father is doing labor reform in Xinjiang, your mother is in a cadre school, and your grandma's class status is bad.' Pulling Grandma's bony hand from her mouth, Lingzi asked secretively, 'What's class status?' Grandma sighed. 'Don't ask. Listen, never tell anybody about the statue.' Lingzi obviously understood the gravity of the situation and she nodded her little head. 'Grandma, I won't. But what about Grandpa Mao?' Grandma said, 'None of your business. I can – Grandma will ask Chairman Mao's forgiveness for you. I can – '

"She racked her brains for suitable words to explain what she could do. While she was muttering, she helped Lingzi get undressed and tucked the shivering child under the quilt. Sitting by the bed, she chanted her plea for forgiveness while patting the child to sleep. As soon as Lingzi fell asleep, Grandma started maneuvering. She took the plaster debris from under the bed and put it in a grocery basket. She caught herself as she was about to leave, realizing her stupidity. At this time of the day, going out with a grocery basket definitely would invite suspicion. Bad idea. She put down the basket and placed the plaster debris into a dustbin. No sooner had she dropped it in than she realized her sacrilege. How could she throw the great leader's sacred statue into a dustbin? When it was discovered, she would be either butchered or shot. Old Grandma was caught in a dilemma. She wanted to cry, but this was no time to cry. She wanted to curse her daughter who was away in a cadre school. But she had enough hardships for one person. Besides, she did not know what was happening here. How could she be held to blame? If Grandma blamed her daughter for having had Lingzi, her daughter could turn around and blame Grandma for having had her.

"In the end, she had no choice but to wrap a few clothes in a sheet, hide the debris inside, and go out, where she ran into her neighbor, Second Aunt Zhang. Her heart jumped to her throat, and she wanted to go back inside, but it was too late. 'Lingzi's Grandma, what are you doing out at night?' 'You see, early tomorrow a colleague of Lingzi's mother is going back to the cadre school. I want him to take a few clothes for her. Even though it's late, I think I'd better make the trip.' 'Has Lingzi gone to sleep yet?' 'Yes.' Feigning neighborliness, Second Aunt Zhang squeezed the wrapped clothes, almost scaring Grandma's soul away. But with a great effort, she steadied herself and moved on. Like a lost soul, Grandma roamed the streets. Although she passed quite a few trash cans, she didn't have the heart to throw the debris into any of them. Pity there was no river in town — she could let the pure water carry the debris away. In the small hours of the morning there wasn't a soul in the street. Occasionally a dog darted out of a trash can and scared Grandma into crying for the goddess of mercy. Calling on the goddess three times, she realized she had committed another crime, slapped her own face, and then recited Chairman Mao's quotation: 'Be resolute. Fear not death and overcome all difficulties to seize victory.' The more you fear the devil, the more likely the devil will catch you. Like a devil digging a well, Grandma found herself in front of her own house after a whole night's wandering. If she did not go in, the day would break, and, if Second Aunt Zhang questioned her whereabouts during the night, she would never be able to explain herself clearly. The first trash can she had seen when she stepped out of the house stood right before her. If she did not throw the debris in now, it would be too late. So she nervously dusted the plaster debris from the folded clothes into the trash tank. Looking around, she saw that no one was watching, so she dashed away as if she had thrown a bomb. There was no one at her door. Inside she found Lingzi still asleep. Thank heavens, she had gotten rid of it at last! 'Sinful, sinful. No. I mustn't say that.' How should she describe her deed? She could not find a fitting expression. She went to bed in her day clothes, murmuring, 'Chairman

Mao, Chairman Mao, tomorrow I'll buy another sacred statue of yours. No, I shouldn't use the vulgar term *buy,* but the respectful term *invite.* I shall invite another sacred statue and restore you to the altar.' She gradually calmed herself down and closed her eyes.

"When she opened her eyes again, she found the sun already high in the sky. She hurried up and got Lingzi dressed, washed, and combed. The radio was cheerfully blasting the song, 'Beijing Has a Golden Sun.' She then went out to stand in line after line for milk and vegetables. She had to wait in three different lines to get cabbage, bean curd, and chicken claws. She could buy only the claws of chickens, not their meat, nor even their necks. Where were all the chicken legs and bodies? It was hard to understand why people in the countryside raised only chicken claws without chickens. It seemed odd. Some people said the chicken breasts were in tins. But where could one buy those tins? They were not sold domestically but were transported to foreign countries in Asia, Africa, and Latin America. Oh, I see, the chicken breasts have gone abroad to carry out a diplomatic mission. They were sacrificed for world revolution. How about chicken legs? They have entered special supply depots. Why are they called *depots* of special supplies? Because they have only a limited quantity of special goods, which are sold only to customers of the proletarian headquarters. How many people can be regarded as customers of the proletarian headquarters? Only a few — a few in the capital, a few in the provinces, a few in the prefectures, and a few in the counties. Because chicken legs are only for the few, why so many chicken claws? Aren't those claws chopped from the chicken legs? Is it possible that one chicken grows ten pairs of claws on a single leg?"

While E was expounding this puzzle in high spirits, A cast a tiny stone right into his mouth. "Why are you digressing? Show-off!"

"Ptui — " Spitting out the stone, E said, "All right. No

more digressions. Let us get to the tale: When Grandma returned with her shopping basket, it was already half past nine. After preparing milk and a few cookies for Lingzi's breakfast, she heated some leftover rice for herself. Lingzi ate slowly, listening to some Beijing opera on the radio: 'Across the sea of clouds and through the snow-covered fields....' Because *across* and *wear* share the same Chinese character, and *the sea of clouds* sounds in Chinese like *yunhai,* Lingzi was puzzled. She asked Grandma: 'What does *wear the sea of clouds* mean?' Having heard the song countless times and without trying to understand its meaning, Grandma said, 'Because the word *chuan* [wear] is used, *yunhai* [the sea of clouds], if not a blouse, must be a sort of trousers. If it were a hat, the word *dai* would be used.' With half a cookie in her mouth, Lingzi thought hard, but with no result. About to ask again, she was stopped by an irritated Grandma. Putting down her chopsticks, Grandma lectured her with a serious face: 'Lingzi, do you know any other children as slow as you? If it takes an hour to finish your breakfast, when can our family find time to be revolutionized? The neighborhood committee is going to ask me to attend their daily study of Chairman Mao's works pretty soon.' Actually, Grandma was saying all this in order to disguise her ignorance. She was afraid that Lingzi might ask her, 'Because one can wear *yunhai,* is it corduroy or Dacron?' A question like that would strike her speechless. Believing her slow eating would affect the revolution, Lingzi inserted the last half cookie into her mouth, and flapped her hands to signal she had finished. Grandma praised the child and gathered up the dishes to wash. After doing the dishes, she sighed with relief and took off her apron. Just then, someone knocked at the door. She knew it must be Chairwoman Qiu from the neighborhood committee. (She had previously been called Aunt Qiu, but since the Cultural Revolution began, everyone had to address her by her official title.) Fumbling for a little stool, Grandma responded quickly,

'I'm coming, Chairwoman. I'm sorry I make you come for me every morning. I should study Chairman Mao's works more actively. I'm a bit late because of my housework. You see, it takes almost an hour to feed little Lingzi. I'll do some self-criticism. I'll criticize myself in a deep, thorough way.' The moment she grabbed the little stool in her hand, she heard, 'Ma, please open the door.' 'Oh, it's Lingzi's mother. Why did they let you come home before the end of the month? Lingzi, quick! Your mother is home!'

"When she opened the door, her daughter came in, followed by quite a few serious-looking people. Although there was a big crowd, nobody dared draw a loud breath. Lingzi's mother took Lingzi into her arms and the child asked, 'Mama, who are they? Are they all my uncles?' 'Nonsense.' Lingzi retorted, 'It's not nonsense. Doesn't Tiemei say on the stage that our family has numerous uncles but none come until something important is up?' Her legs turning rubbery, Grandma asked her daughter timidly, 'What has brought all these comrades come to our house?' Lingzi's mother replied, 'I don't really know. They brought me back in a car early this morning.'

"Grandma recognized a few among those rare visitors: Second Aunt Zhang, Chairwoman Qiu, and Comrade Liu – a policeman in charge of household registration – and Comrade Wang from the Security Department of her daughter's farm. She saw Second Aunt steal around the house on tiptoe, sweeping every corner with her sharp eyes in the manner of Aunt Hong in the revolutionary ballet opera of that title. A sharp-chinned young man, prematurely wrinkled, with thin hair and invisible eyebrows, looked far from the image of a hero in the model operas, but his words overpowered his enemy all the same. His slitlike eyes never opened wide but remained cast down all the time, fixing on your toes to keep you from escaping. He gave a slight cough. In the dead silence of the house, his cough declared the importance of his presence. He knew perfectly the power of his pause – the silence of the moment speaks louder than words. After the pause, he said, 'Comrades of the proletarian revolutionary factions.' This address revealed the gravity of the situation. In China, the manner of addressing your audience is extremely important. Whether or not one is willing to call you a comrade is indicative of your status as one of the people. If you are addressed as 'mister,' you are put in the category of the bourgeoisie or bourgeois intellectuals. If the speaker addresses the whole audience as 'revolutionary comrades' or simply 'comrades,' the atmosphere will be relaxed. The rank of comrades of the proletarian revolutionary factions is more restrictive, excluding people like Lingzi's mother and grandmother.

"The authority of the proletarian revolutionary factions continued, 'Supreme directive: "The reactionaries will not perish of themselves." In the name of the combined revolutionary committee of police, public prosecutor, and court, I announce – ' The combined committee of police, public prosecutor, and court seemed to suit China best, because, even in the past when each had been a separate institution, they had acted uniformly under one man's direction. Sorry, I'm footnoting again. The authority went on to say, 'Today we cracked a big case, a serious case. Are there any cases bigger than this one? More serious than this one?' Poor Grandma's face turned ghastly pale. 'Our party's policy remains: "Leniency to those who confess and severe punishment to those who resist." Now, Comrade Zhang, the security chief of the neighborhood committee, will interrogate the suspect.' Sitting on the corner of the square table, the Second Aunt Zhang began, 'Supreme directive: "Clouds and waves are raging over the four seas; wind and thunders are storming across the five continents." At this moment my mind rages and storms like the four seas. Beware, you cow ghosts and snake-spirits. We will gather the thunderbolts of the five continents to blast every corner of your dark liver and rotten lungs. Guo-He shi!' Who was this Guo-He shi?

It was none other than Grandma, who was born without a name and to whom they could attach only the surnames of her husband's family (Guo) and of her mother's family (He) together as her name in the household registration. This name was used only in formal occasions. Because she had never heard this name before, she did not respond. Her clever daughter, elbowing her, said, 'Mother, they're calling you.' 'Here!' No one knew where Grandma had gotten her military training, but she answered crisply like a soldier, even clicking her heels together. 'Do you have a sacred statue of Chairman Mao in the house?' Dear me! Now what? Too busy this morning to invite another one in. The pitiful old woman's lips quivered for a minute and a half before she replied, 'Yes. Whose family doesn't have Chairman Mao's sacred statue?' 'Where is yours, then?' Grandma's head was spinning. 'Who – who – who knows – where it went to?' 'Who knows? Who knows what happened in your house? You are the person who knows.' Believing they had no criminal evidence, Grandma tried denial. 'I really don't know – really don't know.' 'Well, let her know then. Show it to her!' Following the command, Comrade Liu took out a red packet. Behind the paper, Grandma could see it was the plaster debris she had thrown into the trash can. The broken pieces were pretty big. As soon as the paper was unfolded, one could discern the partial features of Chairman Mao's face. Who in China is not familiar with Chairman Mao's features? Broad brows and square face, an appearance of good fortune, with a mole on the lower chin. Grandma started shaking. With her daughter's support, she remained standing. She thought suddenly, Why didn't I smash it into tiny bits? Of course she had not dared. She would die first before gaining the nerve to do it. 'Is this what you dumped into the trash can in the middle of the night? Listen, we can find you guilty with or without a confession. In the late hours last night you stole onto the street with a bundle. You tried to deceive me by saying you were asking someone to take a few clothes to your daughter in the cadre school. Who did you ask? Where does she live? Can you give us her name? As a revolutionary, my vigilance is very high. I followed you and immediately saw that something was up by the way you wobbled. No sooner did your reactionary head touch your pillow than I invited our great leader back piece by piece. Comrades of the proletarian revolutionary factions, you must know how sad I feel. The proletarian Cultural Revolution has been carried on for so long, yet it took us till now to dig up a malicious enemy like her. Chairman Mao is the leader of the people of the whole world – the reddest, reddest sun in our hearts. Whoever dares to sabotage the image of Chairman Mao will be denounced and slain by the party, the nation, and the human race. How vicious is your wolfish ambition!' The voice of Second Aunt Zhang, rising higher and higher, jumped two octaves at the last word and left a jarring sound, like scratching glass with an iron flint. The crowd around her was aroused in great indignation and shouted, 'Long live, long, long live Chairman Mao!' Grandma collapsed at her daughter's feet.

"The representative from the combined committee of police, prosecutor, and court seemed to direct policy well. A slight gesture from him subdued the waves of slogans. 'Help her to her feet. And let her make a confession. Confess her motives, her criminal action, and her abettor.'

"Supported by her daughter, Grandma got to her feet, her face covered with tears and snot. The representative showed an even higher level of policy direction: 'Give her a glass of water.' But without touching the water, Grandma howled hysterically, 'I'll confess – confess everything. Comrades, I deserve death ten thousand times over.' Her address was denounced immediately. Who would be a comrade of yours? 'Chieftains, the crime was not committed by me. It was – Lingzi, Lingzi who did it. She's an ignorant child, a child who still eats her own shit. She's too young to be responsible.' Second Aunt Zhang rose in a rage. 'Old fox, how dare you shunt your guilt onto the child!' A wave from the representative shut her up.

"'All right. Because you said it was done by the child, let me cross-examine her. Lingzi, your Grandma says you broke Chairman Mao's sacred statue. Is that true?' Lingzi looked around wide-eyed. Having no experience in such a grave situation, she was first scared and then fascinated. The grown-ups who spoke in strange tones and looked at people so mysteriously, were paying so much attention and were staring at her without blinking and waiting patiently. Grandma was dead stiff, and her eyes flickered at Lingzi with a light in which pity and despair were mixed. The mother fixed her eyes of love on Lingzi's little mouth. Pursing her lips, Lingzi laughed. Looking this way and that, she asked, 'What are you all talking about?' The authority from the public prosecutor gave a detailed explanation with gestures, including the measures of the statue and its material. But Lingzi said, 'I don't know.' Grandma was worried nearly to death. She suddenly knew what to do and said hurriedly, 'Lingzi, it's about your Grandpa Mao!' Now Lingzi understood. She smiled shyly and, pointing to the dimple on her cheek with the right thumb, she said, 'I broke Grandpa Mao's statue. I wanted to put a cap on his head. One touch, and he fell to the floor. Grandma asked me not to tell anyone.' All eyes turned to Grandma, who suffered another wave of dizziness. The representative made his decision: 'Chairman Mao teaches us: "Seek truth from the facts." Now the case is clear. Lingzi is the chief criminal, and her accomplice is Guo-He Shi. Guo Yunling – Lingzi's mother – should be criticized for her irresponsible education of the child. Now I will pronounce judgment: Guo Yunling, although not punishable by law, will return to her unit for disciplinary action. Guo-He Shi will receive labor reform by sweeping the public streets under the supervision of the masses. Guo Lingzi's crime is serious, and the means she used to commit the crime are malicious. Although her attitude is good and she has made a confession, yet – ' Sweeping everyone's face with the sword of his eyes as if they were all criminals, he continued, 'for such a hideous crime, no one can escape the law. No matter how high her position, no matter how many years she has worked for the revolution, no matter how long she has been a party member' – now his cruel eyes fell on Lingzi – 'and no matter how young a child she is, we must give her due punishment. We cannot calm the popular anger without sentencing her to prison. Because she is still a child, it is decided that Guo Lingzi be sentenced to just two years' imprisonment. The decision is effective immediately.' When these words fell, Comrade Liu, the policeman, seized Guo Lingzi immediately from her mother's arms. Lingzi kicked and screamed at the top of her lungs. Grandma, with courage coming from an unknown source, dashed over to take the child and begged aloud, 'Please take me. I'm guilty. It was I who committed this crime.' Guo Yunling also pleaded, 'Please let me go to jail, instead of my child. Staying in the cadre school is not much different from sitting in jail.' The man of authority pounded the table. 'Don't you have any respect for the law? Being steady, accurate, and merciless is our principle. We punish only the convicted criminal. During which dynasty in Chinese history can a mother go to jail in place of her daughter?' Guo Yunling pleaded more earnestly, 'Please let me accompany her to jail, then. I would be happier with her in jail than worrying about her at the cadre school. Please, please grant me this favor.' Supporting his head with a fist, like Rodin's *The Thinker,* the man of authority thought for three seconds and said with a decisive hand wave, 'Okay!' That was a year ago, and our prison has hosted the world's youngest prisoner with her mother ever since."

A said, "You're sure long-winded. Aren't you thirsty?"

"Can you give me a bowl of water?"

"I have only a bladder full of urine."

"Take it out. If you dare take it out, I will drink."

B said, "All right. No more kidding. E, how can you tell the story in so much detail, not having seen it yourself? You must have added a lot of soy sauce and vinegar to the recipe."

"Inevitable for oral literature. But Lingzi stands right before us; so does her mother. This means that no one has added any seasoning to its factual plot or theme. The facts are irrefutable."

C said with a sigh, "That's true. They are right before our eyes."

A said, "How did the big country girl to the left of the mother get here? She's quite pretty."

E said, "A mute. She and Lingzi are charged with the same kind of crime."

B said, "How come you know everything?"

"Living in a prison, you must keep your eyes open six ways and your ears pricked in eight directions; otherwise, you will rot."

C said, "How could a mute – ? I thought misfortune came from the mouth, and wished I were a mute because people can neither catch your words nor grope for what you're thinking. They can't seize your pigtail since you grow none."

"That's only one side of the truth. Besides speaking, a person can also act. If his action is wrong, he will be caught the same way. Little Lingzi, who feared that the great leader might catch cold, did not invite her misfortune by mouth."

D said, "Tell me then. What rule did the mute break and how serious was it?"

"She was given a life sentence."

A, B, C, and D cried out in surprise at once: "That serious!"

"Her crime is grave."

"What crime?"

"The same sort of crime."

A said, "We know they committed the same sort of

crime. But the circumstances were not the same, were they?"

"Hard to say."

B said, "I bet you don't know. If you do, don't keep us guessing."

"I know the whole story."

"Then please tell us."

"Well, it happened like this: The mute girl is a peasant's daughter. One day about six years ago, her mother asked her to go to a fair in town. Her task was very simple — to sell firewood and to 'invite' home a sacred statue of Chairman Mao. Peasants in the south use a shoulder pole to carry firewood, with two pointed ends sharp as daggers. Things went smoothly for the mute girl. As soon as she entered the town she sold the firewood. It was not hard to invite Chairman Mao's sacred statue, either. She got one in a stationer's for 2.50 yuan, the price of her firewood. But bringing home the sacred statue was hard for the mute girl. She did not have a basket and thought it indecent for a big girl to carry a man's statue in her arms. And she could not place it steadily on her head. While she stood racking her brains, a one-and-a-half-foot length of hemp on the road suddenly brightened her eyes. She picked it up and hung the statue with it from one end of the shoulder pole — "

B cut in. "Wait a minute. I didn't get that. How did she tie the statue? By which part?"

"I'd rather not say."

C said, "You don't have to hold anything back. Spit it out. We won't report you. We have suffered enough together."

"Can't you guess? It's obvious, there's only one spot she could tie it to. That is — " Still E could not say it, merely making a hanging gesture around his own neck. "In broad daylight, in the public eye, how could such a criminal escape? She was seized immediately. Just imagine the shock and rage the crime aroused in the crowds at that moment.

The people nearly trampled the mute girl to death right on the spot."

Sticking out their tongues with horror, they said simultaneously, "People were really generous with her. Otherwise – "

Silence followed. Our group was also lost in silence. I guessed the listeners were visualizing close-ups of the whole surging scene in which the masses of people who love their great leader were spurred on by their boiling anger, plunging forward to crush her with their stamping feet and forests of raised arms. The stormy scene of roars, shouts, and cries was truly heart stirring. If I had been there, I, too, would have trampled her and waved my fists with tearful cries. I would have had a guilty conscience, grieving over the existence of such reactionaries in China.

While I was deep in thought, the whistle blew to signal the end of work. My first reaction was to feel that time had passed too fast. I stood up and stamped my feet, numbed by a whole day of sitting on a tiny stool.

I gaze at her window. In the past, it was pasted over with black paper; now a cloth curtain with tiny blue flowers hangs there.

After supper, the appearance of a young female guard surprised us in cell number 10045. She signaled me to come with her. Like a white ghost, she hooked my soul away – now to my death. I heard several prisoners had been called to execution by a female guard. I immediately switched on the computer in my body to search for signs that would lead to such a catastrophe. The result of the search was nothing. But who says one cannot be killed without signs? There are lots of historical precedents. Maybe I was just being transferred to a single cell. Or maybe, with a sudden wishful thought, I was being set free. Standing up, I asked, "Shall I take my belongings with me?" She shook the forefinger that had been used as a hook and the flickering of my hope was nipped in the bud. With a funereal eye, I bade my inmates farewell: Goodbye, take care. The cell I had found cramped and smelly, the imprisoned days I had found hard to get through, and those inmates with faces swollen like buns soaked in sewage, all this became gloriously warm to me, hard for me to tear myself away from. Moreover, every inmate had a fantastic tale I could enjoy while chipping stones. And every inmate was an interesting book that enhanced my knowledge, spurred my thinking and opened my appetite. Of course, all things serving as appetizers here were not much different from poison – a defect of prison life. As the female guard was turning to leave, with tears in my eyes I clapped one fist in the other palm to bow to the inmates, like an ancient hero, then followed her out with my head held high. No matter how low I sank, I was a man and must act like one in front of a woman.

When a man reaches his end, what awaits him is death. What is death? Although I had not acquired its flavor, I had tasted the sourness, sweetness, and bitterness of human life; relishing it afterward, I found, was far more delicious than actually experiencing it. My affair with Yunqian was the best example. Could I still relish all this after death? I took the memory relished after death as the most valuable.

I followed the guard. It was a pity I hadn't noticed her face. Was it pretty, or ugly, or somewhere in between? When she hooked me with a finger, she had instantly become the goddess of death in my mind. I felt no need to see the face of the goddess of death; instead, all my attention focused on her finger. Now, even if she had a cruel face I could no longer see it. Only the outline of her back was visible. Although she wore a uniform too loose for her body, to a sketcher like me the outlines of her body were still clear. She was no more than twenty-five years old, five feet three inches in height, with well-developed breasts, slender limbs, and firm buttocks. If her face wasn't too ugly, I would have willingly embraced this seductive body before my death. I could grab her shoulders from behind, cover her breasts with both my hands. My fantasy suddenly soured. How could a man faced with death still produce such life-seeking fantasies? Prison is a wharf leading to death, which dangles a man between the boat of death and the bank of life, a place devoid of sensual colors or bodies of the other sex.

By accident, I found that, although I could tell male prisoners wearing the same gray prison clothes at a distance, when trying to watch a female prisoner my vision was poor. Such a long-distance attraction made us suffer the pangs of sexual starvation more keenly. It would have been better had I never lived with a woman. But unfortunately, I had experienced romance with Yunqian in the cocoon. Like those lusty men who cannot pass a day without talking about sex, I was burning with sexual desire. I swore secretly that once out of prison I would write a book about prison life, regardless of its publishability. In it, I would tell free men what tortures and depresses a man most when he loses his freedom. All prison corridors are long and damp. In the past I had seen them only in movies, but now I was treading along one of them. I followed the young guard closely. If someone had filmed us for a movie, a foreign audience would expect a dramatic scene of violence. But the Chinese audience would not. The Chinese guard did not need to be on guard, and she did not need to carry a pistol. A prisoner in China does not dare to act out the scenarios he has rehearsed many times in his imagination. It is not simply a matter of courage; it is because every Chinese is mentally imprisoned.

The woman ahead of me stopped suddenly and I nearly bumped into her. She pushed open the door of a small room for visitors. Turning to me, she ordered, "Enter!"

Now I had a clear view of her face: not ugly, but actually quite pretty in my view, perhaps because I had not been close to a woman for so long. I could hear her breathing, the sweet breathing of a female. She looked at me, without malignance, actually with a shred of the normal intuitive reaction between a woman and a man. Her zipped lips betrayed a little smile that roused the passionate drives of a primitive man. But it was too late. First, I realized I was not on a ship of death; second, another person was sitting inside the room, also a female, wearing a large face mask, with her army cap pulled very low.

The guard said to me, "A person has come to investigate. Please answer all her questions honestly or you will be punished severely."

"Yes." I lowered my head, the orgies of a natural man after impulsive excitement having subsided.

"Take a seat." The guard pointed to the rough bench opposite the visitor. Having not touched a chair or a bench for a long time, I sat on it with a delicious sigh. The guard went over to the visitor and whispered into her ear, "You may ask your questions now. I have some business elsewhere. But he's okay, you don't need to worry."

Her voice was tiny, yet I heard every word. I was convinced of the increasing sensitivity of my ears. I thought to myself quite complacently, "Now I have become an old jail-bird." Her impression that I was okay proved it was hard to gauge a man's psyche even under extreme stress. I didn't think I was okay, because I was often mad for freedom and sex – the desires of a not-so-okay man. But they couldn't see through me. The guard left. I lowered my head, waiting to be questioned. Who was she investigating? My parents? Was it possible to overturn the verdict in their case? Gui Renzhong? Yunqian? Was she in trouble? The visitor held her tongue patiently. I could sense her removing her mouth cover and cap. Strange, why didn't she ask me anything? I raised my head. Yunqian! "How did you find me here? And how did you get in here?"

"I have a letter of introduction from a powerful man, under the pretext of investigating the cause of your parents' death. But never mind that. Tell me about your case."

After I gave a brief account of my case, she said with a frown: "How could you let others hold anything in your handwriting? If you had only said those things to Gui Renzhong, you could easily deny them. You are as naive as a three-year-old, having done such a silly thing behind my back."

"I did it out of a good heart."

"How much money is a good heart worth? All right. Don't try to defend yourself any more." She sighed. "I really don't know how to get you out of this prison. Most of the prisoners here are political criminals. Without a drastic change in China, you can't dream of getting out. Whether you are convicted or not, you will have to wear out the bottom of the prison. That's not just a threat."

"I know. Do you think China will have a drastic change soon?"

"Hard to say. The Lin Biao affair was big, wasn't it? Yet its occurrence brought no change."

"You mean, China needs an even more drastic change?"

"Yes. Waiting cannot be rewarded by any change. Only the fool knows nothing but waiting...waiting...." She looked at me with tears in her eyes. "No thinner than before. You look puffy. Although I know you're starved here, I can't bring you a sack of buns. Here are a couple of candy bars, pretty hard to buy in shops." She threw four fifty-gram bars of chocolate across the table. "Hide them quickly."

Long starved as I was, the sight of food made me tremble. My shivering hands fumbled several times before picking up the candy bars and shoving them into my pants.

"Listen, I'll pretend to ask you to write a report about your parents so I can come here to get it. Next time I may be unable to see you, especially to see you alone."

I reached out to her under the table. She held my hand in hers. My dear Yunqian – she still belonged to me. I groped for her legs, and she helped me find them. I was still searching for the place that I had searched for hundreds of times during my longing hours for her. She was generous enough to offer it – the door creaked. Quickly I withdrew my hand and stood up when the guard and the warden walked in.

"Have you finished?" asked the guard.

"Yes." Taking out a notepad from her army satchel, Yunqian said, "I am leaving this for him to write a report."

"No problem. Is it urgent?"

"No. Let him take his time. I'll come and get it in a few days."

"Good." The warden took the pad and passed it to me.

"You may leave now. You are allowed three days absence from labor."

"Yes, sir." I turned and walked out of the visitors' room without a chance to cast Yunqian a tender glance.

In the long, damp corridor, the guard followed me. Now our positions had been switched. I was not the one who visualized the other's body through the uniform. Perhaps she never noticed me as a human body because prisoners do not belong to the human race. It was hard to say. After all, I was a healthy male. I was trying to figure out whether she could visualize my body through my prison clothes and what my body looked like in the eye of this woman wrapped in a guard uniform. I had an impulse to look over my shoulder and catch her facial expression at the moment, but dared not take the risk.

I gaze at her window. In the past, it was pasted over with black paper; now a cloth curtain with tiny blue flowers hangs there.

17

At dawn, several large white clouds floated low over Xienami. Five or six wild ducks darted across the lake to the other bank. In the center of the lake, an old man and a little girl seated in a canoe gathered in the nets they had put into the water the night before. Although the sun was still on the other side of the mountain, a faint redness was already starting to appear and spread about in the dark blue of the lake, as though someone had squeezed a drop of red ink into a blue ink bottle.

Two horses and three people broke the tranquility by the lake. Sunamei had left home. She had really left home. The extended family had discussed the matter for three days and nights before reaching a final decision. All the villagers had taken part in the discussion. A few supporters had opposed the majority, who were against her. Luo Ren had become the target of blame, an outcast. Some had even called him a slave trader. Ami Cai'er alone understood Sunamei's heart. The more people opposed her going, the more determined she was to go, even if she had to leap over a sea of flames.

Finally, narrowing her eyes into a sweet smile, Sunamei declared to the whole family, "I am leaving tomorrow morning," as if nobody had ever questioned her going.

Who was going to see her off? On hearing the news, her former *axiao* Longbu came with fifteen horses. Yingzhi, who had no horse, was willing to carry her on his back. But Sunamei declined both of them. She chose her uncle Awu Luruo as her guide to the county. He prepared two horses and they set out before daybreak, without waking elders or children. No one in the village knew they would leave so early. Yingzhi stayed in Sunamei's *huagu* for the last night. His words flowed in buckets, and his tears wet Sunamei's beautiful hair. But Sunamei did not let him persuade her not to go to a strange land. She chased him out of bed early and did not allow him to see her off. "Find another *axiao*," she said. "Better an ugly one so that you won't forget me."

"Don't worry. Once you are gone, all the girls remaining will be ugly."

"I don't want to hear your pretty words. I want you to listen to me and go home. If I catch you following me on the road, I will never speak to you again. Please go, go back to your own *yishe*." Yingzhi submissively stomped out of Sunamei's *huagu*.

Only Ami, her big white cat in her arms, saw her daughter off. She put Sunamei on horseback and followed her a long way. Mother and daughter were silent. Luo Ren, too. And so was Awu Luruo. The eight horses' hooves said continuously to the road of her hometown: Gone, gone, gone, gone!

It was light when they approached the lake. On a ridge Sunamei jumped off the horse and drew a line across the road. Then she said to her *ami*, "Ami, please stop here. From this height you will see far away. You will see your Sunamei again soon. Please stop here. One step beyond this line and your daughter will lose a year of life. If you do not love your daughter, go ahead and cross this line." After these words, Sunamei got on her horse with a carefree laugh. She whipped the horse with the pine switch with which she had drawn the line. The horse galloped away like a trail of smoke. Standing behind the line with the big white cat, Ami followed the horse and Sunamei with eyes blurred by tears. How could she know that Sunamei's laughter was rolling out together with her tears. Laughing while crying expresses a person's saddest emotion. Sunamei's heart was empty, as if in drawing that line she had cut all ties between her hometown and herself. What were these ties, anyway? Before her birth, her umbilical cord had been attached to Ami's body. At that time, she was unconscious, because all senses were blocked. Now that her senses were alive again she tasted the pain of separation, as if all the feelings of affection and love had been severed. She wished she could tumble off the horse and lie on this land. From here she could still see her Mosuo village. The smoke from the fireplace of each *yishe* formed a thin layer of purple mist over the village. Yet she did not tumble off the horse. Instead, she straightened up and kept her eyes forward, in spite of the tears streaming down onto the horse's mane.

How she wished at that moment that Yingzhi was following her. Maybe he was tramping through the woods beside the road, keeping pace with her. But he could see her in the dark; she could not see him. Yingzhi was too submissive. If he were boldly to stop her horse, could she really ignore him? Of course not. She would dismount. Holding the horse, she would say to Yingzhi, "I'm not leaving. I want to go back, go back to the *huagu* you've visited and never leave again, ever." But Yingzhi did not appear. He was faithful to her. Being such an honest man, even if he were following he would not dare show his face. Thoughts like these made the tears trickle down her face. She did not wipe them away, nor did she want to check them. Let them flow, flow. The wind on the journey would dry them in time.

Luo Ren rode on, never turning his head. Awu Luruo followed the horse loaded with baggage and food. He was a smart old man, filled with jokes and tales. But now he was walking mechanically with his eyes downcast, staring at the tip of the horse's swaying tail.

"Awu Luruo," Sunamei called in a tone mixing sadness with loneliness. "Awu Luruo, why don't you say something?"

"Ah." Awu Luruo poked at his wirelike gray hair with

the tip of his whip. The sound of *ah* seemed to have opened his windpipe.

"Please tell me a story, Awu Luruo." Sunamei implored.

"Ah." Still no text followed.

Sunamei waited, riding another couple of miles. "Awu Luruo, if you don't want to tell stories, tell me something about yourself. You've been on long trips, haven't you?"

"True, I have journeyed far, to Lhasa and also to India and Calcutta."

"Were you happy when you left home, Awu Luruo?"

"No. I felt the way you are feeling now, Sunamei."

"How about later?"

"Later, the farther I went, the more outlandish things and people I met. Gradually, I forgot Xienami, our *yishe,* and even my *axiao.*"

"Did you enjoy the outside world?"

"Yes, very much."

"No longer missed home?"

"No."

"I can't understand how one could not miss home anymore?"

"It did occur in time, Sunamei."

"Really? Awu Luruo, please tell me how you came to enjoy it."

"When I left home, I was only seventeen. I had an *axiao* named Muzhami, who tried to keep me at home. But finding nothing around me attractive, I ran away from my *yishe.* Jiacuo, a Tibetan horse trader, had told me that the outside world had women as it had flowers – and the women were more playful. I regretted my decision as soon as I took to the road, but it was too late because I had agreed to help Jiacuo with his horses, for which he would feed me and take me to Lhasa so that the living Buddha could touch my forehead and bless me with a hundred years' longevity. Jiacuo's trade was quite successful. He even took me to India once. He said that India had a big river called the Ganges, and, while

Indian women were bathing in the river, one could choose any one of them, the beautiful or the tender. But the road to Lhasa led not to paradise but to hell. We drove fifty horses: two were lost in a snowslide; three were lost on a slippery slope in a heavy rain; one was carried away by flood; and one was killed by a leopard. Although I risked my nine lives, they were exciting times. I was strong, stronger than horses and stronger than Jiacuo, and fiercer than the leopards that winced before me. Even a flood couldn't wash me away. Dozens of times I escaped whirlpools. At night I fell asleep as soon as my head touched the ground, but a drop of rain woke me instantly. Although it took half a year to get to Lhasa, Jiacuo made an enormous amount of money when we got there, because what was buried in the snow or lost in the flood had been cheap stuff. The expensive tea and jewels arrived safely. After making a fortune, Jiacuo bought me a leather coat, with borders decorated with leopard fur, and a pair of Indian boots. He knew his journey could not have succeeded without me and that without me he would have been long dead. Twice I had dug him out of the snow. With a caravan of fifty horses, every morning and night I had to load and unload so many goods. I was a ball of energy then. I could gobble up five pounds of veal.

"When Jiacuo took me to the Potala Palace, I presented a *hada* to the living Buddha and he touched the center of my head. While I was standing in the octagonal square, many Tibetans took me as the prince of a former Tibetan lord. At the height of his career, Jiacuo asked me to take a fifty-horse caravan to India. India was a terribly hot place, extremely poor and extremely rich. Jiacuo was right that you could see thousands of women bathing in the Ganges, their sandalwood skin soft and smooth, their eyes slender, and a vermilion dot imprinted between their eyebrows. Some even wore gold flowers on their noses. They came out of the water in veils, their bodies half revealed and half concealed, like the moon in the clouds. I forgot where I came from and where I was going. Calcutta is a large city. People there were more crowded together than fish in a bucket, and all sorts of vehicles were ready to run you down. We bought some cattle from the suburbs and shipped them to the city by truck. We stayed in hotels that were perfumed daily. Jiacuo had made a great deal of money with his Tibetan products, which he had exchanged for gold and jewelry. Being a generous man, he gave me a lot of Indian rupees and told me to spend them in the market. He told me Indian silk was very famous and that numerous restaurants in Calcutta served all kinds of delicious food. But I dared not go out, for I could speak neither Bengali nor English. One morning Jiacuo, covered with a satin quilt, couldn't get up from his bed. Falling from the peak of his fortune, he had been struck by plague. The doctors refused to see him and the hotel servants dared not serve him food. I alone waited on him by his bedside. Realizing that his days were numbered, he offered all his possessions to me out of gratitude. I declined his offer and said I would take his gold and jewelry back to Tibet and give them to his wife. I swore this beside his deathbed. Before Jiacuo gasped his last breath, the Indian government sent the police to take him away from me and burn him with his clothes and quilt. They also stripped me and burned my clothes. However, I had plenty of money and could afford many new clothes and more luxury hotels. Although I did not speak Bengali, my money spoke Bengali, English, and all other human tongues. At that time I was crazy for money; the Indians would have nothing to do with me unless they saw my money. They had first thought I was a poor horse driver from Tibet, stinking with dung. When I took out my rupees, their eyes lit up and the corners of their eyes and mouths rose. They could hardly wait to kiss my smelly toes.

"While I was paying the bills and getting ready to go home – oh my heavens – an Indian girl came to see me. What a celestial being, what a beauty! Every one of her movements was like dance. Although she did not understand my words, she knew what I meant. Counting on her tapered fingers, she told me she was only fifteen. She was wearing a pair of sandals made of stringed pearls, revealing her red toenails. Through her transparent veil I could see her breasts. They were not the breasts of a fifteen-year-old girl, but those of a twenty-five-year-old woman. I could also see her delicate, round navel. Although I could not understand her words, I could easily guess her intentions. I knew she wanted to be my *axiao*. It was like a moon flying into my door shining on me. The faint shadow of Muzhami vanished in her presence, nothing left....

"Because I had not touched a woman for a long time, I grabbed her, tearing open her clothes. She attempted to struggle free from my arms, but how could she, confronted with a man who had subdued leopards and whose desire was lit like a pine torch? She was definitely not a child. Instead of struggling, she caressed my face with her tiny hands and calmed me down. Then she took off my clothes and led me like a lamb to a bathroom. Actually, I had not realized there was a bathroom in my suite. She filled a tub with hot water and let me lie down in it. Then, before me and the large mirror, she stripped. Good heavens, I was stunned. Her body was pure and smooth like brown ivory; she looked like the jade fairy waiting on the living Buddha in his private pavilion. My body, covered with scars, contrasted sharply with hers, which was spotless and pure. I was ashamed and wanted to ask her to leave me. Yet I seemed to be paralyzed. She came to me and bent down to wash my body. I was embarrassed to watch a layer of black dirt being scrubbed off my caravan-man body and the water being instantly dyed black. She changed the water; it took three tubs to get me clean. When she lowered her body to dry mine, my face touched her breast accidentally, and I did not even dare to breathe. After drying me with a long white cloth, she led me to bed, and she herself went back to take a bath. I heard her water splashing for a long time. I did not know what she had to wash away, because there wasn't even a speck of dust on her body. When she came to my bed in a veil, I could not press her roughly under my weight as I had done to Muzhami. She approached me gradually. Sunamei, my dear little sister. I guess the goddess would not do it better than she. She knew what a man wanted, and she knew how to play. And she could make me jump up like a leopard at any moment. Since I had Lida — yes, her name was Lida, an elf — since I had her, whatever I wanted to eat or wear she had sent to my room and I spent my days like the prince of Nepal. But by the end of the month, Lida gave me a stack of slips. As I did not know what those slips were for, she told me they were bills for clothes, food, and other things we had ordered. Of course, I had to pay for them. I had plenty of gold and paid her instantly, although I did not expect them to be so expensive, wiping out half of Jiacuo's wealth. The following day, Lida gave me another slip. What expense was this? She explained to me that it was what I owed *her.* I was confused. When had I borrowed money from her? Why should I pay money to her? I had bought a lot of expensive clothes and jewelry for her. She said I must pay the money she had earned with her body. I could not understand why one has to pay to make *axiao.* I also had a body. Why didn't she pay me? I asked her how much she wanted. She showed me a number on her fingers that took my breath away. She cost almost all the fortune I had. That is to say, I would have to beg my way home to Tibet. I explained to her in words like our Mosuo singing: We made *axiao* like a female and a male bird coming together. You gave me your passion, and I gave you my feeling; you gave me your gratefulness and I gave you my love; you gave me your heart, and I gave you my liver; and you gave me blood, and I gave you tears. Why do you ask me for so much money? She suddenly turned into a dumb brute without a shred of human understanding. She could not understand even one word of what I had said. I decided that I could not give her money. If I did, what would she become? Could she be still counted as a human being? Wouldn't she be reduced to a creature without a soul? A beast without human feelings? Her tenderness for me, her smiles, her tears, her screams stimulated by my strong love, her little mouth that had kissed my body, and her body marked by my mouth – could all these be bought for money? I liked her, loved her, and she was my *axiao*. I could not pay her. I told her, 'You are my *axiao*. *Axiao* are not ordinary friends. *Xiao* means lying down together like newly born babies, my dear *axiao*, Lida!' But Sunamei, she was unable to understand me. She became a stranger. No, a thing, a thing without feelings, without a heart.

"In order to get money from me, her whole family came, barking around me like dogs. Later, a swarm of police came like wolves, trying to tear me into pieces. Among those dogs and wolves, Lida glared at me with clenched teeth. I had to throw all my gold, silver, and pearls at their feet. Crawling on the ground, Lida, like a dog or wolf fighting for bones, fought for the scattered jewels. I had nothing left but a little money to pay my way to Tibet. As I was leaving Calcutta, I did not say good-bye, for in such a huge city you could not find a soul worthy of your farewell. I had once taken Lida as my dearest, yet she preferred to become an object. On my return route, I could no longer see any beauty in the city women. Perhaps their faces were as beautiful as Lida's or even surpassed hers; I did not wish to see them. When you were penniless, they became icy cold, like things without souls. They were merely beasts, dogs, and wolves. When I reached Tibet, feeling ashamed to visit Jiacuo's family, I buried his bones in the Himalayas and read a thousand Buddhist sutras for him. Bidding his soul good-bye, I rushed toward my hometown, toward our Mosuo Xienami. As I was approaching Xienami, the face of Muzhami became clearer and clearer. At the sight of the lake, I felt I could almost touch her face. In the whole world, only

Mosuo women on the banks of Xienami are women, not objects. They are women of flesh and blood, women of feelings and heart, women of gratitude and love, women with souls, and women of beauty. Only among the Mosuo women on the banks of Xienami can one find a true *axiao.* Hooray, I have come home!"

"Awu Luruo, did Muzhami still open her *huagu* to you?"

"I think she would have, except her – her *huagu* already held somebody else. Although, despite all hardships I had brought her a pair of silver bracelets inlaid with diamonds, I did not give them to her, because I could not use things like money to buy her away from the man she loved. I dropped the bracelets into Lake Xienami."

"What happened later, Awu Luruo?" Like a little girl, Sunamei asked impatiently, "Did you find any *axiao?*"

"No problem, my little sister. I have had eight *axiao* since. Yet I've never given them a thing. You know, Sunamei, it is not because I am a miser."

"I know, Awu Luruo."

"I have not taken anything from them, not even a waistband. I've told them: 'What I give you is my heart, and you should give yours in return. I treasure a person's heart, and nothing else.'"

"Awu Luruo, if you were still a young man, I would be your *axiao,* too."

"I believe so."

Sunamei stopped asking questions, and Awu Luruo grew silent. Only the eight horse hooves kept chanting on the road: Gone, gone, gone, gone…

Evening came. The three people and two horses camped in a warm valley. Awu Luruo took down the packs from the horses and set a bonfire to boil tea. After shackling the horses' hooves, Luo Ren went to the stream to wash his face. Sunamei tagged along. Squatting by his side, she asked, "Did you hear all of Awu Luruo's story?"

"Yes."

"Your ears are really sharp."

"My ears are not so sharp, but the mountain path is too still."

"Brother Luo Ren, if I give you my heart, will you give me yours?"

Luo Ren shook his head.

"Why? Aren't I good enough for you?"

"It's not that."

"You don't have a heart?"

"Yes. But my heart is tied with many strings."

"Nonsense."

"I never tell a lie."

"Then please tell me, what are the strings?"

"Later. Wait until you live in the city for some time. If I tried to tell you now, you would not understand."

"Because I am too silly?"

"No. I'm afraid I cannot explain clearly."

"Are there things in the world that cannot be explained clearly?"

"Yes, many things."

Luo Ren led Sunamei by the hand to the bonfire to help Awu Luruo cook some corn. Before the corn was ready, they sat silently drinking tea. Sunamei murmured to herself from time to time, "Are there things in the world that cannot be explained clearly?"

After the meal, Awu Luruo spread a large piece of felt on the grass, and the three of them lay down on it, with Luo Ren sandwiched between Awu Luruo and Sunamei. Wrapping himself with a horsehide blanket, Awu Luruo was snoring away in no time. Covering herself and Luo Ren with a *cha'erwa,* Sunamei lay awake, staring at the stars, but after a while she put her arm around Luo Ren's neck and also fell asleep. Luo Ren simply could not sleep. Although his body was burning hot, he dared not make a turn. Sunamei's red lips breathed rhythmically across his neck. He was receiving the most severe punishment – he was nailed on a strange cross, with an iron loop around his neck. He was not released until dawn, when Sunamei woke up.

Sunamei uttered in surprise, "Brother Luo Ren, you slept like a log."

"Yes!" Scampering up to the stream, Luo Ren dipped his dizzy head into the flow of the icy water.

18

I gaze at her window. In the past it was pasted over with black paper; now a cloth curtain with tiny blue flowers hangs there.

I felt lonely not participating in hard labor for three days. Actually, it took only three hours to write a report on my parents' deaths, but I had to hold on to it for three days to show my serious attitude. After handing in the report, I rejoined the others who were breaking stones. It was an endless job, because "dig tunnels deep" was part of the long-term strategy of the party and the nation, part of the grand policy of "preparing for war and natural disasters in the interest of the people." Once a nuclear war broke out, all humankind would perish, except for the Chinese, who would have had the foresight to stay in their tunnels to avoid the shock waves, radiation, and the pollution of the nuclear explosion. According to the warden, there must be a seat for every prisoner in the tunnel, because those who lived to see the outbreak of a nuclear war would be much cleaner than any Western devil. Even they would be superior humans. Being so valuable, they must be put into the tunnels for protection. The warden's words were truly encouraging and raised the prisoners' spirits.

He added, "How can I prove my theory? The fact is that in Western capitalist society, even a junior high school student can indulge in sex – Luan [reckless] gao!" The Chinese character *gao* is a magical word. It can be used to describe the most splendid movement, as in "to purge all the counterrevolutionaries we must *gao* [launch] a mass campaign." It can also be used to describe things too vulgar for words, such as adultery and rape. In the warden's speech, it became a euphemism for fucking. "You (referring to us prisoners)! During your time of forced labor, you have no problems with your lifestyle." (By *lifestyle* he meant extramarital sex.) The Chinese characters for *lifestyle* literally mean *make* and *wind*. I could not help turning a wry smile: true, things here are airtight. How could anyone make wind? While both the warden and I were vouching for the purity of our imprisoned life, an incident occurred that not only damaged the warden's prestige but also gave me a shock. For all the prisoners, the incident became sensational news that seemed to carry more artistic value than all the gossip in circulation.

Without coincidences, books would never be written. The incident happened right in our cell number 10045. Its hero was number 809998, next number to mine, the riddle Kang Sheng had failed to solve. On the night after I handed in my report, the warden suddenly came in person to our cell number 10045. We all stood up to show our respect. The beloved warden, all smiles, pointed at number 98 with his right forefinger. Number 98 was overwhelmed by such an unexpected favor. What was he dreaming? Nobody knew. But I believed he was not expecting much more than the hero, with a pack of dynamite in his hand, ready to blow up an enemy bunker. His face swelled red, his eyes shone like those of a rat when its tail is caught, and his hands nervously rubbed the seams of his pants. The warden asked: "Number 98, is your father a carpenter?"

"Yes, sir!" Number 98 answered like a soldier. "My father is a carpenter, my grandfather was a carpenter, and my great-grandfather was also a carpenter." He knew three generations of workers or poor peasants could aid a person's political credibility. When he had traced his lineage back to the third generation, the warden cut him short with a wave of his hand. Enough was enough. The warden must believe ten generations were no different from three, because even an air force pilot's enrollment form required only three generations.

"Come with me."

"Shall I take my things?"

"No." The warden's negative response informed us as well as number 98: this was not a release from prison. The slightly raised heels of number 98 now dropped to the ground, and his red face started fading into whiteness. The warden walked ahead with his hands clasped behind his back. Number 98 followed him. I gloated somewhat over his misfortune: number 98 could watch only a dull outline that inspired no fantasies.

Number 98 was gone with the warden. The four inmates left behind started trying to solve the riddle. No one could. The clock on the faraway tower told us 9:00 p.m. had passed, then 10:00, 11:00, and 12:00. At about 12:42 (number 97 had a precision clock in his brain, never as much as a minute off. If he said the clock in the tower was going to strike, it struck in fewer than ten seconds. I once imagined all people being able to do like number 97: the clock and watch industry would go bankrupt) number 98 returned. When the guard opened the door and locked it behind him, we all sat up as if on command. "What's up?" I bet the prisoners in the cells on our left and right also pricked up their ears. But number 98 gave no reply. Taking off his clothes with a deliberate rustling noise, he slipped wordlessly under his quilt. Everyone could feel his complacency.

"Have you been struck dumb, young fellow?" Unable to check his curiosity, number 97 nudged him. "What did you do over there?"

"Confidential." With this, he covered his head with the quilt. The message was clear: no questions. "What I did cannot be told to anyone."

"Damn you." We lay our heads on our wooden blocks and stopped questioning him. But our minds were still guessing furiously. Such guesswork was torture because the answer was sleeping right beside me, yet I was unable to grasp it. That night, I bet, except for number 98, we all suffered from insomnia.

During the day, number 98 still broke stones in the yard, but every night he was taken out. All the male prisoners cast their eyes at him whenever they could, and some female prisoners also gazed at him. Our curiosity increased daily. Although he and I slept bottom to bottom in the same cell, I could not find out what he was doing over there – sometimes for three hours, sometimes for four hours, and each time seemed even longer. What was he doing? That devil guarded his mouth like a sealed bottle. It was damned annoying – especially because his spirits had improved greatly, not just a bit, and they were getting better and better. The four of us wished we could press him on the floor and dig the words out of his throat with our fingers. Of course, this was only a wish, and no one dared do it. One night something abnormal occurred. Number 98 did not come back at twelve o'clock – even at one, two, or three. We four lay awake as the riddle became more and more puzzling. At half past three, number 98 was brought back like a drunkard, supported by two guards. His face was puffy as a basketball. As soon as the guards left, we sat up. We waited wide-eyed and silent. "What happened?" we finally demanded. "Torture? Have you been on trial every night?"

Number 98 shook his head and said with a sigh, "No." Although his face was swollen, his tongue was still slippery. "I have been doing carpentry work every night."

We were all annoyed. What was the need of hiding a job like carpentry?

"I worked in the women's cells." This seemed to be a sound reason.

"The female cells were not part of the prison at first, but

a vocational school of technology. The school was changed later." A good change, indeed! Culture counted for nothing compared with dictatorship.

"The windows and doors over there are made of wood." Chinese women could easily be locked in with paper doors and windows, let alone wooden ones.

"The warden asked me to repair the rotting ones." A good chance to have his eyes. He probably even talked or flirted with the women.

Once the dam burst, he could not hold back any longer.

"The night before last, I was changing the door frame in a small cell occupied by three females, all pretty young. The eldest was no more than forty, and the youngest only a bit over twenty. The guard watching me had a sudden craving for tobacco. Fumbling in his pockets, he fished out an empty box, so he went to look for a cigarette. Don't think I saw those three females clearly at the beginning. I wasn't clear about what they were like until the guard had gone. During his absence, the older woman smiled at me as the second tugged on my trouser leg, inviting me to talk with them. But I didn't dare." Obviously, he was not telling the truth.

"If I'm lying, call me a dog! The youngest, covering her face with a bed sheet, stared at me with burning, charcoal eyes. They were all okay looking." Too ambiguous. "Okay looking"? After three years' imprisonment one could take an old swine for a great beauty. He must have been blind.

"Honest. In the eyes of men in our situation, every one of them was a sylph. I fixed my eyes on them while hammering the nails. I don't know why, but I desperately wanted to memorize their looks so I could take them like three boxes of candy back to our world of male prisoners and savor them slowly." He sounded quite sincere.

"The eldest chirped into the ear of the second. The second nodded and then whispered to the youngest, who neither nodded nor shook her head. The second bent over and said to me in an anxious voice, 'Brother, our window can slide open. Please don't nail it shut. You can make it look bolted, but please leave it movable.' I glanced at her suspiciously: 'Why? Do you want to escape? Why do you assume that I have the nerves of a leopard?!' I simply dared not do as she asked. She said, 'Brother, we don't intend to run away. The window is for you.' For me? Why for me? She made eyes at me. 'Leave a door for yourself.' Her words struck the secret place in my heart. Although I knew my chances were slim, perhaps only one in ten thousand, my desire was still aroused. If I had never had the nerves of a leopard before, now her words gave them to me. Just then, the guard returned and asked me to repair the window when the door was done. I said yes, I could do that. After fixing the door, I made a special gadget for the window. Although it was obvious to the three females, the guard, who was smoking outside the cell, saw nothing. I don't know what egged me on. I was ready to take the risk. Even if there was only the slimmest chance, I'd squeeze in." If it were me, I would have hoped for the one-in-ten-thousand chance, too.

"Fortunately, my chance came on the third night. The guard supervising me said, 'You've been doing a good job. Tonight I'll let you repair the doors of the storerooms by yourself, and you'll be free when the work is done. I'll be waiting for you in the guard room. Come to me at twelve so I can take you back. As he spoke, my heart throbbed aloud. I was afraid he might hear it. He gave me two keys and left without a care. I enjoyed the freedom of moving around without being watched. Just think — what luck. If not for the two storeroom doors, or, if the two storerooms weren't empty, the guard would not have given me the keys. It was nearly eleven o'clock when I finished the doors. The small cell containing the three females, being a makeshift little cell, was hidden in the shade of oleanders. I stole into that shade as if my soul were seized by a ghost." We four listeners seemed more tense than he was at that moment. Our heads bent over his face like four unshaded light bulbs in an operating room.

"Then — what happened then is obvious. They were devils, out-and-out vixens. When I was through with the eldest and the second, the clock struck twelve and I got up to go. But the youngest held me by my leg: "Don't go. It's my turn. If you go, I'll scream!" In a palm-sized cell, it would be easy for her to grab his leg. Before them, he had had nothing for so long; she was scorched with the flames of his desire. Even a stone would be burned red. Once, twice, but not the third time, as she was expecting.

"Even if you keep me here, what good am I? I'm too scared to get it up." And next? What happened next?

"Next, the guard caught me in the cell. Next, I became what you see here. They beat my lower parts, and my face they forced me to slap myself." After hearing his tale, we lay motionless for a long time. I felt stifled, instead of having a vicarious release after hearing about a scandalous romance. I couldn't make out whether it was a tale about human beings or about beasts, a tale of the past, one from a distant land, or one from my side. I pitied him and the three females. I felt disgusted by him as well as by them. I also admired all of them for the chance they took and for their courage. I didn't know, if I had a chance like that with three vixens, whether I would dare to do it. Could my story also develop like his? Suppose a guard, or the warden, or any gentleman of high rank who supports severe punishment for those miscreants, after a long imprisonment like ours, chanced on an opportunity like number 98 had, would they dare to do it? Would their story develop in the same way?

The following day, a pole ten meters long stood in the yard when the prisoners separated into two large crowds by sex, southeast and northwest. Beneath the long pole stood the warden and the guards. Five minutes passed, but no one issued a command. Then the warden, knowing the power of silence, inserted his right hand in his coat between the second button and the third, unwittingly imitating Napoleon and Hitler. Even if he were aware of their mannerisms, so what? Here, before the mass of prisoners, only he had the right to speak; the others could not utter a sound. Here, he was Napoleon, he was Hitler.

"Number 809998!" Only in the gravest circumstances was a full number called. "Stand forward!" Even knowing it had nothing to do with me, I still shuddered, and my legs nearly buckled.

Dragging his wounded legs, number 98 walked out from the ranks behind me and struggled over to the warden.

"Don't face me — face the crowd!" Number 98 tried to make a perfect right turn in military style but couldn't because his wobbly left leg failed to serve as the center of a circle. He nearly fell in spite of his efforts. "Tell the assembled prisoners about your, your — " He could not find a suitable term. Finally he spit out a word: "Romance!"

Number 98 stuttered and murmured and found it extremely hard to get the words out. The warden stepped over and gave him a loud slap on his left, unswollen cheek. "Why can't you say what you've done?" Number 98 started five times. But each beginning was cut off by the warden. "That won't do. Details, more details!" Many men of power have a hobby of listening to two wild ducks in a snare confessing in minute detail how they have secretly mated with each other. Number 98, although stammering, churned literary and biological elements together and demonstrated his intercourse with the three women with the thoroughness of a slow-motion picture. The yard was dead still. The male prisoners tightly zipped their lips, motionless but attentive. The reaction of the guards was just the opposite. Their mouths gaped wide; their chins protruded half an inch forward; and their hands stretched like duck wings. Why did two groups of people behave so differently? Because I haven't done research in this area, I cannot explain. Looking at the female prisoners in the distance, I saw their faces were uniformly ashen with eyes like black beans, resembling the sparrows drawn in ink and water by famous Chinese masters. I could not distinguish old from young, beautiful from ugly, although I was dying to make out who was the eldest, the second, and the youngest, as described by number 98.

When number 98 had finished, the warden said, "Here is the answer to the riddle Comrade Kang Sheng could not solve! I have guessed it today!" With his eyes bulging and his face purple, the warden was the picture of indignation. Like a general, he drew his hand from between the second and the third button and raised it to the sky.

"String him up!"

The guards knew their profession to perfection, and in the wink of an eye number 98 was strung from the pole top. His feet dangled seven meters from the ground. Number 98 did not even groan; like an old patient in the constant care of a skilled nurse, he could no longer feel the pain of injections.

Were women's hearts softer or their emotions richer? They lowered their heads almost simultaneously, except for three of them, who raised their pale faces and stared with six black beans. Were these the eldest, the middle, and the youngest?

Number 98 seemed to be looking down at those three uplifted faces.

Late that night, everyone was sleeping soundly. Even number 98, who had bravely survived the torture of hanging and beating, was no longer moaning; perhaps he was lost in deep sleep or a coma. I was wide-eyed, enjoying being the only one awake in a world of dead sleep. I longed to hear some sound in the stillness of prison death. But aside from the monotonous snoring of the prisoners, I heard nothing, not even a mosquito buzzing — strange, summer wasn't over yet. Could the mosquitoes have already lost interest in buzzing their wings? Being satiated, they could not fly anymore. Their unrestricted sucking of the prisoners' blood made them sluggish. They must have been digesting our blood slowly on the wall. Yes, there was some noise. What was it? Gentle steps, approaching from the north end of the long corridor. The walker was attempting to make his steps inaudible; I tried to stretch the sensitivity of my ears to their limit. I could hear clearly now. The steps, moving from north to south, grew clearer and clearer. Something was fishy: a guard on duty had no need to tiptoe. Walking into the prison was like entering a pigsty; no one would take this amount of care so as not to disturb the sweet dreams of pigs. More often they deliberately let their hobnailed leather boots play an unscrupulous march. Was this man a guard? If not, he must be a prisoner. Could he possibly be a prisoner? At this moment, I started worrying about him. He must have walked out of his cell at midnight to run away. What a fool! How dare he take such a chance after the lesson that had just been displayed on a pole top? He had to pass at least ten iron doors to get out of the secure area. The footfalls stopped at the iron bars of our cell. I fully mobilized my eyes and ears. In the dim light coming from the gray, narrow sky, I saw a dark shadow, that of a familiar, clumsy, fat man – the warden. My worry was replaced by curiosity. What had he come here for? Why was he behaving so abnormally? Had he stolen in here to detect number 98, or to eavesdrop on our comments? It seemed unlikely because he had never before cared about our attitudes toward anything. Our attitudes – good, bad, or rebellious – seemed to have nothing to do with him. Bars beyond iron bars, iron door after iron door, the moment a criminal stepped into the prison, he was the unshakable authority of their fate. He had nothing to worry about. But it was he. It was absolutely impossible for me to mistake the shadow of this tyrant.

He came stealthily to our iron bars. What was he going to do? He took out something I couldn't see clearly. Grasping the things in his hand, he threw them accurately onto number 96's bed sheet – one, two – that's all. The shadow vanished; the steps faded away. When I sat up to see the two things thrown in, they had already disappeared. In fact, I was not a loner at all; number 96 had not been sleeping, either. He hid the two things under his sheet quick as lightning. Oh, now I saw them: two extra-large tubes of White Jade toothpaste.

I gaze at her window. In the past it was pasted over with black paper; now a cloth curtain with tiny blue flowers hangs there.

Yunqian was not coming any more. She was not allowed to come, and was unwilling, anyway! My carefree spiritual world, achieved after complete despair, helplessness, and insult, had been destroyed by her surprising visit. Although I always felt tired, I was often sleepless. People say one suffers insomnia in old age. Had I grown old? With only a faucet and no mirror or wash basin, it was impossible for me to check. The chorus of chirping insects at night told me unmistakably that summer had passed. Autumn crept over the prison wall and through the layers of iron doors and bars and started pulling at my thin blanket. I no longer wished for the night sounds. Although apart from the inmates' snoring a variety of insects also sang, a satiety of listening had dulled my ears and thrust me into empty, heavy stillness. Even if I could have heard Tchaikovsky's *Pathétique,* I doubt that it would have thrilled as it had at each listening in the cocoon. Then I had enjoyed the small world of the cocoon, love, fuzzy expectations, and two persons' freedom. Although every cell of the body was still agitated, in a situation where I hoped stubbornly in spite of the impossibility of hope, Tchaikovsky's music was powerless to rescue my soul.

Suddenly, I jumped up in the empty stillness. Something sounded like gunfire in the distance. What was it? After ten years of the Cultural Revolution, were people still fighting with guns? No, It didn't sound like firing, for it was too dense to make out individual shots. Was it a storm? All my cell mates sat up. No, it was no storm. If it were, our bed sheets would be wet with raindrops, as the iron bars could block out only men, not the rain and wind. The world sank in the booming sound dense as a steel wall and impossible to penetrate. I had never heard such a sound in my life before. We – the ones shut behind the iron bars – felt both excited and confused on hearing such overwhelmingly strange sounds. No one could figure out what was happening and why it was happening at the darkest moment and in the most sorrowful space. Men and animals in utter despair might be excited by this abnormal phenomenon and subconsciously wish for it to signal change. I believe all the prisoners were wide awake, with staring eyes and gaping mouths, like cattle shut in a field watching in panic the invasion of a raging fire. Our number 95, that fifteen-year-old renegade – no, he was no longer fifteen; two years had passed behind bars – tugged at my sleeve and said, "It's like fireworks."

"That's right." He had reminded me and all the other prisoners. It was the sound of fireworks. But today was not Chinese New Year, and it had been years since the Chinese had ceased using firecrackers. The Chinese had lost their traditional festivals. Children did not know even what the gift money given on New Year's Day was for, what the wrapped rice on the fifth day of the fifth lunar month was, or what New Years' cakes were. On December 26, every Chinese was allotted half a *jin* of noodles and two ounces of meat to prepare a feast. The prison was no exception, although those within the high walls were deprived of the two ounces of meat.

Indeed, it was firecrackers. But what were they for? What did they signify? We behind the iron bars had no right to know of the changes outside because the sun, moon, and stars no longer belonged to us, and we had even forgotten that the earth was round and revolving all the time. Were we happy or sad? The thick, heavy, tireless firecrackers boomed through the whole night and did not die down until dawn. Nobody blew the whistle for getting up, no one served us porridge, and no one hurried us to the yard to break stones. A shaft of sunshine met us, squeezing in from the crack between the high walls every morning, and ten pale hands stretched into that warm (perhaps warmed only by our hopeful feelings) lovely sunshine. In the bright sunshine our hands looked especially pale, like rotten Chinese cabbage from a cellar.

Suddenly – after the fireworks, everything occurred suddenly – the warden appeared in the corridor, assuming an image we had never seen before. He was all naive, childish smiles, red face, red, thick neck, unbuttoned collar, capless, his bald scalp encircled by flying gray hair, his leather belt loose like the jade belt of an ancient Chinese judge, his feet dragging not a pair of heavy, metal-tipped boots but slippers, one foot stockinged, the other bare. From a distance, we could smell the alcohol. Drunk – the warden was drunk. His drunkenness made me shudder because I was not accustomed to see him as a drunkard. My eyes and every nerve refused to see him as anything other than a dignified general inserting his right hand between the second and the third buttons of his coat or ejecting willful shouts as he suddenly withdrew that hand: "String him up! Beat him with double clubs!" Now his legs were like those of a panda, the left one barely moving forward with an inward bent; the right one followed in the same manner. His hands, swaying from side to side, resembled the pendulums of a peddler's drum.

A guard tried to support him but was shoved away. The drunkard behaved like a toddler who refused any adult's help in order to show off. Was *he* the warden? Was he *our* warden? Was he *still* our warden? How could our warden behave like this? He blended neither with the background scene of the prison nor with us as supporting actors. What about his lines? What would he say in this dramatic scene? He began, "At last – at last, one snake and three turtles have been thrown off our backs." Counting on his fingers, he betrayed four distinguished VIPs: "Wang Hongwen, a rebel; Zhang Chunqiao, the damned military adviser and partisan backbone; Yao Wenyuan, a small hack scribbler; and Jiang Qing. That damned woman bothers me most. Arresting that evil woman is of vital importance. Vital importance, do you understand? She is different from the others." He wagged his tongue at us petrified prisoners and chuckled oddly. "Rebellion! Rebellion! They have tortured nearly all the founding generals of the nation to death. Smashing the institutions of police, prosecutor, and court! What's the outcome? Do *they* win the final victory, or do *we?* Not them. Instead of smashing us, they will be punished by the police, prosecutor, and court. Ha!" He flailed his arms, as if catching flies. Then he tightened his fist and threw the imaginary flies one by one into his mouth, where he ground them up with his teeth. After spitting them to the ground, he stamped on them with his feet as in a ritual dance. His superb performance finally revived us petrified prisoners, and the heavy, gloomy atmosphere gradually relaxed. But suddenly – again suddenly – the warden's mood changed, and he turned the spear of his words on us. "But you! I mean you the prisoners. Never dare to hope. The crimes of the Gang of Four are theirs; your crimes are yours. Each one of you will settle his own score! Don't entertain the idea that you will be released because of their arrest! Quit daydreaming! It's true that some of you were arrested for offending Jiang Qing. But to offend Jiang Qing then was to break the law. At that time, Zhang Chunqiao, Yao Wenyuan, and Wang Hongwen embodied the party's leadership, and you couldn't offend them simply because they were appointed by our great leader Chairman Mao to carry out his policies. They might have smuggled in their own goods, but no one could tell the sham from the genuine. Watch out, you prisoners. Do not forget who you are as you listen to the firecrackers. Holidays people take in order to celebrate their victory will be days of suffering for you counterrevolutionaries. In order to cool your heads, I hereby issue an order: no meals for you all day today, not a single grain of food or a sip of water. Scientists have proved that men who don't eat or drink never become muddleheaded."

On hearing the order of "no meals today," the saliva oozed out from number 95's mouth, and my limbs turned so soft I had to grab the iron bars to avoid falling. Our stomachs also reacted candidly with their rumbling complaints. According to the scientists' observation, as expressed by the warden, we starved prisoners all kept a cool head; he alone was muddleheaded because of his excessive drinking and eating. He continued to talk nonsense:

"Let's have a toast, a big, big, big toast! Our party comes to another critical moment, a turning point as important as the Zunyi Conference. Our victory proves the invincibility of Mao Zedong thought and the correctness and greatness of our party. Glorious! Great! Great, great, great! Long live Chairman Mao! Long, long, long live – eh, right. Chairman Mao passed away more than a month ago." All of a sudden, he realized the contradiction in his words. He was not completely muddleheaded after all. "But his spirit will never die. Long live Chairman Mao's spirit! Long, long live Mao Zedong thought!" The warden ran about with fists raised high, shouting slogans at the top of his voice. His clumsy feet soon began to stumble, struggling to keep the huge body upright. The warden swayed and finally collapsed to the ground. His slippers flew away like a pair of butterflies. The guards rushed over to lift him and drag him away. Yet his tongue kept going all the time.

"Great – glorious!" (chuckle) "Long live! – You! Let me immunize you: Do not entertain any dreams! The only thing for you – is to serve out your sentences submissively. Leniency to those who confess and severe punishment to those who resist."

The farce ended like that. I could not laugh; nor could the rest of the prisoners. Were we too numb, or too sober? Was it because the warden had drugged us? We did not realize how much information and what profound meanings his monologue contained until the warden had disappeared with his guards. I had learned for the first time that Chairman Mao had passed away. Although over a month ago I had seen the guards wearing black armbands, I dared not associate them with Mao's death. How could he possibly die? Just to think of his death was to commit a crime. I had believed it a sort of coincidence: the older guards had all died simultaneously, or the guards, being brothers of the same clan, were mourning for their shared patriarch. The latter convinced me more because the guards all dressed, acted, and yelled the same, including their style of smoking and of blowing smoke rings. Now I realized I had made a mistake. I wished now I could make up the grief I had failed to show because of my ignorance, but the nerves governing sarcastic humor, excited by the news of the Gang of Four's arrest, pinched my mourning nerves.

Overnight Jiang Qing and her followers had joined our ranks, wearing prisoner clothes and having their hair shaved off like us. Perhaps, being a female, Jiang Qing would be allowed to keep her hair, but no supply of French perfume anymore. How could the distance be so close between criminals and the four most, most, most … loyal pupils of Chairman Mao (more superlatives are replaced by "…" to avoid having readers accuse the author of gaining more royalties for the book); the four most, most, most … thorough proletarian revolutionary statespersons, the four most, most, most … resolute soldiers in following Chairman Mao's revolutionary line, and the four most, most, most … outstanding authorities of the proletarian revolution? Between Zhongnanhai and the prison there seemed to exist only a door. Pushing the door open, one could see prison cells right on the marble steps leading to Tiananmen Square. The difference between heroes and clowns seemed a mere matter of standing before or behind the screen. We ordinary people's falling into prison was like falling from a roof; the imprisonment of the citizens of paradise was like falling from heaven. Because the heights from which we and they fell were vastly different, the terrors each experienced must also be different. How amusing it was for me to measure, from their perspective, the psychological and biological burdens of their sudden, high-speed fall. On the other hand, they had climbed on my back to realize their ambitions. When they reigned over the nation and had it in their power to kill thousands of people without lifting a finger, had they ever thought one second about us as we struggled like ants to survive?

How would the two events I had just heard affect my personal life? (I did not want to call them great events, because there were too many great events happening in our era. I measured things simply according to their relation to me as an individual. Therefore, I had not thought of the significance they would have on our national history. Moreover, I was still a cog in the gears of state dictatorship.) If, as the warden had said, we and the Gang of Four each had to serve out his own sentence, and, if the right and wrong of one moment had nothing to do with the next, then the prison would have to be expanded yearly. In some dozens of years, the area devoted to prisons would cover the whole 9,600,000 square kilometers of Chinese territory. By that time there would be no difference between being inside and outside of prison, between law-abiding citizens and criminals or aliens. Perhaps all inveterate, hateful opponents would become reconciled, playing their joyful game like A, B, C, D, and E in our neighboring cell number 10046. Then, humankind would reach its one-world utopia. Truly, every road leads to Moscow. I had never thought there was such an easy path to the one-world utopia. Miaohuzhe? Miaozheyao! [Is that great? Truly great!] The classical interjections I learned in middle school slipped past my tongue. This proved that my memory had not deteriorated that much. So I prepared for more suffering.

I gaze at her window. In the past it was pasted over with black paper; now a cloth curtain with tiny blue flowers hangs there.

19

Six months had passed since Sunamei joined the county singing and dancing troupe. When she was applying makeup before a mirror for a performance or winning thunderous applause from the audience, she forgot Xienami, forgot Ami, forgot Yingzhi, forgot the serpentine mountain path from which she had come as well as the memories associated with it, such as the collective dance beat, the laughter of the threshers and the witty remarks they threw each other during harvesting in the millet fields, the gently rolling stones cast on the roof by the *axiao* at midnight, stealthy steps, and hugging and touching in the dark. But in the still of night when she, although tired, was unable to sleep, or when she was undergoing basic dance training on a beam, or when she was practicing monotonous musical scales, the scenes of her hometown flowed past her eyes and ears. Memory drowned reality. She grew absent-minded, often taking a wrong step, singing out of tune, or sighing in bed. She found it especially hard to control her imaginative recollections during the hours of political study and the criticism meetings. Because she did not quite understand the Chinese language, she found it even harder to comprehend political concepts, devoid as they were of color, smell, interest, and sexual stimulation. Some criticism meetings seemed to have no end, like rivers flowing on and on. Why hold such long meetings? Sometimes it was simply because a male singer and a female dancer had walked together for a while at night holding each other's hand. Yet at the meeting everyone was enraged, roaring at the pair, some even pounding on the desk. Their stern criticism made the lad want to hide his head between his legs and the girl wet a stack of kerchiefs with her tears. Sunamei understood neither why those people were so fierce nor what they were shouting. She hated the informer. Look what an ugly scene he had made. Why did he report them to the woman head of the troupe? And why did she have to lose her temper like that? They dealt with them so seriously, as if the man had attempted to murder the woman and the woman wanted to eat the man. After the criticism meeting, if the man stood in line for his meal, the woman dared not stand in the same line for fear of the public eye. Once, when Sunamei dragged her over and made her stand right behind the man, the girl did not dare to lift her eyes, and her face turned ghastly pale in spite of her willingness to be close to him.

After a criticism meeting like that, Sunamei felt depressed for days. She felt it was too hard to be a human being in this world full of prohibitions. What is the meaning of such a bleak existence? People should belong to themselves. It's my business whom I want to give my body to. If you want to give yourself to me, okay, if I am willing to accept you. A hand, a foot, even the whole body and the heart, whatever I want to give is for me to decide. Why do others need to interfere? Why are they so angry? The anger over the matter should be exclusively his or hers. It surprised Sunamei most when the next couple was caught and the earlier victims also roared at them and delivered tedious speeches at their criticism meeting. The meeting went on so long that Sunamei fell asleep. When she woke up, it was still going on.

But what depressed her most were not other people's affairs or the confusion caused by them, but things concerning herself. In her hometown, men's eyes focused on her like shafts of light when she was soloing on the stage. Not merely their eyes, men's footfalls and songs followed her wherever she went. Even when Yingzhi was with her in the room, there were still pebbles rolling on the roof and men with a ray of hope waiting outside the wall or gate. But here she could detect only men's stealthy eyes, which were not candid and passionate like those of Mosuo men. These eyes hid in the darkness or a faraway corner like thieves. When she met their gaze with hers, theirs immediately turned away or simply died out. It was not men who followed her all the time like a shadow but a female, a Han girl called Jiang Jiying. The very day Sunamei joined the troupe, the head of the troupe assigned her to share Jiang Jiying's room and said to her: Jiang Jiying is your elder sister, and she will take care of you.

Jiang Jiying was a small girl with thin bones and limbs. Only her eyes were large. Whether in real life or on stage, she was equally obscure. Yet she always watched over others wisely. She took good care of Sunamei, telling her where to fetch water, where to take a bath, and where to wash her clothes. And she even bought a brassiere for her and told her, "Girls must wear brassieres." Although Jiang had almost no breasts herself, she wore a type of brassiere with sponge-rubber padding. When Sunamei first put on her bra, she laughed into the mirror. But soon she felt stifled and cast it aside. Jiang reminded her time and again to wear it. This matter affected their friendship. Sometimes they didn't speak to each other for days on end. Jiang was fastidious about many things. For instance, she said when a girl sat in public, she should not open her legs but should keep them tightly closed.

"Why?"

"Ugly."

"I think it's pretty."

"Shameless."

"What shame is there?"

"A girl is not supposed to behave like that."

And, she said, "When a man looks at you, you should not look back at him."

"But I want to look back. Why can he gaze at me and I cannot do the same to him?"

"Because you are a woman."

"Isn't a woman human?"

"She is human, but not the same as a man."

"How do they differ? Is it because a woman does not have a penis?"

Stamping her feet, the embarrassed Jiang screamed, "Oh, have you no shame? How ugly, how dirty! How could a little girl say that word!"

But Sunamei insisted on saying it. Holding Jiang in her arms, she repeated it many times aloud. In a rage, Jiang slapped Sunamei's face, and Sunamei slapped hers in return. Again they stopped speaking to each other. Jiang still followed her around mutely, like a shadow.

A few days later they returned to their speaking relationship. But soon they quarreled again, this time because Sunamei wanted to ask Manager Tao about the sexual relationship between men and women, but Jiang forbade her to do so.

"Why can't I ask?"

"Because it's not a good thing."

"If it's not good, why do people do it?"

"Nonsense."

"If people didn't do it, where would babies come from?"

Covering her ears, Jiang shouted, "Shame on you!"

"Why shouldn't I ask about something I don't understand?"

"Even if you don't understand, being a girl, you should never ask."

Sunamei tried to get rid of her guardian, but not very successfully. Jiang bought two pairs of panties and asked Sunamei to wear them. When they were dirty, Jiang offered to wash them for her, but did not allow her to dry either the panties or the brassiere in the yard. They had to be dried inside.

"Why?"

"It's bad for men to see them."

"Why?"

"Because. Please don't ask."

"I want to dry them in the yard, in the warm sunlight."

"No! These things are too dirty."

"But you've already washed them for me. They are now white as snow."

"Women's underwear can never be washed clean."

Clapping her hands and beating her thighs, Sunamei laughed, "Men's underwear is much harder to clean because their bodies sweat oil every day."

Jiang Jiying was so annoyed with Sunamei she even shed tears over her ignorance. Jiang reported everything to Manager Tao, even trifling things the size of a sesame seed. So Manager Tao often talked patiently to Sunamei. Unfortunately, Sunamei could hardly understand what she was saying. The hazy impression Sunamei got from all her speeches was that her behavior and ideas did not suit the social codes.

Sunamei thought to herself: "Why do people have to make so many codes? If I followed them, what kind of person would I become?" She thought at once of Jiang — the model Manager Tao set for her — and burst out laughing.

Manager Tao was shocked by her reaction and warned her severely, "Comrade Sunamei, this is for your own good." Although Sunamei had almost checked her laughter, on hearing the last sentence she had a second bout of laughing. Angrily turning to look up at the ceiling, Manager Tao used her greatest patience to wait until Sunamei stopped her fit of laughter with tears and a sobbing breath. "A girl should know what is proper and learn to be decent. I believe, with our hard efforts, you will change." Sunamei finally checked her laughing by pinching her own thigh. Tao Zhengfang thought her patient teaching had at last produced some effect. One cannot be impatient with a girl born in a primitive society. Patting Sunamei's head affectionately, she made a gesture for Jiang to leave.

Gradually, Sunamei realized that Jiang Jiying had been sent by the authorities to supervise her, and that all the males in the dancing and singing troupe had been warned not to associate with her. "So, you are playing games with me in the dark," she thought. "I'm not stupid." She started playing hide-and-seek with Jiang. Taking advantage of Jiang's sound sleep, Sunamei stole out of the dorm. Jiang woke up at midnight in a cold sweat. She immediately reported Sunamei's absence to Manager Tao, who sent out a dozen men to search in town, almost like taking a census. The county was stirred up with the tale of catching a spy. In the morning, they found Sunamei practicing singing in a woods on the hilltop overlooking the county. "Why did you all get up so early?" she asked with affected surprise.

Jiang retorted, "Why did *you* get up so early?"

"I couldn't sleep."

"What have you been doing the whole night long?"

"Training my voice."

How could anyone find fault in someone training her voice? The earlier she got up, the harder she trained herself for revolution.

Once, when they were shopping on the street, Sunamei disappeared when Jiang blinked. Jiang searched everywhere among the crowds and was on the verge of tears when she asked an old granny who was selling preserved turnips. "Old Granny, have you seen Sunamei?"

"Which Sunamei?"

"The girl who sang 'I Am Waiting for You by the River' on the stage."

"Oh, that Mosuo girl."

"Yes, that's right."

"She's right behind you, isn't she?"

"Oh!" Turning her head, she found Sunamei right behind her, smiling. "Where have you been?"

"Behind you."

"I've been looking for you everywhere. Why didn't you say anything?"

"How should I know you were looking for me? You were running so anxiously, and my feet got sore running after you. I thought you were looking for a man."

Jiang was so angry that tears swam in her eyes.

"Jiang, you must be very tired." Sunamei hopped lightly to lead the way. Jiang, wiping her eyes, hurried to follow for fear of losing sight of her again.

One night, Jiang and Sunamei were lying in bed awake. Jiang suddenly asked a question she should not have asked: "Sunamei, do you have a daddy at home?"

"What's a *daddy?*" Sunamei asked deliberately.

"Daddy is your father – your mother's husband."

"My family does not have fathers, and my *ami* does not have a husband."

"I mean the man who lives with your mother so as to bring you into this world."

"If no man had slept with my mother, how could I have been born?"

"Look how obscene your words are!"

"If you have better words, please teach them to me. If *sleep* isn't right, then let's say they played with each other."

"Even more disgusting! All right, I want to sleep now."

Sunamei giggled naughtily. "You want to sleep, but I want to talk. Let me tell you, our families do not have fathers. A father is not a member of our family, for he has his own family. Mine only came to look for my mother at night and sleep with her. They played together."

Jiang covered her head in protest. But Sunamei did not stop explaining. She told in detail how Mosuo people make *axiao* and express their love, related her own experience of having Longbu and Yingzhi and even described vividly the pleasures of her sexual life. Because she did not have a vocabulary of euphemism or ambiguity, she told everything candidly, crudely, and incompletely. Jiang seemed to have fallen asleep. Sunamei called to her: "Jiang! Would you like to go with me to my hometown and have a look some day?"

All of a sudden a pillow flew over and hit Sunamei, making her break into a laugh. As expected, Jiang was not sleeping and had heard Sunamei's every word. Jumping out of bed naked, Sunamei lifted Jiang's head gently and placed the pillow under it.

20

I gaze at her window. In the past it was pasted over with black paper; now a cloth curtain with tiny blue flowers hangs there.

The drizzling rain feels nice. Lifting my face, I try to receive as many drops as I can. The longer I stand here, the more I seem to gain strength. I try my legs. Good! I do not need the support of the tree any more.

There are few cars and people on the street; it is pretty late. I lift the baggage at my feet. Actually, it is not baggage, being dirtier and more worn out than the rags people pick up from the garbage. When the warden announced my release, and I stretched out my hand for something like a document, he misunderstood me and thought I was asking for any belongings confiscated on my arrival at the prison. In fact, I had brought nothing to prison. Never expecting we would get out of prison alive, the warden had dumped all the prisoners' belongings in a leaky storeroom, and they gradually became a moldy hill. He took some of them and passed them to me at the end of a rope.

I said, "I don't want them because I brought nothing here."

He said, "Don't stand on ceremony. I know you are homeless."

I said, "I have a girlfriend."

He shook his head with a sigh. "Young fellow, you are

your most dependable friend. As a released convict, do you expect to be received like a returning hero? Take it with you. Don't worry, it cost me nothing. Perhaps its owner has already gone to the other world."

I accepted the goodwill of the dead owner and asked again for a release document.

He explained, "Because you came in without a warrant, you are now freed without an official paper. Just leave. No need to worry about technicalities. The important thing is your freedom. For now just leave."

I had a good laugh over that. A man being imprisoned and released for no reason is a technicality.

Yes, I have a girlfriend. She and I once shared the sweet world of a cocoon. She had once pretended to be an investigator to see me in jail. Although it was only one visit, it's the reason I'm looking for her now. She won't refuse me, because adversity had brought us together. We knew each other so well that her personality, her voice, her smile, and her eagerness for my kiss at the most unforgettable moments flash before me as if they had occurred yesterday and we had parted only this morning. With a few vigorous strides, I cross the street. I gasp all the way upstairs, reaching the third floor to stand before her door. I lean against the door for a while to catch my breath. The door opens at my knock and I use my hand to shade my eyes from the sharp light from inside.

"Who are you looking for?" asks the grudging voice of a middle-aged woman.

"I'm looking for Yunqian." As my eyes gradually adapt themselves to the light, Yunqian comes over, uttering in surprise: "Oh, it's you, Liang Rui!" She waves at the plump, middle-aged woman with her hand to provide introductions: "My mother and father." She points to a gray-haired old man sitting in the midst of crowded furniture. Her father seems to recognize the name *Liang Rui*. Straightening his back with his hands pressed against his knees, he watches me attentively. The first response from the mother is a loud complaint.

"Sorry, but please leave your stuff outside the door. The mayor's skin is terribly delicate. If a flea is brought in, it would be disastrous." She dumps my stuff outside and adds a smile. "Don't worry. It won't get lost; nobody would want it."

I swallow the insult, for my stuff really is a mess. Looking around the apartment, I find it has lost the magic vision of our cocoon, as it is now crammed with floor lamps, electric fans, plates, and bowls.

Yunqian explains: "My mother has brought back our old furniture. We are moving into a house soon. The new house is being whitewashed; things are a mess at the moment." I had hoped to find something familiar in her voice, but unfortunately there is nothing. As if standing in a waste-land, I suddenly feel lonely.

Her father says nothing, and her mother, after getting rid of my dirty stuff, disappears into the kitchen, perhaps to wash her chubby hands. By recollection and association of the past and present, it becomes clear to me that Yunqian's stepmother, who had rebelled against the family, has returned of her own accord. Her tactic is truly admirable. For ten years she suffered nothing, and in the end simply came back to assume her role of mistress. In addition, she kept her interest in the family property. She could be said to be the heroine who has saved the family – in a round-about way.

Finally, my eyes fall on Yunqian. Although the spring is chilly, she is wearing close-fitting wool pants of a light gray color, a white silk blouse, and a rose-colored lamb's wool sweater, unbuttoned. In spite of her placid face, her gently undulating chest betrays the turmoil in her heart. Her expression is cool. To be fair, her eyes do show signs of con-trolled affection. But I can't imagine the body thus clothed as the one I had once embraced. The distance between us has become a hundred thousand times greater than the distance between us in my memory. I no longer feel weak, and my vision and hearing have regained their sensitivity.

The little room is still filled with Tchaikovsky's Sixth Symphony, not an illusion but real notes hanging in the air. I notice that the album no longer makes the needle jump at every revolution. There are no extra quarter notes or intervals of a sixth. The symphony is now complete. Perhaps the tune flowing through Tchaikovsky's brain when he was composing it had been like this: fluent, sonorous, cheerful and sorrowful. I suppress my weak soul, called up by this music. Saying nothing – actually I had nothing to say – like a foreign military officer, I arrogantly march out the door. Picking up my stuff like a fancy suitcase, I quickly zoom downstairs.

I heard Yunqian's steps following me closely. "Liang Rui, Liang Rui, Liang Rui!"

I walked to the street and heard the window open. Yunqian's parents were calling together. "Yunqian, Yunqian! Please come back, come back!"

Yunqian ignored them, and I ignored her. She caught up with me and walked beside me, saying, "Liang Rui, you are too proud."

I gazed at my path, illuminated by two rows of street lamps.

"Liang Rui, where are you going to settle down?"

The path ahead was endless.

"I can help you. Now my father will probably be rehabilitated. I can help you."

I felt proud that I could walk so steadily and so fast by myself.

"You should forgive me, because now everything has become normal again."

Everything has become normal? Thank heavens. Thanks to this generous drizzle that nurtured my parched lips. In prison I never got to drink such pure water, nor could I lift my face freely like this.

"You know I love you – " The word *love,* tumbling from her mouth at that moment, seemed out of place. If the street lamps could say love, and the raindrops could say love, and any stranger coming toward me could say love, it would seem more apt.

"It's a pity we have only love and nothing – nothing else."

My stride quickened.

"If nothing else but love, love alone. But I love you."

Having been released, I wanted to whistle. Human beings die so easily and are resurrected so quickly.

Her steps became slower and slower. The distance between us grew greater and greater, from the measurable to the immeasurable. How simple, much simpler than falling in love at first sight. Fortunately, I was not a romantic. The sharp blade of night cut off the road behind me. I would never again look up at that window. I regretted not anticipating the consequences when I was gazing at the window, where a cloth curtain with tiny blue flowers now hung.

The world of humanity was merciful and considerate. Thinking of food, I found a small wonton shop on the street. It sold baked cakes, too. I had 2.25 yuan, given me by number 97. He was the first in cell number 45 to be released from prison. In his excitement he had taken out the cash hidden in the sole of his shoe, 11.25 yuan in all. Divided into five shares, each inmate got 2.25 yuan. Everyone had to accept it, because he said it was good luck and wished we all could be released like him. So I accepted, and he permitted no thanks. Now the money would be put to good use. Before I entered the shop, I really did not know how the manager and its customers would treat me. I immediately recalled Hugo's *Les Misérables,* a book Yunqian and I had read together, in which Jean Valjean could not buy any food with the money in his hand after being released from prison. Now how about the currency in my hand? I stood hesitantly at the entrance. I wanted to tell the manager that I did have money. Crowded with customers, the shop seemed to have no vacant seat. From their eyes, I could see how filthy and fearful I looked. The manager in the kitchen was a young, good-hearted woman. She was stretching her white arms into the oven to remove baked cakes; she looked at me with pity. Pity was of course better than disgust, although I did not need either.

She said, "Tsk, tsk! What a poor man. If he is not fresh from jail, he must be going up to make an appeal."

The customers pushed back to make room for me, and I sat down unceremoniously. They were huddled together; I had all the space I needed. I tried to order like a wealthy man who frequents restaurants. "Four bowls of wonton and four cakes."

"Okay," the manager answered with an affected calm. In less than a minute, she and a waiter brought me the food: not four but eight bowls of wonton, not four but eight cakes, doubling my order. I looked at her with a puzzled look.

She said, "Eat more. Eat all you can. Half this order is on me. Free."

Swallowing the saliva oozing into my mouth, I folded two cakes one on top of the other and took giant bites. I felt all the customers in the shop put down their bowls and chopsticks and stop chewing. I could hear only my own loud munching. But I couldn't be bothered. In my life I had never eaten such crisp, tasty cakes. Before I knew it, the eight cakes were gone. Then I started in on the soup. Two and a half mouthfuls a bowl – no more than ten seconds each – and eight empty bowls were stacked on the table. In the end, I even picked up the scattered sesame seeds with my sticky, dirty fingers and popped them into my mouth for a good chew. I heard a commotion of surprise and admiration from the onlookers.

The woman manager, quietly picking up the eight bowls, asked me, "Do you want more?"

"That's enough. Here's the money." I passed all my money to her, as I had no knowledge of the price of things in the human world. After a while, she gave me my change wrapped in a neat square of clean paper. I took it, stood up, pulled aside the bench, and nodded goodbye. I was too full to bow to her. "Thanks."

"Don't mention it. Take care, take care."

No sooner did I go out than all the customers in the shop started talking as if someone had hit a beehive. I could not hear what they were saying, nor did I wish to.

The endless road belonged to me again. The rain let up. Standing in the middle of the street, I saw that nearly all the shops had closed and that the lights from the windows by the street were drastically reduced. Each light extinguished meant one person or one couple, or a whole family taking their nightly rest, enjoying warm quilts, the warm breath of their loved ones, and warm dreams. I heard a voice of protest from my heart to this world. "Is there a place for me to go? Is there a place I can stay?"

A tiny tobacco shop in the distance was still open, casting a spot of yellow light on the street. I suddenly felt a craving for a smoke. As I had never smoked before, I did not know the taste of tobacco. Why did I want to smoke? Perhaps my stomach was full. When the stomach is full, does a man have more desires? Smoking must be a special kind of joy. Shutting my eyes, I recalled many smokers' delight. Narrowing the eyes, one lit up a cigarette, inhaled half the smoke and exhaled the other half from the nostrils. Even the way a man knocks the ash from his cigarette conveys pleasure. I stood at the glass shop counter, dazzled by the rich, colorful brands.

Measuring me with surprised eyes, the girl behind the counter asked, "Cigarettes?"

"Yes." I handed her my money.

"What brand?"

"Eh…" Suddenly the brand Great China caught my eye and slipped from my tongue. "Great China, if I have enough money."

Unwrapping the paper, the girl told me, "More than enough. You have five yuan here."

Five yuan? Impossible. How could I have that much money? "Look, one one-yuan bill and two two-yuan bills. Doesn't that make five?"

"Oh." Now I realized that the woman manager must have given me the money. I wanted to laugh at myself. She had treated me like Han Xin [a man of the Three Kingdoms who early in his life had been insulted by being forced to crawl between others' legs, but eventually became a great general]. Yet I had never thought of seeking favors from anyone. The girl gave me a packet of Zhonghua cigarettes. She handed me a matchbox with my change. I took out a cigarette. With a long sigh, I kissed the golden characters of Zhonghua, which gave the girl a big scare.

I struck a match as I was walking to light the cigarette dangling from my lips. I dared not pull hard but had to puff cautiously. As soon as the smoke entered my mouth, I spit it out. Awful! Maybe it took a big mouthful to get the right taste. So I took a deep drag. When the smoke rushed into my throat, a peppery sensation made me cough. It took a while to suppress the cough. I found it hard to understand why so many people in the world smoke this sort of thing, using their mouths and noses as chimneys. I tossed the cigarette from my mouth into a ditch and pocketed the other nineteen.

Not a single random soul was wandering about; my feet alone engaged in a tedious dialogue with the long, long street. After walking and walking, finally I saw a man standing like a statue. Under a street lamp on the verge of falling as it rattled in the wind, the small old man was attentively reading the newspaper he held in his hands. As the source of light came from above, his face was not clearly illuminated. His forehead blocked the light from his eyes; his nose blocked it from his mouth, and his shoulders blocked it from his torso. Only his white hair received the full light, like a blazing torch. The whole image of the man was distorted. At my approach, he laid down his paper and glanced at me. Then he quickly covered his face with the paper. I knew he had seen me clearly because I was facing the light. After a while, his eyes peeked over the top of the paper. I halted right in front of him. Again he covered his face with the paper. Seeing he was a rare being like me in the street, I felt the common link of birds in a flock and had a natural desire to communicate with him. Yet he shunned me. Partitioned merely by a sheet of paper, he and I stood silent for ninety seconds. He couldn't take it any longer. Folding his paper, he ran away. With that motion, the light on him changed radically. The angle of the cone of light expanded and its luminosity weakened, but the contour of the man became clear. When the angle reached thirty degrees, I recognized him: Gui Renzhong! Old turtle egg! My blood started boiling. I sprang on him, strangling him with my plierlike hands. He was unable to make a sound; his face turned from white to red, his hands holding the newspaper fluttered in the air, and his eyes pleaded with me in fright. When the soul's light flickering in his pupils was about to die out, my heart contracted in pain and my fingers relaxed. In the twinkling of an eye, his eyes shaped into a smile, that naive, childlike, and trustful smile I had seen before. My hands moved to his bony back, embracing him tightly. I kissed his icy cheeks. As he pressed his old lips together, tears showered from his hazy eyes. Like a woman, he wept in my arms, his body gradually sliding down till he was kneeling in front of me. With the strength given me by eight bowls of wonton and eight baked cakes, I jerked him to his feet and said, "Old man, what's the use of crying? If blood is worthless, how much money can tears be worth?

How are things now? Are you all right? I'm asking about your present, not your past. Why are you reading a newspaper alone in the street at midnight? Something important?"

No reply. Where to start? He simply passed the paper to me. I saw the front page was filled with Hua Guofeng's corpulent face and a speech.

"Ai!" I gave a loud sigh, tearing the paper to shreds.

Gui Renzhong said nervously, "It carries the portrait of Chairman Hua and his latest instructions. Don't you know, Chairman Mao told him before he passed away, 'With you in charge, I am at ease.'"

"I care for nothing at the moment. I want only to know where I can find a nest and have a good sleep."

"Come to my house," he offered immediately. "I have many rooms."

"Many rooms? Then why do you read the paper under the streetlight at midnight?"

"The old lady is too mean. She doesn't give me a moment's peace."

"Old lady? Did you marry again?"

"Same woman, same house."

"So, another American friend of yours is visiting you, is that right?"

"Not one, but several groups already."

"Because they come now and then, you don't need to move in and out any more."

"That's right. Okay, let's go. With you there, I bet that woman will behave better."

"Can I step into the Gui residence in rags like this?"

"Stop kidding me, little Liang. Let's go." We left, our arms around each other's shoulders.

At the entrance to the Gui residence Gui Renzhong took a key out of his pants pocket and opened the gate, turning on the yard light. The door was unlocked and opened with a gentle push. He turned on all the lights in the sitting room, and the room brightened magnificently. Instantly, Xie Li roared from upstairs, "You aren't blind yet, so why turn on so many lights?"

"We have a guest," said Gui timidly.

"What guest? The American president? They installed a new electric meter, and we have to pay the bill ourselves. Did you know that, dirty pig?"

"Yes, I knew – " He was going to turn off the lights when I stopped him.

Hurried footsteps resounded on the stairs. In less than a second, the raging Xie Li appeared before us. A blue-striped bathrobe hung from her shoulders, and her brassiere and briefs and garter belt for stockings of an unknown age showed. With curlers all over her head, she looked like an angry Pekingese. Looking me over from head to foot, she howled and stamped her feet. "Beasts! You are nothing but selfish animals!"

Old Gui hid behind me. "What's the matter?" I asked calmly.

"Do you need to ask? Look at your feet, they're pig's feet. How could you set them on the carpet of our house?!" Raising her eyebrows and glaring at me with her apricot eyes, she looked as if she were about to tear me to pieces.

I stared at her and said softly: "Don't you remember? 'Without cow dung on your feet, you cannot be called a revolutionary.' Do not soil your own face."

"Who are you?" She was obviously irritated at the truth in my words.

"He is – " Old Gui was about to introduce me, but I stopped him.

"Who *are* you?" Obviously she didn't remember me. They say it's hard for a person who has made his fortune to remember his old acquaintances. The dark shadow of two years' imprisonment also had changed me enormously, and we had met only once before.

"You don't know me?"

"No."

"But I know you."

"You know me?"

"Of course, I know you. You're Xie Li, whose grand name was linked to important titles in the first, second, and third Headquarters of the East-Is-Red Red Guards' Rebellion, the Headquarters of the Workers Rebelling to the End, the Regiment of the Lord's Whip, the Writers' Association Defending Jiang Qing, and militant groups such as the Magic Club and the Ambitious Men, and the propaganda team of the Great Union.... Shall I continue?"

"You!" Her voice quaked. "You – want to persecute me?"

"I want you to know that I am in possession of all your records."

"All of them?"

"All of them, including some things only one or two people know."

"Let's open the window and be frank. What do you want?"

"For now, I want to sleep. You can wait and see my next move."

"Sleep, fine. I can tidy up a room for you."

"Don't bother. I'll share a bed with old Gui tonight. Let's go, old Gui. Upstairs." I dragged him upstairs to the large master bedroom. Xie Li, following me nervously, took her clothes and sneaked downstairs.

I shut the bedroom door. "Look, old Gui. I've harnessed her, haven't I? One has to use the devil's tricks against a devil. She has a mean face, so your face has to be even meaner. Old Gui, look at yourself!" Suddenly feeling my weariness, I said, "I must take a bath."

"Fine, there's the hot water. That woman heats water for her bath every day. Take it in the bathroom. I'll find some clean clothes for you."

I went into the bathroom and filled the tub with hot water, and then soaked off a pound of oily dirt. When I emerged from the bath, old Gui jumped with joy. "Old brother, you look really refreshed. Quick, get under the quilt, warmed by that woman's body."

I got under the warm quilt. By the time old Gui came to bed, I was utterly exhausted. He asked, "Old brother, you need some plans. What's your first step, a job or – ?"

"No. My first step is to help you get rid of that tigress – " Those were my last words before falling asleep.

21

The interstate bus was crawling along the desolate mountain road. I rested my forehead on the back of the seat before me. The bus looked like a remodeled liberation truck of the fifties. A piston in its engine was already loose. Going uphill, its body trembled and the engine coughed like an old asthmatic. I was afraid it would break down at any moment. The seats were close together and my legs were doubled up miserably.

This was supposed to be the last day of my journey: three days by train, with two transfers, plus four days by bus. If I didn't reach my destination soon, my legs would break. Raising my head from the seat back, I saw that all the other passengers were dozing. The early summer sun heated the bus roof like the lid of a steamer. The national minority passengers, in heavy clothing, looked especially hot. Then there were the women of the Li nationality with their long, wide, ruffled skirts, and the Tibetan men in leather coats. Seeing those passengers reminded me that I was already near China's southwestern border.

How did I get here? Released from prison, then losing the love of the cocoon...eight bowls of wonton and eight baked cakes...running into old Gui in the street...my first sound sleep outside prison...a month's thorough investigation to expose all of Xie Li's activities during the Cultural Revolution. We bombarded her with all the evidence and asked her to choose official or private settlement.

She asked, "What do you mean, *official or private?*"

"By *official,* we mean we will submit all your material to the Office of Investigation, Examination, and Sentencing; by *private,* we mean you simply hand us the marriage certificate – a forged document anyway. It, too, is proof of your illegal activity."

After thinking it over for a day and a night, the woman handed over the marriage certificate. I burned it in front of old Gui. Xie Li took her bedroll and left the Gui residence submissively. Having the tigress driven away would give old Gui a better chance of survival. The victory built up my self-confidence, so I went to the party committee of the Institute of Fine Arts, demanding a reversal of my verdict, restitution of my financial loss, and a job. After an investigation, the committee concluded, "Your imprisonment was an error. Because there was no verdict, there is nothing to reverse. During the ten years of turmoil, more than ten thousand people have suffered financial loss. We hope you understand the hard times the party and the state are facing. Assigning you a job is routine work. Although you have not completed your studies, we can still give you a diploma. As to the place of occupation, you must make a request first. Then the institute will try its best to accommodate your choice. But it is hard to stay in Beijing or Shanghai because control of the residence registrations for these two cities is in the hands of higher departments."

To my amusement, when I told them my choice – to work in the most remote, most primitive place, better still a place in a prehistoric state – they thought I had gone mad.

"Are you showing your anger?"

"No. I'm quite calm."

"You suffered a nervous breakdown when you were wronged."

"No, I'm not crazy. You may ask a doctor from the mental hospital to give me a checkup."

"If we approve your choice, you will accuse us of finding a new way to persecute you."

"I'll write my choice down."

"You'll live to regret it."

"It's too late for regrets. A person like me should never have been born."

"Don't talk like that. We'd still like you to think it over carefully."

"I've been thinking it over for ten years. Some people say the ten years passed in vain. I don't agree. Wisdom comes from setbacks. After so many setbacks, shouldn't I have gained some true wisdom? I've made up my mind."

"So this is a rational decision."

"Right. It would be impossible for me to make a purely emotional decision, even if you wanted it that way, because my feelings have dried up."

The other procedures went smoothly. In China going down, like a flowing river, is much easier than climbing up. All men want to go upstream; men like me, who prefer to go downstream, are nearly extinct. So all the officials and passengers I met on my descent were astonished and found me incomprehensible. In fact, I was quite easy to comprehend. Being tired of noise, one simply wants a quiet place; after turning somersaults all one's life, one longs for a place to stand up; after being scorched by fire, one wants to roll in the snow. I was no odd fish, just an ordinary man.

The lofty mountain peaks outside the window had become a paper-cut silhouette. A sliver of sun from between the mountains cast a shaft of hazy redness eastward. The bus, as if stricken by a heart attack, collapsed to a stop. All the passengers fought to get out – all but me. Let them all out, and I would become conspicuous. I had been told that a county representative would meet me at the bus station. I tried to get rid of the dust blocking my vision by blowing upward along my nose. Then I held my straw hat and baggage and got off the bus. The other passengers, welcomed by their friends and relatives, gradually dispersed. The station was deserted. I looked around to view my new world. It seemed to be taking my measure, too. What was I like in the eye of this world – of a so-called town with a single dimly lit intersection? The sky looked very high. I thought the stars here would be bigger; actually they looked about the same, although perhaps brighter. Had no one come to meet me? No matter, since I had little baggage and the town was tiny. I could search for my work unit.

"Are you Liang Rui?" A man in a faded army cap suddenly stood before me, as if he had popped out of the ground. He was not tall, and looked like a low-ranking cadre.

"Yes. And you?"

"I am Luo Ren, head of the County Cultural Bureau." He neither shook my hand nor helped me with my baggage. "Come with me."

I followed the bureau chief into the town. He was a quiet man. The town was a quiet place where people tuck in early. A street lamp on a short post shone at the intersection and an old granny squatted on the ground, selling rice noodle soup.

We stopped at the gate beneath a sign that said County Cultural Bureau. Perhaps inspired by the photos in a pictorial spread, the architect had designed the gate in a mock-European style. The bureau chief groped for his key and opened the gate. We entered the beaten-earth yard. He pushed open a door on the western wing and flicked on the light. The light was dim and shaky, perhaps because of the generator's throbbing. Actually, it was only half a room; the other half was shut off by a wall of sun-dried bricks. The half room was about seven meters square. On a board supported by two benches were heaped some cracked tongs, drums with holes in them, and instruments with broken strings. On the floor there was a coverless wooden trunk stuffed with old flags. One thing among them was new – a color picture of Hua Guofeng's corpulent face. By the window stood a drawerless desk.

He asked me to sit, but I did not know where. Aware of my problem, he wiped the board with his sleeve and all the instruments tumbled to the ground in a loud chorus. They sounded cheerful, as if they had seldom had a chance like this to show their existence. I put my straw hat, baggage, and bottom on the board. He seated himself on the edge of the coverless trunk.

"Hungry?" He asked me kindly.

"Past the peak of hunger, I guess."

"It's hard to find food and boiled water at this hour of the night. All the shops are closed."

"I'm not thirsty." I licked my chapped lips.

Either because he dared not ask more questions or because he was not a man of words, he was silent for five minutes before taking out a wrinkled cigarette packet. "Have a smoke."

"Sorry, I don't smoke. I tried it once, but it's not for me."

Tucking a cigarette into his mouth, he asked, "Did you study painting?"

"Yes, a little. Later, the Cultural Revolution – "

"I heard you – " I knew what he was asking.

"I've been in prison."

"I know. I read your files. You were wronged, but why did you – ?" I could guess what puzzled him.

"I came here of my own accord."

"Oh?" He looked at me askance.

"Before I came I read a lot of books about this area in a library."

"Our city is a poor, backward place."

"I know that. But no matter how poor and backward it is, it's much better than any prison made by technology."

"Of course."

"According to the written records, a country of women

existed here in the past." I was merely trying to keep the conversation going.

"Not just in the past. The Mosuo people are still a matrilineal, extended-family community."

"Still?"

"Yes. Along Lake Lugu, not far from here — "

"Wow!"

"You can rest now. The conditions of our Cultural Bureau are just as you see them. The bureau is still discussing your assignment. Better stay here for a while. Tomorrow the county dining hall will open at seven — still dark in this area." He turned to leave. I posed myself a mathematical problem: how many fifths of ten square meters are there in seven square meters? I even expressed it as an equation: seven divided by ten fifths equals 3.5. Satisfied with the result, I happily went to sleep.

Early in the morning, a heavy knocking at my window woke me up. It was not yet light. Pushing the window open from outside, Bureau Chief Luo handed me a bowl and chopsticks. He held an aluminum pot in his arms. "It's time to buy your meal, otherwise you'll miss it. I'll show you the ropes."

Taking up the bowl and chopsticks, I couldn't help thinking that prison was more convenient, because there you ate what you were given. There were no problems of overeating or leftovers, and you never needed to pick your teeth or worry about a bone sticking in your throat because fish and meat were not served. Now I had to buy my own meal tickets and plan every meal — a real bother. But all this was still simpler than frequenting banquets. I tumbled off the board, and my feet slipped right into my shoes. Bowl and chopsticks in hand, I walked into the yard. The whole process took three seconds.

"Already dressed?" the bureau chief asked.

"I never undressed."

"Don't you wash your face?" He pointed to the water tap in a corner of the yard.

"Sure." Turning on the water, I splashed some water on my face then dried it with my sleeves: another three seconds. The deadpan face of the bureau chief cracked into a faint smile.

The bureau chief introduced me to the staff members and showed them my papers and let them check my ID. Having bought the tickets, I followed Luo to wait in three lines for three items: a bowl of porridge, two Chinese potatoes, and a little rock salt. As he was about to tell me to take my time with breakfast because he had to feed his wife and children at home, he found that my huge bowl of porridge and two potatoes and the salt had disappeared in the twinkling of an eye: another three seconds.

"Wonderful!" Apparently he found my swiftness satisfactory. "Nothing has been planned for you today. You may look around our town."

"Fine." I accepted his suggestion joyfully.

Back at the Culture Bureau, I washed my dishes, brushed my teeth (no time to do this before breakfast), and then went out into the street. The town consisted of two intersecting main streets and several lanes. At a regular walking speed, a tour around it took ten minutes. (By the way, at our parting old Gui had given me a fashionable and expensive electronic watch, a suitable present for a lazy boy like me.) My impression of the town was that, like a sparrow, although small, it had all the requisite organs. It had everything a town should have: a county revolutionary committee, a county committee of the Communist party, a league committee, a trade union, a federal association of women, a Bureau of Education, a Building Bureau, a Security Department, a prosecutor, a court, a first prison, a second prison, and a detention cell, a gas station, a post office, a movie theater, restaurants, an interurban bus station, a weather station, a fire department, an agricultural development post. I counted one hundred and seventy-two placards, each hanging at the entrance of a unit. Apart from the few people taking care of food stands, kiosks for cigarettes, and portable barber baskets, I wondered whether there were any others who did not live off of the government. Perhaps this was a typical feature of socialist nationalization. My second tour of the town was done in deliberate slow motion. It took me two hours and six minutes to carefully study all the gates – their styles, locations, distance from one to the other, and so on. Like a scout, I drew a detailed map in my mind. At noon I ate two bowls of peppery rice noodles, which gave me a good sweat, in the largest restaurant of the town, Four New Things.

Strolling out of the town, I entered a fir forest. A stream rushed to welcome me with its singing. By the stream were several tents put up by the Tibetan caravan men, who were resting around bonfires. Two Tibetan girls, lying prone on the ground, were whispering to each other, their long pigtails draped down their backs. An old man wearing a silver shield sat at the foot of the hill, shaking his prayer stick and silently chanting the name of Buddha. Their horses grazed freely beside the green stream. The azaleas in the woods were burning red like tongues of wild fire. Oh, this was the arcadia that had seduced me from thousands of miles away.

I walked over to the bonfire of the two Tibetan girls and nodded a greeting. One of them winked back at me naughtily. I boldly sat down before them and they immediately sat up and threw me a saddle to sit on. Then they picked up a big bronze kettle and poured some cocoa like liquid into a wooden bowl for me. They were both beautiful, with high noses and big eyes, and they looked like sisters. The liquid had a strange taste. They laughed at me and said something to the praying man at the foot of the hill. They must have been talking about my odd look when I drank the hot liquid. "Buttered tea – buttered tea – " The younger girl pointed to the wooden bowl and stammered in Mandarin.

"Good drink – good drink – " I had heard of buttered tea before but did not know it tasted like this. I can't say it was tasty.

The elder one took the wooden bowl to feed me, but I took it back from her. She said, "Drink some more – the more you drink the better it tastes." I took another sip and found it better than the first one; the bitterness left on the tongue became sweet. Closing my eyes, I took a large mouthful. The girls laughed so hard they rolled on the grass. Then they got up and filled my bowl again. Leaning against the saddle, I watched these two hospitable hostesses, who were so delighted with my quick adaptation to the buttered tea. Actually, they did not know I had once adapted my taste to food even a pig would turn its nose up at; later it even became a delicacy I dreamed about day and night. The two were whispering again, obviously about me. They had forgotten that even if they spoke loudly I couldn't understand a word they said. They then poured some toasted barley flour out of a lambskin sack and kneaded it with buttered tea for me. I never expected that such an unpleasant food could stimulate my appetite so much that I drank a dozen bowls of buttered tea and consumed half their sack of barley flour. The more I drank and ate, the happier they looked. They quickly boiled another kettle of tea and poured it into a bamboo cylinder. After adding some butter and salt, they whipped it with a special stick until tea and butter lost their own identity and mixed into one cocoa-colored liquid. Because they did the work in turns, laughing and talking all the time in their heavy clothes, their faces flamed. The heavy smell of Tibetan girls' sweat enshrouded me. As with the buttered tea, I was repulsed at first but gradually got used to it. Then my nose was drawn to that sour and butter-flavored, intoxicating smell. I wanted to take a nap by the fire, but with my eyes wide open because I could not tear my eyes from the girls. Maybe they noticed my tiredness. Exchanging glances, they took out a dented army flask, and as soon as it was open I smelled wine. They passed it to me. Not wishing to decline their offer, I took a drink. The elder sister took one and the younger one took one. Then she passed it to me again. We drank several rounds like this. The wine, made from barley grown in Tibet and Qinghai, was delicious. We passed it around without a word, but with laughter and shifting eyes. Gradually, drowsiness overwhelmed me, although I tried desperately to keep my eyes open. I wished them to never stop passing me the wine and blocking my view of the emotions conveyed by their beautiful eyes, playful hands, and mischievous lips. My fumbling hands could not grasp the flask any more. The girls pressed it back into my hands. Gradually, my fingers lost their hold, and the flask dropped to the ground. In spite of my resolve against the drooping of my eyelids, my vision was soon blurred, like an abstract painting. Next I knew nothing.

When I woke up, the two sisters' merry laughter intruded into my consciousness, followed by a warm feeling. I saw I was covered with a piece of thick sheepskin, and the bonfire was blazing. The old man had also moved to the fireside, still praying. Seeing me wake up, he paused a second to pass a word to the two sisters, who immediately poured me a bowl of hot buttered tea. I mumbled in embarrassment, "Sorry, I got drunk – drunk. Thank you, but I must be leaving now. It's getting dark."

The elder sister said, "Have some tea."

The younger one tried a bit of humor in Mandarin. "Not drunk – fell asleep." The sisters burst into another bout of laughter. After drinking the tea, I stood up. When I was three yards away from the fire, I realized it was pitch dark, and I couldn't tell which way to go.

The sisters came to help me up, and I realized it was the first time I had been so close to a member of the opposite sex since leaving prison. The younger sister took my right hand and the elder my left; they saw me onto the road and out of the forest. The lights in the town twinkled.

"I know how to get home – "

"We can take you."

"No, thanks." After all, I was a man.

"We'll take you home."

"No." Take me home? Did I have a home? Was that half room my home? "No, but thanks." I bid a firm good-bye to the two nameless Tibetan girls. I even ran a few steps to show them I was sober.

The cool night wind blew against my face and my heart enjoyed unspeakable happiness. My happiness affirmed the strength of an individual's belief and judgment. It was here I saw the unspoiled people who preserved human nature and elemental feelings, unpolluted by the commercial world. They had not asked my name, profession, education, or political status, and I had not asked them theirs. They had no knowledge of the tortuous road I had traveled or that I was a newly released prisoner. We had not talked about world affairs, politics, society, family, philosophy, or human experience. Because of the language barrier, we could express only simple responses to eating and drinking, pleasure and joy. Like a bird of a different flock, I had accidentally landed near their nest for a while and had flown away again. Following that old man, perhaps their grandpa, they would help the caravan safely reach the inland or Tibet. Although their road was also long and tortuous, it was only under their feet. I had to struggle down mine both with my feet and with a bleeding heart. Looking over my shoulder, I could still see the bonfires in the woods yet could hardly believe they were real. Perhaps it had all been a dream, including the girls.

Luo Ren was waiting for me at the entrance to the Culture Bureau. He must have thought I was lost. But he merely asked, "Have you eaten?"

"Yes. I met some caravan Tibetans in the woods. They are really hospitable."

"Oh, I see." As he accompanied me to my room, he said, "Today the county has made a decision on your job. By coincidence, Manager Ding of the movie house passed away, and you can step into his shoes. After a long deliberation, the county found this job is closest to your specialty."

"Really?"

"The movie house team is quite small."

"How many people?"

"Besides the projectionist, the other one is you."

"Only two?"

"Yes. It's sort of a hard job. You have to do everything yourself: selling and collecting tickets, ushering, cleaning the theater. But it has only five hundred seats. It's closed during the day and has two shows every night. The power plant stops producing electricity at midnight. The box office will be both your bedroom and your office. You can move in tomorrow. There are two advertising boards you can use to show your talents."

"I'm happy with this arrangement. Thank the leadership for their consideration. It's nice to have a job." I was truly content with my job. Although the work might be physically demanding, there would not be a lot of human complications. In fact, I would be my own boss. The projectionist would only show movies upstairs, while downstairs I would sell tickets, usher, and sweep the floor. It was not likely we would meddle with each other's business. My day in the woods was a pleasant dream, and my appointment was another; the doubled pleasure thrilled me indeed. I moved to the box office the following morning. Fortunately, I had arrived only the day before and had not done any shopping, so I did not need a truck for my belongings.

The box office was rectangular with a floor area of ten square meters. Entering it, two mathematical equations popped into my head: ten divided by ten fifths equals five;

and ten divided by seven equals 1.428, that is, four feet eight inches. It only had a small ticket window, below which stood a desk with three drawers. Against the back wall was a single bed. As soon as I came in, I saw traces of the late Manager Ding all over the place. From the sunken straw mattress I could easily figure out his height and weight. Numerous black dots made by cigarette butts on the wall told me that he had suffered from insomnia and was a heavy smoker. The gobs of dried spit on the floor proved he had a phlegmy cough. A drawer full of medicine bottles told me the root of his disease was in the liver and lungs. The drawer on the left was filled with his self-criticism and minutes of criticism meetings, all written in neat brush strokes, about a million characters in all. A quick leafing through them would give a comprehensive knowledge of his history and spiritual development. The middle drawer, used for movie tickets, showed that the public interest occupied the center of his mind. Replacing a dead per-son so fast upset me a bit; however, recollection of the past helped relieve my mind. When I was put in cell number 10045, I was told that three previous cell mates had been shot recently. People say being shot belongs to the category of brutal death: a man who dies in that manner will turn into an avenging ghost. But a man who dies of illness is merely an ordinary ghost. If I had not feared an avenging ghost, how could I be afraid of an ordinary one? Besides, given the length of human history, which house has not witnessed a person's death and which inch of land has not buried a dead soul? I didn't even bother to give the room a thorough cleaning. I even used his old straw mattress.

Xiao He, the projectionist, had welcomed me at the entrance as my underling and colleague. One could tell at a glance that he was a talented young man born at the wrong time. He told me that he was born in a city twice the size of this town and that his father was a middle-level cadre. Because of the Cultural Revolution, he was forced to discontinue his education. Last year he had graduated from the prefectural technological training class as a projectionist with an official diploma and license. But during the job-distribution period he had offended his supervisor and was sent to work in a town half the size of his hometown and two hundred miles farther from Beijing. Nevertheless, technicians like him were rare in this place. Apart from showing two movies a night, he had to rewind the reels, clean the projectors, adjust the amplifiers, make repairs, study new technology, restack movie introduction booklets, and make slides for family planning education. If that weren't enough, he lived on the eastern street and had to rush back and forth.

"I am almost crushed by all these duties. Manager Ding appreciated my efforts."

I was no fool. I knew what he was driving at. Being a technician, he did not have time to clean the theater, and as manager I could easily assign myself this task. To avoid damaging his enthusiasm for the job, I said, "I know it's not easy to take care of the work upstairs. I'll take complete charge of everything downstairs. You can plan your spare time around your hobby."

"I love writing poetry."

"Then go ahead and write." The complicated relationship between the ruler and the ruled, and between the cooperators, was solved with a few words. He never expected it could be so simple. He even felt he had wasted a cannon ball to kill a mosquito, that he had taken me for an airplane and wasted his energy in detecting, calculating, aiming, and the like.

The first big event after I assumed office was a memorial meeting for the late manager. The county attached enormous importance to it. Not only would the chief of the Bureau of Education give a memorial speech and the vice secretary of the county committee be present, but representatives from all walks of life in the county would also attend. All of them had seen movies and received education in the theater under Ding's charge, though few of them had known he was the manager. People saw him only sweeping inside and outside. Even a child of three would call him old Ding, as did the first secretary of the county. My task was to draw his posthumous portrait. For this purpose, I collected three of his pictures: one was a landscape where the trees were clear but the man was a blur; another was a scene from the Cultural Revolution – with Ding kneeling at the theater entrance. It was pretty clear, but his face was invisible, as he was not allowed to lift his head; the last one, taken on his deathbed, did present his face clearly. But even after my beautification, he still looked haggard and miserable. But when I sent it to the Bureau of Education and Propaganda Department for approval, all the leaders praised me to the skies, saying it caught not only his image but also his spirit.

The memorial meeting started at two o'clock in the afternoon. It was a solemn meeting, because the night before, the Personnel Department's recommendation of Comrade Ding Gu's posthumous promotion had been approved by the county committee: Comrade Ding Gu would receive the designation of vice office head. They did not say how he had been treated before his death. Since he was now dead, his treatment when alive became meaningless. Although the memorial was originally to be held in the yard of the Cultural Bureau, out of respect for old Ding's promotion it was moved to the theater. The number of people who came to the memorial was unexpectedly large because the whole county, old and young, knew Ding Gu, and also because they had heard through the grapevine that the portrait of Ding Gu drawn by the prodigiously talented new sweeper looked like the real man. Many children came only to see the portrait. Because I had not known Ding Gu personally, and the theater was full, I retreated to the box office, where I could hear everything happening at the meeting. As the funeral music began, a feeling of desolate grief seized my heart. I took Ding Gu's notebook out of the left-hand drawer. In it were minutes of some criticism meeting directed at him. In addition to year, month, and date, he had also written down each speaker's name. Opening the first page, I saw the speaker was Liu Shouhua. Wasn't he the newly appointed chief of the Bureau of Education? What position did he hold at that time? Who knows? But according to the law of progress, he could not have been a bureau chief. I suddenly remembered that today Bureau Chief Liu Shouhua was delivering the memorial speech. The voice from the loudspeaker was his. I wanted to close Ding's notebook to concentrate on his present voice, yet half of me still clung to his past voice. Fortunately his present voice, owing to sorrow, was extremely slow, so I could attend to both voices simultaneously.

Liu Shouhua's past voice (indignant): "Comrades in arms of the proletarian revolutionary factions, 'the monkey king wields his magic club, and the whole world is purged of dust!' The revolutionary rebels of our county have rooted out a deeply hidden counterrevolutionary element! His dog name is Ding Gu! This is good news, a great festival for our revolutionary masses."

Liu Shouhua's present voice (sorrowful and deep): "Comrades, friends. Unfortunately, illness has claimed the life of Comrade Ding Gu, paradigm of the outstanding revolutionary intellectuals. His death is a great loss to our cultural affairs, and he is mourned by all the people of this county. We have lost a beloved comrade in arms."

"Ding Gu was born into a cruel family of landlords."

"Comrade Ding Gu was born into a traditional family of scholars."

"From childhood, he sucked the blood of peasants and made up his mind to succeed his father on the orthodox Confucian path of becoming a lord riding herd over the people."

"During his school days he was inclined to progress and determined to divorce himself from the bourgeoisie and throw himself into revolution."

"After worming his way into the revolutionary ranks, he refused to be remolded and lost his soul in the reactionary cultures of feudalism, capitalism, and revisionism."

"After joining the revolution, he actively studied Marxism-Leninism-Mao Zedong thought and gained great academic achievements, publishing many essays on the subject of national cultures."

"He has been severely criticized by the revolutionary masses in every political campaign."

"Owing to historical reasons, the research of Comrade Ding Gu has not received the evaluation it deserves."

"After being sent to our county, instead of turning over a new leaf, he committed even more serious crimes. Taking advantage of the movie theater, he opened the gate for all sorts of weeds to poison the minds of the masses."

"He voluntarily came to work in our county. Although our county is located on the border and transportation is poor, he neither feared hardships nor complained. In order to enliven the cultural life of the masses and enable them to see more performances and movies, he accepted all tasks, from sweeping the floor to organizing a program, from getting movies to introducing them, in order to guarantee that the people of our county receive the best education."

"Counterrevolutionary black gang member Ding Gu pretended to work hard to win the trust of the masses."

"Comrade Ding Gu sacrificed himself to the revolution, without regard to fame, money, or position. Comrade Ding Gu will be respected by the people of our county and will live forever in our hearts."

"His crimes are hideous and he deserves punishment more severe than death."

"No one can deny his great contributions."

"Let us criticize him until he becomes infamous, trample on him, and keep him down forever!"

"While we are expressing our sorrow for him, let us study his spirit of serving the people. Eternal glory to Comrade Ding Gu!"

"Down with Ding Gu! Down with the counterrevolutionary black gang member Ding Gu!"

"Rest in peace, our beloved Comrade Ding Gu! We shall use concrete deeds in socialist revolution and construction to console your soul down in the yellow springs."

Liu Shouhua's words fell with tears and his sobbing finally overwhelmed him. The memorial was extremely successful, more touching than a melodrama. People left the theater wiping away their tears.

The small theater of about five hundred seats turned out to be a perfect cosmos for me. During show time, the entrance was as crowded as a cosmopolitan city and all the celebrities of the county gathered here, to everyone's excitement. During the day it was so quiet that one could catch lazy sparrows. A dozen bats, permanent residents of the theater, flew high and low regardless of the time. Sweeping the floor, selling and collecting tickets, ushering, sweeping again after the show – although my job was not very interesting, it was quite regular, half hard work, half rest. It followed an ancient maxim perfectly: the way of civil and military art, one moment of intensity followed by one of relaxation.

More than a month had passed since my arrival. But we had shown only one movie, *The Pine Ridge*. Children who had seen it countless times could reproduce its dialogue, sound, and gestures to perfection. When May Fourth youth day came, the singing and dancing troupe of the county would be putting on a show in the theater. Because those tickets were distributed by the league committee, it saved me the trouble of having to sell tickets. When I was collecting tickets at the entrance, some of the children pointed at me and shouted, "He came here to replace the dead old Ding."

To the ordinary ear, this statement sounds dreadful, and it would be better with slight modification. For instance, "He came to take over old Ding's work." But I didn't care. It sounded all right to me, because all men must die, and the living replace the dead. In a sense, the children's words carried more truth. So I encouraged them. "Well said! I came here to replace that dead old Ding."

It had been years since I had last seen a live performance. I was excited, believing it must be fresh and interesting. After my ushering duties were finished, I leaned against the doorpost and watched. The first dance looked familiar: men and women sang and danced with a bunch of rice stalks in each hand. Their clothes were gaudy and their faces simpering. In the end, the change of formation produced a portrait that used to be Chairman Mao and was now Chairman Hua. The joyful men and women split into two teams like wild geese. Some stood and others knelt as they stretched the rice toward the portrait, as if singing, "We have more rice than we can eat. Come look if you don't believe it." The audience was thrilled as usual, applauding thunderously. The next performance was similar to the first, like an old acquaintance popping up after a number of years. I lost interest, and, before it was half over, I returned to the box office. I'd rather stay there and read old Ding's notebook and self-criticism. His dignified words, soaked with the blood of human life, were instructive. Although I never met him while he was alive, in death I found in him a bosom friend. I was soon caught up in my reading. Before I knew it, the show was over, and the audience had disappeared. Now my show started. My first performance, the hardest and most skillful one, was sweeping the floor of the theater. The space between the rows was so narrow the broom hardly fit. I had to dig out melon seeds and colored candy wrappers from under every seat. Occasionally, I picked up a coded billet-doux dropped by a careless lover. But never any money. This performance had me sweaty all over. My second performance was cleaning up the stage and backstage area, where the used tissues, cheap powders, and greasepaint made me nauseous. As I was tidying up the stage, Manager Tao of the singing and dancing troupe led a dozen men and women performers back to the theater like a cyclone. All were dressed for workouts in Chinese lantern-like loose pants and tight tops; they were tense and breathless. Ignoring me, they acted their roles of a general and his guards in a model opera. When General Tao said, "Search," the guards split into two rows and went separately backstage, then returned through the entrance, reporting in unison, "Nothing." General Tao said, "Go!" In a wink, they vanished like ghosts. I stood in the middle of the stage, holding my broom, dumbfounded. The scene and the excitement I had witnessed would have been perfect for a painting.

"Hey!" A cry, a female voice, made my hair stand on end. Was it a ghost? My well-trained ears could tell the cry came from above. Raising my head, I saw a girl in minority national dress perched on the iron beam of the left spotlight, waving and grinning at me. How did she get up there? During the performance there had been a folding ladder. But it was the property of the troupe, and after the show it had been removed along with all the cosmetics, costumes, and instruments. As I racked my brain for an answer, she shouted, "Catch me!" She fell as she shouted. Instinctively I threw away the broom and stepped forward to catch her. She caught my neck and knocked me to the floor, luckily landing astride me. Showing no fear, she got up giggling. Still sitting on the stage, I looked her up and down. She was wearing a dark-blue satin top with buttons slanting to one side, an embroidered white linen shirt, and pointed red shoes shaped like boats. Her hair was entangled with fluffy false pigtails and silk tassels, and she had an innocent face, mature big eyes, a straight, high nose, slightly meaty lips, and glistening white teeth. She stopped laughing and offered her hand to pull me up. She beat the dust off my back and bottom. I asked her nothing, but she volunteered the answer: "I'm just having a good time with them." Her Chinese was a bit awkward.

"Why?"

"They always have someone follow me."

"Why?"

"They are worried about me."

"Why?"

"Why? You know why, don't you? I am a Mosuo girl."

"A Mosuo girl!" My eyes lit up, with a surprise that I had lost for many years. Was she dressed Mosuo style? Was the girl standing right before me from the country of women? I defended myself. "I really don't know."

"Did you drop from the sky?"

"Well, I came from a faraway place."

"Oh, I see. I've heard of you."

"What?"

"They say you can paint portraits, and Ding Gu's portrait was your work. They also say you have been in jail and have a mental illness. You were a college graduate, but instead of staying in a big city you insisted on coming to our small border county."

"Is that so?" Now I knew the county was small. Any outsider here would become the talk of the town. On the other hand, no one paid any attention to the newspapers or broadcasts.

"I'm not going back to the troupe."

"But they're searching for you."

"Let them search! Why stop them? I often play with them like this. But I'm not going back, no matter what."

"But there's no place for you to sleep in the theater."

"Don't you have a bed?"

"Yes. But if I give it to you, where can I sleep?"

"Oh." She seemed to gain a sudden insight. "Yes, I know, you have rules."

Not only rules, we had laws.

"All right!" She said with a sigh. "I'm leaving."

"Back to the troupe?"

"By no means."

"Where to?"

"To the mountain. I will sleep in the woods, making a bonfire."

"That won't do!" My compassion was stirred. "You can stay in my box office and bolt the door. I'll sleep on the stage. There is a tumbling mat to sleep on and stage curtains for covers."

"You have a good heart, don't you?"

I smiled and said nothing.

"With such a good heart, how could you have been in prison?"

Still I did not answer, looking at her deep in thought.

She murmured to herself: "Perhaps you were in prison just for your good heart. Is that so?"

I just said, "Let's go. I'll take you to the box office."

"Let's go."

After closing and bolting the theater doors, I took her to the box office. The moment I shut the ticket window, the electricity went out, a signal that it was midnight. I lit a lamp. Now I suddenly remembered I should ask her name. "Little sister, what are you called?"

"Sunamei."

"Sunamei – what a beautiful name. I am called Liang Rui."

"Liang Rui, Liang Rui," she repeated several times softly.

"I am leaving now."

"You are leaving?"

"Yes, I am leaving," I said in a no-nonsense manner.

"Then – you – " she gazed at me without blinking. After a long while, she said, "Well, please leave then."

I walked out, shutting the door behind me, and groped my way to the stage. Even though there were probably no lice, as there had been in prison, I stripped naked out of habit and lay down on the spongy mattress, covering myself with the stage curtain. Pillowed on my hands, my head was clear and sleepless. I was thinking, "Is it proper for me to keep her here? If people learn the truth, what will they say? The rumor will circulate that I have hidden her in the theater. In less than an hour, the whole city will be gossiping about me. Because I am a newcomer, what punishment will they dole out?" Thinking about the consequences calmed me unexpectedly. At most they would strip me of my position and criticize me at a public meeting. Then they would have to give me another job. For a man who had been to prison, criticism meetings didn't mean much. They would have to give me a rice bowl after all the trouble they took, wouldn't they? Besides, the meal tickets are in my hands, so there's no danger of my going hungry. I'm sleeping alone on a mat on the stage. So what's there to worry about? Those thoughts soothed me. And I even gained a sense of pride, for the one I had supported and helped was a rebel, an adventurer. These complacent thoughts relaxed me to sleepiness. Although the mattress was too soft for a man used to sleeping on the hard concrete floor of a prison cell, I eventually fell asleep.

Feelings of comfort and excitement were teasing my sleep. I tried to resist them, yet they were stubborn and gradually drove away the haziness of my dream. A hand, I felt a hand groping along my naked body. Another naked body lay down beside me. I awoke suddenly, aroused body and soul. There arose a sexual impulse that had been suppressed for so long. It was her! I knew clearly it was her. She embraced me. I was frightened. She, so quick, embraced the whole universe. And I enabled her to stretch her wings and sing like a bird, as if we were not on an empty stage, but in a dense forest, two birds hooked to each other's claws, turning and gliding. Her sensitivity stimulated my desire and my desire doubled her sensitivity. Yunqian had never given me so much. Now I made a firm decision: From now on, I could not live without her, this Mosuo girl who had fallen into my lap from heaven, no matter whether she be fairy or demon.

22

From then on, Sunamei and I wished the singing and dancing troupe could perform in the theater more often. Every two shows she could escape successfully once from the troupe. Her frequent absences at night caused a great sensation in the town. There were a lot of mysterious stories about her. The most popular one said Sunamei was a spirit and had the art of invisibility. The moment she sucked in a breath and vanished, her corporeal body stole into a home and into some man's bed. Even without legs, this tale sped through town, making females so nervous that they closed their doors at dusk and felt around for a naked woman beside their husbands at night. The males were also on the alert. When their wives weren't looking, they would unbolt the doors, hoping for a miracle — the visit of a female spirit. Once a man's devious intentions were discovered by his wife, a horrible fight would disturb the sleep of their neighbors.

Sunamei's absence caused both husbands and wives a loss of sleep. But no one imagined she would be with me. I was a stranger, a mental patient, and a taciturn sweeper. Sunamei slept peacefully in my place, as if the little bed and the man both belonged to her. The troupe was helpless. The army of men they summoned to search the surrounding woods never found anything. Not until the morning would they find Sunamei in the woods practicing her singing in the foggy morning sun, as if nothing had happened. The headache was that they never discovered a suspicious man with her, and they were not allowed to force anyone to make a confession, as during the purge of the May sixth counterrevolutionaries.

A controversy over Sunamei brewed among the members of the troupe. Some thought, "Since Mosuo girls are born that way, it would be better to send her home." Others thought, "Never mind her, because Mosuo girls are simply intractable. We may as well tolerate her behavior with one eye open and the other shut. But it is not wise to let her go because she is the best actress of the troupe, and losing her means losing half the show." Some even said, "Like dealing with a flood, one can only channel it but not block it. Find her a husband, and she will be tamed." The latter was fiercely opposed on the ground that the Mosuo do not marry and so no husband could tame her. Owing to those different opinions, the case of Sunamei hung in the air. As the farce caused by Sunamei's absences occurred repeatedly, the troupe gradually lost interest and did not even bother to look for her. However, this lucky, chancy success still made me anxious. Once the cat of our secret love was let out of the bag, I would lose her completely. I had an idea: I wanted to marry her. The notion, "Once married she will be naturally tamed," fit well into my plans. I proposed to her many times, and each time she said, "Isn't it enough for us to be together like this?"

"No, you should belong to me."

"You should belong to me." I thought she was merely repeating my words.

"Then let's get married."

Then she would giggle for a long time over my silly idea and play all sorts of tricks to banish it from my rational mind. Or, she would explain to me the customs and rituals of the Mosuo people's matrilineal extended family and their way of making *axiao*. I hated listening to this, because it included her own experiences. But at the same time, I was enchanted by her descriptions, because what she said was surprisingly new and carried an irrefutable logic.

Finally I decided to talk with Luo Ren. I found him in the Cultural Bureau compound. I said to him, "I want to talk to you about something."

He took me to the half room where I had spent my first night in the county. He offered me the board, and he himself took the coverless trunk as a bench. "Bureau Chief Luo, you know I have no acquaintances here. You're the first person I met and the one who introduced me to this town."

Rolling a cigarette with his fingers, he did not look at me but listened attentively, without interruption.

"You see, I am no longer young, over thirty already. My former years were tortuous." I didn't know how to bring up the subject. Such a hypocrite. Forget it. Then it slipped out: "I want to marry."

"Marry?" Now he looked at me. "Do you have someone in mind?"

"Yes. A girl has caught my eye."

"In this county?"

"Yes, right here."

"Sunamei?"

"How did you know?"

"I guessed." I could see in his eyes that it was more than a guess.

"How could you have guessed it?"

"Everyone will know before long, the answer will be found not only by me. That sort of thing will always come out eventually."

I didn't know what to say.

"I brought Sunamei here, and I have been to her hometown. To avoid suspicion, I have stayed clear of her since she joined the singing and dancing troupe. When she comes to look for me, I simply refuse to see her."

"She has told me."

"Do you know what her ethnic group is?"

"Yes, I do."

"They – their relationships between men and women are pretty messy."

"You could call it free."

"Free? Has she told you everything?"

"Yes."

"So what do you think of their family and marriage customs?"

"Quite ancient, like those of ten thousand years ago, but also quite modern."

"Modern?"

"They don't have marriage, but they have love. Many couples in our society have marriage but no love. I think they have better morals than we."

"Morals? How – how can you talk like that?" He frowned, looking hurt.

"I can see that you know the truth, but can't yet voice it."

"Then why do you want marriage?"

"Well, I'm living here, not by Lake Lugu, and I'm not a Mosuo man. If our relationship is not legalized, I'll lose her, and I don't want that. I couldn't bear it. She should belong to me. I love her, and she loves me."

"Really?"

"It's true. I love her deeply and she loves me deeply, too."

"Are you sure she loves only you?"

"Of course."

"Can you really tame her?"

"I think I can. I'll try to change her."

"You have great confidence, don't you?" His tone was one of doubt.

"No one but me can know how much she loves me."

"Have you learned everything about her past?" He stared at me with a different expression.

"Yes. She has told me everything."

"It's easy to admire things from the outside. Once you are involved, it won't be so easy."

"I don't understand."

"My friend – " He hesitated. "Tell me, what do you want from me?"

"Please talk to Manager Tao of the singing and dancing troupe on my behalf."

"All right. Because you have made up your mind to marry, go ahead. But before you're married you shouldn't see each other too often. If people learn of your intimacy, they not only will disapprove of your marriage but will try to keep you apart. Chinese moral principles. As to talking them around, you leave that to me."

Luo Ren's persuasive work was carried out smoothly. The troupe's opinion was mobilized, and Manager Tao came to realize that what the restless girl needed was a husband. Her naughty shrewishness was due to the lack of a husband, a master. When Luo Ren offered to be my go-between, Manager Tao was afraid I might not agree. Goodness, how men differ from one another. When Luo Ren saw me he repeated their conversation with enthusiasm.

"How could a university graduate want a Mosuo girl? A Mosuo girl starts having *axiao* at the age of thirteen, and this one was deflowered long ago."

Luo Ren said slowly, "Well, give him a try. Maybe he'll agree because Sunamei is so beautiful."

"Has he seen her yet?"

"He should have; your troupe often performs in the theater."

"But Sunamei has never seen him."

"If he likes the idea, we'll give them a chance to meet."

"Thank you very much, then."

"Wait until I succeed. I hope your troupe will perform the wedding ceremony."

"No problem. We'll take care of it."

Lying is the key to success: the maxim seems to hold water. For fear of prematurely revealing our intimacy, Luo Ren took me to Tao's office the very next day to see Sunamei. Of course, Luo Ren had already informed Sunamei. As soon as she entered the office and saw how I pretended not to recognize her, she nearly burst out laughing. Fortunately, Manager Tao thought it a typical feature of her personality and ignored it. Manager Tao asked her opinion of me. She nodded her head several times and asked aloud, "Can I move my bedroll to his place now?"

"Nonsense!" Manager Tao covered her mouth hurriedly. "Not so fast! You haven't got a marriage certificate yet."

After Sunamei had gone, Tao Zhengfang asked me my opinion, and I put on an excellent show. Hesitating for quite a while, I turned to Luo Ren and asked him, "What do you think, Bureau Chief Luo?" I never expected I could be so crafty.

"You have to make your own decision."

"Manager Tao, how about letting us see each other for a while to cultivate our mutual love? She is a girl of minority nationality. Who knows whether we are fit for each other?"

"That sounds like a good idea." Luo Ren also acted his part. "We can't impose marriage on them. Let them court each other first, and then marry."

"But – " Tao Zhengfang said shyly. "We can't allow you to keep her for the night – "

"Of course not! I'll send her back in the evening."

"That's right. One must behave according to the moral codes."

After this official introduction, Sunamei and I could see each other openly. However, in the evening I had to coax her to leave in spite of her unwillingness, unhappiness, and incomprehension. After being constrained in this way for two months, I told Tao Zhengfang, "The love between Sunamei and me has been cultivated, and I agree to marry her." Tao Zhengfang was very glad because the two months' practice had proved the truth of Luo Ren's proposal. Sunamei started listening to others and had not been reported missing once, even without being watched.

The singing and dancing troupe performed at our solemn, noisy, and boring wedding. That night I was merely wearing a smile as I anxiously awaited the end of the wedding. Sunamei's smile was genuine. She later told me: Everything was fun, much better than the skirt ceremony. During the skirt ceremony, she was the sole protagonist, but at the wedding there were two. People even hung an apple for the newlyweds to bite into at the same time. There were a lot of games like that. At the tedious, noisy wedding banquet, people used wine for toasting and certain games for teasing. They swapped the bride and groom's glasses for fun. When it all finally came to an end, Manager Tao asked us to show our marriage certificate and lectured us: "This is a marriage certificate. Don't ever lose it. It will allow you to live together all your life without anybody interfering."

At the moment I found her words comic. Why did she have to make such a statement?

Several members of the troupe followed us, helping Sunamei move her belongings to the newly whitewashed box office. We were lucky that the young men who had planned to play practical jokes on the bride had lost interest because the room was small and eighty percent of it was occupied by Sunamei's baggage and wedding presents. Besides, the electricity had gone out and the little oil lamp failed to produce a celebratory atmosphere. In the narrow space of the box office, only Sunamei and I remained. Tugging at my brand new Mao suit, she said, "Take it off! You look so awkward." She was wearing the same minority national dress she used for her stage performances. While taking it off she recalled the speeches, practical jokes, and wild drinking.

I didn't know why, but, even though a moment earlier I had found Tao Zhengfang's statement about the marriage certificate comic and superfluous, it now created a solemn emotion in my heart. It seemed important to take the opportunity of our wedding to say a few earnest words to Sunamei. All words from me, of course, coming as they did from the bottom of my heart, were neither comic nor super-fluous but absolutely necessary. Taking the marriage certificate out of my pocket, I said, "Sunamei!" I knew my voice was quivering. "Have you taken a careful look at the marriage certificate?"

"Why look at it?" She was undoing the heavy headdress. "It's just a couple of flags, not a single human figure on it."

"Do you realize that this means you and I are legal spouses? Legal, do you understand? It means our being together is enforced by law." On the one hand I felt my words were tedious, and on the other I felt the importance of what I had to say.

"That means tonight I don't have to go back to the troupe, and no one will come to catch us." She didn't seem to be joking. I felt like slapping her.

"Not just tonight, it means our whole life," I corrected her.

"Our whole life?" She was greatly surprised. "That long?"

"That's right. You and I will love each other until our hair turns gray. We love each of our own free will and have freely become one. We will respect each other, love each other, and take care of each other. No one is allowed to destroy our marriage." I found my own lecture boring, yet without saying these things my heart would not be at ease. What an awkward situation.

Sunamei was taking off her underwear. On hearing my words, she simply hung her slip on my head. "Are you giving a stage monologue?"

"Don't be flippant." I pulled her slip off my face and said with some anger, "Be serious! Marriage, which concerns a man's entire life, is no joke. Sunamei, please tell me, can you be forever – "

Before I could finish my sentence, Sunamei opened the ticket window and threw the oil lamp into the street. Our room sank into darkness and I nearly lost my temper. Sunamei jumped into bed, holding my neck with her smooth arms and pressing my head to her breasts until I could hardly breathe, let alone speak. She was strong, lifting me up and knocking me down on the bed. Then she said in an agitated tone, "You damned fool, what are you asking? You ask me but I never ask you. I do not ask you, and I do not want you to ask me. Asking means disbelieving. Disbelief leads to questions. I believe, so I do not ask. I do not ask. I do not ask...." Her words tapered off. What followed next were her groans, screams, and tears of ecstasy. Although she was young, I felt she was much more mature, beautiful, and pure than the body in my arms.

Our married life was wonderful. The whole county was witness to our happiness. People said my color improved, and I grew plucky. What a wonder occurs when a depressed man long tired of life suddenly sees a bright future. Like a torch, she shone on me and purified me. I even helped her wash dishes and clothes, including her briefs and brassieres, which I insisted on her wearing after we were married, to which she agreed. Meanwhile, I tried to influence and educate her. I told her that a married woman should be more staid, not flirty like a little girl. Every time I talked to her like this I told her it was because I loved her. Men flirted with her, but she ignored them. By and by she heard some men saying nasty things about her.

"Look at her. I guess she's no longer a Mosuo woman."

"Hey, Sunamei, who is your daddy?"

"Sunamei, how many daddies do you have?"

"Who do you think you're fooling? A whore from the age of thirteen."

"Let's make *axiao*. I'll come to you when your man is out."

Sunamei did not know the nastiness of these words, since she seemed not to hear them. After a few days, the men, properly snubbed, stopped slandering her. But they were waiting, enviously, for a big scandal. Meanwhile Sunamei's reputation was constantly improving with the women.

"Who would take her for a Mosuo girl? She's like a perfect Han wife."

"After marriage, that elf has turned into a decent woman. No one follows the rules better than she."

"When she wears our clothes, who would take her for a Mosuo?"

"A person can change. Her husband is a university graduate, which makes all the difference."

"When a person knows what's good for her, she turns out fine. Just look at Sunamei."

"Sunamei sings better now than in the past, when she made eyes at one man after another and so teased those bad men that they made a scene."

We had a wonderful time together, peaceful, harmonious and affectionate, and adapted to our surroundings perfectly. If something marred our perfect happiness, it was Sunamei's nostalgia for her hometown that sometimes dampened her spirits. It thrilled her to talk about the boats collecting pig weeds on Xienami, the cranes on the sea of grass, and pilgrims worshiping the goddess on Mount Ganmu with incense. Whenever she mentioned the names of Awu Luruo, Amiji Zhima, her childhood friend Geruoma, her former *axiao* Longbu and Yingzhi, and Ami Cai'er and old Asi, her eyes would fill with glistening tears. Although she received one or two letters, with their poor literacy the scribes could hardly say anything. In fact, no matter how high a writer's education is, he could never satisfy a Mosuo girl's nostalgia. Who could describe the home of her dreams? Who could relate all the things about her old friends in the community? She missed the paths she had walked, the trees by the road, the black dog following behind her, the cat squatting by the fireplace, the river singing day and night, the fragrance of the soil she alone could smell, and the music only she could hear played by the wind passing through the trees. I truly admired her because I did not have a hometown like hers that deserved my dreams and nostalgic feelings. Every tree and blade of grass of her hometown gave life to her poetic imagination.

Finally I said to her, "Sunamei, why don't you and I pay a visit to your hometown?"

"Go home?" Her eyes shone in ecstasy.

"Yes. Your home, Lake Lugu."

"Really?"

"We can ask for a leave of absence."

"Really?" She cried softly.

"We should write to Ami first."

"When Ami hears that her Sunamei is coming home, she will send Awu Luruo with a large team of horses to get me."

"Me, too."

"How could they leave you out? My *axiao*."

"What, am I your *axiao?*" I had taught her to call me her husband.

"No." She corrected herself. "My husband."

"That's right."

"Will they let us go?"

"They have no reason to refuse. We haven't taken any leave since our marriage."

"True. Let's write a letter quickly."

"I'll do it now."

"Don't scribble. The letter must be written neatly stroke by stroke. In our place few people read Mandarin."

"What shall I write?"

"Well, simply write, 'Sunamei is homesick.' Ami will understand we are coming and will send Awu Luruo with horses to get us."

The following day, a letter containing only three words was mailed out.

23

My request for leave was quickly approved by the Cultural Bureau of the county "on principle," with the condition that I must wait until an acting manager was found. In the process of searching for the acting manager, leaders at various levels came to realize what a loss Ding Gu's death had been to the county's cultural affairs, how noble an intellectual from the big city like me was, and how decent my work attitude was. Meanwhile, they regretted giving their approval so quickly, because no one wanted the position of manager, and it was hard to find anyone who was willing to take over even for a few days, including the service workers who boiled water or did housecleaning in the county hotel, for they knew more clearly than any leaders how heavy my job was. Searching, discussing, and persuading went on for a dozen days until they finally found two people to share my job. As soon as the horses sent by Sunamei's Ami arrived, we would set out.

One morning, as I was stamping dates on the movie tickets, the ruddy face of a middle-aged man appeared at the ticket window. A black moustache with some gray stubble, like a curved brush, covered his face, his head was decorated with a red kerchief, and his eyes were slightly bloodshot. Winking at me mischievously like an old friend, he asked in a deep voice, "You are Liang?"

"Yes." Guessing he was Sunamei's Awu Luruo, I immediately walked out to meet him. As expected, he was a caravan man, with six leather wallets around his broad waist belt, a whip in his hand, and a pair of tall red and black riding boots on his feet.

"You are Awu Luruo?"

"No. I am Longbu."

"Longbu?" The name sounded familiar. Longbu? All my blood rushed to my face. Wasn't he Sunamei's first *axiao?* He was the first man to possess Sunamei! Sunamei had described their affairs minutely. Why was he laughing, looking at me so complacently? I was ashamed of my delicate features, for he was so robust, smelling of overpowering masculinity.

"Awu Luruo is away to Li Jiang with a caravan, so I made the trip here." He knew what was bothering me. I tried to build up my courage: Be self-confident. Be self-confident! You are Sunamei's husband! Although he was a Mosuo man, he had spent a lot of time in the outside world with caravans, so should know what a husband was and what a husband meant to his wife. I said calmly, "Sunamei is with the singing and dancing troupe. We have been waiting for you." I thought it was brave of me to say *"We* have been waiting for you."

"Let's go find her."

I took Longbu to the troupe and called Sunamei out from the exercise hall. I could tell she was surprised at seeing Longbu, although she seemed calm and merely said, "Oh, it's you, Longbu. Why didn't Awu Luruo come?"

Longbu shifted to their native tongue to answer her. Not knowing what they were saying, I found their language repulsive. He talked a lot; Sunamei listened carefully and punched him playfully in the chest. They were still intimate.

"Shall we invite Longbu to have some wine?" I suggested.

"Yes. Longbu, we want to invite you to have some wine." Like a modern lady she held my hand, and I caressed hers in an assured manner. Longbu nodded his acceptance. Sunamei took Longbu's hand; like me, he caressed her hand tenderly. The psychological balance I was trying to keep was shaken again. Sunamei, in high spirits, walked faster than both of us, as if dragging us along.

As soon as we entered the restaurant, Longbu took a full wallet off his belt and gave it to the fat woman cashier. "The best food and the best wine, please."

I scrambled to get my money out, but Sunamei held me back and said, "Longbu has money. If he is willing to pay, let him do it." Longbu smiled proudly, and I felt humiliated.

Sunamei chatted with Longbu the whole time, leaving me in a cold corner. I tried to figure out what they were talking about, and it seemed that Sunamei was asking about her hometown: one moment of surprise, another of ecstasy or anger or grief. When our order came, Sunamei poured me half a bowl of wine and fed me a piece of pork lovingly with chopsticks to show she had not forgotten me yet. Then they went on talking, drinking, and laughing, and I had to drink by myself. Occasionally, Sunamei would stroke me affectionately; otherwise, I would have smashed my bowl. Longbu was a big eater, wolfing down large amounts of meat and wine. Wiping off the sweat from time to time, he unbuttoned his shirt, exposing a bronzed, hairy chest. Finally, he held out his wine bowl to me and said in Mandarin, "Liang, what a lucky man you are!" He banged my wine bowl so hard that it nearly broke. "Cheers!"

I had drunk enough wine, but I was determined to accept his toast and show my mettle. I was about halfway finished with the last bowl when Sunamei grabbed it and poured it down her own throat. Longbu pointed at her and laughed. "You really do like him." Sunamei cast a proud sidelong glance.

Seeing a hint of sadness in Longbu's eyes, I perked up. He drank until his eyes were bloodshot and bleary. His insobriety was my liberation. Sunamei and I supported him to his hotel. Tears glistened beneath his droopy eyelids, and the minute his head touched the pillow, he was snoring thunderously. Sunamei sat and gazed down at him for a long time. Was he still that attractive to her? Perhaps she was worried he had drunk too much. She seemed obsessed with some emotion. Nostalgia? Friendship? Love? It was impossible for me to tell. She didn't realize I was beside her until I said, "Let's go and let him sleep in peace."

"Okay." She buttoned up his shirt and walked out with me.

That night I asked Sunamei, "What has Longbu been telling you?"

With a sigh, she said, "Well, all sorts of things about my hometown. Asi passed away and called my name before she shut her eyes. They tried not to let me know. And our black dog got rabies and was clubbed to death. The white cat ran away with a tomcat. Amiji Zhima is having a child soon. He also told me things about my friends and their *axiao.*"

"Did he say anything about us?"

"Yes. He asked me, 'I heard you got married, didn't you?' I said yes. 'How much money did he spend on you?' 'He has no money.' 'Are you going to live with him all you life?' 'We have a marriage certificate.' 'Ami is not happy because you did not write to tell her beforehand. Don't forget you are the root of your family line.' He also asked me, 'Is Liang a good man?'"

"What did you say to him?"

"I said, 'Very good – good at everything, better than you.'"

"Did you really?"

"Do I ever lie to you? He said he still wants to come to me and be my *axiao,* but I said, I am a married woman." True, she had never told me a lie. I embraced her, and we fell asleep.

We started out early the next morning. Longbu's dozen horses, carrying almost no goods, had come especially for us.

He asked Sunamei and me to ride; he preferred to walk because he was used to it. Because he wouldn't ride, I jumped off, too. Sunamei rode a tame white horse. Longbu followed her horse, and I followed him. They seemed to have an endless supply of words, talking more heatedly than in the restaurant. Sometimes Longbu could not help touching Sunamei's thigh with his hand, and Sunamei did not try to stop him. Longbu deliberately whipped the white horse and let it gallop away with Sunamei so as to lengthen the distance between us. When, gasping for breath, I caught up with them, he would crack his whip again. I was unaccustomed to running on rough terrain, whereas Longbu, like a horse of the Liang Mountains, followed Sunamei effortlessly and I could hardly hear him breathing. I was gasping the whole time. He turned from time to time and sneered at me. I returned a malignant glare. If he ran, I ran. No matter how tired I got, I wouldn't take a break. Sunamei also turned to look at me from time to time. The faster her horse ran, the more fun she seemed to have. When I was about to ask her to stop for a rest, she and Longbu started singing their dialogue. I couldn't understand the words, but the tune was frivolous. All those sudden portamentos! If they weren't flirting, what were they? Despite my hatred, I had to admit that he sang skillfully and gracefully, matching Sunamei well.

Apart from the mountains and fields, he alone could fit into her antiphonal singing style and bring out the beauty of her art. On stage, the young lad of the singing and dancing troupe could use his half-male and half-female voice with exquisite charm, but it lacked the beauty of bold freedom. At this moment, Sunamei was singing not for an audience but to reveal her heart. Their voices were so liberated and engaging that even the woods seemed to listen.

Here, every tree, every cloud, even the vulture gliding above the clouds merged into one harmonious picture in which I seemed to be an accidental splotch of ink. I was the only discordant note in this symphony. How wonderful if I were Chaliapin and could use a sonorous, powerful, beautiful voice to drown out theirs! However, I soon realized that even if I were Chaliapin, there would be no way for me to drown out their singing, because our types of singing, belonging to two different categories, could not be compared.

At last, they stopped. Sunamei got off the horse. While Longbu was stopping the other horses, she drank spring water from her cupped hands and washed her face. I sat on a boulder, still panting.

"Sunamei!" I called to her, trying to suppress the tone of complaint in my voice. Turning her dripping face, she found me ghastly pale and hurried over to me with water in her cupped hands. I did not drink, and the water leaked between her fingers. She could tell I was angry. Back at the spring, she scooped up some more water for me, and this time I did not have the heart to refuse, so I put my mouth to her palms. I would not let her hands go when I finished and buried my face in her palms.

"We walked too fast," she said apologetically. "You should have ridden."

"No!" I said angrily.

We rested by the spring for a long time. Longbu made a bonfire and boiled tea. Sunamei took out some cookies bought in town. No one spoke. Finally, Longbu spoke to Sunamei, but she seemed not to hear him, silently drinking tea and nibbling cookies.

Leaning against a slope, I gazed at Sunamei. I had never found her so precious before. Today, in my eyes, she was the most beautiful and bewitching woman I had ever seen. Taking out my drawing board, paper, and pencil, I sketched her portrait. I had never done a picture of her because I had nearly stopped drawing altogether. It required a special state of mind, and now I had the right inspiration. With one stroke, her contour came out vividly, the curve I knew by heart, running from her round forehead past her straight nose, across the groove of her upper lip to the delicate twist between two slightly meaty lips, down to the two arcs of the upper and lower lips, and finally to the childlike chin linked with her smooth neck. Longbu stepped behind me with curiosity. When I finished this first line, he was astonished and could not help uttering, *"Ami!"* This was a Mosuo word I understood. It meant "mother." I knew he was marveling at the precision of the line.

His interjection disturbed the meditating Sunamei. She turned her face, but Longbu told her in the Mosuo tongue, "Don't move. Sit like you did a moment ago." Then I focused all my attention and drew the second, the third, the fourth lines, while Longbu cheered each of them. I was extremely happy – the delicious taste of revenge. Now it was time to display my superiority. Now *he* was the superfluous ink splotch. Could he reproduce Sunamei's beauty on paper? If he tried, it would not be a beautiful Sunamei. Who knows how ugly it might look? I turned all my appreciation of beauty and love for Sunamei into artistic lines, and soon finished the drawing. A three-dimensional portrait of Sunamei appeared on the white sheet. I put down the pencil; Longbu called Sunamei over. Amazed by the drawing, she squatted by my side gently, tucking the hair at her temple into the mirror of my drawing. Then she seized my right forefinger and sucked it into her mouth. Longbu held the portrait with both hands like the icon of a god, and mumbled reverently. It was the first time Sunamei had seen one of my drawings and the first time she knew the magic art of my figures. Rather than praise me, she nibbled on my finger that was tired from drawing, comforting me. Then she gave it a sudden bite. Withdrawing my finger intuitively, I raised my hand, pretending to beat her.

For the remainder of our journey, Longbu insisted on carrying Sunamei's portrait on his back. He did not run anymore, nor did they continue with their dialogue singing.

When night came, we camped in a mountain valley. Sunamei and I lay under a row of small trees, sharing one *cha'erwa*. The exhausted Sunamei slept soundly. But I could not sleep. With my eyes close to the ground, I watched Longbu, who had not yet gone to bed. He first added fodder to the bags under each horse as they strolled along the river bank and then made a fire upstream from us. The flames stretched his shadow long and large and swayed it over the grass. Sometimes it seemed to cover Sunamei and me completely and gave me a feeling of depression and horror. I did not know why he was walking around, with no intention of going to sleep. Finally, he sat down. Sometimes he blew on a tree leaf, and the emerging tune was sad, so unlike what I expected from a sanguine man like Longbu. How could such a wailing, sorrowful sound come from such a robust body? I took a look at Sunamei; she was sleeping soundly. I could not watch anymore. Things before my eyes started blurring. Soon I saw Longbu stand before me, beckoning Sunamei with a smile to sit up. After glancing at me, she extended her hands to Longbu. I wanted to scream. I wanted to stand up. Yet I had no strength and could not even utter a sound or move a limb as I helplessly watched Longbu lift Sunamei and carry her away. I desperately wanted to hit myself, yet I could not raise my hand. I gathered all my strength to cry and scream. At last I let out a call: "Sunamei!" I sat up from the ground, only to find Sunamei still lying by my side. The day was already light. Opening her drowsy eyes, she looked at me puzzled.

The mist was floating on the small river, and by the riverside Longbu was calling to his horses.

24

It was already dark when we arrived at the Youjiwa Village. As though several thousand years of human history had not passed, at the moment that night fell the whole village was shrouded by smoke and mist. All the people were inside; not even an idle dog wandered about. Stars began floating on the tops of distant mountains and rising into the sky. When we came to the small road inside the village, we at once saw light. A crowd of people holding torches rushed through the gate.

Sunamei, who had already dismounted, said quietly, "Our family already knows we've arrived. Look."

I wondered, "How did they find out?"

Sunamei said, "Well, people in the mountains have their tricks. Some children have climbed the trees to watch for us."

Before we reached the gate, a swarm of people, men and women, old and young, like giants, snatched Sunamei away from me and then, like the moon surrounded by stars, she was escorted into the gate, leaving Longbu and me, horses, and baggage outside.

Unloading sacks and saddles, he chuckled malignantly, as if to say, "See – does Sunamei's family take you for a man?" While I was feeling lost, Sunamei and a big-bellied, beautiful woman came out of the gate. I guessed the woman must be her sister, Zhima. They dragged me into their front hall, called the *yimei*. The dim oil lamplight, flickering in smoke, seemed about to go out any minute. Although a huge crowd of people had squeezed into the hall, in a minute they all sat in front of the fireplace with legs crossed in an orderly fashion. It is said that Mosuo people give priority to the right side. So the women sat on the right side of the fireplace and the men on the left. As an exception, I was placed by Sunamei's side, perhaps because I did not know their tongue and needed Sunamei as my interpreter.

By the fireplace were all sorts of snacks: melon seeds, sugarcoated popcorn, wine, and milk. There were more than thirty people in Sunamei's family, and every one of them tried to ask us questions. Sunamei couldn't answer everyone; yet no one gave up. They vied with each other in shouting and gesticulating to catch Sunamei's attention. Smiling with tears of joy, Sunamei tried to hear everyone's greetings and questions, but in vain. The noisy prelude lasted until Ami Cai'er stepped into the *yimei,* followed by Longbu carrying the presents we had brought in his arms and Sunamei's portrait on his back. Ami Cai'er sat at the head of the fireplace and invited Longbu to sit in the first place on the male side to express their gratitude to him.

Longbu passed our presents – clothes, boxes of cookies, and lumps of tea – to Sunamei, who in turn passed them to Dabu Ami Cai'er with words of gratitude and love. She cried, and so did all her family members. Although I could not understand Sunamei's words, their open feelings moved me almost to tears. Dabu Ami Cai'er unfolded clothes and opened boxes of cookies and showed them around. After that she packed them again and used the key only she had the right to use to open the closet in the back wall and store them inside. The closet had a square door just big enough for a person to crawl through. As if to lighten the mood, Dabu Ami Cai'er asked me something in the Mosuo language and Sunamei translated: "Ami is asking you, I heard you Han men beat women at the slightest irritation, is that true?"

I answered, "Yes, there are men like that."

Ami continued, "You must be careful! In our place, women beat men, more fiercely than you Han men. They strip them and beat them."

Dabu Ami Cai'er's words triggered uproarious laughter all through the hall.

Sunamei whispered into my ear, "Ami is trying to scare you. She is kidding. We Mosuo people do not fight."

"I know."

Dabu raised her wine bowl to me and more than thirty others rose up to toast me. Through Sunamei, Ami said solemnly to me, "Our Mosuo *yishe* is the most harmonious *yishe*. All people of our line are not like people of other nationalities, who split over a needle. Even a hail of golden stones cannot knock our *yishe* apart. Although you are not a member of our family, because our kin Sunamei loves you and chooses you, we all love you and choose you. We will treat you as well as you have treated Sunamei. Isn't that true, Sunamei?"

Sunamei said sincerely, "Yes, Ami. He has treated me very well. He always accommodates himself to me, like an *amu*."

"Thank you." Cai'er said to me, "Sunamei has been in the outside world, a Han place full of dishonesty and turmoil. Because you have taken care of her, we can feel at ease now." Although she spoke in a gentle voice, her words thundered in me. She was so dignified. Her face was furrowed from hard work, but every line revealed honesty, confidence, decisiveness, patience, and maternal severity and love. I wanted very much to draw a portrait of her, with the title "Dabu Ami Cai'er."

She asked Sunamei, "Sunamei, is he an honest and kind Han man?"

"Yes, Ami." Sunamei's affirmation thrilled me.

"You haven't made a mistake, have you, Sunamei?"

"No mistake, Ami. He knows that a man should be honest and kind, because he has suffered a lot in his life."

"Ah!" Dabu took my hands and caressed them. "My child, suffering teaches a person wisdom." This simple maternal love soothed my soul, and I believe even my eyes turned softer.

"He is very intelligent," Longbu said respectfully to Ami. Taking the drawing folder from his back, he showed Sunamei's portrait to Ami. "He finished it before one could smoke a pipe of tobacco."

"Oh!" More than thirty pairs of eyes brightened. Ami took the folder. One look at the portrait and another at Sunamei, and she was all smiles. After looking at it for a long time, she passed the portrait around, saying, "Don't touch it with your dirty hands." After Sunamei's portrait had been passed around, Longbu tidied it up in the folder and returned it to me.

After a couple of bowls of wine, Cai'er distributed food, soup, and preserved pork with a long ladle; I was given a share like everyone else. The eating noise like the patter of rain lasted for quite some time. Girls and boys watched me with inquisitive eyes throughout the meal because I was different from them, an inscrutable Han man who could draw.

At night, Sunamei and I stayed in her *huagu*. That little room had been a hazy scene in her love stories, but now it became almost too real. The fireplace by which lovers drank tea and wine was still warm, like all the times she had been with Longbu or Yingzhi. Only the big white cat was missing. The flames dancing on the wall formed with their dark shadows a waterfall of red and black fluid along the wall. The red wooden trunk stood by the fireplace like a silent witness, its bronze lock grinning mysteriously. A wooden plank bed, no bigger than the one in my box office, was covered with an old straw mattress and two hand-knit black wool blankets. Perhaps in the modern world no lovers would meet in such a crude place. The Mosuo were not rich, but they could have made their surroundings cleaner and more attractive. Material objects held little attraction for her. Here in the *huagu,* the most important thing was one naked person next to another. I did not really want Sunamei to enter that *huagu* again, particularly to sleep there, because I would think too much and she would have too many memories.

As if she had never left her *huagu,* Sunamei boiled tea and served me wine. She smiled tenderly and mutely, unbuttoned my clothes, blew out the lamp, led me by my hand to the bed, and laid me flat on it. Then, facing the fireplace, she slowly removed her head ornaments, bracelets, necklace, and clothes, piece by piece. I saw only a dark silhouette against the red flames. Every motion so shocked me that I felt like a voyeur. I was observing every detail and every line for somebody else. And my expectation was another's expectation, and my sudden sexual urge was another's impulse. Like a tide suddenly ebbing, my desire deflated with a shudder. Sunamei was surprised to see that I did not reach out to her. She lay beside me and said softly, "You must be tired."

"Eh. . . ." I muttered ambiguously as I rolled over.

She bent over my back and said mysteriously, "Don't you want to see how young girls receive their *axiao* in the dark?"

"Not anymore."

"All right."

How could she know what I had thought and what I was thinking? Believing I was tired, she stopped teasing me and soon was sleeping against my back, her mouth releasing sweet air against my ear, a bit itchy. I lay awake the whole time. The *huagu* beyond the partition was originally Zhima's, but, because she was about to deliver a child and had moved to the *yimei* to sleep by Cai'er, her *huagu* had been occupied by another *amiji* called Sheruo. I could hear everything happening on the other side of the partition clearly. And I could imagine how much Amiji Sheruo and Sunamei had in common. They were both sensitive and encouraging. But Sheruo was much more sexually aggressive than Sunamei. I did not feel sleepy until the man in the neighboring *huagu* started snoring like a bull. And his snoring shook me several times from my dreams. It was hard to pass the night in a little *huagu*. I urged Sunamei to go back to town nearly every day. But she would not hear of it.

She took me to visit her childhood friends. During the day, I could see more clearly that every Mosuo courtyard was too dirty for me to set foot in. Everywhere there was manure, and the worn-out clothing of the children and the elderly seemed to have never been washed. Although beautiful girls wore beautiful clothes, their necks were dirty. Supposing I had met Sunamei here but not in town: could I have brought myself to kiss her?

Sunamei took me to the mountains. In the woods where she used to cut firewood, she searched for a string of glass beads she had lost at the age of thirteen. Of course, she was really looking not for those glass beads but for her childhood. Pointing to a row of little religious banners, she said secretively: once when she was small she had peed on them. She had come down with a terrible headache that very night and had not recovered until a lama prayed for her. "Can I have a try?" I asked playfully. Her answer was to push me down the slope.

She took me to the riverside where, at the age of thirteen, she and other girls of her age had gathered. Apparently she was still cherishing the girlhood she had lost long ago.

Sunamei said, "I was so foolish then I did not even know why a woman needs an *axiao* and what he could do."

In the shallows of the river, swarms of fish fry the size of grains of wheat swam on the surface. Sunamei caught several in her hands. She had not really lost her childhood yet. Sometimes she even held one knee cupped in her hands and hopped on the narrow field path. Her undiminished passion for her hometown and her happiness in searching for her childhood contaminated me eventually, and I no longer urged her to go back.

One morning, on awakening we heard the cry of a newborn baby coming from the *yimei,* along with the laughter of adults and the prayers of the *daba.* Someone was killing a chicken that was screeching its last. Sunamei cried with joy, "Amiji Zhima has borne a child."

After getting up, we went to the *yimei.* People surrounded the *daba,* watching him do his oracle. A tall, thin old man with a sallow face, he sat on the upper left corner below the fireplace, with two oyster shells pinched between his fingers. Murmuring incantations, he threw the shells into a wooden plate. Then, according to the direction of the fallen shells and the hour of delivery, he determined the name of the newborn. The shells pointed northeast, the direction of the cow, so Daba named the baby Yimu, daughter of the cow. He stretched his hand to Zhima lying on a mattress by the fireplace. Zhima passed the child to him. He called three times to Yimu and Zhima and, bending over, answered three times on behalf of the baby. He then smeared some butter on the baby's forehead and wished her good luck and happiness in an odd voice that scared the baby into crying. Out of curiosity, I touched the baby's crumpled little crown. Dabu Ami Cai'er laid out twelve bowls of various foods, but Zhima, who had no appetite, was greeting the congratulating visitors with gentle, calm smiles.

That night, Sunamei brought Ami Cai'er to our *huagu* to inform me that Awu Luruo had come back from River Li. "Tomorrow he will accompany you two to worship Jiumulu. Before Daba leaves, let him go with you." Sunamei told me that Ami had come to inform us, not to seek our opinion. After Ami had left, I asked Sunamei, "What is Jiumulu? Is Jiumulu a god or something?"

Pressing her lips into a smile, she said, "You will recognize it as soon as you see it."

"Why do we need to worship Jiumulu?"

"Because Ami thinks I should have a child, now that Zhima has borne one."

"What's having a child got to do with Jiumulu? We're newlyweds, aren't we?" At once the unpleasant thought occurred to me that she had associated with *axiao* long before leaving home, and Ami must have been counting days from then.

"If Ami asks us to go, we have to go."

Yes, Ami was also Dabu, the highest authority, so we had to go. I truly loved her as the head of the family, anyway, even worshiped her a little. So I might as well regard it as a field trip to collect folklore.

At daybreak, Awu Luruo had a brown horse ready. It was our first meeting.

"Awu Luruo!"

Like an English gentleman, he touched the rim of his bowler hat and said in Mandarin, "How are you?"

Wearing a long brown cloak, Daba held a sheepskin drum in one hand and a drumstick in the other. Awu Luruo put Sunamei on horseback and we set out. Just outside the gate we heard three loud bangs from the neighboring yard.

"The *apu* of the Agupozhe family has passed away."

Daba told Awu Luruo to hurry up, or the Agupozhes would hold him back for the funeral. Now it was hard to find a *daba* and even harder to find god images and religious instruments. Pulling the reins of Sunamei's horse, Awu Luruo dashed off like a stallion. Daba and I ran after them. Once out of the village and onto the mountain path, Daba started chanting incantations to the beat of a drum. Sunamei told me what Daba was chanting: "A lucky woman is coming. Please make way for her, all road-blocking monsters and beasts. Please make way, a lucky woman is coming. She is searching for her descendants, who are with the goddess. The goddess, having all her daughters and sons in Jiumulu, is waiting for her. Jiumulu waits for her, too."

After a long trip along the serpentine path, we reached a mountain called Abulingu. On its northeast slope was a rectangular cavern, about fifteen meters in length and seven meters in width. Water on its western side had formed a pool, and a platform in the center was covered with burning incense. A stalagmite rising from the western side was shaped like a mountain peak. Daba told us the peak was the goddess Jizhema. Where was Jiumulu then? Awu Luruo pointed to the column-shaped stalagmite on the platform: This is Jiumulu. I immediately grasped their imagery – a gigantic phallus, protruding upward to a height of two feet seven inches. A dent on its tip, receiving the drippings from a stalactite hanging from the roof, was constantly filled with clear water. While I was carefully observing this stalagmite made sacred by the human imagination, Daba lit the cypress twigs as incense. Following Daba's instructions, Awu Luruo asked us to face east and kowtow to Jiumulu again and again in front of the burning incense. The solemn looks of Sunamei, Daba, and Awu Luruo soon infected me, washing away my hidden laughter.

Daba was chanting all the time. Later Sunamei told me what he chanted: "May Heaven let you bear children. May earth let you bear children. May river let you bear children. May mountain let you bear children. May the wind, the sun, the moon, and the star all let you bear children. May your neighbors let you bear children. May the Mosuo people let you bear children. May the Tibetans and the Li let you bear children. May goddess let you bear children. She will bless you with a firm belly that will bear you many, many daughters and sons."

We knelt until Daba finished his prayer. My knees ached from the rocky ground, but Sunamei looked self-possessed and beamed with happiness. Next, Daba and I squatted by a fire. He continued praying and asked me to add cypress twigs to the fire while Sunamei, following Daba's instruction, stripped naked and walked into the pool, where she bathed herself from head to toe before getting dressed again. Then Daba gave her a reed tube and asked to close her eyes and touch Jiumulu gently with her hand while sucking water three times through the reed tube from the dent on its tip. I shuddered at this moment, my body turning cold. When Daba took back the reed tube, the ceremony was over. We made a bonfire outside the cavern, boiled water, and had a picnic. Before eating, Daba said solemnly to Sunamei and me, "Tonight you two must sleep together, holding each other tightly and chanting the name of Jizhema for a long, long time. You must give yourself to her and she to you – then you will have a child." It seemed that even Daba did not believe that the strength of the goddess and sacred water alone could make a woman pregnant.

Sunamei answered Daba solemnly, "Yes, I will obey you."

In order to get back while it was still light, we started home immediately after the picnic. On the way, I asked Sunamei, "Do you believe all that stuff?"

"Yes, I do."

"Why?"

"Because this is what we Mosuo people have believed for thousands of years."

Should one believe anything simply because it has been believed for thousands of years? "I don't believe it."

Sunamei, on horseback, kicked me nervously. "Do not say things like that. How terrible it would be if Ami heard you. Awu Luruo, you understand some Mandarin, but please do not tell Ami. Okay?"

Awu Luruo laughed. "I do not understand Mandarin."

"My good Awu."

It was dusk when we reached the river outside the village. The shadows of the western mountains appeared blue, and their peaks thrust right into the river. A flood of light red sunshine remained on the eastern bank of the river. Suddenly, as if in a dreamland, I saw two men in ancient armor by the riverside, each wearing a helmet, a leather coat of mail, with a sword on his back. One was pouring water with a wooden bowl into the pail on the back of the other. Seeing my amazement, Sunamei said to me, "These two men are fetching water to wash the dead body in the Agupozhe family."

We made way for the two young men, who passed silently with sorrowful strides toward the Agupozhes. One of them paused a moment at Sunamei's horse, raising his eyes to Sunamei, while Sunamei shut hers.

An aged woman, coming out from the Agupozhe home, stopped Daba and begged until he bid good-bye to Awu Luruo and followed her into the mourning yard, which was crowded with mourners from the same *siri,* all of them holding flags of red, blue, and white. Did they know these are the three primary colors of the universe, or did they have some other significance? When we got home, I asked Awu Luruo why Daba had to attend the funeral. He who did not speak Mandarin said, "Oh, he is very important. His most important function is to guide the dead person's soul away. Although a person's body is dead, his soul still exists. Invisible to our naked eyes, the soul will never die." (The Mosuo believe in the immortality of the soul.) "Daba will guide the dead person's soul back to the homes of our ancestors, quite far away. *Daba's Bible of the Road* has recorded several hundred such places. Every Mosuo *er* has a line stretching from the ancient time up to now. It is like a long string, and each place the ancestors lived becomes a knot on the string. The route of our *er* is tortuous, having a lot of circles, going back and forth from the golden Sand River several times. We came from north of Muli and Sichuan to the foot of Kala Kunlun Mountains." (They are a nomadic race, moving from north to south.) "Our ancestor was the master of the the Kala Kunlun Mountains. She raised ten thousand white horses, ten thousand white cows, and ten thousand white sheep." (He believed his ancestor was rich.) "Later, owing to the growing population, the oversized family was divided into six er – Xi er, Hu er, Ya er, E er, Bu er, and Guo er. The six er were subdivided into numerous siri, and we are no longer rich."

I asked Awu Luruo how Daba guided the soul onto the route. He told me, "Daba calls out the dead person's name and says, 'Care no longer, do not care about the things of the living. Because you cannot run their affairs, do not care about them anymore.'" (Obviously they fear that the ghosts of the dead make trouble for them.) "'Can't you hear with your ears? Now I come to open the path for you. Because we have given you every share you deserve and you have enjoyed your happy life, please go away with a relieved heart. Stepping out of the gate is the first step. Right, go out of the village, following the route of our ancestors. Don't complain that the route is long and tortuous. Don't try to take a shortcut, because our ancestors, no matter what hardships they confronted, blazed their own path and paved their own way. Their path was new; yet the path you are returning on is already old, marked with black stones at each turn. The places you should pass are – ' Daba intoned more than a hundred place-names. 'Now you have arrived at the place your ancestors are living. The room upstairs is a shrine. The dirty one downstairs is for the cattle. Don't go in that one. Here in the middle live your ami and amu. Please go in and stay there. Never come back. Do not worry about the younger generations; they are leading a happy life. Do not worry about the cattle. We have someone to look after them, feed them, and take them out for exercise. Please do not try to take them away. When you are settled there comfortably, during the wheat harvest in summer and the time of making rice cakes or the festival of butchering pigs, we will call you back and let you sit with us in a circle for a feast. Until then you should sit properly, stand properly, and live peacefully with our ancestors. Never come back unless we call you. Never, ever.'" People are afraid of the dead. Even the return of dead relatives is a fearful event.

I was carried away by Awu Luruo's words. The elders and children in the *yimei* were snoring heartily, and Awu Luruo had added firewood several times. He suggested: "If you're so interested in stuff like this, why don't you go to the Agupozhes and watch how they wash the dead body and how Daba washes the horse? It's very interesting."

"I don't think I can, because I am a stranger."

"Oh, that's true. You are an outsider from a faraway place. Your visit may scare the dead person's soul, as they believe."

Ami Cai'er, lying by the fireplace, sat up with Zhima's baby in her arms and grunted a signal at Awu Luruo, who immediately whispered to me, "Liang, please hurry back to Sunamei's *huagu*. Watch out for other *axiao*."

I knew he was joking, and Ami Cai'er scolded him for his rudeness. Still I had some qualms. After running to the stairs leading to Sunamei's *huagu,* I slowed down and tiptoed, trying to hear whether there was a man in her room. Absolutely still, not a sound. The door was ajar. I pushed it open and saw that Sunamei was in bed and the lamp already blown out. She turned to face me. I scolded her, "Why don't you bolt the door?"

"What for?"

"If a man came in – "

"Do not think our Mosuo men behave like you Han men who risk jail to break into a woman's room. We are a different people. If a Mosuo woman says, 'Out,' a Mosuo man goes out submissively. I was about to ask whether you went to the wrong *huagu*."

"I was chatting with Awu Luruo, listening to him talk about Daba."

"I know. I got up three times to look for you at the *yimei* entrance."

"Then, why didn't you call me?"

"Where have you heard that a Mosuo woman goes out to call a man?"

"So that's it?"

"Do you think I would lower myself as a Han woman does? If her husband does not come back at night, she searches high and low; if the man does not want her any more, she cries as if the sky is falling. Once in town I met such a Han woman wailing. I asked her, 'Sister, why are you crying?' She screamed, 'That man of mine, who deserves to be butchered, has abandoned me! That heartless beast!' It sounded more like singing than cursing. I said to her, 'Sister, if he has abandoned you, why don't you abandon him?' She was horrified by my words. Blinking her eyes for a moment, she wailed even louder: 'Oh, my heaven! My earth! My life!'"

Sunamei had teased a laugh out of me. Sitting by the fireplace, I poked the fire to boil a kettle of tea. Sunamei said aloud, "Have you forgotten that?"

"What?"

"What Daba has bidden you?"

"Daba?" I didn't know what she was talking about. I had forgotten completely.

"Think hard."

"Sorry, I can't recall. Tell me."

"Daba says, tonight – now do you remember?"

I remembered but pretended I didn't. "No."

"Daba says, tonight you and I must sleep together."

"And what else?"

"Hold each other tight."

"What else?"

"For a long, long time."

"What else?" I laughed.

Now Sunamei realized that I was teasing her. Jumping out of bed, she picked up the earthen kettle and tossed it out the window. When I hugged her in the darkness, kissing her face, I tasted her tears.

25

When I opened my eyes in the morning, I saw that Sunamei was already awake; she seemed to have something on her mind. She turned to me and said, "I saw Yingzhi."

"Yingzhi?" Of course I knew who she was talking about. "Where? Did he come?"

"You saw him, too."

"Me? No."

"Yesterday, on our way back from worshiping Jiumulu, we saw two men carrying water for the funeral, didn't we?"

"Do you mean the two wearing leather helmets and armor?"

"Yes. The one carrying a pail on his back was Yingzhi."

"Why didn't you greet each other?"

"Anyone carrying water for washing the dead is not allowed to speak."

"Oh – I didn't notice him."

"Ah."

"What's the matter?"

"Nothing."

She said no more, so I didn't give our exchange much thought.

After getting up, we fitted out two horses for sightseeing along Lake Xienami. Declining any guide or company, Sunamei and I went alone. It was the happiest day of my stay there. We rode toward Xienami at a leisurely pace at the foot of lofty Mount Lion. As Lake Xienami seemed to open itself wider and wider in the mountain valley, a vision suddenly came to me. In a remote time, perhaps the Neolithic Age, ancestors of the Mosuo people crossed a long distance from the north to the south, as I had done only recently, and discovered Mount Lion, whose peak resembles a lion and is even more majestic than a real one, thrusting its head into the vast blue as if ready to leap. Farther south, a huge lake gradually came into view. It was so blue they had trouble believing it was water. Those ancestors cheered with excitement and sat by the wooded lakeside. Several clan chieftains met together, recalling the difficult mountains they had passed. All agreed that this was the most beautiful and richly endowed of all the places on which generations and generations of Mosuo had set their feet, and they decided to settle here. They burned their tents, built wooden houses, and hollowed out tree trunks for canoes. They grew grain, fished, and hunted. They named the lake Xienami (mother sea). Yes, mother sea – the sea of our mother. What do the Mosuo people respect more than the mother? So they gave this most respectable name to this matchless, pure blue lake.

At the lakeside we borrowed a canoe from the fishermen. Paddling out to the center of the lake, we saw small fish glistening like silver on the surface. A snow-white bird dived right in front of us to catch fish. Lying on her back in the canoe, Sunamei looked at the sky and said emotionally: "Liang Rui, I am a Mosuo girl after all."

"Of course. That goes without saying."

She dipped her hands into the water, splashing playfully. "I don't know why I ever moved to town!"

"I understand your feelings. If I were Mosuo, I would not want to leave here, either."

"You." She eyed me sadly. "But you are not Mosuo."

"Now the greater part of me has already turned Mosuo."

"The greater part? Far from it. Even your smallest part hasn't turned Mosuo yet."

"Not even the smallest part of me? How much I love your home village now, Sunamei! When I first arrived I was not accustomed to its way of life, but now I never want to leave."

"What do you love about my home village?"

"Everything. The mountains, the waters, the forests, Mount Lion, and the people, your kinsmen Ami Cai'er, Awu Luruo, and you, my dear Sunamei. Even Longbu, he's a pretty decent fellow when I think about him calmly."

"Do you like Longbu?"

"Sort of, but not completely..."

Sunamei giggled heartily. We canoed in a large semicircle back to shore. Then we went over to the fishermen's bonfire for some tea. An old fisherman roasted some small fish on bamboo sticks over the flames. When the fish were sizzling and dripping grease, he sprinkled some salt on them. They are delicious when eaten hot. Sunamei and I each ate a dozen. After paying and saying good-bye to the fishermen, we were ready to get back on our horses.

Suddenly, the old man stopped Sunamei and asked her, "Is this Han your – ?"

Sunamei had no term for husband. So she replied, "He and I have a marriage certificate."

Narrowing his eyes into a smile, he said "Ah, he is truly *ga!*" Because I could not understand the Mosuo word *ga,* I asked Sunamei for help. She told me, "He said how brave you are!"

"Of course I am!" With great pride I jumped into the saddle.

Sunamei was silent on our way back to the village; I talked endlessly. With my mind purified by nature, I became intoxicated, talking about my visions of the history and future of their nation and about my impressions of their matrilineal, extended-family customs. I talked on and on as if delivering a lecture. I wanted to pour out all my feelings. My conclusion was mainly encomium: "Here I witness a matrilineal society that should have existed only in antiquity. Yet it exists today. No outside pressure has the power to change it. The Mosuo people live and love solemnly according to their own primitive way of existence. Although modern men cannot appreciate their sexual permissiveness, nobody can deny the fact that among them there is no murder for love, no jealousy and hatred between mothers-in-law and daughters-in-law or between aunts and sisters, nor even any family quarrels. In their extended family there is no power struggle over inheritances and no selling of the body for money or position. Mosuo women are their own masters on earth. Only they have the right to love or not to love, to want or not to want, to accept or to refuse. They are independent of men. In their world, there are no spouses in bondage, no lonely old men, no homeless orphans – and, of course, no modernization."

Sunamei said nothing, only smiling at my excited, lofty speech. Her smile contained ridicule, happiness, and melancholy; it was hard for me to read her thoughts.

That evening, the eve of the funeral of the Agupozhe family, I wanted to see their ritual of chasing ghosts and the dance of the spinning plates, but Sunamei wished to talk with Ami. They had a lot to talk over, for they had been separated from each other for a long time and were going to be again. Nevertheless, I was glad to get out all by myself for once, to be an observer of their strange rituals and customs. The ritual of chasing ghosts was simple enough, but quite a noisy and exciting scene. When I went to the crowded courtyard of the Agupozhes, Daba's voice, already hoarse, was still chanting incantations. He swept the ghosts, which remained invisible to all the others, from every corner and instructed a large group of family members to take down several boards from their roof. Then he picked up a bowl of rice and ran about as if he were chasing a flock of chickens. He seemed to keep a host of ghosts in sight, muttering as he drove them out the door, out of the village, and over the bamboo bridge. People felt suddenly relieved, for they believed that the ghosts had really been driven away.

The dance of the spinning plates followed. The dancers were a group of handsome young men in helmets and leather armor. Their armor was hung with many little bells. When they danced, the bells rang out rhythmically and their beat was quite distinctive – ding-a-ling, ding-a-ling. Every dancer carried a long sword diagonally across his back. The edge of his scabbard as well as of his coat and pants were decorated with yak hair. Holding long spears and swords, the dancers imitated the movements of tigers, yaks, and leopards, turning somersaults and jumping rhythmically. Their dance attracted all the children of the village, who saw no connection between this dance and the mourning. The children followed the dancers around, laughing and shouting battle cries. I was enchanted by this barbaric dance and meanwhile was trying to spot Yingzhi among those young men. Of course my efforts were in vain, because I did not know him. One glance at a stranger doesn't leave much of an impression, and I had noticed only his outfit when he passed us at the riverside. This group of young dancers looked as if they were born from one mother. Their armor made it even harder for me to tell one from the other.

After the dance, the young men all went to the Agupozhe house to take off their armor for a feast, and the children gradually dispersed. Glancing at my watch, I was surprised to see the hour hand already pointing to two. Sunamei must be awaiting me anxiously. How could I have behaved like a child? Mosuo women never go out to look for men – this custom I had already learned. Looking off into the funeral ground, I saw that a pine pyre in the shape of the Chinese character 井 was being put up by torchlight. The torches shone through the pyre; shadow and light changed like a mirage to produce various mysterious beams and spots. However, I contained my curiosity and walked off. I found the gate bolted. Worse still, I dared not shout for someone to come open it. Seeing that the enclosing wall was not high, I followed the example of Mosuo women's *axiao* and climbed over it. Fortunately, they had not yet got another dog after their black one had been killed. I jumped smoothly into the courtyard. The night was exceptionally still. In the Agu-pozhe home, Daba was reading sacred texts in a loud voice; maybe half the village could hear his voice. I tiptoed up the stairs to the *huagu*. As I was about to push the door open, I heard a man's voice and noticed there was no light inside. My heart nearly jumped out of my chest. Desperately holding my composure, I put my ear to the crack between the door and its frame, listening intensely. The man was still speaking. Although his voice was soft, I could sense that he was lying on the bed. Then I peeped through the crack. The embers in the fireplace were still burning, and Sunamei had already stripped off her clothes. Against the background of the dark-red flames, the black shadow of her naked body flashed by. She must have jumped into bed. Shutting my eyes, I turned away from the door. Oh, my God! What should I do? Although I had shut my eyes and covered my ears, I knew what was happening as if I could see it and hear it. I was too familiar with the scene: she flutters her wings with cries of joy, and then groans, screams – weeps.

Suddenly, I swung back toward the door. Now my behavior was no longer controlled by the reason of a civilized man – or perhaps only a so-called civilized man could behave like me. I burst through the door. Sunamei jumped shamelessly up from the bed without a stitch of clothing. Unexpectedly, the naked young man – Yingzhi, no doubt – took his time putting on his clothes, and nodded to me as if nothing had happened. Sunamei perceived the coming disaster in my face. Certainly she could see that I was shaking violently. She grabbed her clothes and slipped them on in a hurry. But before she could button up, I dashed over and slapped her. I had never hit a woman before and was unconscious of how my hand stretched out and slapped her so fiercely. I did not notice my violence until Sunamei uttered a piercing shriek. Yingzhi did not expect the matter to be so serious that it would lead to my slapping Sunamei. Stepping forward, he protected her with his body and yelled at me. I could not understand his words, but his meaning was only too clear. How could I tolerate a lecture from a man who had just insulted me? What right do you have, you scoundrel? What right do you have to steal into *my* room, to get into *my* bed, and to seduce *my* wife? I will punish you mercilessly. I picked up a piece of oak heavy enough to smash his head. The weight of the wood gave me a pleasurable thrill. As I lifted it to strike at Yingzhi, Sunamei uttered a scream, a strange scream, a soul-tearing cry like that of a wounded beast. She grabbed Yingzhi and dashed out. I turned, but they had already rushed downstairs. I flung the wood into the fireplace. The earthen pot and burning wood flew to the ceiling, and the room was quickly engulfed by flames. Walls, beams, and panels were burning; tongues of flame licked at the small window, at the wool blanket, and at the straw mattress. Staring at the orange tongues of flame, I did not understand what had happened. When the flames began consuming the door frame, I walked slowly out of the room. From the landing I saw the whole Mosuo community – men and women, old and young – standing in the yard below, an enormous, dark crowd. Sunamei was not among them. Dabu Ami Cai'er, standing in the middle, head held high, watched the burning wing of the cottage with great indignation. She uttered only a single word in a low voice, and the crowd dispersed at once to fetch pails, basins, and bowls to put out the fire. With nowhere to go, I stood downstairs, drenched by their water. Let it pour.

The fire woke up the whole village. Soon all the villagers came to the rescue with pails and basins. Awu Luruo climbed to the collapsing eastern wing and pushed down the wall that was burning most furiously. Once the fire was put out, the village resumed its tranquility. I asked every member of the family about Sunamei. "Sunamei? Where is Sunamei?"

From Ami Cai'er and Awu Luruo down to a child of three, no one answered me, nor did they even look at me – it was as if I were mute and invisible. How recently I had stressed the existence of *I* – I, I, I! Now, did *I* still exist? I searched all the rooms and asked anyone I met about Sunamei, but no one answered me. Zhima, who was breast-feeding her newborn baby, ignored me. Even the baby Yimu denied my existence; her entire consciousness was filled with milk.

Awu Luruo took several men into the yard and began sawing boards to repair the house. I was knocked here and there by the wood they were carrying, but they showed no perception that their wood had touched me. I became a human obstacle. Outside the gate, I took to the village path, circling around the yard of every family, hoping to chance on Sunamei. She would not ignore me, I believed. She would be the last person to ignore me in this place. But I had no luck. What I met was a troop of the Agupozhe mourners. I quickly stepped aside to make way. The vanguard of the funeral parade was a robust man carrying a bamboo basket on his back, who was spreading food and grain along the way. Behind him came a pair of men holding torches, pairs holding flags, and pairs wearing armor like ancient warriors. They led a horse, carrying the gilded clothes for the dead, sacrificial artifacts, and pheasants' tail feathers. They held their spears high and kept their faces straight and stern. The relatives of the dead, wearing linen robes for the occasion, brought up the rear, following a square coffin more than a meter high. They were silent, shedding tears with lowered heads, slipping past me endlessly like shadows. No. Maybe I was the shadow. Maybe I had already gone deaf. Following the end of the funeral parade out of the village, I sat on the lawn, watching as they went to the crematorium and removed the body from a white linen sack. Then they placed the sacrificial artifacts and the body, which seemed to be in a sitting position, into the pyre prepared the night before. As the flames rose from the pyre, my ears suddenly recovered their hearing. I heard the cries of grief piercing the sky. I had never heard so many people cry together, and their wails were sincere, wild, and free beyond description. Some of them rolled on the ground, some beat the earth, some attempted to jump into the flames, and some hammered themselves with their fists. This scene showed that they shared with the dead a life of profound happiness and love. If they behaved so sorrowfully at the loss of a beloved family member, how should I behave at losing a lively, young companion? Their beloved had been taken by heaven; I myself had discarded my Sunamei. But I did not cry, not a single teardrop. They could complain to the heavens, to the earth, to their gods and ghosts, turning complaints into sorrow, sorrow into grief. To whom could I complain?

It was broad daylight when the mourners left the crematorium. The swirling wind formed the ashes into a couple of dark cylinders. Were these the last traces of a man?

With heavy steps, I dragged myself back to the village. Entering Sunamei's yard, I was surprised to find that the burned east wing of the cottage was already mended, just like the original, although its color was a bit lighter. Awu Luruo was repairing the door frame of Sunamei's *huagu*. I went over and asked him the same question, thinking they would see me and hear me in the morning. But still no one answered me and I began to panic. A little girl dropped my drawing folder from the east wing. Picking up the folder, I found that, although its corner was burned, the portrait of Sunamei's silhouette inside was still intact. Refusing to admit defeat, I shouted loudly to them again, "Where is Sunamei? Sunamei?"

They responded with the silence of a ten-thousand-year-old, snow-covered mountain. I wished they would curse me, beat me, smash me with an ax; but they simply could not see me or hear me. Standing in the yard, I howled desperately, "Sunamei! Sunamei!"

No one heard my howling but a flock of scared chickens that fled noisily. Their flight proved that my vocal cords still worked.

The sun came out; a ray of sunlight beamed on the cottage roof. Suddenly, a kindled pine torch was thrown out from the *yimei*. Dabu Ami Cai'er, with Zhima's baby in her left arm and a sickle, a flax stalk, and a page of sacred text in her right, stepped out the door of the *yimei* with Zhima and entered the yard. The sunlight fell on Ami's head; several silvery hairs fell over her brows. Narrowing her eyes, she looked up at the great mother sun of all creatures. The sun moved fast, and after a while sunlight bathed the three of them. Ami Cai'er held the baby toward the sun, which was climbing over the other side of the roof, spreading a layer of golden powder on little Yimu. Little Yimu kicked her legs and cried; Dabu Ami Cai'er smiled happily, tears glistening in her eyes. Zhima unbuttoned her blouse with a sweet smile and exposed a full, round breast. Taking her daughter from Dabu Ami Cai'er, she inserted into the baby's mouth a pink nipple that was oozing white milk, and the baby immediately stopped crying. Both Dabu and Zhima beheld the baby suckling with all her heart and soul. Suddenly Dabu leaned her face to the little feet of the baby and kissed them for a long, long time. What Sunamei had once said sank in at last: the third day after a Mosuo baby's birth, if the baby can be bathed in the rising sun, she will enjoy longevity, happiness, and health all her life under the loving care of the mother sun.

Why stay any longer? I walked past them, past their courtyard, and past their village. I walked away from their world; there was no place for me among them, their courtyard, or their village. I walked away as an outsider, a miserable exile. Now I experienced the true agony of exile. I was returning to the boring, hateful world I had once known and loved so well. In that world, at least I could still sell tickets, collect tickets, and guide moviegoers to their seats. Occasionally, I could still take a look at boring reruns and hear the audience laugh, applaud, and cheer. In China, no matter how vulgar a movie might be, an audience somewhere will cheer it.

I left, carrying on my back the drawing folder with my perpetual meditation on Sunamei pressed inside. My shadow grew gradually smaller and then gradually bigger. I knew I was leaving a beautiful dream behind. What future lay before me?

Every person has a sun over his head. But doesn't a single, common sun shine over yours, his, hers, and mine?

Glossary

Ada: father.

Ami: mother.

Amiji: mother's younger sister; literally means "little mother."

Amizhi: mother's elder sister; also called "big mother."

Amu: elder brother or sister.

Apu: granduncle on the maternal side.

Asi: great-grandmother.

Awu: mother's brother; uncle.

Axiao: the sexual friend. *Xiao* means "lying down." *Axiao* can be translated as "friends of different sexes lying down together."

Ayi: mother's mother; or the sister of mother's mother.

Cha'erwa: a long cloak that can also be used as a blanket.

Daba: shaman. The Mosuo maintain their own traditional pantheon of gods, but, under Tibetan influence, they also believe in Lamaism.

Dabu: the head of the Mosuo extended family.

Er: clan.

Ganmu Mountain: the mountain of the goddess. Located near Lake Lugu, it has the shape of a lion.

Hada: a piece of silk used as a greeting gift among the Tibetans and Mongolians.

Huagu: a boudoir assigned to a Mosuo woman when she reaches the age of thirteen, where she receives her *axiao.*

Kouxuan: a type of mouth organ.

Mo: daughter. The character used by Bai also means "model."

Siri: subdivision (moiety) within a matrilineal clan.

Xienami: mother sea; also known as Lake Lugu.

Yimei: the central, large sitting room, which also serves as a

communal dining room and meeting room, and as a
sleeping room for the elderly and children.

Yishe: a matrilineal extended family.

Youshemei: a backbone column of the house; known as the
female pillar.

Zhaijie: the skirt-dressing ceremony for a Mosuo girl at the
age of thirteen. A literal translation of *zhaijie* is "heroine
of the house." Before the ritual of receiving skirts and
pants, which occurs at the age of thirteen, Mosuo boys
and girls wear unisex shirts that look like oversized
blouses or undersized gowns.

About the Mosuo Communities

The Mosuo communities, known as the country of women, were recorded in history as early as the Jin dynasty (A.D. 265–420). Also known as the Naxi nationality, the Mosuo people spread along the Jinsha River and around Lake Lugu in the provinces of Sichuan and Yunnan.

In 1981 Zhan Chengxu and three other anthropologists published the results of their investigations of the Mosuo community in a book titled *Azhu Marriage and Matrilineal Family among the Yongning Naxi*. In 1983 Yan Yuxian and Song Zhaolin published a similar book, *Matrilineality in Yongning Naxi Nationality*. Inspired by the matrilineal model described in these studies, Bai Hua made two visits to the Mosuo community along Lake Lugu in 1985 and 1986. "Even today," he observes, "the Mosuo people still maintain a prehistoric family structure and marital form. They regard the female as the root and trunk and the male as the branches and leaves."

In *The Remote Country of Women,* Bai Hua "intended to use the past as a mirror to see the present," that is, "to use the values of his matrilineal model to challenge our conventional evaluations regarding the primitive versus the modern, and the barbarous versus the civilized. After *The Remote Country of Women,* he wrote two other long novels, *Xishui, Leishui* (Streams, Tears) and *Aimodala Xin Weisi* (The Heart of Aimodala Is Not Dead), continuing his reflection on the future of humanity in the value conflicts between the primitive and the civilized. But *The Remote Country of Women* remains Bai Hua's most significant work because of his powerful recapitulation of Mosuo community—a utopia, remote but in existence.

About the Author

Bai Hua was born Chen Youhua in Xinyang, a small city of Henan Province, in 1930. He joined the People's Liberation Army in 1947 and began to write poems, short stories, and screenplays in 1951. In 1961 he became an editor and screenplay writer for the Shanghai Petrel Film Company. He started his career as a freelance writer in 1964 and has been residing in Shanghai since 1985.

An internationally renowned writer, Bai Hua has been a cause célèbre because of his dissidence and his involvement in the human rights movement in China. As early as 1979, he used humanism to challenge Communist authoritarianism in his screenplay *Bitter Love,* which was made into the movie *The Sun and Man* in 1980. Consequently, Deng Xiaoping made him the chief target of the first post-Mao antibourgeois liberalization campaign in 1981. *The Remote Country of Women,* published in 1988, is Bai Hua's first long novel, satirizing the warping banality of totalitarianism and establishing him as a pioneering and subversive writer of great power.

About the Translators

Qingyun Wu is assistant professor of Chinese and director of the Chinese Studies Center at California State University, Los Angeles. Her publications include an English translation of Wang Meng's "Anecdotes of Minister Maimaiti: A Uygur Man's Black Humor," which first appeared in the journal *Translation* and then was collected in *Return Trip Tango and Other Stories Abroad* (1992), and *Transformations of Female Rule: Chinese and English Feminist Utopias*, which devotes a chapter to the study of Bai Hua's *The Remote Country of Women*.

Thomas O. Beebee is associate professor of comparative literature and German at Penn State University. His full-length translation study, *Clarissa on the Continent: Translation and Seduction*, was published in 1990. He has published widely on modern Western literature and theory.